Janna
Mysteries
BOOKS ONE AND TWO

T0340825

Rosemary
FOR
Remembrance
Rue
FOR
Repentance

FELICITY PULMAN

RANDOM HOUSE AUSTRALIA

Random House Australia Pty Ltd
Level 3, 100 Pacific Highway, North Sydney NSW 2060
http://www.randomhouse.com.au

Sydney   New York   Toronto
London   Auckland   Johannesburg

Rosemary for Remembrance first published by Random House
Australia in 2005
Rue for Repentance first published by Random House
Australia in 2006
This bindup edition first published in 2007

Copyright © Felicity Pulman 2005–7

National Library of Australia
Cataloguing-in-Publication Entry

Pulman, Felicity, 1945–.
Janna mysteries 1 & 2 bindup.

ISBN 978 1 74166 251 1 (pbk.).

I. Title. (Series: Pulman, Felicity, 1945–
Janna mysteries; 1 & 2).

A823.3

Cover design by saso content & design pty ltd
Internal illustration and design by Pigs Might Fly Productions
Typeset by Midland Typesetters, Australia
Printed and bound by Griffin Press, South Australia

10 9 8 7 6 5 4 3 2 1

Janna
Mysteries
BOOK ONE

Rosemary
FOR
Remembrance

FELICITY PULMAN

RANDOM HOUSE AUSTRALIA

ONE

THE WOLF'S HOWL shattered the dark, secretive forest. Startled, Janna spun around, straining to pinpoint the direction of the sound. At the sudden movement, the flame of her torch flickered and almost died. Fighting panic, she cupped her fingers around the flame to protect and steady it. The light gave her an illusion of safety and she took courage from it, for she was alone out here, with no protection against the prowling predators of the forest. No protection against wolves.

Janna cursed the quick temper which had sent her fleeing into the night without bringing even a knife to defend herself. She raised the torch higher, watching for movement, listening intently for a telltale rustling.

All was still. Her gaze moved up to the full moon, which floated above her in a blaze of radiant silver light. It brightened the sky almost to daylight. Yet even the moon's brilliance could not penetrate the tree-shadowed darkness that surrounded her. It was heavy with mystery and threat.

The sudden crackle of dry leaves set her heart racing. A deer? A fox? Not loud enough to be a wild boar – but a wolf would move quietly, stealing up on its prey. At once Janna's imagination conjured up the beast creeping through the forest towards her. Her first impulse was to run, to put as much distance between her and the wolf as possible, but she remembered her mother's warning: 'Never turn your back on a wild animal.' She kept still, knowing that she could never outpace a wolf – never.

She swallowed hard, gulping down fear. The thin trail she followed ran deep into the forest, into the wild and tangled places where the wolf was surely lurking. Should she go on, or go back to the cottage? The immense forest closed around her, hushed and still. Nothing moved; there was no sound now to break the silence. The wolf's howl wasn't very loud, she thought. Perhaps it was too far away to be any real threat.

Janna set off once more, leaves crunching, twigs snapping under her boots. If she hurried, she could pick the wild strawberries and get out of the forest before the wolf even knew she was there. She couldn't just abandon her mission, for the strawberries were important. Her mother needed them for a special potion. They had planned to pick them together, tonight.

'It's a foul-tasting mixture. The fruits will add sweetness and strengthen the blood, but we must go tonight for there will be no time to pick them before my visitor comes tomorrow,' Eadgyth had fussed, all the while pulling from the shelf the other ingredients she would need. It was a mix to bring on a woman's monthly courses and so prevent an unwanted child from developing in the womb. The church forbade the practice and most women remained obedient to both the priest and their husbands. Sometimes, however, worn out with childbirth and with already too many mouths to feed, they were desperate enough to seek Eadgyth's help. Even then, she acted only if she was truly convinced of their need. From Eadgyth's preparations this evening, it was clear she was sympathetic to the woman's cause and prepared to help her.

'Who is she?' Janna had asked, but her mother hadn't answered, saying only, 'I want you out of the cottage by the time she arrives.'

'Why won't you let me stay and help you?'

'Not this time.'

'You never let me help!' Janna scowled at her mother.

Eadgyth had sighed impatiently. 'You have enough to do. You tend the herb garden and help me prepare my mixtures and potions. That's quite enough to keep you busy.'

'I don't want to just keep busy. I want to *learn*.'

'I've already taught you everything I know.'

'But knowledge isn't enough! I need experience too. How will I ever get that if you won't let me help look after the people who come here?'

'You know enough for now.' Eadgyth had turned back to her decoction. Janna knew, from long experience, that the subject was closed. She seethed with resentment. She was sixteen years old. When would her mother start treating her like an adult?

''Tis well it's a full moon tonight. Picked at midnight, the strawberries will carry the moon's power,' Eadgyth had fussed on. At that point Janna had stopped listening. If it wasn't the moon, it was the time of day or night, or the alignment of the planets that must be favourable. She'd heard her mother say the same sorts of thing a thousand times in the past. Doubtless she'd be saying the same things to Fulk in the future. Once she went into partnership with him. Janna's mouth pulled down into a sour scowl, while her mind went back to the scene from which she had fled.

The loud knocking had startled both Janna and her mother. Eadgyth paused in the act of pulling on her boots. 'Who could that be?' She'd flashed a sly smile at Janna. 'Are you expecting a suitor to come calling? Godric, maybe?'

'No!' Even as Janna issued the denial, Godric's face flashed into her mind, and her cheeks heated at the memory. He, too, had come calling late at night, seeking aid for his ailing mother. But his mother had made a good recovery, so Eadgyth had said.

'I saw the way Godric looked at you. I think you've taken his fancy, Janna.' There was a twinkle in Eadgyth's eyes as she teased her daughter.

Janna flushed under her mother's scrutiny, and kept on fastening her cloak.

'He is a fine, well-set fellow. You could do worse,' Eadgyth observed. Another knock came, more urgent this time. 'Likely it's some poor soul in trouble. Go to the door, Janna. See who it is.' She bent to her boots once more.

Janna opened the door. Her welcoming smile died and her heartbeat slowed to normal. Not Godric but Master Fulk the apothecary. Eadgyth sometimes bought supplies from his shop in Wiltune to make up her own medicaments and creams. For the moment, however, he was staying at Babestoche Manor, having been summoned to attend Dame

Alice during the last few weeks of her pregnancy. Local gossip said that Fulk divided his time between the manor, his shop, and the alehouses in Wiltune, where he boasted of his skill and his noble patronage to any who might listen. What on earth could he want with them?

'Good evening, Johanna. Is your mother home? Might I have a word?' Master Fulk pulled a large square of yellow silk from his purse and mopped his red, sweating face. Their small cottage was some distance from Babestoche Manor, and the journey had obviously taken its toll on the apothecary's constitution.

Janna bobbed her head and made way for him to enter. His large presence dominated the small, smoke-filled room, which was lit only by the flickering light of the fire at its centre. In unusual deference, the apothecary bowed to Eadgyth.

Janna saw that her mother wore a smile of chilly politeness as she greeted him. She grinned inwardly, knowing her mother's opinion of Fulk both as a man and as an apothecary. '*Wortwyf* I may be called,' Janna's mother had declared when news of his presence at the manor became known, 'but as a herbwife I know far more of women's troubles than that turnip head! Even Aldith, the midwife, knows more than him. He's a posturing ignoramus. What does he know of the difficulties of carrying and birthing children? What does any man know, or care? In my opinion, Janna, if Fulk was even half so skilled as he claims, he would surely be ministering to King Stephen himself instead of selling his nostrums to any wealthy enough to pay for the privilege of being gulled by him!'

Eadgyth kept her smile firmly in place as Fulk pushed Alfred, their big black cat, off the heavy wooden chair by the fire. The chair had been crafted by Eadgyth herself, along with the stuffed cushions that provided extra comfort. With a grimace of distaste, the apothecary brushed off black cat hairs then sank down, expelling a sigh of relief.

Janna picked up Alfred and settled onto a stool nearby, waiting eagerly for Fulk's explanation of this unusual visit. His opening was unexpected.

'My dear Eadgyth, I am come here to make you an offer which I am sure can work only to your advantage.'

Fulk paused, perhaps waiting for Eadgyth's delighted response. When it was not forthcoming, he continued. 'You will have heard that I am skilled in the art of healing . . .' He stopped, frowning at Janna's barely suppressed snort. Eadgyth kept silent, giving him no help at all.

'Of course, my knowledge is far greater than yours for I have taken instruction in *scientia* from scholars in Oxford. Small wonder that the infirm and elderly come from far and wide to consult me, knowing that they will benefit from my plasters and poultices, my pills, tonics and mixtures.'

And when those fail, they come to my mother! With difficulty, Janna kept her thoughts to herself.

Fulk looked expectantly at Eadgyth, searching for an acknowledgment of the honour of his presence here in their cottage. She tilted her head, and waited for him to continue. A heavy silence settled, broken eventually by the apothecary. 'However, there are still many mysteries concerning the human body which are known only to God.'

'And perhaps to me. Is that why you're here?' Eadgyth

suggested, tiring suddenly of the charade. 'Are you here to ask my advice, Master Fulk?'

'No, no, of course not.' With an airy laugh, the apothecary dismissed the thought.

'Then why, pray, do you come knocking at my door so late at night?' She settled onto a stool opposite Fulk, and stared at him intently.

'Because . . . because I have an offer for you to consider. We both practise the healing arts. I thought you might care to share my knowledge.'

'You're offering to teach me?' Eadgyth lifted an eyebrow in surprise.

'I expect there is also something I might learn from you.' Fulk's face flushed a darker shade than before. 'For example, some women's troubles may be beyond my ken . . .'

'So you're actually asking *me* to teach *you*?' Eadgyth gave him a glacial smile.

Fulk shifted uncomfortably. 'You must know there's talk about you in the village,' he said, changing the subject. 'If you come under my tutelage, it would give you a high position in Wiltune.' He leaned towards Eadgyth. 'It would also help me. I am so busy with customers I have too little time for mixing up those remedies that my patients seek. I'm here to offer you –'

'A partnership?'

'No! No, not quite that. After all, I have my reputation to consider.' At the sight of Eadgyth's ferocious glare, Fulk extracted the yellow kerchief and mopped his brow once more. 'I'm offering you a chance to sell your potions through my shop, and your help in the preparation of my own remedies under my guidance. It would give you a reputable outlet for your medicaments and bring you in a steady income. Of course, I could not put my name to any concoction of yours unless I knew that it was quite sound.'

'And how would *you* be able to tell?'

The contempt behind Eadgyth's question was lost on Fulk. 'Why . . . I would need to know all the ingredients, of course,' he blustered.

'And so you would learn my herbal lore under the guise of helping me?'

'You mistake me, mistress. I thought you would be delighted by my offer. It works far more to your advantage than to mine.' Janna noted that Fulk's condescending tone didn't quite match the worried expression on his face.

'Delighted by your offer? Delighted to be patronised by a man who knows little but would steal my knowledge under the guise of helping me? I think not!' Eadgyth surged to her feet, indicating that Fulk had worn out his welcome. He stayed seated, sweat beading his brow.

'I assure you, Mistress Eadgyth, a business relationship would benefit both of us.'

Eadgyth studied him narrowly while she assessed the worth of his offer. 'A business relationship, no. A partnership – perhaps.'

Aghast, Janna stared at her mother. She could hardly believe what she was hearing. Eadgyth despised Fulk. How could she bear to contemplate a working relationship with such a loathsome toad?

Fulk's face, already red, now turned a deep crimson. 'You believe yourself to be my equal?' He spat the words as if they were bitter gall in his mouth. And yet, Janna noted, he seemed to be considering the idea in spite of Eadgyth's cutting assessment of his ability. She was sure Fulk wasn't telling them the real reason he'd come knocking on their door so late at night. She wondered what it could be.

'Come with me to see Dame Alice.' The invitation seemed more of a command than a suggestion. 'Bring with you one of your nostrums. Let us see if you are as good as people say you are.' His words were measured, but Janna sensed the urgency behind them, and saw it in the fingers that twisted together in barely concealed impatience. She had her answer: Dame Alice was the reason he was here.

'What sort of nostrum? Is Dame Alice having difficulty birthing her babe?' Eadgyth asked sharply.

'Not at all,' Fulk said proudly. 'Thanks to my ministrations, my lady has given birth to a fine son, when it's common knowledge she's lost every other child since the birth of her first little boy. That is why the midwife was put off and why my lord Robert summoned me to see ma dame through this pregnancy.' He puffed out his chest, swollen with self-importance.

'Why then do you come to see me, Master Fulk?'

Fulk's eyes slid sideways. He would not look at Eadgyth. 'Ma dame needs a mixture for something of which I have limited experience. Something to stop excessive bleeding after childbirth,' he mumbled.

'Have you massaged her back with goosegrease and given her herbs to help her expel the remains of the afterbirth?' A glance at Fulk's face confirmed that he had no notion what she was talking about.

9

'Then I must see her before infection sets in. I wish that you had told me this at once, Master Fulk, instead of wasting time like this.' Eadgyth jumped to her feet and moved towards the bunches of aromatic herbs hanging from the rafters of the thatched roof. Their spicy fragrance scented the air as she began to pick them. 'Tell me, Master Fulk, what have you done to help Dame Alice since the birth of her child?'

'I have purged my lady and placed a triangle of agate on her forehead, but she continues to bleed,' Fulk confessed. 'She is too weak to take nourishment, and she burns with fever. I have tried all that I may to bring her to good health, but to little avail. Reluctantly, mistress, I must come to you for help.'

'Hardly the words to make me believe in your offer of a partnership, Master Fulk, but at least we now have the truth of the matter.' Eadgyth pulled a mortar and pestle from the shelf, then carefully lifted down a small pair of scales. While she measured out and weighed the herbs, Janna tipped the cat off her lap and moved to hook a pan of water over the fire.

The apothecary watched intently. 'What herbs do you use, mistress?' he asked, unable to contain his curiosity any longer.

Eadgyth laughed and shook her head. 'You will not learn my secrets, Master Fulk. You may have been trained in Oxford, but my knowledge comes from the lore of my ancestors, the leechcraft of the Saxons, which I have combined with the healing arts practised by Jews, Greeks and Arabs as well as by our Norman masters. I will not share a knowledge so hardly won.'

'And where did you learn such mysteries?' There was a small measure of respect now in Fulk's tone.

But Eadgyth compressed her lips and answered only: 'My herbs will help my lady finish the birthing process and inhibit the bleeding, you have my word on it. I will also give her a mite of poppy syrup and some willowbark to reduce her fever. I presume you know of them, for they are common enough.' As she spoke, she ground the herbs into a fine powder. 'I shall add a little honey to sweeten the mixture, and some ale which will help my lady to relax. I shall also massage her back and her stomach to help her expel the remains of the afterbirth. You may go home to Wiltune, Master Fulk. I can help Dame Alice recover, I know it.'

'She will only see you if she believes you respectable,' Fulk warned.

Eadgyth gave a contemptuous snort and continued about her business.

'I'll have to tell Dame Alice that you are in my employ and that I am training you,' Fulk persisted.

Eadgyth dropped the bowl of herbs and turned to face him. 'Then you may take me to the manor and introduce me as your new partner,' she said evenly. 'You can also tell Dame Alice that, in the future, I shall be taking care of all the women who come to your shop, no matter what their troubles might be.'

Not believing what she was hearing, Janna spun around from the fire to confront her mother. A level glance from fine grey eyes showed Janna that her mother was in deadly earnest. It seemed she was prepared to abandon Janna, and all those villagers who had come to rely on her help, in order to cut a fine figure at the apothecary's shop in Wiltune. It was too much to bear. Pausing only to snatch up the flaming resin torch brought by the apothecary to light his path to their cottage, Janna raced out into the moonlit night and plunged into the forest.

TWO

ANOTHER HIGH, WILD cry shattered the silence. Was the wolf alone? Hunger might make it bold, but she'd have a better chance of survival than if it was hunting as part of a pack. Janna stopped once more to listen. A secretive rustle, the hoot of an owl, then silence. Go on – or turn back? She tilted her head upwards, and the moonlight fell on her face like a blessing. 'Keep me safe,' she whispered, then hurriedly crossed herself, knowing she should more properly be asking God for help, or even St Edith, the young patron saint of nearby Wiltune Abbey. Yet she felt comforted as she held the torch a little higher and hurried on.

The trail dwindled to little more than a thin depression of flattened leaves and grass. It was barely discernible among the shadows. Although Janna knew this part of the forest well, it looked quite different on this dark, shining night. She kept her head bent, looking for the signs that told her she was going the right way. She had walked this path only yesterday, hoping to snare a small something to add to the pot for their dinner, although she would have given the king's forester a different answer if she'd been caught by him so close to the king's hunting lodge.

She had seen the wild strawberries growing amid a tangle of bindweed and the beautiful blue flowers whose shape gave deadly monkshood its common name and her mother the ingredients for an ointment to ease stiff and aching joints. Knowing the importance of her find, for it was still early in the season, Janna had told her mother, and Eagyth had vowed to visit the place, to dig up some strawberry plants and repot them in their own herb garden.

'God's bones!' Janna muttered crossly now as she realised that, in her haste to leave the cottage, she'd also left behind a digging trowel and a bag to hold the plants. She would have to make do with picking only the berries that her mother needed to add to the concoction. She patted the woven purse that hung from her girdle. There was room enough. If she packed them in carefully it would suffice to carry the fruits home without squashing them.

She was moving uphill into a dense grove of beech and oak. Great branches closed over her head, their leafy mantle blocking the moon's light. The flare from the torch seemed bright in the darkness as, step by cautious step, she traced her way towards the small, fruiting plants.

There was a rustle, the crunching of dry leaves and then, sudden and shocking, several sharp explosions of snapping twigs. They sounded alarmingly close. Fighting fear, Janna cast about for signs of the strawberries. With a gasp of relief, she saw the patch of blue flowers. Knowing she was near, for this was the only place she'd ever seen monkshood growing wild, she set the torch down, then fell to her knees to look for the sweet, wild strawberries. They were small, hidden among the leaves, but she was too impatient and too frightened to seek them out. Instead, she pulled them off in clumps, leaves and strawberries together, and stuffed them into her purse, desperate to be gone.

She seized up the torch once more and sprang to her feet. Now the whole forest seemed loud with sounds: a hooting owl, squeaks, a snuffling grunt, crackling twigs, and a steady thumping that terrified Janna until she realised it was her own heartbeats reverberating in her chest. Yet there was something else, she realised, as her ears isolated and identified each sound. Something large was blundering through the forest without care or thought of danger. A grunting squeal confirmed Janna's fear. A wild boar was coming her way. Should it find her in its path, it would attack her. She had no knife to defend herself; she had nothing but her wits – and a pair of swift feet. Without stopping to think where she was going, she began to run. With each flying step she imagined the huge beast charging behind her, closer, closer, spearing her with its sharp tusks, bringing her down, trampling over her. She lost all sense of direction as she ducked and weaved through the trees in a desperate effort to get away.

She found herself in a hazel thicket. The trees grew close together, their thin branches interweaving into traps that caught and held her. She tried to zigzag around them. Tall weeds and dry leaves covered the ground, shrouding sharp flints and unexpected hollows. She had to slow down; it was too hard to keep her footing. Her cloak snagged on brambles and the sharp points of holly leaves as she blundered on. Her breath came in great sobbing gasps. She knew that she was utterly lost, but she dare not stop. She could hear the boar crashing through the undergrowth. It sounded much closer now; she must be running in circles. Fear surged through her body, urging her to a speed she couldn't sustain. She tripped and fell. At once she staggered to her feet, but the stabbing pain in her side told her she could not go on. She looked about her, seeking safety in a tall tree.

She stood in a small, moonlit clearing. There was nowhere to hide. She would have to face the boar, and fight for her survival. She could hear it coming towards her; she could even smell it now. Sobbing with fear, Janna snatched up a thin branch from the rotting remains of a fallen tree. She held her torch to the leaves and dry twigs at its tip. Her hand was shaking so badly she could hardly connect flame to tinder.

A tinge of red, a thin wisp of smoke, and then the flame caught. As the boar hurtled into the clearing towards her, squealing with rage, Janna leapt aside and thrust the burning brand into its face. Responding to a fear more urgent than its need to attack, it skidded to a halt. It began to back away, keeping a wary distance between itself and the source of fire.

Feeling somewhat comforted that her strategy had worked, Janna held aloft the flaming torch and the fiery branch, one in each hand, and considered what to do next. Pointless to go on when every step might take her further from home – yet she couldn't stand here all night either. If only she knew which way to go, the branch might burn long enough for her to reach safety. Undecided, she risked another glance upwards, wondering if she might tell her direction from the stars. But the moon's radiant aura outshone even the brightest of them, while those few stars visible in the darkness above the trees beyond were too far and too scattered for Janna to make sense of them.

Coming back to her present danger, she made a quick rush at the boar and shouted loudly, hoping that the noise and the fire might be enough to scare the beast away so that she could revert to her original plan of climbing a tree to seek refuge and direction. The boar gave an angry squeal and retreated a few steps, but its eyes stayed fixed on Janna.

'Help!' she called, but without much hope. The royal forest of Gravelinges belonged to King Stephen, but he seldom used his hunting lodge for, in this year of our lord 1140, he was busy defending his kingdom against its rightful heir, his cousin Matilda. Few other than the king were allowed into the forest, and no-one was likely to be around at this time of night, at least not legally. Poachers risked death if they were caught, although hunger sometimes drove them into the forest. Those who sought to escape the king's justice might also hide themselves here. Janna was filled with new fear. A boar, an outlaw, or the king's forester? None would show her mercy.

Without warning, the boar suddenly charged at Janna. 'Help!' she screamed as she tried to leap out of its way. Its bristles grazed her as it passed; its rank smell filled her nostrils. She whirled to face it, circling the flaming torches in a wide arc in the hope of frightening it.

Was that a faint cry? Janna listened intently. Should she shout again? The boar had turned, ready to charge once more. Its eyes glowed bright in the silvery moonlight.

'*Help!*' Janna didn't care who heard her now, so long as someone did.

'Who goes there?'

'Janna! I'm being attacked by a wild boar.' Her voice shrilled upwards with fear.

'Janna! Keep calling so that I may find you.'

A man's voice. It sounded familiar. 'I'm here, I'm here in a clearing,' she shouted. 'Please, *please* hurry!' The boar hunched up its bulk in front of Janna. Its dark form blended against the undergrowth at the edge of the clearing so she could see only its eyes, but she could sense its rage at being thwarted, sense that it was gathering power to launch itself at her once more. 'Begone!' she yelled, thrusting the burning brands towards it.

With an enraged squeal, it rushed at her. She tried to leap aside, but its shoulder caught her. Knocked off-balance, Janna staggered and fell. 'Help!' she screamed.

A man burst out from the darkness of the forest. He paused to get his bearings. It seemed to Janna that the moment stretched to an eternity. Why didn't he come after the boar; why didn't he help her? Terrified, she lay helpless among the grass and weeds, waiting for the boar to trample and gore her to death.

She could hear its angry squeals as it turned, hear the crunch and crackle of leaves and twigs under its feet. Suddenly it erupted into the moonlit clearing. It was coming at her, coming at speed. She heard a grunting cough. The boar staggered, but its momentum carried it on towards her. Janna shrank back in a last desperate effort to keep out of its way. It kept on coming, closer and closer, but she could see now that something was desperately wrong. As it reached her, it skewed sideways then tottered and crashed to the ground. Speechless, Janna's gaze moved from it to the man racing towards her. He was coiling a sling as he came. Janna noticed the glint of a blade as he fumbled at his belt.

Realising at last that she was safe, Janna picked up her fallen torch and scrambled to her feet. The man's voice had sounded familiar. Who was he? She held the torch aloft so that she could see the face of her saviour.

ChREE

GODRIC! A GREAT smile spread over Janna's face as she recognised him. She was so happy to see him, she could have kissed him. But she had no chance to embarrass either herself or him, for he'd made straight for the fallen animal. He kicked it, and the boar shifted and tried to struggle to its feet.

'Don't!' Janna reached out a hand to stop him. Although upset and hurting, she knew that the creature had acted only according to the rules of nature, obeying its instinct for survival. She shuddered as she looked down at the great hairy beast.

'It's a wild pig, not a relative.' Godric leaned over the boar. His arm rose and, with a swift movement, he slit its throat. Blood spurted. Janna jerked back with a cry of horror.

Godric wiped his knife clean on a patch of moss, then sheathed it at his waist. 'I had no true aim in the dark,' he explained. 'I had to see if I'd killed it or if it was still conscious. It was lucky I managed to strike it hard enough to stop its charge.'

'You didn't have to kill it!'

'Yes, I did. It was ready to get up and go for us again. My knife would have been no defence against it at all.'

Speechless with shock, Janna could only nod in understanding.

'Are you all right?' Godric placed a steadying arm around her shoulders.

'It knocked my breath from my body, but it didn't hurt me.' She leaned against him briefly, grateful for his warmth, his solid comfort. 'Thank you,' she said. 'You've saved my life tonight.'

'What are you doing out in the forest so late?' he asked.

'Gathering strawberries.' Janna touched the purse hanging from her belt. She'd fallen backwards. Hopefully the fruit hadn't been crushed when she fell. 'What about you? Why are you here?'

'Unlike you, I have permission from both my lord Robert and the abbess to come into the forest.' His laughing eyes belied his tone of reproof.

'How so?' Janna asked, intrigued that a common villein like Godric, tied as he was to the lord of Babestoche Manor, should be given the freedom to roam about in a royal hunting forest.

'I've been leading lost souls.' Seeing Janna's frown of puzzlement, Godric grinned. 'Today I escorted a group of pilgrims from Wiltune Abbey on their way to Glastingberie,' he explained. 'There's an ancient road built by the Romans that crosses the full length of the forest from east to west, but it's visible only to those who know that it's there. If the forester is about some other business, I am often asked to lead travellers through the forest to save them from getting lost.'

'How do you know about the Roman road?' Janna asked curiously.

'My forefathers were huntsmen here at the time of the Saxons. Their knowledge has been passed down from father to son, through many generations. So shall I pass on the knowledge to my sons, and I'll show them too, when it's time.' Godric nodded to himself, confirming his intention.

'So you acted as a guide today. What about tonight?' Janna searched the surrounding forest for signs of the pilgrims, but could see no-one.

Godric laughed. 'I'm still on my way home, should ill luck bring the forester my way.'

'The knife is for your protection, of course.' Janna indicated the sheath hanging from his belt.

'Of course. He gestured around the forest. 'I might meet outlaws, wolves, wild boar or even young damsels in need of protection.'

'You might also have to protect yourself against a savage rabbit or two,' Janna ventured.

Godric's mouth twitched. 'That's certainly possible.'

He must have abandoned his catch to come to her rescue, Janna thought, feeling sorry that he'd lost his dinner on her account. She stared down at the beast that had so frightened her. Its legs were coated black with mud and dung, and so was its nose from a lifetime of rooting about for its food. It stank, and yet Janna couldn't help feeling a pang of pity – and then fear as she realised the consequences of their night's work.

'What are we going to do with it?' she asked, pointing at the dead boar.

'I can think of several things.' Godric licked his lips in hungry anticipation. 'Collops of bacon. Chops. A leg roasted on a spit . . .'

'Have you taken leave of your wits?' Suddenly becoming conscious of the noise they were making and the need for secrecy, Janna lowered her voice as she continued. 'The forester will be told you've been in Gravelinges today. You'd be caught with blood on your hands, and brought before the forest court. You could lose your hands, your eyes, possibly even your life! You know how harsh the laws are. Oh, Godric, I fear that I have put you in far more danger than I ever was.'

Godric frowned. 'Then we'll leave the body here for the creatures of the forest to pick the flesh off its bones,' he said regretfully, after a moment's reflection.

'We can't,' Janna contradicted firmly. 'If the forester comes this way and spies it, he'll suspect you, he'll make you the scapegoat. We have to bury the boar, Godric. We can't trust the forest to keep our secret safe.'

'I'd much rather eat it than bury it,' Godric grumbled.

'Eat it, and we could be burying you!' Janna retorted.

Godric heaved a sigh, and bent to take hold of the beast's front legs. He began to drag it towards an overgrown thicket. 'I have only my knife to dig with,' he said, looking over his shoulder at Janna. 'We need to find a place where the soil is moist and the growth thick enough to hide the evidence.'

Janna nodded in understanding. Lifting her torch higher to cast a better light, she led Godric into the darkness under the trees.

She knelt beside him and helped him dig the grave, using a stout stick and her bare hands as tools. A silence fell between them as they concentrated on their task, yet Janna was acutely conscious of his presence beside her. She recalled her mother's teasing words, and her cheeks burned. If Godric had taken a fancy to her, it would be true to say that she had also found him worth looking at. She stole a quick glance. How old was Godric? Seventeen, maybe eighteen. Not much older than her, anyway.

As she dug deeper into the earth, Janna's thoughts went back to their first meeting only a few weeks ago. He had come, in a fright, for a cure for his mother. She was shaking with ague, he'd said. She could hardly breathe. He didn't know what to do for her. Could someone please come at once?

Eadgyth had sent Janna to gather fresh herbs, and Godric had followed her out into their herb garden, looking as if he wasn't quite sure where to plant his feet. Fearing for the delicate herbs, which were her responsibility, Janna bade him stand still and hold what she picked. Although he'd stayed where she'd put him, there was a contained restlessness about him that told her Godric was a man more used to action, and that he chafed at standing still. She was conscious that he watched her, and she tried to make sure he didn't catch her looking at him. Yet he was pleasing to look at, being tall and well built, with the fair hair and blue eyes of the Saxons. She'd been disappointed when Eadgyth bade her stay home to keep an eye on a mixture she had simmering over the fire, rather than allowing Janna to accompany them to the sick woman's cottage.

'What do you know of Godric and his mother?' she'd asked, when her mother returned home. Eadgyth had chuckled, not deceived by the casual question or the real focus of Janna's interest.

'They live over at Babestoche Manor,' she said. 'Godric owes his allegiance to Dame Alice and her lord.'

'Not to the abbess?' Janna was surprised. The Abbess of Wiltune owned vast tracts along the Nadder River, including the land their own cottage was on. Godric must have walked several miles across the downs to seek them out.

'The manor's lands adjoin those belonging to the abbess. Godric's mother has told me about his position there, and his prospects. He sounds like a good and honourable man, Janna.'

'He's not married then?'

'No. But his mother would be glad to see him take a wife.' Janna wondered now if Eadgyth shared that ambition, and if she'd been left behind on purpose, so that her mother could check out Godric's suitability as a husband. Yet Eadgyth often left her behind while she went out to minister to her patients. It was an old grudge, and the injustice of it angered Janna anew.

'How is your mother?' she asked Godric, thinking that she should make use of this time to get to know him while Eadgyth wasn't around to interfere. 'Is she quite recovered now?'

'She is very well, I thank you.' Godric paused for a moment and studied Janna. 'It was a blessed day that brought me to your door.'

And what did that mean? Was he thankful for his mother's cure, or was he glad of their meeting? Janna wanted to ask him, but was afraid where the question might lead. To a proposal of marriage? She smiled in the darkness, telling herself not to let her imagination run away with her.

'This is not how I imagined our second meeting would be.' Godric continued to dig while he elaborated on his earlier observation. 'I had intended to ask your mother if I might call on you.'

'Do you need more medication for your mother?' Sudden panic prompted Janna to deliberately misunderstand Godric's meaning. At once she wished she could retrieve her words. He'd already told her his mother was well. He'd think her a witless idiot.

Godric laughed. 'I think you understand me well enough, Janna,' he said cheerfully. To her relief, he straightened then, and said, 'The hole is deep enough. Hold up the torch so that I can see what I'm doing.'

He grabbed hold of the boar. 'What a waste of good meat,' he said as he tugged and pushed it into the deep hole they'd dug. Suddenly hopeful, he whipped his knife out of its sheath. 'Couldn't I just slice off a little . . .?'

'Don't even think about it.' Quickly, before he had time to put the thought into action, Janna scooped up a handful of earth and threw it over the animal. With a shrug of resignation, Godric sheathed his knife and set to helping her cover the boar.

Godric wanted to come calling on her! As Janna heaped earth over the dead animal, she reflected what that meant. Courtship. Marriage. No! Although she liked Godric – liked him a lot – she did not want to wed, not yet anyway.

True, she was of an age to marry. Other young women of her age in the hamlets nearby were either betrothed or wed. One was even expecting her first child, and wore the bump of her belly like a badge of honour.

26

Instinctively, Janna shrank from the knowledge of what had gone before to bring their love to such a conclusion. This was not for her. She was not yet ready to share her body or her life with someone else. There was still so much she wanted to experience for herself, so many new places she wanted to explore. She could not, would not plight her troth to Godric, nor to any other, nor keep a home and bear children at the price of her own freedom, and her own dreams for the future.

Yet what were those dreams, exactly?

Janna couldn't say, knew only that at times she sensed that a world beyond the forest awaited her, a world full of promise for the future. At such times a great longing seized her, a longing for adventure, a longing to be gone. She and Eadgyth eked out an existence from their small plot of land, and knew hunger if the season went against them. It was a hard life, but they were free to leave, to go anywhere they wished, whereas Godric, like all villeins, was bound to a liege lord and had to spend his days in service on the land so that he might have enough food to eat, and sufficient left over to pay his dues. If she wed Godric, she too would be stuck here for ever. She would never know if there was something else out there, waiting for her.

Common sense told Janna she was nothing. A nobody. Her only identity came from being Eadgyth's daughter, while her occupation, her reason for living, lay in tending their garden and animals, growing the vegetables which fed them, and the flowers and herbs for the concoctions that made up their livelihood. It was unlikely she'd ever go anywhere. In fact, she'd be lucky to find a husband at all, let alone someone as kind and as brave as Godric.

Lost in her thoughts as she was, Janna was startled when Godric straightened and wiped his muddy hands down his tunic. 'Do you know where we are?' she asked, as she clambered to her feet and took hold of the resin torch.

'Of course. I told you, I know this forest.' He plucked off a small leafy branch of hazel and swept it around the grave to hide all trace of their illicit activity, while Janna scattered armfuls of dead leaves on top, to further disguise the spot.

'Stay close to me. I'll look after you.' Godric took Janna's hand to guide her. He began to push his way through the trees. It seemed to Janna that they were setting off in the wrong direction, but she held her peace, trusting him. Fallen logs and hidden tree roots tripped her. Several times her feet sank into boggy patches, unseen traps under the nettles, dock and bracken that carpeted the forest floor. She would have fallen without Godric's hand to steady her. Did he really know where he was going? He didn't seem to be following a set path; in fact she was sure they had turned through at least one circle. Once or twice he stopped, bidding her shine the torch ahead. He was following the signs of his passage, she realised suddenly, recognising then the significance of bruised and trampled plants, a muddy footprint, broken twigs. At last he bent and picked up a dead hare. He slung it over his shoulders and took her hand once more, this time walking ahead in a straight, sure line.

Janna was pleased that saving her hadn't interfered with his real night's work. All the same, she felt uneasy. She should say something, just to have things clear between them. How could she let him know how she felt without hurting his feelings?

28

It's not my fault I don't want to marry yet, she thought crossly. Why can't he court Gytha instead? Or Elfreda or Wulfrun? They would surely be pleased to have an offer of marriage from such a fine fellow!

The memory of her ordeal did little to add to Janna's peace of mind as she trudged along. Her heart pumped faster and she broke into a clammy sweat as she relived the terror of the chase. She could have died tonight. Without Godric, all her fine dreams for the future would have counted for nothing. There was no getting around the fact that she owed him her life, and that she would always be in his debt. She hated that feeling of obligation, and what it might mean for her future. In fact, Janna felt thoroughly uncomfortable by the time they came to a part of the forest she recognised. She was not so very far from home after all.

'Thank you, Godric.' She stopped and let go of his hand, wanting to put an end to her indebtedness to him, and to her own uneasy thoughts. 'Thank you for saving my life tonight. I know where I am now. I can find my way from here.'

'I will see you safe home.' He kept on walking in the direction of the cottage.

'I know this part of the forest. I'm used to walking it alone,' Janna protested.

Godric smiled at her. 'I just want to make sure you are safe,' he said simply, and kept on going. With a sigh of resignation, Janna followed him.

The cottage was in darkness when they reached it. Janna pushed open the door, hoping to find her mother back home and sleeping within. But the only sign of life was the black cat, which stirred and blinked one sleepy eye at them. A faint warmth came from the turfed-down fire; thin wisps of smoke added to the already choking atmosphere. Janna flung open a shutter to let some fresh air into the smoky room, while Godric crouched down and blew on the embers, helping to bring the flame to life with a handful of dry leaves and twigs kept in a crock beside the fireplace.

As the flames caught and held, the small cottage became illuminated in their glow. Janna poured some water into a bowl and added a few leaves of soapwort to clean her filthy hands. She beckoned Godric to join her.

'Where is your mother?' he asked, once he'd dried his hands on the cloth Janna offered him.

'Gone to look after Dame Alice.' Janna scowled at the memory.

'Is something amiss with ma dame?'

Janna remembered that the lady's husband was Godric's liege lord. 'My mother has gone to help my lady recover from the birth of her babe,' she said briefly, not wanting to fuel the situation with wild rumours.

'Will you be all right out here on your own? Shall I stay with you until your mother returns?'

'No! I'm quite used to being alone.' Janna turned from him, willing him to be gone. Her thoughts were in turmoil, and he was standing far too close for comfort. She could feel the heat from his body, and shivered as his sleeve brushed hers.

The black cat uncoiled and began to weave around Godric's ankles. He nudged it aside with his boot. 'Don't!' Janna remonstrated as the cat gave an affronted growl.

Godric looked up then, his expression serious. 'I know your mother has skill with herbs, and I have good reason to

30

be grateful. Dame Alice's patronage must also be seen as a mark of respect. But take care, Janna. There is talk in the village and in the hamlets around here, much talk about this cat and about your mother.'

'What nonsense is this?' Janna snatched up Alfred and stroked him, soothing his dignity along with her own agitation.

'The new priest speaks against you for refusing to come to his church. He says that you meddle in matters which should better be left to God.'

'I suppose he would rather a woman die in childbirth than seek help,' Janna said scornfully.

'I understand that you and your mother seek only to heal, to bring relief to those in need, but there is a midwife at Berford. Why not leave such things to her?'

'My mother has far more skill and knowledge than Mistress Aldith,' Janna retorted. 'She says the midwife knows more about burying mothers than bringing babies into the world. That's why Master Fulk was summoned to the manor house. And that's why he came to fetch my mother and not Mistress Aldith tonight.' Janna stopped abruptly as she remembered Godric's position at the manor house. 'If Aldith has been speaking against us, it is because most women respect my mother's knowledge and seek her out rather than place their safety in the hands of an ignorant woman!' she added hastily.

'I have not heard Mistress Aldith blacken your mother's name, but others do. There is talk that your mother communes with the dead, and that she is even able to take on their appearance.' Godric pointed at the cat in Janna's arms. ''Tis also said by some that this is the devil in your home.'

'Alfred?' Janna's arms tightened around the cat. 'You can't be serious!'

'And that's another thing,' Godric said awkwardly. 'They're also angry that you've given your cat the name of the greatest king that Wessex has ever known.' He smiled then. 'Couldn't you just call it Fluffy, or something?'

'No, I could not.' It was because of the villagers that she'd come to name the cat Alfred. She wouldn't change the name for anything.

'Well.' Godric moved towards the door. 'I mean no harm in repeating what people are saying. It's nonsense anyway. I just wanted to warn you. But perhaps a warning isn't necessary if Dame Alice has called on your mother's skill to aid her. That should be enough to stop any ill-natured tattle.'

He opened the door, then quickly turned, seized Janna's hand and kissed it, blushing deeply as he did so. 'Goodbye,' he muttered. 'God be with you, Janna.'

'Goodbye, Godric. Thank you for saving me tonight.' Janna felt his kiss burn through her skin, through all the bones and muscles of her body.

'Shall I ask for a reward?' he said cheerfully. His face brightened as he added, 'Shall I ask for more than just your thanks?'

Janna's face flamed scarlet. Godric grinned at her. 'We shall meet again, Janna, and soon,' he promised, and padded off into the night.

FOUR

THE COTTAGE SEEMED too quiet after Godric had gone. Janna stared into the golden heart of the fire, reflecting on his words. Did the villagers really fear them, fear Alfred? She set him down, then sat down herself, for her legs felt trembling and weak all of a sudden. She still felt shaken after her encounter with the boar, but she felt even more shaken after her encounter with Godric. There was no doubt as to his intention, but what did she really owe him for his deed this night? Was she willing to pay with her heart, her body, her life and loyalty?

Alfred nudged her hand, his intention plain. Janna bent to stroke him and he purred loudly. She smiled down at him, remembering how, so many months ago, she'd found him struggling in the river, along with the rest of the litter that had been thrown in to drown. She had tried to save them all. This was the only kitten to survive, so she'd decided to call him Alfred after the great king who had never given up, who had continued to fight the Danes until he'd succeeded in driving them out of Wessex.

Patiently she had set out to befriend the cat, and tame him. Step by step, Alfred had allowed Janna to touch him, to stroke his fur, to pick him up for a cuddle. Shut in on the long winter evenings, he had finally come to Janna in the midnight hours, when the fire had died down and the cottage was cold. Together and warm, they had slept through the night.

She picked him up and plopped him down on the straw pallet where she and Eadgyth slept. Next, she unfastened her girdle of plaited fibres and laid the purse of strawberries upon the table. They had cost her dear – how dear she could not tell her mother, for she knew the questions that would follow if she spoke of her encounter with Godric. She would not answer to her mother, or Godric, until she knew the truth of her own heart, she decided.

She removed the long, coarsely woven grey kirtle that covered her under-tunic and lay down beside the cat. She shivered suddenly, and pulled an old moth-eaten fur coverlet over her body, snuggling into its folds for warmth and comfort. The black cat curled up beside her, purring loudly. She raised a hand to stroke his glossy fur, then gave a sudden snort of laughter as she recalled Godric's warning. Could the villagers truly believe that Alfred was the devil? How could they be so ignorant, so superstitious! She longed to be free of them all, free to follow her destiny. What fun it would be to travel to royal Winchestre and have adventures. She could find work along the way. It wouldn't matter what she did, so long as she could earn her keep. And if she worked hard, perhaps she might even become a somebody instead of a nobody. She might meet a handsome nobleman . . . or even the king himself . . .

Janna's hand stilled upon the cat's soft fur. There was a

half-smile upon her face as daydreams dissolved into the phantasmagoria of sleep.

The cottage was still empty when she awoke. She sat up, feeling a moment's alarm until she realised that her mother must still be with Dame Alice. It meant things must be going badly for, with an important visitor to see this morning, her mother would surely have returned by now. Unless she and Fulk were busy making plans for their new partnership? Janna scowled at the thought, but it was followed quickly by another, more interesting idea. If Eadgyth spent most of her days in Wiltune looking after Fulk's patients, wouldn't that give her, Janna, more freedom to look after the villagers here on her own?

Janna felt excited by the prospect. She began to regret her hasty exit the night before.

Alfred was waiting by the door. Janna jumped up to let him out, then followed him outside to peer across the green downs in the direction of Babestoche Manor. A distant figure told her that Eadgyth was on her way home. She set about rekindling the fire, and hung a pot of water to boil, while she waited impatiently to question her mother about their future.

'And did you gather the strawberries after you left us so rudely, Janna?' Eadgyth's tone, as she opened the door, was cool, unforgiving. She did not look at her daughter but instead busied herself untying her cloak and hanging it from a peg.

Janna's face flushed with embarrassment. 'And are you now in partnership with Fulk the apothecary, mother?' She mimicked Eadgyth's tone, sulky with resentment.

'Hold your tongue, foolish girl.' Her mother caught sight of the purse and moved towards the table to inspect its contents. The night's adventure was still vivid in Janna's mind. She wanted to tell her mother how dangerous gathering strawberries had proved, and ask her advice about Godric. But her mother had cautioned her to be silent and so she would. She, too, could keep secrets.

'I have spent the night with Dame Alice, although Fulk would have been present in my lady's chamber if he'd had his way, if I had allowed it.' Eadgyth relented somewhat, pride loosening her tongue.

'How is it with the lady? And the new babe?' If Eadgyth was trying to make peace, then Janna was prepared to meet her mother halfway.

Eadgyth frowned. 'Dame Alice is recovering her health and her spirits, but I worry that the baby may not survive. He is weak after the lady's long labour and will not suckle. I suspect there may be more wrong with him even than that. I've done what I can to make him comfortable, and I shall make up a special tonic for him and call in after noon to see how they both fare. Indeed, I would rather have stayed on at the manor and made my physic there if it were not that I have agreed to see . . .' She caught herself before she said the name.

'You must go to the mill at Bredecumbe, Janna,' she said instead. 'We are in need of flour. You may take the usual crock of honey in payment.' She considered for a moment.

'It would be best if you speak to the miller's wife. I'll give you a balm of comfrey for her ulcers, for I know the poor woman suffers sorely.'

'And why may I not stay and meet Mistress Whoever-she-is?' Janna said hotly, resentful at being sent away when her errand was not so very urgent.

'Because she has impressed upon me the need for the greatest secrecy. No-one must know of her coming, she told me. No-one. That includes you, Janna. Now go out and pick me some rue and pennyroyal before you go, and houseleek too. Oh, and bring me tansy and lavender to freshen the rushes on the floor. Instead of being quarrelsome, make yourself useful.'

'What of Fulk? How do matters rest with him?'

Eadgyth gave a short laugh. 'Dame Alice knows my true worth, even if Fulk does not. I discovered that it was she who sent Fulk to fetch me. All that talk of wanting me to work in his shop was to cover his ignorance and bolster his pride. The man is a turnip head. I could never work with him, I have far too much to lose. So I've sent him on his way, with a flea in his ear for how he has treated his patient and instructions to summon me earlier next time he is called on to deal with such problems.' She gave her daughter a brief, bright smile. 'You and I will continue as we were, Janna, as we have always been.'

As we have always been. Janna felt a sharp stab of disappointment as her brief dream of independence was snatched away. 'I had thought, with you in Wiltune, that you might trust me at last to take care of the villagers on my own,' she ventured.

'You are too young. They would have no respect for you.'

'They'll never respect me if I don't know what I'm doing. And I'll never find out if you won't let me try!'

'I've already taught you everything I know,' Eadgyth protested.

'Then let me use that knowledge to help people. You may be the greatest healer around here, but I could be too if you'd only give me a chance.'

'I swear that tongue of yours has been sharpened by the devil!' Eadgyth gave her daughter a good, hard shake. 'Soon enough you will marry, have children, be happy. That's the future I wish for you.'

'And what about my wishes?' Janna flashed. 'I don't want to marry, at least not yet.'

'Why not? You are certainly old enough to wed. Far better a life with a good husband than the hard life we live here.'

'I want something more than to become some man's drudge and a nursemaid to his children.'

'There's much more to wedlock than that!' Eadgyth retorted. Seeing her daughter blush, she added, 'As well as bedgames, a good husband would give you security. Safely wed, you'd be both respectable and respected.'

'And how would you know, Mother?' Janna seized the opportunity Eadgyth had given her. 'Were you ever safely wed? What was between you and my father? Why will you never speak of him? Are you ashamed of him, or is it your past that shames you?'

'It is because of him that I would see you wed.'

Janna read the pain in her mother's eyes, but the devil snapped at her heels. She had to go on, to push for answers to the questions that would not go away. 'Tell me about him, please,' she begged.

It wasn't the first time she'd asked the question. Her father had died just before her birth, or so her mother had told her. Janna had often wondered if Eadgyth was telling the truth, or trying to cover the fact that she'd never been wed – that Janna's birth, in fact, had been an accident. This thought nagged Janna like a sore tooth, but after she'd seen how talking about her father so distressed Eadgyth, she'd stopped asking after him. She knew anyway that Eadgyth never answered her questions. Nor did she now. She turned to her task, dismissing Janna with a brief, 'See to the herbs, girl.'

Frustrated and resentful, Janna stamped outside. Their garden was a small, awkwardly shaped piece of land that had come with the cottage because it didn't fit in to the long strips of fields worked by the villeins. The hives that provided honey for her mother's salves and potions were tucked into one corner. Janna was protective of her bees and took good care of them, for their honey was like liquid gold when silver was always in short supply. The bees lived in straw skeps, woven and crafted by Janna herself, and usually she stopped and talked to them, following a long tradition of telling them about the doings of the household. Today she did not take her usual comfort from the soothing buzz that marked their industry. Instead, she slapped angrily at a lone bee that circled close to her nose, and seethed with the injustice of being treated like a child when she no longer considered herself to be one.

She stomped on past the dew pond that provided them with water, past rows of turnips, cabbages, leeks and broad beans that put food on their table, past bushes of alecost which they used to flavour ale, and past flax plants which were boiled into decoctions to ease various ailments, or stripped and woven into cloth.

Janna looked beyond the neat lines of plants to the wattle fence that penned their two goats, Nellie and Gruff, along with Fussy, Greedy, Rusty and Laet, their hens. The goats bleated anxiously, reminding her that they still needed to be fed. She stooped over the clusters of herbs that formed the basis of her mother's healing mixtures, forgetting her sulks for the moment as she concentrated on her task. She could not afford to make any mistakes if she wanted her mother to treat her like an adult, someone more fitting than Fulk to be her partner.

First, Janna stripped off several leafy sprigs of tansy and put them in her scrip. It was a useful plant. The flowers made a fine golden dye, while the bitter, aromatic leaves served as a repellent for lice and fleas. Janna turned next to the fleshy leaves of houseleek and the other herbs her mother had requested, but once they were gathered her mind returned to her grievances. Why would her mother not speak of her father? Was it sorrow that kept her tight-lipped, or was it the shame of bearing a daughter out of wedlock? Janna knew her mother's lips would stay stubbornly closed unless she could come up with some new strategy to persuade her to unlock the secrets of her heart. Could she perhaps threaten to go elsewhere for information? Who might know the truth?

Her mind ranged over possibilities. They were few indeed. Her mother had no close friends, no-one in whom she might confide if she would not confide in her daughter. For the first time it occurred to Janna how lonely her mother must be. Where was her own family? She didn't think Eadgyth had always lived here, on the edge of the forest, yet this place was all Janna could remember, so her mother must surely have come here before giving birth. That being so, people might have seen or heard something, might remember something of that time. If so, why had they never spoken? Had her mother sworn everyone to secrecy? Who was she trying to protect? Her daughter – or herself? Janna knew that Eadgyth was proud, and that she kept her secrets well. Yet if Janna was now old enough to marry, she was surely old enough to be told the truth!

Janna rushed indoors, determined to try out this new argument.

She found Eadgyth, cheeks flushed from the rising steam, stirring a concoction over the fire. Absorbed in her task, she was humming quietly to herself. The tune was familiar to Janna. It sounded rather solemn and sad. She'd once asked Eadgyth to teach her the song, but her mother had silenced her with a sharp look and an angry refusal. Janna had never asked again, thinking there must be something shameful in the practice for Eadgyth had looked so guilty when caught. Yet she'd heard her mother sing the tune several times since; it seemed that Eadgyth sang only when she was preoccupied with something else.

'Tell me about my father.' Janna dumped the herbs in front of her mother. 'You say I'm old enough to marry, so that makes me old enough to know the truth about my birth.'

Startled, Eadgyth stopped humming and glared at her daughter. 'I haven't got time for another argument. The lady will be coming shortly. You must go now.'

'I still have to feed the hens and goats.'

'I'll do it.' Eadgyth jerked her thumb in the direction of the door. 'I want your promise that you'll not linger to watch, but that you will go directly about the business I have given you, and speak to no-one of my business back here.' She eyed her defiant daughter, and sighed. 'As well as visiting the miller, you have my permission to walk on to Wiltune. Today is market day. Take the beeswax candles and some of my special scented creams and rinses to sell there. They'll fetch a few pennies, so you may buy a hot pie for your dinner. I don't want you to leave Wiltune until you hear the abbey bells ring the hour of nones.'

Janna's face brightened. Going to the market was a rare treat, even if she knew her mother's offer stemmed from a need to keep her away for most of the day. 'I don't want to argue with you. I just want you to tell me my father's name,' she said, refusing to be diverted from her purpose. She avoided her mother's eye, instead collecting up the goods she would sell and setting them carefully in a woven basket. She hoped that the beeswax stoppers were thick and tight enough to prevent the precious liquids from leaking out but, to make sure, she wedged fat scented candles around them to keep them in place. All the while, she waited for her mother to speak, but Eadgyth remained silent. Janna hefted the strap over her shoulder. The basket was heavy but she would carry it without protest, so long as her mother gave her something in return. Determined not to leave without an answer, she confronted Eadgyth.

'There may not be time to talk now, but I insist that you tell me my father's name at least.'

'Janna!' Her mother threw down the spoon and, hands on hips, turned to glare at her daughter.

'Who was he? Where did you meet him?'

'That's enough, Johanna!' Her mother only called Janna by her full name when she was in serious trouble. Otherwise Janna was known by her baby name, which was what she'd called herself when she was just learning how to talk. Being called 'Johanna' made her feel uncomfortable, as if she was someone different, someone who didn't belong in the only world she knew. Now Janna felt torn between her usual obedience to her mother's wishes and a wild impatience to know more. She opened her mouth, then quickly closed it as she struggled to find the best words to change her mother's mind. Dismissing her daughter, Eadgyth turned back to the fire and picked up the spoon to give her decoction another stir.

Janna pulled a face at her mother's back, then instantly regretted her action. She wasn't a child any more. How could she convince her mother of that if she still behaved like one? She scooped up the crock of honey and jar of healing salve her mother had placed on the table, then paused at the doorway, determined to speak her mind.

'I am sorry if the memory distresses you, Mother, but if you won't tell me about my father then you force me to ask others for information.'

Eadgyth's hand stilled. Her whole body went rigid with shock. 'Questions, questions!' she snapped. 'Why do you always plague me with questions?'

'Because you taught me to question everything! Why, then, should I not question the mystery of my father?' Janna met her mother's hard stare, determined that this time she would not back down. For a long moment they defied each other. Finally, Eadgyth nodded slightly. 'If you must hear of it, then 'tis better I tell you in my own words. Those who do not know the truth of the matter might not be so kind.' She paused, weighing her words carefully. 'You believe your father to be dead, but in truth and for all I know, he may still be alive.'

'My father lives?' Janna's eyes widened in amazement. 'Why did you not tell me this before?'

'I wanted to protect you.' Eadgyth touched Janna's cheek in a rare gesture of affection. 'I have many regrets in my life, but the one thing I shall never regret is giving birth to you. I'll do anything to save you making the same mistakes that I made.'

For a moment Janna was silenced by her mother's un-expected tenderness. Yet her will to learn the truth was strong; she felt impatient with her mother's desire to protect her. 'All my life I have kept silent, thinking my father was dead and that it grieved you to speak of him. For all these years, you have let me believe a lie!'

'It does grieve me to speak of him. I loved your father. That's why I –'

A timid knock interrupted Eadgyth. Startled, she glanced from Janna to the door. 'Wait here,' she said, and went quickly outside, slamming the door shut behind her. Janna heard the soft murmur of voices. She moved towards the door, listening hard. The door was suddenly flung open, catching her by surprise.

'Go now.' Eadgyth was in too much of a hurry to repri-mand her daughter for eavesdropping. 'We will speak later.' She pushed Janna outside, then followed her out and moved towards the back of the cottage. 'Go!' she shouted, as she noticed that Janna had stopped to watch.

Having secured her mother's promise, Janna did as she was told, but she couldn't resist a last look behind. Too late, she realised, as she heard the door slam. Her mother and the visitor were now both safely inside and out of sight. She turned then and walked on towards the small village of Berford. The day was cloudy; there was a hint of rain in the air, but Janna's spirits rose as she sniffed the fresh air, smiled at peacefully grazing sheep and listened to the melodious whistle of a lone blackbird.

Her path followed the contours of the gently sloping downs, taking her down towards the Nadder River and Berford. A straggle of thatched cottages came into view, set along a track of beaten earth close to the river. Like Janna's own home, the cottages were made from panels of woven wattle set between wooden posts and pasted over with a mixture of clay, dung and straw daub to keep out wind and rain. While still having only one room, these cottages were larger than the small cot Janna shared with her mother. Most of them boasted henhouses, vegetable gardens, goats and sometimes even a cow or pig. Beyond the settlement and above the water meadows were the open fields where villeins grew crops in their allotted strips, both for themselves and for the abbey.

The track was littered with human and vegetable waste. Pigs, goats, hens and ducks walked free, noisily scuffling for pickings among the rotting vegetation. Pools of scummy water added their stench to the ripe air. Janna picked her way past the worst of it, following the path that would bring her to the water mill and, by way of several small hamlets, to Wiltune itself. Near Bredecumbe she forded the river, splashing through clear pebbled shallows to the water meadows on the other side. She walked on to where the chalk stream divided and pooled into a small lake, turning the swiftly flowing tributary into the rushing torrent which powered the mill when the waters were released. Two low stone arches spanned the frothing water; above them was a thatched wattle and daub building where the grinding of the grain actually took place. Janna could hear now the thunder of the great wheel churning below. She stopped, charmed by the sight of a mother duck paddling upstream, with a string of babies behind it. Her pleasure in the sight quickly changed to alarm as she noticed that one of the ducklings had lagged behind and become caught in the undertow. In spite of its efforts it was being dragged closer and closer to the powerful wheel. She looked about for a net or a bucket, anything to save it, but even those few seconds had taken all the time that was left. As she turned back to the river, the duckling disappeared from view.

Janna swallowed hard, and hoisted up the honeypot so that it fitted more snugly under her arm. This was nature's way; it was stupid to get upset about it, she told herself as she walked up to the open door and peered in. The miller's wife, hand to her back and heavy with child, stood beside the chattering pit wheel, watching as brown, gritty flour poured down through the chute into the grain bin. Above her head, Janna could hear the heavy tread of the miller as he hoisted another sack of corn to feed into the hopper. The millstones ground the corn with a dull roar. Janna sneezed as a spray of fine flour dust tickled her nose. The sound alerted the miller's wife to the fact that she had company.

She swung around. As she recognised her visitor, an expression of alarm flitted across her face. She took a quick step backwards, and crossed herself.

Surprised, Janna held out the jar of salve, fixing a smile on her face as she did so. 'I have here some ointment for you, Mistress Hilde. For the sores on your skin. My mother said I was to bring it to you.'

The woman made no move to take the jar. Instead she scratched her arm while she took the time to look Janna over. Janna felt sorry for her. It was common knowledge that the miller strayed from home, and that he spread his favours among several women. 'Her jealousy is eating away at her skin as well as her heart,' Eadgyth had said once. 'I can soothe her sores, but she will never be free of them unless her husband stops straying or she ceases to care about it.'

'But surely he will stay at home now that his wife is with child?'

Eadgyth had given her daughter a cynical smile. 'It's at this time, when wives are large with child and become unwilling partners in bedgames, that most men are tempted to look elsewhere. Unfortunately for Hilde, her husband has already had a lot of practice in the art of straying. Nothing is likely to change him now.'

Her mother must have thought her comments naive, Janna realised, yet she truly believed that a marriage should be for love, and for ever. She would never settle for a husband who strayed, whose tomcatting left her vulnerable and despairing, and an object of pity and scorn to others.

Janna felt a great sympathy for this hurting, discontented woman.

'Please, take the salve,' she said, thrusting it into Hilde's hand. She kept her eyes fixed on Hilde's face so that she wouldn't have to look at the weeping sores on the woman's arm. Her mother had told her that there were sores on Hilde's legs as well – another reason for the miller to stray.

Hilde's fingers closed around the rough, home-made pot.

'I have also this crock of honey.' Janna placed it on the table. 'My mother wishes to exchange it for a bag of flour as usual, if you please.'

The miller's wife gave a grudging nod. Janna wondered if she might ask a final favour.

'I am bound for the market at Wiltune, mistress,' she said. 'May I fetch the flour later?'

Undecided, the miller's wife looked upwards as if seeking advice from her husband. Janna heard a loud rattling noise as the miller fed grain into the chute; the millstones began to grind once more. Coarse flour poured down into the grain bin. For the moment, the miller was safely occupied. Hilde's tight expression eased somewhat. 'You may come for it on your way home.' She gave Janna a push towards the door.

With a light heart, looking forward to her treat, Janna turned and left. It was going to be a wonderful day, she just knew it. Whether it rained or no, the birds sang and whistled about their business, the river chattered merrily beside her, and the frights of the night seemed long ago and far away.

FIVE

ALTHOUGH JANNA HAD been to Wiltune several times, it had always been in the company of her mother. Now she enjoyed a new sense of freedom as she looked about her, fascinated by all that she saw. The abbess held the barony over just about all of the land she was walking through. Her villeins were out in the fields, working her lands and paying rent for the privilege of having a home and employment. Some, like the miller, paid rent and rendered services, while others paid their dues in labour. Every year Janna's mother grumbled about having to find the fee for the abbess for, although they were free to leave if they wished, while they stayed they must pay for their cottage and the land that came with it. In bad seasons, payment caused hardship for everyone. Fortunately, this year had started well and promised fair, unless the civil war between the king and his cousin came close enough to upset smiling nature and wreck the harvest to come.

The sun had poked through the clouds. It burned Janna's face and dried her mouth. She shifted the strap of her basket from one shoulder to the other; her back ached from carrying it. She turned towards the river, squelching through

49

mud and pushing through sharp reeds to get to the water's edge. There, she bent to scoop a handful of cold, clear liquid into her mouth, relishing the moisture as it slipped down her parched throat.

She drank her fill and set off once more, coming at last to the high stone walls that encircled the abbey. Janna followed them around, heading for the market square outside the abbey's main portal. She heard the noise long before she got there: shouts of pedlars, the shrill cries of children, yapping dogs and squealing, clucking livestock, and the rise and fall of voices as shoppers and traders bargained hard to get the better of each other. Janna sighed with pleasure. This is where I want to be, she thought. This is where real life is happening!

Pleasant odours wafted towards her – hot pies, spiced wine and gingerbread – but they were offset by the stink of sewage, newly tanned leather and salted fish. Travelling merchants had set up stalls among the more usual goods for trade. Janna stopped to admire a display of soft leather gloves and slippers, then moved on to inspect trays of ribbons, cheap trinkets, bone combs and buttons, strings of amber and glass beads and finely wrought brooches. She fingered her empty purse, imagining how it would feel to have enough money to buy whatever she wanted. With a small sigh, she moved on to join a group gathered around a juggler. As she came closer, two women stepped out of her way, neither acknowledging her nor meeting her eye. Janna recognised them and was puzzled. One of them, the wife of a weaver from Berford, had made the journey to the edge of the forest several times to consult her mother. Surely she would not be influenced by the priest's prejudice against them?

'I give you good day, Mistress Bertha,' she said, as she came closer.

'God be with you, Janna.' Bertha didn't look at her, seeming absorbed instead in the antics of the juggler, who had now added a flaming sword to the three balls he was keeping in the air so skilfully.

Janna pulled a face behind Bertha's back as the woman kept on walking, then chided herself for being silly. She would not allow anyone to spoil her pleasure in the day. So she watched the juggler, and clapped his performance when he was done. She wished she had some coins to put in his cap for he'd entertained and delighted her with his skill.

She was about to move on when she recognised another familiar face. There, in the marketplace, his black cloak flapping around his short, thin frame so that he looked like an old crow as he swooped about, was the priest from Berford. What was he doing here? Probably making sure none of his flock managed to enjoy themselves, Janna thought with a grin, and edged away out of his notice. There was so much to see and do; she had no intention of being waylaid and lectured by the priest.

She ambled on, fascinated by all the products for sale: fruits and vegetables, sparrows, pigeons and hens, woven cloth of varying quality, fresh bread, candles and soap, crocks of honey and blocks of cheese. Her nose twitched as she smelled once more the fragrance of hot meat pies. She had come out in such a rush that she'd not yet broken her fast. Her empty stomach rumbled to remind her of the fact.

As soon as she had sold her wares, she would visit the pieman. She looked about for a space to set out her scented candles, creams and rinses, enjoying her new feeling of independence. The thud of a horse's hooves and the jingle of a bridle alerted her to the presence of a stranger coming towards her.

The first detail Janna noticed was the horse, a huge black destrier such as a soldier or a crusader might ride into battle. It was a sleek beast, quite unlike the shaggy ponies and plodding carthorses she usually saw in the fields. The horse's glossy coat shone, and Janna shielded her eyes from the bright sunlight the better to admire it.

She became aware of its owner next, as he reined his mount to a standstill and surveyed the market scene before him. Dark shoulder-length hair and clean-shaven in the old Norman fashion. A long and decorated tunic, the sort worn by the nobility. A faint smile curled his mouth. Seeing it, Janna clenched her fingers into fists, feeling hot indignation on Wiltune's behalf. Condescending *bricon*, she thought, automatically assigning to him the Norman word for 'fool'. He must surely be one of them for no Saxon would sneer at the villagers as he was sneering now.

As if becoming aware of her gaze, and her judgment, the man glanced down at Janna. The smile died on his lips, burnt away perhaps by her furious expression. Feeling no fear, for she had nothing to lose, she continued to glower up at him. A smile twitched his lips once more as he nodded to her from his horse and called out, '*Bonjour, ma belle petite.*'

Janna bridled anew. She tilted her head back and glared at him. Pretty girl indeed!

'Can you give me directions to the manor house at Babestoche?' The man continued his careful inspection of Janna. There was warmth in his gaze; a smile of appreciation curved his mouth.

For a moment, Janna thought to send him off in the wrong direction entirely, but she had the sense that, in fact, the stranger already knew the way and was using this merely as a ruse to speak to her. Telling herself she wasn't in the least flattered, she said, 'Follow the river to Berford, then ask again.' Although the stranger had asked directions in her own tongue, pride prompted Janna to answer him in the language of the Normans, taught to her by Eadgyth. She jerked her head in the direction the stranger should ride, and walked away, conscious that his eyes still watched her. Belying her cool manner, her mind was full of a jumble of impressions, not least of which was the stranger's easy assurance, his fine tunic and hose and, yes, she was forced to admit it, his handsome face and strong physique.

Frowning, Janna considered the matter. Some years older than her, perhaps in his mid-twenties, she thought. She could sense the experience behind his ease, the experience that told him his worth in terms of his birth but also in matters of life – and death. This was a man sure of himself, someone not to be disregarded or put aside. A scar down one cheek spoke of his having tested himself in combat, either of a personal nature or on the battlefield. A man of courage, then. A man's man. A lady's man too. Janna felt herself grow hot as she recalled how his bold glance had raked her body. He'd called her a pretty girl, but she was a Saxon serf and therefore unworthy of his notice. He was merely teasing her. This was a man who could pick and choose among women – and most probably did, for who could not fail to be impressed by that proud, handsome face, that confident demeanour?

Janna was surprised how much she had noticed – and remembered – on such a short appraisal. Who was he? And what could he want up at the manor? These were troubled times for travellers – and for all of England. King Stephen had usurped the throne and was now forced to defend his position against his cousin, the Empress Matilda. Janna had a secret admiration for the empress. Enraged by Stephen's action and determined not to give up the throne, Matilda had gathered her own army of supporters and come to England to fight for her rights. Her claim seemed just, for she had been named heir by her father, King Henry. He himself was the son of the Norman bastard, William the Conqueror, who had taken England for his own and established the line of Norman rule. There had already been several skirmishes between Stephen's army and Matilda's supporters. Was the stranger here on Stephen's behalf, to demand from the abbess and the manor house the knight service due to the king?

Telling herself his business was none of her concern, Janna found a space next to a traveller, a spice merchant. Keeping a sharp lookout for the shire reeve, for she had no permission to sell her wares, Janna pulled a clean linen cloth from her pack and spread it on the ground, having first cleared straw and assorted rubbish out of the way. Carefully, she laid out her goods for sale. 'Creams to perfume your skin, ladies!' she called out, gesturing towards the pots on the ground as she continued: 'Smell like a rose for your husband tonight. I also have rosemary and chamomile rinses to cleanse and lighten your hair. I have fragrant lavender for your linen, and a mint rinse to freshen your breath. Farthing a jar.'

Frowning, the spice merchant leaned over and inspected the pots, calculating whether or not their presence would damage his own business. In turn, Janna stared at his portable table, fascinated by the strange seeds, berries and plants upon it. She bent over and inhaled, savouring their fragrance. 'What are these?' she asked, pointing at a pile of light brown sticks.

'Cinnamon.' He gestured towards a crock of small black balls. 'And those are cloves.' His manner thawing in the face of Janna's interest, he kept pointing out various spices, perhaps hoping that she might buy something. 'My wares come from across the sea, from the east,' he told her, speaking loudly so that his voice might be heard above the hubbub of the marketplace. 'It is a long journey, and my spices are highly prized because of it. See – I have yellow saffron, cardamom, peppercorns and caraway seeds.' While he answered Janna's questions, the merchant kept a sharp eye out for passing trade. She became aware that he was using his answers to her questions as a means to tempt others to inspect his wares. His ruse was working, for first one and then another woman drew closer. There was quite a crowd of observers around when Janna pointed to a small phial of brownish oil, and asked its purpose.

'It is a marvel, a miracle cure, most efficacious for aching joints. A little of this oil rubbed in at night, and you'll be as agile as a young spring lamb come morning.' His eyes twinkled. 'Not that you'll need it for quite a while yet, lass.'

'But what is in the oil?' Janna persisted, refusing to be either diverted or beguiled by his flattery.

The man hesitated for a moment, then said, 'It is a substance of such danger that I am loath to sell it to any other than those who are skilled in the art of healing and who know well the care that must be taken in its employment.'

Was he sincere, or was he merely building up the mystery and therefore the desirability of his liniment? Janna wasn't sure, and didn't really care. Curiosity drove her on. 'My mother is a healer, and would be interested to learn more of such a substance. Pray do tell me what is in the oil?'

The man folded his lips together, and would not speak.

'Answer the lass,' said Bertha.

Janna hid a smile. No doubt Bertha was after the secret ingredient so she could cure her own aching back rather than continue coming to Eadgyth for special liniment.

A sergeant-at-arms had joined the swelling crowd around the spice merchant, and now he stepped up close to the man. 'Give us your answer. Tell it true or I'll send you on your way. There's no place for quacks and charlatans here in Wiltune.'

'I mean no harm, I mean merely to warn.' The spice merchant stood his ground, looking self-righteous.

'Then warn away, and tell us what it is we need to fear.' The sergeant moved even closer, dwarfing the spice merchant by many inches both in height and width.

'*Aconitum napellus*. The root is ground and mixed with oil and hot mustard and then rubbed into aching joints. It brings almost instant relief. It really is a wonder cure.' The man was anxious to ingratiate himself now – and perhaps to make a sale in spite of his warning.

Aconitum. Aconite. The man was making the herb sound more important by giving it the Latin name – unless it was a ploy to keep a common plant a secret? Janna was willing to wager that no-one present knew what it was – but she knew what he was talking about. Her mother had instructed her well in the properties of herbs and the art of healing. The merchant could not bluff Janna with fancy Latin names. *Aconitum* was known by several common names: monks-hood, blue rocket, wolfsbane, helmet flower. Janna sup-pressed a shudder as she recalled the last time she'd seen it. It was the plant that grew near the strawberries she had risked so much to pick.

There was no secret here, for her mother already knew the properties of aconite, and no doubt the weaver's wife had felt its benefit on more than one occasion. Janna felt some satisfaction in thinking that Bertha would have to continue relying on Eadgyth for relief if she wasn't prepared to ask any more questions.

The sergeant nodded, and walked away. Janna breathed a sigh of relief that her own modest wares had not attracted his attention, but perhaps the sergeant had assumed that her pots were part of the merchant's display. The trader was busy with other customers now. They all wanted to finger his spices, and smell them before making a purchase. Taking advantage of the crowd, Janna sang out a temptation to the women to inspect her own wares. As she did so, she noticed that Bertha had taken her turn to hand over a coin, receiving from the spice seller a small phial of the rubbing oil. Had things come to such a pass that Bertha would rather hand over good silver than visit the *wortwyf*, who would treat her in return for a piece of woven woollen cloth or the gift of a few eggs?

Bertha hurried off, but several other women turned to Janna after making their purchases from the spice merchant. She congratulated herself on choosing such a good position as she smeared a dab of cream perfumed with violets onto her skin so that the women might smell it. Judging from the stench of perspiration and unwashed clothes emanating from some of them, they might well benefit from its application, she thought, as she held out her wrist to a new customer to take a sniff. 'The cream is good for your skin, too, it'll make it soft as a baby's cheek,' she said persuasively when the woman hesitated.

Strangers bought from Janna; some who knew her hurried on, crossing themselves or making a sign against her to ward off evil. Janna comforted herself by calling out, 'Buy my special perfumed candles for the church. Real beeswax, they'll burn for hours and hours and save your souls from damnation!'

As her purse swelled and supplies dwindled, Janna's thoughts turned again to the handsome man on horseback. Would she ever see him again? The thought stirred her blood, bringing an unexpected heat to her cheeks and body. Blushing, although she knew not why, she sang her song of temptation once more, loud enough to drown out the thoughts that would not lie quiet in her mind.

'Lavender and roses to perfume your skin! Mint balm to refresh tired feet and hands! Comb out the tangles and add sunlight to your hair with a chamomile rinse.'

The last jar and the last candle were finally sold. Janna folded the linen square, now filthy from the dirt and dust of the street and the animal dung that had left its mark. She placed the fabric carefully in her empty basket. It would have to be washed and bleached before it could be used again. Coins and tokens jangled in her purse as she moved. She smiled, feeling well pleased with the day's trade.

Her stomach grumbled, reminding her that she hadn't yet broken her fast. She pulled a token from her purse and set off towards the pieman.

Munching hungrily, she walked on then to the sundial in the centre of the market square and inspected the shadow cast by the marker. Only a little past the hour of one. She felt tired and she had a raging thirst. She was ready to go home, but dared not until she heard the abbey bells ring the three hours of nones. She would not risk her mother's anger – not when there was so much at stake. If she annoyed her mother by coming home early, then the secret of her father's identity might well stay locked in Eadgyth's heart.

Nor would she need to hurry home at nones either, she realised with some dismay. Once her mother's visitor left, surely Eadgyth would go straight to Dame Alice, to take her the concoction she'd prepared for the new infant. It could be hours before she came home to answer questions as she'd promised. Janna decided that she might as well relax and enjoy her small holiday. She glanced about the marketplace and the small shops that hedged it in. Master Fulk's shop was closed. Dame Alice must be paying him well for the business he was losing by attending her. Close to his shop was an alehouse, its purpose made clear by the bush tied to a pole outside the door, the same sign which marked the premises of several other alehouses in Wiltune. She fingered her bulging purse, and nodded to herself. She had never been to an alehouse before, but was curious to see inside. If she was old enough to wed, she was surely old enough to brave the louts who were hanging around outside, and who seemed to have made the alehouse their headquarters. She would go in, sit down, and have a jug of cool ale to slake her thirst. While she was resting, she would listen to the market gossip. Perchance she might overhear the identity of the man on horseback, and the mission that had brought him to Babestoche Manor.

Her first thought, when she stepped over the threshold, was to turn and run. The room was dark, having only a couple of window spaces to let in the light. Although there was no fire, stale smoke hung heavy in the air. It was mixed with the smell of sweat and unwashed clothes, and a lingering odour of animal waste brought in on boots and smeared over the already filthy straw strewed over the earthen floor. Janna placed her hand over her nose and coughed, debating whether she should leave. The bold glances of the patrons inside, and a lewd invitation for her to join some drinkers at their table, eroded her confidence even further. The only other women in the alehouse seemed to be harlots looking out for business. Yet pride made her defiant. She was not a coward; she would not turn and run. She had as much right to be there as any of them. She would find a seat and take some refreshment and the devil take them if they didn't like it. So Janna forced herself to keep on walking past the crowded tables until, mercifully, she spied an empty stool at the back of the room.

The alewife appeared from the brewhouse behind. She paused at the door to let her eyes grow accustomed to the dim light. She bustled over then and looked Janna up and down, mouth pursed in disapproval.

'Good day, mistress,' Janna said, continuing in a rush before she lost her nerve, 'I'm very thirsty. Bring me a jug of your good ale, if you please.'

The alewife didn't budge. Quickly, Janna produced a token and slapped it down on the rough wooden tabletop.

The woman waited until Janna produced another token. Then she nodded, slipped the tokens into a purse at her waist and disappeared through the crowd. Janna wondered if she'd ever see her again. She stretched out her legs and leaned back against the rough plastered wall of the alehouse, glad to rest as she waited to see what would happen next. Realising that they would get no fun out of her, the other patrons of the alehouse stopped their stares and resumed talking among themselves and flirting with the harlots.

Janna relaxed further when a wooden bowl was shoved in front of her. The alewife filled it from a leather bottle, the liquid sloshing over the brim. Janna muttered her thanks and bent over to slurp up a mouthful so that she could then lift the bowl without wasting any more ale. The alewife ignored her and kept on circulating around the tables, refilling and clearing as she went. Janna wasn't sure if the woman had taken against her because of her youth, or because she suspected Janna wasn't here only to slake her thirst. She decided she didn't care. She was thirsty and determined to enjoy her drink. She lifted the bowl and gulped down a couple of mouthfuls.

She smacked her lips, savouring the cool liquid as it slipped down her dry throat. She swallowed again, and then again more slowly, holding the ale briefly in her mouth as she thought about its taste. Janna helped her mother brew their own ale from the barley and herbs growing in their garden. Its taste was familiar to her, for like most villagers they broke their fast each morning with ale and a hunk of bread. She sipped again. The difference was subtle, but it was there: this ale was stronger in flavour and not nearly so sweet as their own. Eadgyth tended to have a liberal hand with honey. Was that the only difference? Perhaps there was something else added, other herbs that gave the ale its special flavour? Janna sipped and sipped again, trying to decide what it was that left the faintly unpleasant aftertaste in her mouth. Could it be that the water used by the alewife was not quite so fresh as the water Eadgyth always insisted that they collect from the most swiftly flowing stretch of the river to brew their own ale? In the past Janna had grumbled about having to carry the water uphill in heavy buckets, but she thought now that the effort was worthwhile if it made such a difference to the taste.

Having analysed the ale to her satisfaction, Janna sat back to survey the room. Her eyes had adjusted to the dim light, and she realised that a couple of the drinkers were known to her. She wondered if Fulk the apothecary was among the crowd, but after a careful scrutiny she concluded that his new patient must be keeping him occupied up at the manor. She just hoped he was not undoing all the good her mother had done.

In need of diversion, she began to listen to the

62

conversations going on around her. To her surprise, almost the first thing she heard was her own name.

'. . . growing into a real beauty by all accounts.' The man gave a sharp grunting laugh, unaware he had an extra pair of ears listening in. 'I'd be glad to take her on, if it wasn't for . . .' He stopped abruptly as his companion gave him a hard nudge and jerked a thumb at Janna. Undeterred, the man winked at her, then took a thirsty swig of ale.

Janna looked away, not sure whether to be amused or upset. Ulf the blacksmith was recently widowed and had a number of motherless children. No wonder he was in the market for a wife. She wondered what stopped him from approaching Eadgyth to speak of the matter. If it wasn't for . . . what? Her mother's reputation for shape-shifting and communing with the dead? Or Alfred, the devil cat who lived in their home?

'. . . on his way to Babestoche Manor.' Another voice came to Janna's ears. 'Did you see him, Eadric? Anyone would think he was King Stephen himself on that big black horse of his.' Janna shifted her stool closer, eager for news of the handsome stranger.

'Does he come to rally support for the king?' Eadric was a dark, ill-featured man who seemed to be taking no pleasure from either his companion or the drink in front of him. 'Does trouble come our way?'

'I think he comes only to visit his aunt, Dame Alice. He is quite often at the manor.'

'I hope you speak the truth of it, for if he has come to raise an army for the king, there will be trouble.' Eadric gave a loud belch, then patted his stomach. 'The abbess must surely side with the empress, not the king. After all, Matilda's mother spent part of her childhood here at the abbey.'

'The abbess risks everything if she supports the empress. If Stephen can arrest Bishop Roger, throw him into prison and take his palace at Sarisberie, he most surely can arrest our abbess if she supports the wrong side. Mark my words, the abbess will put the abbey's interests first and go with the king. But you are right: if my lord Hugh comes to raise an army, there *will* be trouble.'

'Why?' Eadric plonked an elbow on the table and leaned forward. 'What do you know of Dame Alice's nephew then? Where does his allegiance lie?'

'I had it from that traveller, him with the fancy leather goods for sale, that he's seen my lord Hugh in the company of Earl Robert of Gloucester.'

'Then that makes him the king's man.'

'No, it does not.'

'But Earl Robert has pledged his allegiance to the king.'

'That was after the king seized the throne, but the earl has since changed his mind. After all, he's half-brother to the empress. 'Tis said he's now Matilda's strongest supporter and the leader of her army.'

'So, if our fine lord is here on Matilda's behalf, he'll likely be clapped in irons and handed over to the king.' Eadric smirked at the thought. It was the first time Janna had seen him smile.

'Aye, that's what I told the traveller. "Robert of Babestoche is the king's man," that's what I told him.'

'But is he, though? Robert, I mean?'

The two men buried their faces in their beakers of ale and drank deep as they considered the question. Eadric's friend was the first to put down his pot. 'Tis true Robert of Babestoche hasn't travelled even as far as Sarisberie to pay homage to the king, so who knows where his loyalty lies? Or ours, for that matter?' He cast a quick look over his shoulder to check whether any had heard his words, for they could be construed as treason. Janna quickly averted her gaze and instead studied her hands as if red, chapped skin and ragged nails were the most important things in her life right now.

Eadric drained his beaker and set it down with a determined thud. 'I don't care who supports what, so long as the fighting don't come any closer,' he said. 'I've heard tell there's terrible hard times for those who are in the wrong place at the wrong time. Whole villages burnt, crops and beasts destroyed, people murdered in their beds or left to rot in dungeons. Tortured, even.' He shuddered. 'May the king, his ambitious cousin and those murdering barons keep as far from us as the moon itself, that's what I say. The devil can take them all!' He pushed his stool back and stood up, then lumbered slowly out of the room, followed by his companion.

So the stranger's name was Hugh and he was Dame Alice's nephew. Janna sat back, finding more questions to replace those that the drinkers had already answered. When had Hugh been seen with Earl Robert of Gloucester – before or after Matilda's half-brother had changed sides? Were they in agreement or at odds over the king? And what was his true purpose in coming to the manor? She felt a small shiver of fear run down her back at the thought that he might be running into a trap. Hastily, she consoled herself with the notion that Robert of Babestoche must have his mind on more urgent matters: the birth of his new son and the health of his wife.

The crowd in the alehouse was thinning now as, refreshment taken, people went outside once more to bargain, buy or sell. Janna heard the bells ring out, and counted: one, two, three. It was time for her to change her market tokens into good silver, and go.

Preoccupied as she was with questions about Hugh, and the more pressing matter of her father's identity, Janna almost walked past the mill. Suddenly recalling her errand of the morning, she turned aside and went to the door to collect the bag of flour promised her by the miller's wife. Hilde was not there, but the miller was, and he smiled a welcome as he noticed his visitor. Stockily built, he had the fair hair and beard typical of Saxon men. Women might find him irresistible, Janna thought, as she noted his cocky demeanour, but for herself she'd rather keep company with Godric – or even Hugh! The thought of the handsome stranger brought a rosy blush to her cheek. Hastily, Janna tried to compose herself. 'I . . . I have come for the bag of flour promised me by Mistress Hilde,' she said.

The miller stood by the door, unmoving. His smile grew broader.

'I left the usual crock of honey and some ointment for Mistress Hilde in return for the flour.' Janna waited, wondering why he did not answer.

He made no move to fetch the flour, but instead let his gaze roam over Janna's body. 'I believe I hold the toil of my labour more dearly than my wife does,' he said at last, and stepped closer. 'However, I am sure we can come to an arrangement agreeable to both of us.' Before Janna had time to move, his hand was at her breast. He stroked her shrinking flesh through the fabric of her kirtle.

'No!' Janna backed off, flinging her arms across her chest to protect herself.

The miller laughed softly. 'You are a maid, are you not? It is time for you to grow up, Janna, more than time. I am willing to teach you what it means to be a woman.'

'Save your instruction for your wife!' Janna said tartly, and backed off further. 'Just give me the flour and I'll trouble you no more.'

'I told you – I want something more than honey in return for my labour. I've decided I want something much sweeter.'

'You'll have my silence – and your wife's good humour – in return for not tormenting me further.'

The miller glowered at Janna. Feeling more confident, she stared back defiantly. With a scowl, he turned then and walked away. Janna lingered by the door, savouring her victory. As the miller returned with the sack, she held out her arms to receive it. The weight of it dragged down her arms, leaving her defenceless as the miller suddenly pulled her in close and kissed her hard on the lips.

With a cry of outrage, Janna jerked up her knee. The miller's face darkened with anger as he doubled over in pain. Janna swung around, ready to run. She found Hilde waddling towards her, grim-faced, holding her hands over her belly as if to protect her unborn child.

Janna tried to find the words to explain the scene that Hilde must surely have witnessed, but she had no chance to say anything for the woman shouldered her aside with an oath and stormed into the cottage, hurling a torrent of abuse at her husband as she did so.

Janna was sorry that Hilde had further proof of her husband's nature, yet she was also relieved that Hilde had arrived in time to prevent the miller from chasing after her to vent his anger and frustration. With a wry grimace, she hoisted the heavy bag of flour onto her shoulder and set off once more along the path for home.

SIX

ONCE HOME, JANNA kept busy with chores while she waited for her mother. She dug up some precious carrots and turnips for their dinner and fed the tops to the grateful goats, along with a handful of dock, dandelion and other weeds hastily gathered from the forest's edge. Seeing the tansy and lavender she'd picked that morning still lying on the table, she strewed the aromatic herbs over the floor rushes. Their fragrance scented the smoky room, adding to the rich smell of the vegetable stew which she'd set to bubble in a pot over the fire, awaiting Eadgyth's return. Janna had already used some of the new flour to make two flat bread cakes on the griddle, and now she ladled some of the vegetables onto one of them, too hungry to wait any longer. Alfred mewed, and batted her with his paw. She put some of her dinner down onto the rushes for him, and he scoffed it hungrily.

Why was her mother so late returning? Janna yawned, and wondered if she should go to her bed. Yet she knew she'd be too restless to sleep. Curiosity would keep her awake until she finally found out the truth about her father.

She sat down in her mother's chair beside the fire. Alfred jumped up and turned in a circle. He dug his claws into her kirtle and kneaded her lap, purring loudly as he made himself comfortable.

Janna stared into the flickering flames and pondered her mother's surprising admission. She felt deeply angry that Eadgyth had bought her silence with a lie designed to shut her mouth. Her father might still be alive! Who was he? A common labourer who had moved on, perhaps impelled on his journey by news of her mother's pregnancy? Did he still live in Berford or Babestoche, or even Wiltune, with a wife and children of his own? Janna sifted through all the men she knew, peasant, merchant and labourer, rejecting each one almost as soon as his face came into her mind. She would surely have sensed a bond when they met, or intercepted a special look between her mother and father when they thought no-one was watching. Besides, if he was a local man, Eadgyth would know for sure whether or not he lived.

He must be someone from her mother's past, from a life lived somewhere else. Either that, or her father had moved on rather than deal with the fact of her birth. Would she want to acknowledge someone like that, someone so cowardly that he would leave a maiden – either wed or unwed – to face her ordeal alone?

No, she would not! Neither would her mother – and yet Eadgyth had confessed that she loved him still. What could have gone so wrong between them that he'd abandoned them?

Janna's thoughts were interrupted by the faint drumming of hooves. As she listened, the sounds became louder. A horse from the manor house, bringing her mother home? She tipped Alfred off her lap, then unhooked the pot of vegetables and laid them aside in readiness.

The cat's back arched and its black fur stood on end as it faced the door. 'Scaredy-cat!' Janna scoffed. The sounds of hoof beats died. A loud knock thundered against the door. Not her mother then. Janna knew a moment's alarm. Surely not Fulk! Could it be Godric? No, he wouldn't come on horseback. Just like her, like most of the villeins, he wouldn't know how to ride a horse. She hurried to the door and opened it.

A man stood outside, solidly built and clad in the garb of a servant. Janna's first instinct was to close the door on him, but he jammed a foot against it. 'I am sent to fetch you, mistress,' he said. 'You must come at once.' Janna's heart plummeted as she noticed the compassion in his eyes.

'What has happened?' Instinctively, she took a step backwards, as if to distance herself from what was to come.

'Your mother is taken so ill she is like to die. Dame Alice hopes that you might yet save her.' Without waiting for her reply, he turned and hastened towards his mount.

'But . . . how? What is amiss with my mother?' Dazed and confused, Janna stared after him.

'I know not.' He did not check his stride, nor did he turn to look at her.

Thrown off-balance, too upset even to close the door behind her, Janna scurried after him. Before she had time to protest, the man put his hands around her waist and swung her high onto the horse's back, then vaulted up in front of her. 'Hold tight.' He dug his heels into the horse's flanks and the beast took off across the downs in the direction of Babestoche.

Janna had never been on horseback before. Excitement and terror overrode her modesty. She'd landed astride the horse but she had no time to cover her legs with her kirtle, no time for anything but to throw her arms around the stranger, lean close and hold on for her life.

Her mother so ill she was like to die? Eadgyth had seemed perfectly well when Janna had said goodbye to her. She couldn't believe it, yet the proof was in this race across the downs. Silently, Janna berated herself for not taking the time to select some healing herbs, but how could she know what to bring when she didn't even know what was amiss? Would she have the skill, the ability to heal her mother? Janna closed her eyes. Guilt washed over her as she recalled their argument. Eadgyth was right. She was still too young, too ignorant. She was certainly no healer, not yet, not even when her mother's life depended on it. Yet who else was there to help, if she could not? Perhaps she should have questioned the servant more closely, rather than allowing herself to be swept up by the urgency of his message. The knot of anxiety tightened in Janna's stomach. 'Hurry, hurry,' she whispered in time to the horse's galloping hooves. 'Hurry, hurry!'

They pelted on through the night until they came at last to the gatehouse of Babestoche Manor. The gate was already up and the horse galloped through, not breaking its stride. Janna caught a brief glimpse of the gatekeeper standing by as they rushed past.

The manor house loomed large before them. Made of stone, it was the biggest house Janna had ever seen. She had only a confused impression of bulky darkness below and a faint gleam of candlelight shining through window slits high above, before the servant reined in and dismounted. Without ceremony, he reached up to Janna and swung her down. Trembling, Janna stared about her.

'Come.' He set off at a fast pace across the courtyard, and Janna hastened after him. He bypassed the door that seemed to lead into the manor house, and instead raced up a stone staircase outside the building. Janna followed close on his heels, her heart thumping with fear.

The servant stopped abruptly, and hammered on a door. It was flung open and there, standing dark against the light of the torches behind him, stood the handsome stranger. Surprise flared in his eyes as he recognised Janna from the marketplace, but his face quickly creased into lines of concern. 'You must be Johanna,' he said gravely, dismissing the servant with a flick of his fingers. 'I am Hugh fitz Ranulph. Please come with me.'

Janna hardly had time to make her obeisance before he turned and strode quickly through a long hall with a high beamed ceiling. A fire blazed in a huge fireplace, shedding a soft, dancing light on stone walls and the decorative tapestries which partially covered them. Flaming torches, slotted into high sconces, added a glow to the rich colours of the hunting scenes woven across the walls, but Janna was too intent to do more than glance at them. She followed her guide through the hall and into a smaller room screened off by a leather curtain at the far end. 'Please wait here,' Hugh instructed. He pushed aside the heavy curtain and disappeared from view. 'Alice?' he called. Janna heard a murmured reply then Hugh's head poked out. 'Come,' he said, and vanished again. Janna hastened to obey.

A woman lay upon the large bed which dominated the bedchamber, her figure partially obscured by a number of people gathered around her.

'Mother!' Janna sprang forward without thinking, only to freeze in embarrassment as she realised the reclining figure was a stranger to her.

'Here is Johanna, ma dame, as you requested.' Hugh's deep voice made the introduction. The figure on the bed raised a feeble arm. Just as Janna was debating whether or not she was supposed to kiss the lady's hand, Dame Alice made a dismissive gesture.

'Your mother is through there.' She indicated a small alcove off the bedchamber. 'Pray do what you may for her, for I have great need of her services.'

Dread settled on Janna's heart. She rushed into the alcove, taking in the situation with one agonised glance. With a half-stifled sob, she fell to her knees beside the still form of her mother. She didn't need to be told that Eadgyth was dead. She'd read it instantly in the blueness of her mother's lips and the absence of light in her eyes. Fighting grief, she placed her hand on her mother's chest, willing the heart to beat beneath her fingers. She forced herself to concentrate, to mark off time in a steady beat, but there was no movement. Janna bent her head close to Eadgyth's mouth, listening for a breath, for anything that might mean that her mother lived. The silence, the waiting, seemed to stretch into eternity.

'Mother!' Desperate now, Janna grasped her mother's arm and shook her hard. There was no response. Automatically,

Janna noted that her arm was limp, her body still quite warm, not yet stiffening into death. She had arrived too late, but only just. Bitterly, Janna reproached herself for not making the long journey to the manor house with her mother. If she had seen with her own eyes what had gone amiss, perhaps she might have been able to prevent her death.

Dry-eyed, numb with grief, Janna raised her head and looked about her. The smell of vomit assailed her nostrils. Now she noticed traces of foul matter down the front of her mother's kirtle. Beside the straw pallet lay a basin of stained water and a cloth. Someone, then, had cared enough to wash her mother's face, and try to help. Janna glanced around, catching the gaze of a young woman standing beside Dame Alice's bed. For a heartbeat they stared at each other. The girl's face was pale. She looked strained and ill at ease. She *knows*, Janna thought. *She knows my mother is dead.*

The girl coloured a delicate pink under Janna's gaze. She turned away then and murmured something to the man at her side. Janna bobbed a hasty curtsy as he cast an appraising glance over her. 'Pray see to the *wortwyf*, Master Fulk,' he said curtly.

'Of course, my lord Robert. Right away.' Fulk had been bending over Dame Alice, encouraging her to sup a little broth, but now he straightened obediently and came into the alcove. He peered over Janna's shoulder to look at Eadgyth. 'The *wortwyf* is dead,' he confirmed, and turned to Janna. 'I am sorry for your loss.' His face was tight and cold, yet there was a gleam of triumph in his eyes. With a cursory nod, he swaggered back to Dame Alice's bedside and picked up the bowl of broth.

Cold fury seized Janna. Only last night her mother had saved Fulk's skin, and his reputation. Now, when she was most in need, his concern was all for his wealthy patron. 'You claim to have such great knowledge of the art of healing, Master Fulk,' she flashed, springing to her feet to face him. 'Surely you could have done something to help my mother, to save her life!' Her voice choked on the last word.

Fulk made no reply. Instead he turned his back on Janna, and lifted a spoon of broth to Dame Alice's mouth. She pinched her lips together and turned her head away. Fulk hesitated, then put the bowl down and, instead, picked up the lady's hand and felt the pulse at her wrist.

'You might pretend you don't care about my mother, but last night you were so desperate for help you offered to make her a partner in your shop!'

'The girl is hysterical. Ignore her.' He gave Dame Alice's hand a reassuring pat.

'Tell me what happened to my mother! How did she die?'

'I expect she took one of her own foul potions.' Fulk carefully rested his patient's hand on the fine linen bed sheet. 'It is lucky for you, ma dame, that I came in time,' he told Dame Alice. 'You, too, might have suffered the same fate but for my intervention.'

'Don't be absurd!' Dame Alice raised herself up against the bolster and beckoned Janna forward. 'I am sorry that you did not get here in time to save your mother,' she said. Her voice was high; she sounded somewhat peevish as she continued, 'Eadgyth spoke highly of you. I had hoped you might be able to save her life.'

Janna was less than flattered by the implied compliment. She was beginning to understand that Dame Alice had an entirely selfish reason for summoning her so urgently. 'Fulk was here!' she flashed in reply. 'Why didn't you ask him to save my mother?'

'Keep a civil tongue in your head, girl,' Robert snapped. 'I bade Master Fulk leave his practice in Wiltune to tend my wife – not your mother.' He clicked his fingers, beckoning one of Dame Alice's attendants to his side. It was the girl Janna had noticed earlier. She stepped forward and stood with bowed head before him. 'Ask the steward to arrange for a litter to carry this woman down to the church at Berford.' The girl bobbed her head and hastened from the bed-chamber. Robert walked back to his wife's bedside and bent to kiss her cheek. 'Try not to upset yourself, Alice,' he murmured. 'For the sake of our child, you must stay calm and recover your health.'

Unsure what she was supposed to do, Janna sent a glance of appeal at Hugh.

'Johanna has had a bad shock. Small wonder that she's upset. Why don't I take her to the kitchen for a hot posset?' He moved to her side and took her arm.

'But I . . .' Janna cast a glance at her mother's still form lying on the pallet in the alcove. Before she went anywhere, she wanted to say goodbye.

'Come.' Hugh's firm grip shifted Janna from the room, propelling her through the solar and out into the hall. Feeling his grip slacken slightly, Janna jerked free and faced him. 'If Master Fulk was anywhere near as good as he pretends to be, he could have –'

'You'll achieve naught by accusing the apothecary of neglect,' he cut across her protest. 'Your mother died a hard death. I doubt anyone could have saved her.'

'But that . . . that quack didn't even try, did he?' Janna steeled herself, knowing she could not rest until she heard the worst.

Hugh shrugged apologetically. 'I know not what happened before I arrived, but I heard that your mother poured scorn on Fulk and his treatments this afternoon. It seems he insisted that Dame Alice drink an infusion of his own making, but your mother threw it out. They had a fierce argument about it. Of course, as soon as Fulk heard that your mother was taken ill he lost no time in returning to the bedchamber and putting it about that your mother had brought this illness on herself and that she was not to be trusted. He has his good name to salvage, Johanna, you must understand that.'

Yet Dame Alice had quickly put Fulk in his place when he'd tried to suggest that Eadgyth's potion might have killed her. Janna took some comfort from that, but knew that she must also use her own persuasion to counteract Fulk's accusations.

'My mother was always careful with her mixtures, sire,' she said. 'I have never known her make a mistake, not ever. Besides, if the mistake lay in my mother's potion, it would be Dame Alice lying dead now, not . . .' Janna swallowed hard, unable to finish her sentence.

'What you say makes sense. It may be that you speak the truth of the matter.'

'Then what happened to my mother? She was perfectly

well when I last saw her. There must be a reason for . . .
for . . .'

'I'm sorry, Johanna, I really don't know. All I can tell you
is what I saw towards the end, after Jeanne, one of ma dame's
tiring women, came in search of Fulk and Robert. I was
with Robert at the time and I accompanied him to Alice's
bedchamber for I am her kinsman and so have great concern
for her wellbeing. It is fortunate I was present, for Robert
fell into such distress when he entered the bedchamber that
I thought he might lose his senses altogether. His face
blanched of all colour; he trembled as if with the ague. We
thought his wife was beyond all care, you see. It took some
moments before we realised that, in fact, it was your mother
who was taken ill. Dame Alice insisted that Robert send the
groom to fetch you. He stayed to reassure and comfort her,
while Cecily looked after your mother. She gave her water
and washed her clean, but alas, nothing seemed to help.'

'And Master Fulk? What did he do?'

'He sent Jeanne to the kitchen for one of his possets.
Really, he did his best to help your mother.'

Janna made a rude noise at the back of her throat, knowing
that Fulk's best wasn't worth a dirty straw. She looked up at
Hugh and struggled to put her suspicions into words. 'Did my
mother say anything of what ailed her before she died?' She
didn't believe for one moment that Eadgyth had been affected
by one of her own mixtures, yet something unexpected had
caused her mother to die so quickly and in such distress.
Perhaps her mother had said something, left some clue?

'Let us ask Cecily. She may have spoken to your mother
while she tended her,' Hugh said, as the young tiring woman

entered the hall in company with the steward she had been sent to fetch. He beckoned her forward and she hurried towards them. Janna plaited her fingers together and squeezed them hard as she struggled to keep her emotions under control. She could not give in to grief, not yet. She needed all her wits to find out the truth of her mother's death, and all her courage to get through it.

'My lord?' Cecily bobbed a knee in front of Hugh and waited, her eyes cast down in humble submission. Full of gratitude and forgetting her place, Janna took the young woman's hands in her own. 'Thank you, mistress,' she said. 'Thank you for taking the time to ease my mother's passing.'

Cecily nodded, not speaking. She was much younger than the other attendants, Janna realised. In fact, Cecily looked no more than a year or so older than Janna herself. She had delicate features, set in a heart-shaped face which was framed by a cloud of dark hair. For all that she must be high-born to be a tiring woman to Dame Alice, she seemed afraid. Janna wondered why.

'Can you tell us, did the herbwife, the healer, say anything before she died, Cecily?' Hugh asked the question before Janna could, and she was glad of it for surely the girl would respect him and so would answer more truthfully. Janna felt a rush of warmth towards him as she realised he had called her mother a healer, acknowledging her mother's true worth.

Cecily stole a quick glance at Janna, then looked downwards. 'Mistress Eadgyth complained of feeling cold,' she whispered. 'She said her lips felt numb. She could barely speak or swallow. It was hard to hear her, and to understand her words, but she said your name, Johanna. She called also for a monk, I suppose to give her absolution before she died.'

A monk? Janna frowned, utterly rejecting the notion. If her mother had known she was dying, if she'd wanted absolution, she would have called for the priest. Even that seemed unlikely, given her mother's reaction to him at the first and only service they had attended when the new church opened at Berford, when she had turned her back on the priest and walked out of his church, dragging Janna behind her.

'Thank you, Cecily.' The tiring woman bobbed a curtsy and hastened back to the bedchamber. Hugh shot a glance of concern at Janna. 'Come.' He put his hand under her arm and propelled her down the stairs and out into the night. The dark shapes of other buildings spread out before them under the star-filled sky. Janna hardly had time to wonder as to their purpose before Hugh hurried her on and into a small stone building set close to one side of the timbered palisade that enclosed the manor.

Two great fires, set along one wall, heated the room to an almost unbearable temperature. The cook's sleeves were pushed up to her elbows; her face was red, dripping with perspiration. She was rolling pastry, pressing it down with hard, determined thumps of the rolling pin. A rich scent of food flavoured the air: fresh bread, and the smell of stew from a cooking pot hanging over one of the fires. A joint of beef was being turned on a spit by a scullion who crouched beside the second fire, sweating heavily as he laboured. In spite of her distress, Janna's mouth began to water.

The cook paused in her labours, as did two maids and a young boy who was busy washing vegetables. They all stood to attention as Hugh came forward, propelling Janna ahead of him.

'This is Johanna, daughter of Mistress Eadgyth the *wortwyf*,' he introduced her. 'Treat her kindly for she's had a great shock. Her mother has died most suddenly and unexpectedly. Give her a hot drink and find her a pallet and somewhere to sleep tonight.' To Janna he said, 'You shouldn't be alone. Stay here and I'll escort you home in the morning. You'll need to make burial arrangements with the priest in Berford, but I can help you with that.'

Why was he being so kind? Janna didn't know, could only feel grateful for his understanding and care. 'Thank you, sire,' she whispered, and bobbed a curtsy. He nodded to her and left the kitchen.

At once everyone relaxed. But they did not go back to their labours. Instead they crowded around, staring at Janna as if she'd come down to them from the moon.

'Don't think you can come in here and start telling me what to do like your mother did.' The cook was the first to speak. She smeared huge floured hands down her stained apron in a vain effort to clean them, then stuck them on her hips to confront Janna. 'Giving me all manner of strange berries and roots and ordering me around in my own kitchen. "Boil this, soak that," as if she was Lady Muck of the Manor herself.'

'In truth, I do believe the *wortwyf*'s mixtures helped Dame Alice,' one of the kitchen maids ventured timidly. The cook flashed a glare in her direction.

'Not according to Master Fulk! Now there's a gentleman. We were in absolute agreement over what was needed to help ma dame. In fact, he paid me many compliments on my preparations.' She shot a triumphant glance at Janna. 'Master Fulk threw out your mother's vile potions and 'tis just as well he did, seeing as the woman has now died by her own hand.' She shook a fat finger under Janna's nose. 'You'll not brew any concoctions in my kitchen while you're here,' she warned. 'I'll be watching you.'

Janna drew in a breath, almost too indignant to speak. 'I'll not stay here to be watched,' she retaliated. 'My mother was quite well when she left home this morning. Who is to say it's not something from *your* kitchen that has poisoned her!'

The words were out before she'd thought them through. Poison! Yet Janna knew instinctively that she'd spoken the truth. Her mother must have been poisoned; there was no other explanation for her sudden and untimely death.

The cook's face flushed dark red. She drew herself up, large bosom heaving so hard it seemed she might burst through the fabric of her kirtle. 'How dare you!' she spluttered. 'I keep a fine kitchen and a fine table. My lady has told me so herself.' She picked up a twiggy broom and gave Janna a hard poke in the chest. 'Get out of my kitchen! I'll not stand here to be insulted by an ill-bred brat like you!'

Janna retreated. The cook kept coming forward, jabbing the besom at her until she turned and fled out into the quiet night. Once outside, her steps slowed. She lifted her face to the cool night air, and breathed deeply, trying to settle her agitated spirits. Where was the gate? She looked at the bulky shapes of the buildings around her, trying to make sense of them, to remember the way in. From the smell, Janna judged that some of the buildings must be used to house pigs and other animals.

She spied the gatehouse then, and hurried towards it. To her relief, the gate was still up, and the gatekeeper was nowhere in sight. She scurried outside. Not for anything would she stay at the manor through the night.

She felt exhausted, shattered by grief, as she started the long walk home over the moonlit downs. Questions tormented her. Who and what had killed her mother? How had she come to die such a hard death? Janna drew a shuddering breath. Now was not the time to give in to sorrow. She must be strong. She must concentrate, ask questions, find answers. She would not rest until she had found out the truth.

Eadgyth would never poison herself, not even by accident. Someone must have given her poison; someone must be responsible for what had happened. Someone who held a grudge – like the apothecary, whose position at the manor had been threatened by her mother's greater knowledge and expert treatment of her patient. Or Aldith, who must know that women – and even Dame Alice herself – would rather seek help from clever, knowledgeable Eadgyth than an ignorant village midwife.

Perhaps she should talk to Cecily again. She'd seemed fearful. Perhaps there was something she did not want to say in front of Hugh? Janna resolved to win her confidence and find out all she knew. She would also question the cook, who had run her out of the kitchen in spite of Hugh's instructions to take care of her. Did the cook have something to hide?

No-one would believe her if she spoke her suspicions out loud, Janna realised. She must find proof before she could accuse anyone. So she would ask questions; she would not stop until she had discovered the truth and found the evidence she needed to bring whoever was responsible for her mother's death to justice.

It was a solemn vow, one that Janna knew she must keep if she was ever to know peace of mind again.

SEVEN

THE JOURNEY THAT had flown by on the back of a horse was long and frightening on foot. Spooked by shadows and plagued by dark suspicion, Janna felt shaken and sick at heart. As she came to the cottage she'd shared with her mother, she was surprised to find the door open. She remembered, then, her hasty departure. She walked into the cottage, half-expecting to find her mother stirring something over the fire, or perhaps drowsing sleepily in her fine chair. Grief shook Janna anew as she surveyed the empty room. She felt especially wretched as she recalled the last words they had spoken together.

She'd never been so angry, so outspoken before. Through her childhood she'd trusted and respected her mother's wisdom and her skills with herbs and healing, and had been keen to learn all she could. It was only lately that she'd begun to feel constricted, to feel that she could do more with her life, and that there was much of the outside world for her to learn about and see. Now, when it was too late to explain how she felt, and make amends, she must live forever with the knowledge that she and Eadgyth had not parted on friendly terms. It was too late to apologise.

Worse, it was too late now to learn the secrets of her mother's past.

Hot tears welled in Janna's eyes and spilled down her cheeks. She dashed them away, but they continued to fall until at last she crumpled down into the large chair and buried her head in a cushion to smother her sobs. Even though there was no-one around to hear her, Janna needed to hide the sounds of her own distress from herself. If she could smother her cries and pretend that all was as it should be, then perhaps life might continue as it had always done. The truth of her situation was much too huge and frightening to think about.

Janna cried until she felt sick. She had never, ever, felt so lonely as she did now. There was no-one she could talk to, no-one to whom she could turn for help. She cried until there were no tears left to shed. Exhausted, she blew her nose and mopped her sore eyes one last time. Then she stood up, knowing that she could postpone the future no longer. She would have to face it, no matter how bleak.

One day at a time, she thought to herself. But a day seemed too long and too hard; even an hour was too much of a trial.

Moment by moment then, at least for now.

Janna took up the tinder box and laboured to produce a spark from flint and steel, to ignite the kindling and start the fire going again. Light and warmth seemed a good way to begin the rest of her life. Her task accomplished, she glanced around the room seeking Alfred. She was surprised he hadn't already come to greet her.

The cat was nowhere to be seen. Janna remembered her hasty flight, the open door. He would have escaped outside, delighting in the opportunity to go hunting at night. Janna felt a cold frisson at the thought that, in turn, the cat might find himself hunted. They always kept him shut in at night for that very reason. But Alfred was a survivor, just like the king after whom he'd been named. She went to the door. 'Alfred!' she called.

She listened intently, but there was no answering miaow. 'Alfred! Tssss-sss-sss-sss.' Silence, broken by the lonely hoot of an owl. Janna comforted herself with the thought that, like the owl, Alfred would be busy chasing field mice and voles and other small creatures, and stuffing his belly full of wild food. She looked into the silent forest, its silvered treetops, its dark and secret depths. The moon was low in the west. Soon a new day would dawn. Briefly, passionately, Janna wished that she could turn back time. She would rather face the boar without Godric than face the future alone.

Desolate and despairing, she called the cat one last time, searching the inky blackness for a gleam of silky fur. Through the noises of the forest she strained to catch any sound of the cat's presence. The crunch of leaves made her heart quicken. 'Alfred!' she called again.

'Janna!'

For one wild moment Janna wondered if the cat had answered her, until reason told her that even if Alfred could talk, he wouldn't have answered with Godric's voice.

'Godric?'

He came towards her out of the darkness. 'I'm so sorry to bring you bad news, Janna. Your mother has been taken ill up at the manor.'

'Oh, Godric!' She stretched out her hand to him, then

hurriedly snatched it back as she recalled their parting words. It was not fair to encourage Godric to believe he had a chance with her. 'News travels fast, it seems,' she said warily.

'You know about your mother's illness?'

'I've already been to Babestoche and back tonight.'

Godric looked surprised. 'Everyone is saying your mother has been poisoned by one of her own potions,' he said awkwardly. 'I've told them all that they are mistaken.'

'Of course they are!'

'But you have the knowledge and skill to aid her recovery, I am sure of it.'

'My mother is beyond help, Godric. She is dead.' Janna's throat ached with the pain of saying it.

Godric drew in a quick breath of surprise. 'I am so sorry, Janna. I am so sorry.' Not giving her time to retreat, he threw his arms around her and held her tight. Secure in his embrace, Janna began to cry.

'Sshh. It's all right, everything's going to be all right,' he soothed. 'You mustn't worry, Janna. I'll help you.'

Nothing would ever be all right again, Janna thought. With an effort, she broke free and wiped her eyes.

'You've seen your mother? You are certain there's no hope?' he queried.

Janna nodded, unable to speak.

'But this is so sudden! Was she ailing?'

'No. I believe she was . . .' Janna stopped abruptly. Should she tell Godric of her suspicions?

No, she thought, remembering the vow she'd made to herself. She would speak to no-one until she could prove the truth of her words.

'She was . . .?' Godric prompted.

'. . . quite well this morning. You're right. Her death was very sudden.'

Godric stood back so that he could study Janna more closely. Pity set his feet in motion. He walked into the cottage and fanned the fire into brightness. Once set, he added pieces of wood to keep it burning high. He put aside the vegetables then filled the pot with water from a bucket and hung it over the fire to boil. Then he poked about the few provisions set on a shelf close by. 'You need a hot drink and something to eat,' he said, and held up the leftover griddle cake. Numbly, Janna picked up a jar and pushed it forward. Godric inspected the contents, then pulled out his knife and spread the cake with a paste of honey and crushed hazelnuts.

'Eat,' he commanded.

Janna realised that, in spite of her misery, she was hungry. She gave Godric a shaky smile as she took the cake from him. She crammed a piece into her mouth and chewed, relishing its sweetness. He smiled back at her, and settled down on a stool beside the fire, sneaking glances at Janna as she ate. A soft rustle outside sat him bolt upright, straining his ears to listen.

'What is it?' Janna's voice was indistinct through a mouthful of bread.

'I heard a noise outside.'

'My cat?' Janna jumped up and went to the door. She peered out into the dark night. 'Alfred?' she called.

Godric stood up and looked over her shoulder. 'Fluffy!' he bellowed.

Janna was surprised into laughter. 'He won't come if you insult him like that,' she said. They stayed by the door, looking out into the night. All was silent and still. There was no sign of the big black cat. Finally, Janna shrugged and sat down again. 'There are always noises in the forest at night.' She took a large bite from her bread, and began to chew once more.

Not satisfied, Godric ventured a few paces outside, searching for movement, for the source of the sound. But there was nothing to see and nothing to hear. He waited a few moments, then came back in and closed the door behind him.

'A squirrel, a deer. It could be anything,' Janna said indistinctly, still chewing.

Godric nodded, and settled down beside the fire once more.

Janna stuffed the last of the bread into her mouth. Too late, she wondered if Godric might also be hungry. There were only crumbs left now to offer him. She licked her sticky fingers, then jumped up to attend to the pot of water steaming over the fire. Glad to have something to do, she picked up the dipper and scooped water into two mugs, flavoured the hot drinks with crushed herbs and a spoonful of honey for sweetness.

Godric cleared his throat. 'Janna,' he said, and took hold of her hand. 'I came to escort you to the manor house to see your mother. I'm sorry I arrived too late. Now that I know your mother is gone, I'm worried about you. You are so far from help, should you need it. We don't know each other very well, but I wonder if you'd consider . . .'

'Please don't ask me to be your wife!' Janna snatched her hand away. 'I don't want to marry you, Godric.' The surprise on Godric's face was quickly masked by a guarded expression that told Janna she'd hurt his feelings. 'I don't want to marry anyone – not yet, anyway,' she added hastily.

'I wasn't going to offer marriage,' Godric retorted. 'This is certainly not the time for such a question. But it seems, from what you say, that I would be foolish even to consider such a thing.' There was a rough edge to his voice. Janna deeply regretted her thoughtless outburst. Eadgyth always said that her quick tongue would get her into trouble, and she was for ever being proved right! But Eadgyth would never say such a thing to her again, Janna remembered. Utterly downcast, hardly knowing what to say to redeem the situation, she studied her boots intently.

Godric broke the silence. 'I was actually going to suggest that you stay with my mother and me for a while. For your own safety.'

'Oh.' Janna couldn't look at him for shame and embarrassment. 'This is my home,' she mumbled. 'This is where I must stay.'

'Then I'll trouble you no further.' His earlier warmth was gone, replaced by a cool courtesy. He set down his mug, stood up and moved to the door.

'Thank you, Godric. I'm sorry if I –'

'I thought we were friends, Janna. After last night and tonight, I hoped that one day we might become something more. A fool's dream, I see that now. I shall not trouble you again.' He walked out of the cottage and slammed the door shut behind him.

Godric had every right to be annoyed, Janna thought, remembering how she had clung to him, and how tenderly he had held her. She wished now that she had gone with him, but she didn't want to give him false hope, nor did she want to be beholden to him and his mother. She didn't want to be beholden to anyone. Even though it was frightening to face the world on her own, she knew she must get used to it. Only hours before she had longed for freedom, yet now it had come to her, and so unexpectedly, she shrank from it. She lay down on the straw pallet and pulled the covers over her head. If only she could sleep a little, things might look better in the morning. This thought was followed by a desperate wish: that she might wake to find that today was all a bad dream.

She closed her eyes. Tears began to flow once more. She sniffed and tried to wipe them away, but they continued to flow until, at last, she fell into a troubled sleep.

EIGHT

THE SUN WAS already up when Janna awoke. A beam of light slanting through the window slit brightened the room and warmed her face. Joyously, she sprang from her bed to greet the day. Memory struck her with the force of a body blow. She crumpled back onto the straw pallet, holding her stomach and gasping with the pain of it.

Not for one moment would she accept that her mother had been poisoned by her own potion. Who could have given the poison to her, and why did her mother not recognise what it was? Surely she would have realised the truth when she was dying. Why did she not speak out about it?

Perhaps she had! Janna tried to recall Cecily's words. Eadgyth had complained of feeling cold. Numb. She'd had difficulty speaking, but had called for a monk. Why?

Cold. Numb. Janna searched her memory for her mother's instructions on the herbs she used, particularly her warnings about poisonous plants.

Hemlock was one. It caused paralysis and loss of sight, but Cecily hadn't said anything about her mother going blind.

Deadly nightshade? Her mother sometimes ground the tiniest portion of the plant into a powder to relieve a tooth-

94

ache. Janna knew there'd been no call for such a remedy recently, so it was unlikely that she'd had it to hand – but others might. The plant was common enough, and most people would know that it could be dangerous. If too much was ingested, rapid breathing was followed by convulsions and death.

Not nightshade. Cecily hadn't mentioned anything about panting or fits. She'd said her mother had complained of feeling cold. Numb. And she was vomiting. Cecily had said she could barely speak, but it seemed she'd stayed conscious until the end.

The spice merchant's face flickered into Janna's mind. Why was he important? He'd had a whole selection of herbs and spices on display, exotic substances she'd never seen before, which were on sale to any who could afford them. Could her mother have been poisoned by something like that up at the manor house, something unfamiliar and therefore dangerous?

The only substance the spice merchant had warned about was his rubbing oil. Aconite was common enough. Prized for its pretty blue flowers, it grew in gardens everywhere. Most people would know its poisonous properties, although they would call the plant by its common name: wolfsbane or monkshood.

Monkshood! It caused numbness of the face and tongue, making speech difficult. It also caused nausea and severe pain, leading to death. Eadgyth hadn't called for a monk at all. Her mother was trying to tell someone she'd been poisoned!

Anguish jerked Janna upright, and she cried aloud as she recalled how she'd gone into the forest, how she'd been so afraid of the boar that she'd grabbed at the strawberries and stuffed them into her purse. Had she been so hasty that she'd also pulled off bits of the poisonous plants growing alongside them? Her mother might well have eaten the fruits that were left over from the potion, not noticing as she ate them that she was also swallowing bits of the monkshood that grew close by.

In her mind, Janna had accused everyone but herself. Now, she was faced with the realisation that she alone was responsible for her mother's death. Time and again Eadgyth had scolded her for her clumsiness, and warned her of the need to be careful; warned her that she should never under-estimate the power of the herbs they used. Now her mother had died as a result of her carelessness.

The thought squeezed Janna's heart into a small tight ball. She didn't know how it was possible to feel so much pain and fear, and still be able to breathe. She jumped up from the pallet and rushed over to the shelf that held Eadgyth's medicaments. Her hands shook as she began a desperate search for any sign of the strawberries, and the potion that may have contained them.

A new horror forced itself into Janna's consciousness. Her mother's important visitor! Had she also taken poison along with the strawberry mixture? Was she also lying dead? Desperate to find out the worst, Janna tumbled and almost dropped jars and dishes in her haste to open stoppers and sniff the contents. Some she tasted before setting them aside to continue her search. Her heart gave a sudden lurch as she spied a rough earthenware dish pushed towards the back of the shelf. It contained several small, ripe strawberries.

Janna inspected them carefully. Their bruised, torn flesh bore testimony to the haste in which they'd been collected and bundled into her purse. Yet they were quite clean, sitting in a small puddle of water that indicated they'd been washed.

Relief swept over Janna, leaving her feeling dizzy and light-hearted in spite of all that had happened. She sagged onto a stool, blinking back tears of gratitude. Her mother had washed the strawberries before using them. Of course she had! How many times had Janna witnessed that very act, the careful washing of all roots, leaves, flowers, seeds, fruits and nuts. Her mother had always insisted on it.

Nothing took away from the fact that her mother had been poisoned, though, and not by anything unfamiliar either. Monkshood. Why had her mother not recognised its taste after the first mouthful, and taken steps to protect herself?

Janna poured herself a beaker of ale while she pondered the problem. She remembered the ale she'd supped at the alehouse, how unfamiliar it had tasted. What if it had contained poison? Ignorant of how real ale should taste, she might well have drunk it all, and died as a result. Was that what had happened to her mother? Janna sniffed the ale, then took a cautious sip. It smelled the same, and tasted as it always did. Thoughtfully, she drank it down. Feeling somewhat more composed, she pulled her kirtle on over her shift, raked her fingers through her long hair to tidy it, then walked to the door and opened it.

'Alfred!' she called, expecting to find the cat waiting for her, miaowing and hungry. There was no sign of him, so Janna stepped outside to look around. 'Alfred!' she bellowed, startling a woodlark. Its sweet trilling ended abruptly, replaced by a fluttering of wings as it flew off.

A glimpse of something hanging from a tree in the distance caught her eye. The dark formless shape shifted and changed as she watched. For a moment she stared at the object, not fully comprehending what she was seeing. As her brain caught up with her vision, she let out a long, ragged cry and began to run.

Alfred was tied to the tree, his limbs stiff and his fur stained with blood. A swarm of flies buzzed around him, grouping and regrouping as they searched for wounds to feed on. Janna tried to brush them away so that she could find out how he had died. A cord had been looped around the tree trunk several times so that the cat was stretched out as if crucified. His throat had been cut. He must have died sometime during the night.

Janna began to shiver. Her teeth chattered as she forced herself to touch her pet. Alfred's fur was matted and sticky. She'd disturbed the flies; they buzzed around her in a thick black cloud and then settled once more on the cat's body. Looking down, Janna saw that she'd stepped into a puddle of blood that lay directly beneath the dead animal. Her thoughts splintered into fragments of grief as she tried to come to grips with her pet's fate.

It seemed clear that he had been killed right here, next to the tree, and then strung up straight away. She looked at the smudged footprints around the dark red puddle congealing underneath the cat's body. Her own, or did some of them belong to whoever was responsible for Alfred's death? Janna examined them carefully; the prints of her own small boots were superimposed on other, larger prints. Whose? Large or small, the prints were now so muddled it was impossible to tell. Head bent, Janna traversed the ground nearby, but grass, leaves and weeds all seemed undisturbed. The earth near their cottage bore faint marks of boots: hers and her mother's, and their visitors: the groom from Babestoche Manor, Fulk and Godric. And here, staining a patch of leaves, was another splatter of dark red blood. She looked across to where she'd found the cat, some twenty paces away. Had the killer first cut Alfred's throat, and then looked for a tree from which to hang the dead body so that it would be the first thing Janna saw when she walked out of the cottage? Suddenly anxious, Janna swung around to scan the forest in case the killer was still lurking somewhere nearby. But she could hear only the churring of turtle doves as they puffed themselves up in the warmth of the sun.

Dry-mouthed, trying not to panic, Janna hurried back to Alfred and began to wrestle with the tight knot around his neck. As she tugged and pulled at it, tears began to run down her face. She was crying for the kitten with the will to live, who had struggled so hard to survive. The cat would have had no chance against a man with a knife in his hand, and hatred in his heart. Who could have done such a thing? Who could have anything to gain from Alfred's death?

Godric! The thought was sudden and shocking, and Janna immediately tried to push it out of her mind. It would not go away. Yet she couldn't believe it, didn't want to believe it. Could he betray her like this? Surely it wasn't possible!

The evidence hung before her, grisly and gory and only too real. Who else could have done such a thing, if not

Godric? He had visited her in the night, had held her tight and offered help and comfort. And instead of being grateful, she'd flung his kindness back in his face and made it quite clear that she wouldn't consider him as a husband. Had he taken out his anger on Alfred?

Janna remembered how he'd nudged the animal aside with his boot, and how he'd slit the boar's throat without even blinking. Perhaps, like the villagers, he believed Alfred was the devil and that it would be right to kill him. Tears almost blinded Janna as she tugged and pulled at the knots binding her cat, but a new thought filled her with a scalding anger. With such an act, did Godric think to frighten her out of the cottage and into his arms? She would rather scratch out his eyes! How could Godric have done such a thing to a defenceless animal? She would never forgive him, never!

Unable to vent her anger on Godric, she fought with the knot instead, until finally she managed to untie Alfred and bring him down from the tree. She laid the body carefully on the ground then went off to fetch a spade to dig a grave.

Should she save the body as evidence, in case she could call down justice on Godric's head? She paused, resting on the spade while she thought about it. To whom could she report this crime? Godric's liege lord would not punish him for the killing, not if it came to his word against her own. The villagers certainly wouldn't support her. She was an outcast, and they thought the cat was the devil. It seemed to Janna that if she wanted justice, both for the death of her mother and for Alfred, she would have to find it in her own way.

Starting with Alfred. She didn't need his body to challenge Godric. He would know what she was talking about – and she would make him suffer in every way she could. She began to dig, driving into the earth with angry jabs as she thought of how she might make Godric pay for what he had done.

She had cried all the tears she could cry. Now she felt achingly empty and sad. And angry. Her anger added iron to her backbone and gave her the strength to do what had to be done. She rubbed her cheek against Alfred's soft fur, then tenderly laid him down into the hole she had dug. The cat stared up at her, his wide eyes clouded now by death. Janna leaned down and gently closed them. She stroked Alfred's glossy fur one last time, then covered him over with damp, dark earth. As a last gesture, she gathered up some late blue-bells and red poppies to brighten the grave. So, too, would she find something to place on the grave of her mother.

Her mother! Janna straightened hastily and scanned the sky, noticing the sun's position that told her what time it was. By now, her mother's body would have been brought down to the church and the priest would be waiting for her. She ran inside to wash her dirty hands. She snatched up a basket and hurried outside again.

Her mother's livelihood had come from the herbs and flowers that she cherished, so it was only fitting she have some on her grave for her last journey. Janna made a careful selection: poppies and creamy purple pansies for a splash of colour, and a small plant of rosemary to mark what was in her heart.

Regretting that she hadn't left hours earlier, Janna set off at a run down through the fields towards the village. Although the sun was shining just as it had the day before, she could take no comfort from its warmth. Everything seemed black, full of shadows, full of anger and despair. She hurried on, not pausing to draw breath or ease the stitch in her side, until she came at last to the small stone church in the centre of Berford.

She raced inside, pausing only to cross herself before looking about. There was no sign of her mother's body. Just as Janna's taut muscles relaxed somewhat, the light from the open door was blocked by the batwing form of the priest. He advanced towards her.

'Johanna,' he said. His narrow face was closed and hostile. Janna instinctively recoiled. 'Your mother's body lies outside, beyond the pale. You'll have to go outside the churchyard walls if you wish to say your last farewells to her.'

'Beyond the pale?'

'I cannot bury your mother in consecrated ground. You remember, I am sure, what happened the last time you and your mother came to church.'

Yes, Janna remembered only too well. The trouble with the priest had started as soon as he came to Berford. She and her mother had attended the first service that was held in the new church. Before it was built, a preaching cross had served as a place of worship as well as being a focus for the exchange of news and gossip. An old priest had come regularly from Wiltune to hold a mass in the open air. Gentle and mild, he had welcomed them all and had happily absolved them from sin and given them his blessing every month.

At this, the new priest's first service, he had gazed around his small congregation, taking their measure. It seemed he had taken the trouble to find out about them, for his gaze lingered longest on Eadgyth. His knowledge of the nature of his flock became certain when he began to address them from the pulpit. It was a long rant against the dangers of breaking God's commandments, and it seemed to be aimed directly at Eadgyth. Janna's mother had kneeled on the hard stone floor, listening as the priest warned his flock about those who lived outside God's laws, which he then set out to list. Small choking sounds told Janna how her mother regarded the priest's rules, especially when it came to the servitude of women and their absolute subjugation to their husbands. But it was on his injunction that the villagers must bend always to the will of God and not question it that Eadgyth had come to the end of her patience.

'Surely God gave us a brain in the expectation we would use it,' she hissed under her breath to Janna. 'After all, He gave us the capacity to choose right or wrong, to acquire and use knowledge for the benefit of mankind. If God wanted us to wait around for him to fix everything, we'd have been called "beetles", not "humans".'

'Sshh.' Janna agreed with Eadgyth, but she wished her mother would just let it go for now.

Eadgyth frowned at her. 'Don't tell me you agree with what he's saying? I brought you up to have a mind of your own, Janna. I taught you to question everything.'

'Sshh.' Others now turned on Eadgyth, annoyed that her sibilant whisper was interrupting their devotions. Janna felt embarrassed. The trouble with her mother was that she never let anything lie until she'd argued her own point of view, but now was not the time or place for it.

103

'. . . and if God should cast affliction on us, we must be like Job and bear our troubles with patience and courage.' It seemed almost as if the priest had heard Eadgyth's protests, for he fixed her with a gimlet stare as he continued: 'There are some who would set themselves above God, who believe they have the power of life and death over others. There are some who will even break God's laws to carry out their foul deeds. To you, I say, "Beware, for God is watching and great will be your fall." On the Day of Judgment, when sinners are called to –'

'I've had enough of this.' Eadgyth grabbed Janna's arm. 'Come!' To Janna's intense embarrassment, she pulled her to her feet and marched her down the aisle and out of the church. A tense silence had marked their passage, but Janna heard the priest's voice raised in exhortation once they exited the church.

'You don't need to go to church when God's great cathedral is all around you, Janna,' her mother had said on the way home to their cottage. She'd pointed then at the bright flowers in their garden, the dancing butterflies and furry bumblebees, and the green forest beyond. 'I follow God's law in my own way. I certainly do not need the priest to tell me how to behave, and what I may or may not believe.' Hearing her mother's voice in her mind brought tears to Janna's eyes. Determinedly, she blinked them back. She would not give in to grief in front of the priest.

'Your mother didn't believe in Christ and she didn't come to church. And I know there were times when she broke God's law,' he said now, recalling Janna to the present. She suspected that he was referring to the abortifacients Eadgyth sometimes administered to the desperate women who came to her. She kept silent, knowing that in truth there was no defence against his accusations.

'She was a heretic!' The priest turned from Janna, indicating that their conversation was over.

'That's not true! She believed in God.' Outraged, Janna stood her ground, silently damning him to the hell he was wishing upon her mother.

'She condemned herself out of her own mouth. Indeed, they were almost the last words she spoke to me.'

'When did you see her? When did you speak to her?'

'When I asked her to say her confession. Before she went in to Dame Alice's chamber.'

'You were up at the manor yesterday?'

'Indeed I was. I'd been told of my lady's troubles, and I was ready to administer the last rites should I have cause to do so. It was only fitting that your mother should be in a state of grace before being allowed into the presence of Dame Alice.'

'If my mother said her confession to you, why do you deny her burial now?'

'She did not make her confession. Instead, she told me to get out of her way for she had more important matters to which she had to attend.'

'Like saving Dame Alice's life!'

The priest glowered at Janna. 'Nothing is more important than communion with God.'

'I am sure my mother would have made her confession if time had allowed it.' Janna wasn't sure of any such thing, but she had to fight on her mother's behalf. Not to be buried in consecrated ground would leave her mother condemned by everyone. And if people condemned her mother, they would surely condemn Janna herself.

'She would not!' the priest contradicted sharply. 'She told me to take my blessings and prayers elsewhere for Dame Alice had no need of them.'

'By that, surely she meant that she believed she could make the lady well again.' Janna hated pleading with the priest, but she had no choice. To her surprise, he smiled at her, baring the brown stumps of his teeth.

'I bid you good morrow, sire,' he said.

Realising the smile was not for her, Janna swung around to find Hugh advancing towards them. He looked down at her. His voice was full of concern as he asked, 'Why did you run from the manor? I meant to escort you here today, but they told me you left last night and they haven't seen you since.'

I'll wager they didn't tell you why I left, Janna thought to herself, while acknowledging that she wasn't prepared to enlighten him either. She bobbed a curtsy to him, and said, 'I thank you for your care of me last night, sire, but my place was at home, not up at the manor.'

Hugh studied her for a moment, then turned to the priest. 'I have been specially charged by Dame Alice to see about the burial arrangements for Mistress Eadgyth. Where have you laid her?' He looked about the small, bare church.

The priest looked down at his toes. 'I was just informing Johanna that her mother lies outside the churchyard, beyond the pale.'

'What?' Hugh sounded incredulous. 'Mistress Eadgyth's death was an accident! The *wortwyf* did not knowingly take her own life.'

Hugh's words confirmed that he, too, believed that her mother had been poisoned – but by one of her own concoctions. Before Janna had time to protest, the priest began to defend his decision.

'If the lady died by her own hand it is suicide, and suicide is a sin against God. Even if her death was an accident, as you claim, she died unshriven. She did not come to church. In fact, almost her last words to me were that she had no time for God.'

'She said no such thing!' Janna wouldn't be silenced a moment longer. 'She was in a hurry to see Dame Alice, you told me so yourself.'

'She was in a hurry to go about her devilish practices,' the priest said darkly. 'I have spoken time and again from the pulpit, warning my flock of the dangers of submitting to ancient beliefs about *aelfshot*, and the conviction that diseases may be cured by magic and leechcraft. My flock now repent the error of their ways. They know that they must bend to God's will and seek Christ's blessing on the ills that befall them. Only your mother continued to defy me, brewing her potions and communing with that black cat to summon the dead.'

'She sought merely to heal, to bring comfort and relief!' Janna could hardly speak for rage.

'She took the power of life and death upon her shoulders.' The priest glowered at Janna, silencing her.

Hugh's expression was grave as he turned to the priest. 'Let me remind you of Dame Alice's wishes in this matter, and add my own plea for Mistress Eadgyth. No matter what you may believe, the herbwife was a good woman and as such I ask you to give her the benefit of your Christian charity, to relent and accord her a decent, Christian burial.'

'Never.' The priest drew himself up to his full height, which took him as far as Hugh's shoulder. 'A Christian burial would be an abomination in the sight of God.' His glance at Janna was both spiteful and triumphant.

Janna realised further argument was futile. With a muttered exclamation, she pushed past the two men and ran out into the churchyard. The warmth of the sun fell on her face like a blessing, but Janna was unaware of it, could hardly see for the tears streaming down her cheeks as she hurried past the graves with their rough stone markers, and out through an archway in the stone wall. A shrouded bundle lay in the wasteland beyond. It was a weedy, unkempt bit of ground which housed the unmarked graves of felons and those poor itinerants who had died without kin to identify them.

The grave had already been dug, a rough gaping hole that looked like a greedy mouth waiting to be fed. Eadgyth lay beside it, wrapped in a roughly woven cloth. Janna fell to her knees and gently removed part of the wrapping so that she might see her mother one last time. It seemed important to say goodbye and ask for forgiveness.

Eadgyth's face was calm in repose. Janna kissed the tips of her fingers then put them to her mother's lips. 'I'm sorry I was angry with you,' she whispered. 'Forgive me.' She gazed down as a lifetime of memories crowded into her mind. Her mother had raised her, and had given her the knowledge of the herbal lore and leechcraft that she herself practised. She was not given to praise, nor to demonstrative acts of affection.

In fact, Janna couldn't remember ever being kissed or comforted by her mother, not even as a child. Perhaps Eadgyth's ability to show love had died when Janna's father abandoned them. Now, her mother's hard and lonely life was over, and she would take her secrets with her into the grave.

With bitter regret for all that had come between them, Janna took one last look at Eadgyth, noticing again the traces of vomit on her kirtle and cheeks. Could her mother have taken, by mistake, some of the aconite mixed with oil that she made up as a rubbing lotion? It hardly seemed possible, particularly as her mother only made it fresh when it was needed and always threw out whatever remained, rather than risk having such a deadly poison close to her other preparations.

Janna tried to still her fears with the memory of her search earlier. She'd checked all the jars and had noticed nothing untoward, certainly nothing that resembled the rubbing lotion. The poison must have come from outside, and in a form unknown to her mother, for she would never have taken it willingly. Lost in thought, Janna carefully draped the russet cover over Eadgyth's face once more. 'Goodbye,' she whispered, and rose to her feet. She was startled to realise that she was no longer alone. Hugh was standing some distance away, watching her. As she caught his glance, he walked towards her. She gave her eyes a hasty scrub on the back of her hands, and faced him.

'I've done all I can to change the priest's mind,' he said, as he came closer. 'I even offered him payment, but I'm afraid he remains determined that your mother may not lie in consecrated ground. I'm sorry, Johanna.'

She nodded sadly. 'He's been preaching against us ever since he first arrived here. He knows he will lose face among the villagers if he gives her a burial with all the rites.'

'Was your mother not a Christian, then?'

Janna hesitated, wanting him to be on her side against the priest, wanting him to be sympathetic. Yet she didn't want to lie to him either. 'My mother believed in God, who created our world and who watches over us. She believed that true goodness lies in how we live our lives, and that was how she lived her life – because she believed that healing the sick was a good thing to do. She told me she followed God's law, not the priest's. She disagreed with what he said about women, and she hated the way he told the villagers that anyone who questioned what he said about Jesus and the scriptures would go straight to hell. The priest spoke against my mother's healing powers and her skills with herbs. The villagers listen to him and some of them stopped coming to my mother when they were ill and in need of help. She was very angry about that. She blamed the priest for making the villagers suffer when she could have given them relief.'

Hugh nodded in understanding. 'I know that she saved my aunt's life, for Dame Alice told me herself how your mother helped her when the apothecary could do nothing more.' He tapped the purse hanging from his belt. Janna heard the jingling clink of coins. 'Dame Alice gave me silver to give to the priest for your mother's burial. As he has proved so un-cooperative, I will arrange instead for the bishop to say a mass for your mother up at the abbey. It's the best I can do.'

'And I thank you from my heart, sire. Please also give my thanks to Dame Alice.' No matter how pitiful were the priest's efforts on her mother's behalf, Janna knew that he would expect payment. It was kind of Dame Alice to relieve her of that burden. Now, she struggled to find the words that might yet save her mother's soul. 'Please, tell the bishop there was never anyone so good as my mother. She helped so many people with her healing skills; she saved their lives. She did not deserve to die, nor does she deserve to lie out here in the wasteland. My mother will go to heaven, for certes, and I hope the priest may rot in hell for his deeds this day!'

She turned from Hugh, gulping down sobs as she tried to regain her composure.

'I will speak to the abbess about the priest,' he said firmly. 'And I will make sure your mother has a mass said for the repose of her soul.' He looked at her with kindness. 'God keep you, Johanna,' he said, and stepped back to join the priest and the small group of villagers who had now clustered around the grave.

Janna's glance swept over them. Her face hardened as she recognised Godric. He was standing a little apart from them all. She turned abruptly, so that she would not have to look at him. With head held high, she waited for the priest to step forward, and the funeral rites to commence.

NINE

I T SEEMED TO Janna that there was no more desolate sound in all the world than the scrape of the shovel and the soft thump of falling earth as slowly, so slowly, the cloth-wrapped body of her mother began to disappear from view. Her throat ached from unshed tears. 'I will seek out the truth. I will make sure that justice is done,' she whispered as another shovelful of dark earth dropped into the hole.

Godric was burying her mother. She'd felt shock and rage when the priest had beckoned him forward to fill in the grave. Not content with trying to frighten her into his arms, he was now going to earn a penny or two as a grave digger. She had once thought him honourable, kind and brave. How could she have been so completely wrong? Yet, in spite of everything, her eye was drawn to the tanned skin of his neck, the knotted muscles of his arms as he drove the spade once more into the earth piled beside the grave.

Anxious for distraction, she glanced around the assembled villagers, curious as to why they had come. Mistress Hilde, the miller's wife, stood among them, looking sullen and resentful. As she caught Janna's gaze, she gave her a vicious glare. It seemed the woman really hated her. Could she truly believe that Janna was a threat to her happiness?

Ulf, the blacksmith, and his three children had also come to witness the burial. He was paying no attention to the graveside; he was staring at Janna, his eyes hot and hungry. Uneasy, she shrank into herself, realising suddenly that she no longer had her mother's protection from unwanted suitors. Anyone could come calling. And if they wouldn't go away there was nothing she could do about it, for she was but a girl, no match in strength for any man determined to have his way with her. The cottage was too far away for her to run for help from the village; it was too far for anyone to hear her cry.

Janna was appalled by her predicament; even more appalled to realise how vulnerable she was. Godric had understood. He had offered protection, and she had refused it, had flung his offer in his face. But it was too late to unsay the hasty words that had led to such a shocking outcome. After what Godric had done she wanted nothing more to do with him. He was beyond her forgiveness.

Ulf was smiling at her now. Leering at her. Janna hastily looked away. Her glance fell on the village midwife. Mistress Aldith had no reason to be here; in fact, she had every reason to rejoice in her rival's death. Eadgyth had made no secret of her contempt for the incompetence of the village midwife. She had certainly taken away some of the midwife's business. Had Aldith come to make sure Eadgyth was truly dead and safely interred? Janna watched the woman for a moment, searching her face for any show of triumph or pleasure, but the midwife continued to contemplate the mound of earth steadily piling up in the grave, her expression serious. Perhaps, like so many mourners, she was not thinking of the recently deceased but contemplating instead how brief and fleeting was life on earth, and how long a death awaited them all.

Next to the midwife stood Hugh, with a lady by his side. Janna recognised her. Cecily. Her small face was pale. She looked ill. Was she clinging to Hugh's arm for comfort, or to show possession? Janna felt an unexpected pang of disappointment at the thought of Hugh being already attached and out of reach.

He's always been out of my reach! Janna knew she would do well to remember it. Yet he had been kind to her and she valued that, while acknowledging that it was a kindness he might have shown to anyone, even a stray dog. She eyed Hugh and the tiring woman thoughtfully, and came to the conclusion that he supported the lady from necessity. She seemed in great distress. What was she doing here? Why had they both come to witness this sorry scene? Janna could not pride herself that Hugh had stayed for her sake. It was his commission from Dame Alice to ensure that her mother was properly interred. And Cecily? It must be kindness that had brought her to the graveside, the same kindness that had prompted her to wash her mother's face and try to ease her dying moments.

Janna became aware of silence. She looked from Godric, red-faced and sweating after his exertions, to the newly dug patch of dark, damp earth. Her mother was covered from sight now. She was truly gone.

A shiver of misery shuddered through Janna, but she tilted her chin, defying the motley collection at the graveside. She did not want their pity, she wanted their acknowledgment of her mother's true worth. '*Requiescat in pace*,' she prayed silently, and waited for the priest to echo her words, to commend her mother's soul to God so that she might rest in peace. Surely he could not refuse her this small comfort? But the priest remained silent.

His silence goaded Janna to action. She had meant her ritual to be private, but his petty meanness spurred her to make a public farewell to her mother, to show them all that she honoured her mother's life – and death. She stepped forward, holding the bright flowers that now seemed inappropriate for this sad, rubbish-strewn wilderness. She laid them carefully at the place where she judged her mother's heart to be. Then she straightened and held aloft the rosemary so that all might see what she carried.

'This is rosemary, for remembrance,' she called out, her voice sounding high and clear in the still morning. She knelt down and carefully inserted the plant into the soft, damp earth. She pushed the stem in deeper and patted the earth firm to keep the plant secure, so that it might take root and grow, and mark forever the site of her mother's last resting place.

The assembly was quite silent, waiting to see what might happen next. Janna rose from her knees and faced them. Willing her voice not to tremble, she said, 'With this rosemary, I pledge to remember my mother, just as all of you who knew her will remember her for her healing ways, and for the aid and comfort she has given you over the years.' It was a command, not a wish. Janna hoped they recognised the difference.

She took a deep breath. 'My mother's death was an accident.' She looked directly at the priest, daring him to contradict her. Wisely, he kept silent. Janna wished that she knew the truth, so that she could tell them all, and still their wagging tongues for ever. But it was too early; she didn't know enough yet. She looked down at the rosemary on her mother's grave. This was her pledge to herself: to find out the truth and bring whoever was responsible for her mother's death to justice.

She had one last thing to say. She gave herself a moment to marshal her thoughts. 'Here, under the open sky, I commend my mother's spirit to God, for I know that she believed in Him and that she will find peace out here in His green garden. My mother always told me that God was everywhere around us, and I would rather she rest out here in open space and in the sunlight of His love than be confined by a mean and narrow spirit.' Janna addressed the priest directly, her intent unmistakeable.

'How dare you show so little respect!' His eyes bulging with fury, the priest turned away and stormed off in the direction of the churchyard gate. Seeing that the priest was leaving, the villagers hastily crossed themselves and set off after him. Ulf lingered momentarily, perhaps hoping to press his claim.

'Go away!' Janna tried to keep the fear from showing in her face. He hesitated, took a look at Godric and then hurried off, dragging his children behind him. He was followed by Hugh and Cecily. Janna was left alone to face Godric across her mother's grave.

'I suppose you were paid well for your toil this morning.' Her voice was sharp with contempt.

Shocked, Godric took a step backwards, recoiling as if her words had been a physical blow. 'Janna, I thought it would be some small comfort to you if I . . . if I . . .' Unable to spell out his intentions, he stuttered into silence.

She faced him down. 'I don't want your comfort, Godric. Not after your deeds last night!'

'But . . . but . . .' Now his face showed only bewilderment. 'My offer was kindly meant, Janna. And my mother would have welcomed you, I am sure.'

'I'm not talking about that!'

'What then?' Godric looked at her, waiting for her to enlighten him.

'You crucified my cat!' Janna could not stem the rushing torrent of anger as she relived the horror of finding her pet's dead body. 'You cut its throat and strung it up on a tree, knowing I would find it hanging there in the morning. My cat. A poor, defenceless creature which never did anyone any harm! How could you do that, Godric? How could you?'

'In truth, Janna, I don't know what you're talking about.'

'Don't try to pretend you are innocent of this crime! I found Alfred's dead body this morning. You were in the forest late last night. Who else, if not you?'

'Janna, I swear to you on your mother's grave that I . . .'

'Don't you dare swear on my mother's grave. You are not worthy even to speak of her!' Janna drew a sharp, agonised breath. 'And I never want to speak to you again, either. Go away, Godric. Stay out of my life. I hate you for what you've done.' She whirled around and set off towards the arched doorway in the stone wall of the churchyard, walking with fast, determined steps.

It was over, all over. She'd never felt so alone, so miserable. She wanted to throw back her head and howl like a dog. Instead, she scratched up the tattered remnants of her courage, and steadily marched on.

TEN

'I WOULD SPEAK WITH you, Janna.' The hissed whisper startled Janna. She stopped, wondering who had addressed her.

Aldith stepped out from behind a clump of bushes at the side of the church. She'd obviously been waiting for Janna. Now she put her hand on Janna's arm to draw her behind the bushy screen. Curiosity prompted Janna to follow her.

'What do you want with me?' she asked.

'What are your plans for the future?' the midwife asked in turn.

Janna blinked. She had no plans. There'd been no time to think of the future, no time to think beyond trying to fathom the mystery of her mother's death.

'I had great respect for your mother's knowledge,' the midwife continued, perhaps hoping to ingratiate herself. As Janna still stayed silent, she continued. 'I know you helped your mother prepare her herbal potions. You must have learned a great deal?'

Janna dipped her head in acknowledgment, wondering where this was leading. The midwife sighed. 'Your mother was a proud woman, and arrogant with it. She put me in the

wrong whenever she could for I have only a midwife's
knowledge, whereas she seemed to know almost as much as
any skilled physician in London!'

As Janna sucked in a sharp breath, ready to spring to her
mother's defence, the midwife continued, 'My business is
birthing babies, and Eadgyth had knowledge of herbs and
healing practice that would have helped the mothers
and babies in my care. When I asked if she would teach
me, she said only that I should wash more often. In fact,
she brushed me off as if I was no more than a fly come to
irritate her.' An old resentment soured the midwife's voice.
'I hope you have not inherited your mother's arrogance,
Janna. I'm asking you to share your knowledge with me,
just as I am prepared to share my experience with you.
I'm hoping that perhaps we may work together in the
future?'

'But . . .' Janna struggled to find the words to defend her
mother. 'But . . .' She remembered the impatience and
contempt which her mother had shown both Fulk and the
priest, and the way she had spoken of the midwife. Could
there be some justice in Aldith's claim?

'The villagers will come calling for my services soon
enough. I suspect Fulk will not linger now that Dame Alice
is safely delivered of her child,' Aldith observed.

'It was my mother who saved the lady and her child – not
that weasel!' Janna said hotly.

The midwife nodded in agreement. 'I believe you, but "that
weasel" is doing all in his power to take the credit, while
laying blame on your mother for trying to poison Dame
Alice.'

'My mother would never poison anyone!'

The midwife eyed her steadily. 'I believe you,' she said again.

As she understood what Aldith was saying, Janna could have cried with relief. Here, at last, was vindication for her mother.

'But that will not stop Fulk from spreading what he would have everyone think,' the midwife continued. 'Be careful, Janna. No man likes to be seen as a fool. He was a danger to your mother; he may yet be a danger to you.'

Fulk! He was top of her list of suspects. It was a comfort to have her suspicions echoed by the midwife.

'I advise you to stay in your cottage for a few days, keep well away from him,' Aldith continued. 'He'll be returning to his shop in Wiltune soon enough. With his new exalted opinion of himself, he may even move on to Winchestre to ply his trade!'

Janna's lips twitched to hear her mother's opinion of the apothecary repeated by the midwife. Curiosity prompted her to ask, 'And when Fulk goes, what then would you have me do?'

'Become my assistant,' Aldith answered promptly. 'You lack experience so there is much I can teach you, just as I believe that your mother will have taught you much that I do not know. We can learn from each other.'

Janna hesitated, tempted by Aldith's offer. It seemed far more genuine than Fulk's offer to her mother, and its benefits were manifest. Under Aldith's protection she would find a place and acceptance in the community, as well as gaining the experience she needed. Yet Aldith had been

Eadgyth's rival, and was about to reap the benefits of her death. While her offer might be kindly meant, Janna cautioned herself to stay on guard. Aldith was not off her list of suspects yet.

Aldith was waiting for her answer. Undecided, Janna wondered what her mother would have advised her to do.

She looked down at the midwife's apron. It was clean and freshly laundered, but the kirtle underneath was somewhat grubby and stained. There was her answer – or was it? If Eadgyth had only bothered to explain, the midwife would have understood why cleanliness was so necessary for the health of mothers and their babies. Aldith seemed more than willing to learn – and so was Janna. If sharing their knowledge would benefit the villagers, her offer was surely worth consideration. About to say yes, a further thought stopped Janna. If she accepted, it would tie her to this place just as surely as she'd been tied by her mother and their life here. Was that what she truly wanted?

'It's kind of you to think of me, and I thank you,' she said, searching for the words to frame a more gentle refusal than her mother would have done. 'Please give me time to think about it, for I know not what the future holds for me. It's too soon to make plans. Who knows, I may even marry.' It was an attempt to sound light-hearted, but Aldith nodded in immediate understanding.

'Eadgyth told me once that it was her dearest wish that you would marry and find happiness with a good man.'

'Why should my mother wish for me what she never knew herself?'

'I think because she wanted to keep you from making the same mistake that she did,' Aldith said quietly.

'Did you know my father?' Janna could hardly breathe from excitement.

Reluctantly, Aldith shook her head. 'I never met him,' she admitted. 'I only know the very little your mother confided to me when first she came here, swollen with child and looking for shelter.'

'Where did she come from?'

Aldith shrugged. 'I don't know. She never said.'

'Why did she come here? Did she tell you why she chose this place?'

'She came to see the abbess. She had little money or jewellery to give in return for shelter, but the abbess did well out of the exchange for the cot you live in was derelict, and the small piece of land beside was not large enough to support a villein and his family. Not only did your mother repair the cot and render that land fruitful, she also paid rent to the abbess in return for that act of charity. Your mother was no beggar, Janna.'

'Did she ever speak of her family, or her past? Please, please tell me everything you know,' Janna begged.

'I can't tell you much. Your mother and I weren't close, you know. I gave her shelter while your cottage was repaired, and we exchanged some confidences then. But I think she later regretted even the little she'd told me – and she repaid my kindness by stealing my patients!'

Janna was silenced by the bitterness in Aldith's voice. Her mind teemed with the questions she wanted to ask: questions that Aldith probably couldn't answer. She became aware that Aldith was studying her intently. 'You have your father's eyes,' she said then, unexpectedly.

'How can you know that? I thought you'd never met him.'

'I didn't. But your mother was a Saxon beauty with her fair hair and grey eyes. You have your mother's fair hair, but your eyes are dark brown.'

'Then I must be ugly. I would rather look like my mother than a father I don't know and who doesn't want to know me!'

'I suspect he doesn't know you even exist.'

'Did she tell you that?' Janna was worried now that she'd utterly misjudged her father, was ready to shift the blame for his neglect onto her mother.

'No. From the very little she told me about her circumstances, I gained the impression that your father might be someone wealthy, important. Too important to wed a woman of no consequence like your mother.'

'Surely, if my father was wealthy, he could have helped my mother live a better, more comfortable life than she did!' Janna's anger blew like a straw in the wind as it shifted between her mother and her father. She longed to know the true circumstances of her heritage and her birth.

'Perhaps he was already betrothed to another and would not break off that alliance? Your mother may well have decided to leave rather than beg for his help when she realised she was carrying you!' As she noticed Janna's stricken expression, Aldith's voice softened slightly. 'Your mother did not hold a grudge against your father, for all of that. In fact, she spoke of him with great love – such a love, I think, that prevented her from taking any other man to her bed thereafter.'

Janna nodded slowly as she came to understand the truth behind her mother's lonely life, and her desire for her only daughter to marry and be safe. 'My father's name? Did my mother ever say it?' she asked, eager to learn all that Aldith could tell her.

To her utter disappointment, Aldith shook her head. 'Your mother kept her secrets, Janna.'

'From me, as well as you. And now she's dead, I'll never know the truth about my father.' Janna felt her throat clog up with tears. With a huge effort, she struggled to stay dry-eyed and calm.

She took Aldith's hand. 'I am grateful to you, more grateful than I can say.'

'Think over my offer.' Aldith pressed Janna's hand between her own. Janna felt ashamed of her mother's past treatment of the midwife, for she believed that the woman was kind, and that she meant to bring comfort. 'We'll talk again,' Aldith promised, and slipped away.

Head bowed, Janna stayed motionless, thinking over what she'd just learned. Her father was likely highborn, too important to wed her mother. Which meant that by now he would surely have wed someone else, a lady, and would probably have children of his own. She longed to know more about him. Why had her mother kept his secret, never gone after him, never asked him for anything in spite of the hard times she and Janna had lived through? Pride? Or was it love and the need to protect his good name with his family that had kept her away?

Aldith had told her she had her father's brown eyes. She'd inherited more from him than that, Janna realised, for her

125

fair hair and skill with herbs were her only likeness to her mother. As well as resembling her father, did she have his temperament too? What sort of man could he be to inspire such love and devotion in Eadgyth, and yet abandon her so completely? Janna frowned, rejecting any part of her own nature that could ever be so brutal.

What would her father say, if he knew he had a daughter? Would he welcome her, or was his new family so important to him that he'd deny her and show her the door?

Saddened by her thoughts, Janna walked slowly along the narrow street that led through Berford. It seemed to her that several people turned aside as she passed, or ducked into doorways or down lanes rather than meet her face to face. She looked back to check if her suspicion was true, just in time to see a young boy making the sign of a cross with his fingers, as if to ward off evil. Acting on impulse, Janna made the sign back at him. His eyes widened and he scuttled off. Janna looked after him, feeling troubled and angry that the villagers seemed so against her when her mother had always done her best to help them.

The priest and his sermons, and the fact that he would not bury her mother in consecrated ground: that news must be out already. Truly the priest had succeeded in turning her and her mother into outcasts.

Lost in thought as she was, Janna did not at first pay attention to the slender woman in the long green gown hurrying ahead of her. It was only when the woman glanced behind her, and their gaze met, that Janna realised who she was. Not bound by any notions of maidenly modesty, she picked up her skirts and raced after her.

'Mistress Cecily!' she shouted. 'Please wait!' There was no reason why a highborn tiring lady should pay her any attention or do as she was told. Janna understood that, but her need to ask questions was greater than her need to worry about propriety. 'I want to ask you about my mother,' she called.

The young woman stopped. Slowly, reluctantly, she turned to face Janna. Her face was pale, her eyes red-rimmed as if she'd recently been crying. Janna wondered where Hugh had gone, and if the lady was weeping because of him. She quickly banished that disturbing thought from her mind. She needed all her wits to find out what she could from the last person to see her mother alive.

'Forgive me.' She bobbed an awkward curtsy. 'I called after you because I wanted to thank you again for looking after my mother while she lay dying. I'm trying now to piece together the last hours of her life, so that I may truly understand what happened to her.' The tremor in Janna's voice was real, and Cecily responded with sympathy.

'Your mother did seem ill and out of sorts when she arrived back at the manor, but I put it down to the fact that there was quite an argument between her and Master Fulk over the best potion to help Dame Alice. Fulk had prepared a posset but your mother threw it out and told him to leave the room. Fulk appealed to Dame Alice, but she said he should do what he was told. He was very angry with Eadgyth. He blamed her for everything.' Cecily cast a timid glance at Janna, then modestly lowered her eyes.

'Did my mother have anything to eat or drink when she arrived?'

'I offered her a beaker of water. She'd had a long walk and I thought she must be hot and thirsty.'

'That was kind of you.' Janna hesitated, wondering how to phrase the question without offending Cecily. 'Did she say anything about the water? About its taste?'

'No. She said she was thirsty, and she drank it straight down.'

'So the water couldn't have been . . .' Janna was going to say 'poisoned', but stopped in time. 'Foul? Polluted in some way?'

'Not at all!' Cecily bristled in indignation. 'It was poured from the very jug that Dame Alice herself uses. But your mother was sick almost straight away.'

'Who gave the water to my mother?' Janna had visions of Fulk slipping aconite into the beaker, but then remembered that he'd been banished from the bedchamber.

'I poured the water myself, and brought it to her. She thanked me. She said the water had cooled her. In fact, she complained of feeling cold.' Cecily still looked indignant. Janna knew she could not press the matter further.

'Did my mother take any food or drink before she saw Dame Alice? Could she and the apothecary perhaps have taken some refreshment together?'

'I doubt it!' Cecily gave a brief snort of laughter at the idea. 'There was no love lost between them right from the very beginning. He never wanted your mother to come, it was only that ma dame insisted on it.' She looked up at Janna, suspicion in her eyes. 'Why are you asking me all these questions?'

Janna bit her lip. She was being too blunt. 'Forgive me.

128

I believe my mother's death was an accident, and I'm trying to find out how it happened. Did she swallow any of the decoctions she prepared for Dame Alice?'

'No.'

'So they could not have caused her death?'

'No.'

'Yet Dame Alice took them – and they helped to stop the bleeding and gave her strength?'

'Yes, indeed.' Utterly serious now, Cecily faced Janna. 'We'd heard of your mother's knowledge and skill in the matter of carrying and birthing babes from one of the kitchen maids. That was why . . .' She stopped abruptly, pink washing over her pale face.

'That was why . . .?' Janna prompted, curious to understand why Cecily looked so embarrassed and uncomfortable.

'Why . . . why Dame Alice sent Master Fulk to fetch your mother.' Cecily had hold of her girdle and, with restless fingers, was busily shredding the delicate fibres. Janna wondered at her apparent distress. Before she could question her, Cecily hurried on. 'It was my lord Robert who asked Master Fulk to attend ma dame. She soon saw that he had even less knowledge than the midwife when it came to . . . to . . . and the kitchen maid had said that . . . that . . .'

'I'm glad my mother was able to help Dame Alice,' Janna intervened, taking pity on Cecily's reluctance to speak of womanly matters. 'Did she say anything else before she died? Did she give any clue as to what ailed her?'

Cecily hesitated. 'I wondered if her wits had gone wandering. She said there were ants in the bedchamber, but there never were!' Indignation sharpened Cecily's tone. It seemed she took the accusation personally. '"Ants," she said. "Ants." Her words were quite clear.'

Eadgyth's intention was clear to Janna too. Her mother had told her that symptoms of monkshood poisoning included feeling cold, and also the unpleasant sensation that ants were crawling over your skin. To be sure, she questioned Cecily again.

'You said my mother called for a monk?'

Cecily nodded vigorously. 'That is true. I offered to send for the priest but she shook her head most violently. "Monk," she said. Even though she could hardly talk by then, she was most insistent about it.'

'Are you sure she said monk, not monkshood?'

'You mean the plant with the pretty blue flowers?' Cecily frowned, puzzled. As understanding came, she clasped her fist to her breast in shock. 'But . . . but it's very poisonous!' she stammered.

'Yes. Yes, it is.' Janna was torn between wanting to clear Eadgyth's reputation and keeping her suspicions a secret until she could prove them. 'It was just a silly thought I had. Don't worry about it,' she said quickly.

'Your name was on your mother's lips as she died.' Cecily seemed anxious to switch to a safer topic. 'Johanna.' Her voice softened in sympathy. 'I am sorry you came too late to speak to her.'

'She called me Johanna?' She was only 'Johanna' when she was in trouble. It seemed Eadgyth had taken the anger of their argument to her death. The thought pierced Janna's heart.

'Actually, I thought Eadgyth was calling for "John", but when I questioned who he was, one of the tiring women told me your name. Your real name.'

'Johanna.' Janna felt sick with misery, sick that her mother had died without forgiving her their quarrel.

'I thank you for your time, for answering my questions.' Janna turned away, too dispirited to ask any more. A couple of small, grubby children were scooping mud from a puddle in the lane and carefully fashioning it into a castle. They reminded Janna of one last question. 'Dame Alice's new babe. How does he?'

Cecily's face knotted into a frown. 'He does very poor. When she first arrived at the manor, your mother bade us wash him and rub him with salt, and then wrap him tight. The babe had been cut from his mother, but the cord was not tied and there was a great deal of blood. She took care of that, and took care also to cleanse his mouth and rub his gums with honey. As soon as she was done, the priest came in to Dame Alice to baptise the child in front of his parents. The baby is now in the care of a wet nurse, but he does not thrive. Your mother brought back with her a mixture to stimulate the child and help him suckle, but she fell ill before she could do much other than instruct the nurse as to its use.'

Cecily's voice echoed with misery. Janna felt a flash of warmth towards the tiring woman. She seemed so kind, and so compassionate. Janna wished she could get to know her better, but although Cecily was near her own age, she was so far above her in station that friendship between them could never be possible. Sadly, Janna acknowledged how desperately she wanted, and needed, a friend right now.

'Cecily!' The voice captured Janna's attention. She tried to still a sudden kick of excitement as they both turned in the direction of the sound. It was Hugh.

ELEVEN

UGH WAS LOOKING for Cecily, Janna reminded herself as she watched him lead the huge black destrier towards them, along with a brown horse on a leading rein. The gleam of appreciation in his eyes was for Cecily, not her. She bobbed a curtsy as his gaze swivelled to encompass her. 'Johanna.'

'Sire.' She would have spoken her thanks for his presence at her mother's burial, but he forestalled her.

'I understand that grief may have unbridled your tongue, but it was rash of you to speak as you did beside your mother's grave. I fear you have made an enemy of the priest.'

Janna flushed, shamed by his reproof, yet she was determined that he should understand her. 'The priest is already my enemy,' she said. 'He made himself so when he refused to bury my mother in consecrated ground.'

'Nevertheless, you should not jeopardise your position in the village by public displays of this sort. I understand there has been a lot of hostility directed towards your mother, which might now spill onto you.'

Janna's face darkened in angry resentment. She had thought Hugh an ally, but it seemed she'd been wrong.

'Don't misunderstand me,' he said quickly. 'I agree with you that the priest acted outside his duty of care towards your mother, and I have just told him so. I've also warned him that I'll be speaking to the abbess about it. She holds the barony from the king and has the bishop's ear. You must let them deal with the priest together. You should more properly show concern for your own position in the village now that you no longer have your mother to protect you.'

'I am of an age to protect myself!'

'For certes you have the temper for it,' Hugh retorted, but he smiled as he said the words. Janna blushed anew. Mercifully, he turned his attention then to Cecily, who stood silent by Janna's side.

'I asked you to wait for me until my business with the priest was done so that I might escort you back to the manor,' he said courteously.

'I . . . I thought a walk in the fresh air might revive my spirits, sire.'

'What ails you? Why do you not rest?' There was sympathy in Hugh's eyes as he surveyed the tiring woman.

'I had long enough to rest yesterday morning.' Cecily looked down at her muddy shoes rather than meet his eye.

'Yet you did not rest,' Hugh observed drily. 'Dame Alice said you were gone from the manor all morning. She's worried about you, particularly as you looked so ill on your return. When she realised you had come out again today, she sent this palfrey to me with a messenger. She has asked me to ride home with you.'

'Dame Alice is kind to think of me.' Cecily looked stricken. Her face was so white, Janna thought she might faint.

Hugh led the palfrey to a post nearby. Janna tried to suppress a flash of jealousy as she noticed the care he took while helping Cecily to mount. Did his hand linger unnecessarily on the lady's waist? He kept the leading rein in his hand all the while, gentling the palfrey so that it would not startle and upset Cecily. Their journey back to the manor would be slow and decorous, utterly unlike the wild ride Janna had shared with the groom. She felt a flash of resentment over the lack of respect shown to her, but she had to acknowledge that had she been given a mount of her own, she would not have been able to ride it. She and the groom had been racing against time. When death awaited there were far more urgent considerations than the chance exposure of a lady's ankle or leg.

A lady! Janna made a disgusted noise in her throat. Truly she was reaching far above herself with these thoughts. All the same, she found it hard to smother a pang of envy as she watched how solicitously Hugh settled the tiring woman into the saddle and noticed Cecily's shy smile of thanks in return.

'God be with you, Johanna,' Hugh said then, and mounted his own horse. Slowly, they clip-clopped away.

Janna stayed still, pondering Hugh's words as she watched them depart. So Cecily had lied to her employer. Why? She began to think over all the tiring woman had told her – or not told her – and came to the conclusion that Cecily had perhaps revealed more than she realised. It seemed that Eadgyth's skill with herbs was common knowledge, even at Babestoche Manor, and Fulk had been sent like a common errand boy to fetch her. Not only had Eadgyth refused to salvage Fulk's reputation by going along with his play-acting but, worse, she'd thrown away his preparation and sent him from Dame Alice's bedchamber. She'd publicly exposed Fulk as a charlatan. Small wonder then if he hated her enough to want her out of the way. Monkshood was common enough. It was perfectly possible that Fulk would have access to it.

Janna's head felt crammed with questions. Certainly Cecily's description of her mother's symptoms had dispelled any doubts as to the poison her mother had ingested. Aconite was fast-acting. Janna knew that much from what her mother had told her when warning her about the properties of various poisonous plants. So whatever Cecily believed, her mother must have had some refreshment on her arrival at the manor as well as the water.

A thought stopped Janna. If her mother had taken only a little of the aconite in something well flavoured, there would not have been enough in the taste to warn her, while a tiny amount of poison might take several hours to wreak its damage. If that was so, Eadgyth could have taken the poison even before she arrived at the manor house. Who then might have given it to her?

Janna frowned as she thought about the possibility. She would have to cast her net more widely to encompass everyone her mother might have met on that last fateful morning of her life. She would start with her mother's mysterious visitor. Who was she? Certainly not one of the villagers. Someone highborn. Up until yesterday they'd known no-one like that. Now, they did!

Janna stood stock-still, thinking it through. As the answer came to her, she wondered why it had taken her so

136

long to work it out. The woman visiting her mother had insisted on secrecy. Cecily had tried to fool the household into thinking she was resting at the manor when, in fact, she'd gone out without telling anyone. Cecily knew that Eadgyth had had a long walk to Babestoche. And she looked ill, as she would after Eadgyth's ministrations. If Cecily had visited the *wortwyf* yesterday morning in a desperate attempt to get her out of trouble, it could explain why, in return, she'd tried to look after Eadgyth in the last moments of her suffering, and why she'd come out to see her buried today. More than anything, Janna wished Cecily was still there so that she could offer her comfort, and also ask more questions.

She needed to sit quietly and put her thoughts in order, Janna decided. She must question Cecily to find out if she or anyone else had shared food or a drink with her mother. Someone must know something, and she would not rest until she had found it out.

She set off to climb the downs towards the forest and home, but a hoarse shout stopped her before she'd taken more than a few steps. Turning, she found herself confronted by the miller's wife. Hilde's face was flushed dark red; her eyes were bright with anger as she waddled up to Janna.

'Whore!' she spat. 'Slut! Taking a man to your bed even while your mother was breathing her last!'

'What? What?' Janna could hardly take in the meaning of Hilde's words.

'I suppose you thought you were safe to do as you pleased, with your mother out of the way dispensing her potions and poisons up at the manor?'

'I . . . I don't know what you're talking about!' Janna was at a loss as to how to defend herself against Hilde's wrath. But she couldn't let the last part of her speech go unchallenged. 'My mother was working no poison up at the manor. She was helping to save the life of Dame Alice and her newborn son.'

'Then how did she come to poison herself at the same time?' Hilde's eyes twinkled bright with malicious glee.

'She did not poison herself. She did not!'

But Hilde was no longer listening. She began to scratch at the rash of sores on her arm, unaware that she was drawing blood. 'You leave my husband alone!' she spat. 'He told me he was going out to check his eel traps last night and he didn't come home. I know he was with you and I'm warning you, you will join your mother in her grave if he visits you again.'

'But . . . but I haven't seen your husband!' Janna remembered the scene at the mill, the scene the miller's wife had witnessed. 'Well, I saw him when I went to fetch the bag of flour, but his actions were none of my doing.'

'I don't believe a word of it! I saw you talking to him, leading him on. You invited him to come to you in the night, did you not?'

'No!' Janna found herself blushing at the very thought of it. 'If he was gone from your bed, mistress, I assure you he was not in mine! You must look elsewhere for someone to blame for his roving ways. Perhaps, indeed, you should ask your husband for an explanation!'

Hilde's hand, bloodied from scratching at her arm, moved down to her bulging stomach. She touched its rounded contours with soft fingers. Janna felt a twinge of pity, until she caught Hilde's expression. Stony and unforgiving, her glance raked over Janna. 'I saw you in his arms. I saw you kiss him!'

'He kissed *me* – and I kicked him where it really hurt!' Janna felt sick, poisoned by the woman's suspicion.

Hilde looked momentarily nonplussed. Then she gave a snort of disbelief. 'I am warning you, miss. Do not entice my husband to your bed again.' Shocking in its suddenness, she pulled a small knife from the purse at her girdle, and brandished it in Janna's face. The blade glinted bright in the sunlight. 'Tempt him again and it'll be your turn to feel how sharp this is!'

Janna blinked, hardly able to believe what she was seeing and hearing. Before she had time to respond, Hilde had shouldered her aside and lumbered back down the lane. Janna looked after her, shocked and upset by the unexpected confrontation. That the woman was unbalanced was obvious, yet it was not unknown for pregnant women to become unsettled and take odd fancies. It was certainly true that the miller gave Hilde good cause to worry and fret.

The best plan was to keep out of Hilde's way in future, Janna told herself, as she hurried on. In an effort to banish her disquiet, she turned her mind back to the conversations she'd had with Aldith and Cecily and the handsome Hugh.

Aldith had told her much about her father, but nothing that had shed any light on who had killed her mother. True, she had warned Janna about Fulk, but Janna already had her own suspicions about him. Posturing turnip head that he was, even Fulk would know about the poisonous properties of aconite. Everyone knew, although they might call the plant by another name. What else had Aldith told her?

Or not told her? Janna frowned as she considered the midwife's position. Aldith had a grudge against her mother, that much had become clear. She also had much to gain from Eadgyth's death. Could the midwife be as blameless as she appeared? Janna had been so intent on learning what Aldith knew about her father that she'd neglected to question her about her movements on the day of Eadgyth's death. At the very least, she should find out when Aldith had last seen her mother.

As Janna began to climb the grassy downs, she stared up at the great blue canopy over her head. God's realm, where truth and justice must surely prevail. It was comforting to think that someone watched over her, that someone cared what happened to her. She had a Father in heaven. She might also have a father right here on earth!

It was like an itch that wouldn't go away, this mystery of her father. To know so little was frustrating beyond belief. Yet already she knew far more than she'd ever known before. Why had her mother been so secretive? Because she felt shame? Because she could not bear to talk about the man she loved? Would her mother have honoured her promise to tell Janna the truth, or had she learned more from Aldith than her mother might ever have confessed? The questions kept coming, questions without answer. She could not set her thoughts free.

Feeling sorry that she'd never been given the chance to know her father, or even to understand her mother, Janna continued the climb towards her home.

There were still vegetables left from the night before, the dinner her mother never came home to eat. Although tempted to throw them out, Janna put them in the pot, then hung it over the fire to heat for her dinner later. They were far too good to give to the goats. Instead, she cut some nettles and brambles from the edge of the forest, and grabbed up a handful of grain for the hens. 'Nellie! Gruff!' she called, and the goats bleated and ambled towards her, ready to be milked and fed. The hens came running too. Janna waited until they were all busy feeding before she produced an extra morsel for Laet, who always came last in the race for food. 'It's a hard life,' she told the small, scrawny hen. 'You've got to fight if you want to survive.' It was advice she herself should heed, she realised, as she slowly walked back towards the cottage.

The row of bee skeps under their woven covers brought a pang of remorse as Janna recollected how she'd stomped past them before, and had even tried to smack down a passing bee. Now she stopped beside them to make amends. 'You'll never guess what's happened,' she said, and suddenly found herself pouring out the story of the past couple of days.

There was a relief in talking about it, she found. The bees were coming back to the hive; their busy humming soothed Janna as she poured out her misery. 'I've made a pledge,' she confided. 'I shall not rest until I see my mother's killer brought to justice.' She thought about it. If she could work out who had the means, the motive and the opportunity, she should then know the identity of the killer. 'I'm sure it's Fulk,' she said. 'He had the knowledge, and he also had the motive. He hated my mother. I just have to find out if he had the opportunity to act on that hatred. There's also Cecily. She hasn't told me all she knows. I have to talk to her again.'

The bees hummed quietly about her. Janna continued to marshal her thoughts. 'And there's Aldith,' she said. 'She's a midwife; she'll know about monkshood. I like her, but my mother's death will certainly be to her benefit. I must find out when they last met.'

The priest, Janna thought suddenly. He, too, had been at the manor house. He, too, wished her mother ill. Could a priest know such hatred that he would break God's law and kill someone he thought of as an enemy, even if it was done in the name of Christ?

It was a disturbing thought, made more pressing by Janna's sudden memory of the marketplace in Wiltune. She had seen the priest swooping about there like the carrion crow that he was. Had he been listening when the merchant spoke of the healing effects of his rubbing oil? As a priest, he would have an understanding of Latin and so would be able to identify the plant in question. At the end of the merchant's sales pitch, he would also have a good idea of how dangerous it was.

His motive might be shaky, but he certainly had the knowledge and possibly the opportunity. 'I also need to question the priest,' she told the bees.

Once inside, she put the hot vegetables onto a griddle cake, and sat down to eat. There was no Alfred to share her meal tonight. Janna felt immensely sad, and immensely lonely as she took off her kirtle and lay down on the pallet to sleep. She missed the presence of her mother beside her, and the warm bulk of Alfred at her feet. Tears pricked the back of her eyes, and she gave a forlorn sniffle. Knowing she had a plan for action brought her some comfort, and helped to settle the questions that tumbled endlessly through her mind. Instead of lying awake all night, as she had supposed she would, exhaustion claimed her and she fell into a deep and healing sleep.

ᴄᴡᴇʟᴠᴇ

Janna woke late the next morning, to find the sun already high in the sky. Her long sleep had refreshed her, so that although she felt lonely as she went about her morning chores, she also recognised that this was how things were going to be from now on, and that, in time, she would get used to it.

She found herself humming the tune she'd heard her mother singing, and instantly stopped. For some reason she felt ashamed, although she couldn't think why she should.

She walked outside with an armful of feed for the animals. Their pen was getting somewhat smelly, she realised, as she looked about at the mounds of excrement. She dumped the greens in a corner to entice the goats and hens out of her way then, with a sigh, she took up a spade to shovel the dung out and over the garden.

'Dirt and disease go together,' Eadgyth had said, when Janna had once questioned why their animals were not brought into the cottage at night for safety, as was common practice. 'The fence protects the animals; that is why I made it to close them in. And their waste can be spread among the plants to help them grow, instead of it fouling the rushes on our floor and making us both ill.'

The sound of Eadgyth's voice in her mind brought tears to Janna's eyes. She blinked hard, and kept on digging. Once done, she came back into the cottage and looked about her. She would have to do the work of two if she wanted to survive, she realised. She would need goods to trade for other necessities as well as having to provide enough food for herself. Even with her mother by her side, they had often gone hungry. Janna felt a tremor of fear unsettle her stomach. She had the few coins from her sales at Wiltune market, but there were no goods left; she would have to make more. She should also think about Aldith's offer, although she wouldn't commit herself to anything until she could be sure of the midwife's innocence. In the meantime she should put the word about that she was able to physic the villagers just as her mother had always done.

It wasn't quite true, and Janna felt a momentary anger against her mother. Then she shrugged. It was the way it was, and she would have to make the best of it. She had her mother's knowledge. It was only a matter of time before she gained her experience.

The sound of galloping hooves alerted Janna to the presence of a horseman riding towards the cottage. She opened the door and stepped out into the sunlight, recognising instantly the big black destrier and its rider.

'Johanna.'

'Sire.' She smiled up at Hugh and bobbed a small curtsy. He led a palfrey on a rein behind him, the same palfrey he'd brought for Cecily.

'I am pleased to find you here,' he said, and hurriedly dismounted. 'Dame Alice is distraught. The baby has taken a turn for the worse and is like to die at any moment. Robert has sent for the priest, but Alice won't give up the babe, not yet. She begs you to come with me and do what you may to save him.' Even as he spoke, he planted his hands around Janna's waist, ready to hoist her on to the palfrey's back.

Janna panicked. 'I . . . I can't . . . I don't know how to ride,' she stammered.

'I should have thought of that.' Hugh kept his hand on Janna's waist as he pulled the destrier towards him. 'You can ride with me.' Before Janna had time to protest, he hoisted her up. She landed awkwardly, her legs straddling the beast's back.

She felt a flash of resentment that she had no say in the matter, that in spite of all the tasks she must do to ensure her survival, she was expected instantly to do as she was bid. Her protest was silenced by the urgency of Hugh's message.

'What ails the infant?' she asked instead, trying all the while to pull down her kirtle. Once again it had bunched itself up near her waist.

'I know not.' In spite of the gravity of the situation, Hugh's eyes twinkled as he watched her endeavours to cover her bare legs. 'Dame Alice trusted your mother's knowledge, and hopes that she may have taught you enough to save her baby.' Hugh quickly tied the palfrey to a nearby tree, then pulled himself up in front of her. He turned the destrier and kicked it into a gallop.

As the full enormity of Hugh's words sank in, Janna subsided into a frightened silence. She was expected to save the baby's life, but she no longer had her mother's knowledge and expertise to draw on. If the child died, she alone would be held responsible.

This last thought tightened her grip on Hugh. Sensing the pressure, and perhaps seeking to reassure her, he turned his head to speak to her over his shoulder.

'The baby has been baptised, and the priest now counsels Dame Alice that it will be God's will if the child should die. But Alice won't hear of it. She has had such ill luck since the birth of her first little boy. She had thought, having brought this child to term and borne him alive, that he would thrive. Will you be able to save him, Johanna?'

'No!' It was a cry from the heart, but even as she uttered her fear aloud, Janna knew that she could not give up so easily, not if she meant to honour her mother's name. Besides, if she could save the child, surely it would still the clattering tongues that spoke of poison and devils and such. 'I mean, yes!' she said more loudly, to counteract her denial. And then, as honesty prevailed, she muttered, 'I'll try.' She tried to collect her frightened thoughts. Should she ask Hugh to turn around and go back to the cottage? What was wrong with the babe? What might she need to save his life?

There was no point asking Hugh. He'd already admitted he didn't know. Eadgyth had said that the babe was weakened by the long birth, and would not suckle, but was that all that ailed him? If so, Janna knew what steps to take to ease the problem. If it was something worse, however, she was in trouble, deep trouble. Conscious of time passing, she struggled to decide. Finally she came to the reluctant conclusion that she would not know what to do until she could see the child herself. Hopefully she would recognise the symptoms and be able to find the herbs to treat him in

Dame Alice's own garden. Otherwise she would have to ask Hugh to take her back to the cottage.

Desperately, passionately, Janna wished that her mother was still alive. If only she had her mother's experience. She closed her eyes. 'Help me,' she whispered, her plea unheard against the drumming of the horse's hooves. 'Please, help me.' She wished the ride could go on for ever, so that she would never have to confront the dying child and his distraught mother. But all too soon they were flying through the gate and dismounting in the yard.

Almost the first person Janna saw as she hurried up the stairs and into the great hall was Aldith. She stopped, dismayed. The midwife's apron was clean, but Janna knew the dangers of the grubby skirt beneath. 'What are you doing here?'

Aldith gave her a reproachful glance. 'Tending mothers and their babies is the work of a midwife,' she said, addressing her comments to Hugh. She turned then to Janna. 'Your mother knew that full well, although that didn't stop her pushing her nose in. Now that she's gone, you must allow me, as having more experience than you, Janna, to take care of Dame Alice and her new babe.'

'Dame Alice has asked for me,' Janna retorted. 'That's why I'm here.'

'But I am come prepared to help my lady.' The midwife held up a flask, the movement accompanied by the sound of sloshing liquid. Her lips twitched up in a smile of triumph as she glanced at Janna's empty hands. 'Go home,' she advised. 'There is naught for you to do here.'

Hugh frowned at Aldith. 'You'd better wait here. Dame Alice wishes to see Johanna without delay.' He brushed past the midwife, not waiting to hear any further argument. Janna kept her head bent as she scuttled after him. All her suspicions had been aroused by Aldith's presence at the manor. The midwife had hardly waited to see her rival safely interred before hastening to take her place. Janna hoped she would wait in the hall, as instructed. She had questions to ask the midwife, questions that would reveal either her guilt or her innocence.

Her emotions were so close to the surface that tears of sympathy came to her eyes when she entered the bedchamber. The lady, red-eyed from weeping, clutched the limp body of her baby to her breast. With shaking fingers she was trying to guide his mouth in a desperate effort to suckle the child. 'Please, help us,' she implored as she caught sight of Janna. 'If my child would only feed, I am sure he could be saved.'

'Drink some wine, dearest.' Robert of Babestoche was a handsome man, Janna thought, with his shock of dark hair and the ruddy complexion that spoke of a great enjoyment of all the good things that life at the manor had to offer. With great solicitude, he poured some red liquid from a glass bottle into a silver goblet. Janna looked at the bottle, fascinated by both it and its contents. She had never seen such a beautiful bottle before, nor had she ever tasted wine made from grapes. This looked so fine it must have come by ship from Normandy.

Robert held the goblet out to his wife. 'This will strengthen your blood and, I am sure, give strength to our son as well.'

With an impatient exclamation, Dame Alice knocked his hand away. The goblet fell, spilling its contents in a red stream. The wine looked like blood on the fine linen sheets. Janna gasped, aghast at the waste.

Robert's lips tightened in anger. He bent to retrieve the goblet and set it carefully on a chest close to the bed. 'Try not to distress yourself, my love,' he said, and bent down to brush a kiss on his wife's forehead. 'We are in God's hands now.' He left the room, acknowledging Janna's presence with a brief nod as he passed. It seemed that he, along with the priest, was ready to give up, but Janna was not. She forced her shaking legs to walk to the bedside, while she prepared to fight for the life of Dame Alice's infant.

I must first calm Dame Alice, Janna thought, and cast her mind back to recall what Eadgyth did when faced with an angry or distressed villager. It seemed to Janna that she was taking a great liberty, but nevertheless she laid her hand on Dame Alice's arm and tried not to betray her fear. 'I will do all in my power to help you,' she said, speaking low and slowly. 'First, I need you to tell me all that you have seen and observed since the baby's birth.' She looked down at the infant cradled in his mother's arms. He was swaddled tight in a woollen wrap. A strap kept the wrap in place; it was criss-crossed around his tiny body. His head, too, was covered. Janna could see nothing but his tiny face. What she saw did not reassure her. His eyes seemed blank, without life, and there was a bluish tinge to his lips.

'He was perfect! A beautiful, healthy child who was taken away from me.' The lady sounded desolate, but there was an edge of anger beneath her words. At first, Janna thought the anger was directed at her mother, until she followed Dame Alice's gaze and noticed what she'd missed before. Fulk was standing in a shadowy recess, watching her, watching them both. Now he hurried over to the bedside, ready to defend himself.

'Ma dame, you know right well that it is common practice for ladies of high birth to appoint a wet nurse to suckle their babies.'

'Common practice it may be, but I deeply regret that I did not follow Eadgyth's instructions to suckle the child myself. Now I fear I am too late for he will not feed.' Tears welled up in the lady's eyes and spilled down her cheeks.

'Who's been looking after the baby since his birth?' Janna queried.

A slight young woman stepped forward, looking haggard and careworn. Janna sympathised with her. Should the baby die, she would carry the blame and would likely find herself dismissed. Without permission to leave, she would be unable to find work anywhere else. She must also have a new baby of her own, if it had lived, and would need a husband or her family to support her.

'Tell me about the baby. What did you observe while he was in your care?' she asked. She was sorry to put the woman in a difficult position, but she had to know the answer. She already suspected part of it. Knowing Dame Alice's situation, Eadgyth would not have suggested that the lady suckle her own child unless there was some worry about whether or not he would thrive.

The wet nurse gave a nervous glance around the room, testing how safe it might be to tell the truth. If she confirmed Dame Alice's statement, she would most certainly be blamed should the baby die. If she spoke the truth about its ailments, she risked the wrath of the mother who believed her child perfect in every respect.

Fulk broke the silence with a cough. 'You were in no position to suckle the child yourself, my lady,' he said. 'The birth was long, and very hard. There was an excessive amount of bleeding. Far better that you rest and recover your strength and leave the nourishment of your child to someone else.'

Dame Alice glared at him. 'Get out,' she said. 'Pack your bags and be gone. Had I listened to you alone, and done as you suggested, you would be getting ready to bury me along with my son.'

'But I —'

'Go!' Dame Alice commanded, her voice rising in hysteria as she cried, 'You have done enough harm. I will not see you again.'

Angry and resentful, the apothecary shouldered Janna aside and left the room.

Janna felt her skin crawl at his touch, understanding the anger behind the violent movement. He was her enemy now, as well as her mother's. With an effort, she turned her thoughts back to the more pressing problem. 'Please, tell me everything you can about the baby,' she prompted, needing the nurse to answer her question.

The woman glanced nervously at her mistress, then looked quickly away. 'The child's skin was deadly pale, he was almost blue when I first saw him,' she whispered. 'After she tied the cord, Mistress Eadgyth bade us give him a warm bath and wrap him tight. His skin flushed more pink in the warmth, but he still seemed somewhat distressed. Your mother asked us to place some lavender next to his cradle, which she said would calm him, and she collected herbs for the cook to make into a syrup with some honey. She instructed us to give the baby a small sup of it every few hours.'

'And did you do that?'

'Yes. At once when the mixture was given to me, and again in the morning. The lavender is still beside his cradle.'

'Did you have syrup enough for only two doses?'

'The apothecary ordered me to throw it away. Your mother brought a different potion back with her, but Master Fulk told me to destroy that too.' The girl looked flushed and uncomfortable. Janna wondered if she'd done what she was told. She must have a baby of her own, a child who might also be ailing and in need of a healing potion. Yet Janna was sure the nurse would not give her a straight answer in front of Dame Alice.

She tried another tack. 'What was in the mixture? Did my mother tell you?'

'No.' The girl shook her head, not meeting Janna's eye.

Desperation forced Janna's hand. 'And did you throw it away, as you were bid?'

The girl remained silent.

'Come now, Dame Alice will not punish you if you disobeyed Master Fulk's orders. In fact, I feel sure she will reward you if you can bring the mixture to us now. For certes my mother knew exactly what was needed to save the baby's life.' Janna flicked a glance towards the lady, mutely asking for her support.

Dame Alice leaned forward. 'If you still have it, I beg you to fetch it immediately,' she said.

The girl nodded, and fled. Dame Alice fell back against the pillows, her sigh of relief echoing around the chamber.

Exhilarated by what she saw as a win, Janna called for a jar of honey to be brought. As soon as the girl had returned with the mixture, and the baby had swallowed a few drops of Eadgyth's healing brew, Janna dipped her finger into honey and then, greatly daring, spread the sticky sweetness over Lady Alice's nipple. Another dip into the honey, and this time she picked up the baby and put her finger in his mouth. He turned his head away. She could hear his breath rattle faintly in his chest. The sound alarmed her, for it was the sound made by the dying. But she could not give up, not yet, and so she persisted, dipping her finger into the honey once more. Eventually, the baby responded to the sweetness and began to suck, although with little enthusiasm. At once, Janna removed her finger and lowered him into the lady's waiting arms. Gently, she guided his mouth to the honeyed nipple, willing him to start taking nourishment.

She held her breath. At last his lips moved and he began a feeble sucking. Janna felt her tense muscles unclench. The knot in her stomach began to dissolve.

'I thank you.' Dame Alice didn't look at Janna. Her attention stayed focused on the small bundle in her arms. She bent to kiss the dark fuzz on top of the baby's head. Unsure if she should stay or go, Janna hovered beside the bed. She wondered if she could ask for permission to leave the bedchamber. The baby's rattling breath alarmed her. There were herbs that might alleviate the problem, if she could find any of them growing in the manor's own kitchen garden. Cecily was not here to give her advice; another tiring woman was in attendance. Perhaps Cecily was looking after Dame Alice's little boy. Janna wondered if he'd met his new baby brother yet.

A rattling cough brought Janna's focus back to the bedchamber.

'May I take a walk in your herb garden, my lady?' she asked. 'I hope to find something there to ease your baby's breathing.'

'Yes, go at once, but don't leave the manor.' Dame Alice glanced briefly at Janna. 'I need you here.'

'Yes, my lady. Of course I'll stay as long as you want me.' Janna hurried out into the hall, keeping a lookout for someone to give her directions to the kitchen garden. She hated the thought of asking at the kitchen and having to face the cook once more, but she needed to find the herbs she was seeking.

She set off towards the outside flight of stairs that would take her down to ground level, but before she'd taken more than a few steps across the hall, she heard her name called. Aldith had been lying in wait for her to appear. Now she stood fast, blocking Janna's path. 'So,' she greeted her, 'you have managed to push your way in here just as your mother did.'

A flash of anger heated Janna's blood. 'It was none of my doing. You heard my lord Hugh. Dame Alice sent for me.'

'A green, untried girl. What do you know of women's troubles?'

'I know what my mother taught me. Which is a great deal more than the apothecary knows, and probably more than you know yourself, mistress.' Janna knew she was being rude. Too provoked by Aldith's accusations to guard her tongue, she continued. 'You were very quick to take my mother's place here at the manor. 'Tis certain that my mother's death will be good for *your* business.' She was about to hurry on through the hall, but Aldith's next words stopped her dead.

'Midwifery has always been my business. There is no blame in wanting to help a mother and her new child if they are in need. That's why I offered my services to your mother when I heard where she was bound. She refused my offer, of course. Wanted all the glory for herself, I dare say.'

'You met my mother on her way to the manor?' In spite of her hurry, Janna couldn't lose the opportunity to question Aldith further.

'Indeed I did. She was looking inordinately pleased with herself. I asked where she was bound and she told me.' Aldith put her nose in the air and gave a contemptuous sniff, trying to hide her jealousy.

'And you offered to help? Did you give her advice on what to do to help the lady and her babe?' Janna tried to placate the angry midwife with flattery.

'I offered advice, yes. After all, I have been here before to attend Dame Alice and I have witnessed her troubles.' Aldith hesitated a moment, struggling between boasting or telling the truth. 'Your mother didn't listen, of course. She told me she already knew all there was to know.'

Janna didn't like to point out that Fulk the apothecary had only been called because, under Aldith's care, the babies had all died. 'Did my mother perhaps take any of your syrups or potions even if she wouldn't take your advice?' Janna held her breath. The answer to her mother's death lay in Aldith's reply.

Aldith's face darkened with remembered annoyance. 'She would take no advice, and she spurned the tonic I offered. But she wasn't too proud to ask for some of my special cordial to drink.'

'You gave her some cordial?' Janna made a huge effort to keep her voice under control as she asked, 'Did my mother drink it?' Her hands felt clammy; she sweated with the need to know the truth.

'Of course she drank it! My mint cordial is renowned for its cooling and reviving properties.'

'Of course it is!' Janna agreed hurriedly. 'What herbs do you use, mistress, to make it so special?'

'It's a secret recipe.' Aldith looked coy.

'Mint. And perhaps a few drops of poppy juice?' Janna probed.

'It's a secret! I will not tell you.'

'A little hemlock to dull the senses? A mite of monkshood, perhaps?'

'Are you accusing Mistress Aldith of poisoning your mother?' The deep voice of Robert of Babestoche startled both Janna and Aldith. They had not seen him enter the hall. Janna wondered how long he'd been standing there, listening to their conversation.

Now he strode forward, and pinned Janna with a fierce gaze. Beside her, Aldith had sunk into a deep curtsy. Janna hastily copied the midwife's action.

'I . . . I know my mother was poisoned. I am trying to find out how it happened, sire,' Janna stammered, as she rose to her feet once more. She was dismayed at having to explain herself when she'd hoped to keep her suspicions secret.

'If your mother was poisoned, it was certainly none of my doing.' Aldith drew herself up, looking deeply offended. Janna silently cursed Robert's untimely appearance. She could understand Aldith defending herself, but knew she would come no closer to the truth while Robert was present. Still, she had to defend her mother's reputation in front of him.

'My mother knew and understood herbs and their properties – especially the poisonous ones. She was very particular with her potions; very careful when she collected the ingredients and especially when she mixed them. She would never knowingly have ingested monkshood, and yet she died of its poison.'

'Just so am I particular with my mint cordial.' Aldith glared at Janna. 'You cannot pin your mother's death on me. I vow I will make you sorry if you try!'

Janna looked from Aldith to Robert, seeing anger and condemnation in both their faces.

'You do wrong to spread false accusations,' Robert said coldly. 'I can only thank God that my dear wife has suffered no harm at the careless hands of your mother. Let this be a lesson to you not to meddle with nature or the Lord's will. It was at Dame Alice's request that you were brought here, Johanna, but I will not have you spreading slander and lies about the manor. You may consider yourself dismissed!' Turning on his heel, he strode through the hall in the direction of the bedchamber, leaving the two women to confront each other.

'I offered your mother my advice and my cooling cordial in friendship and as an act of Christian charity, hoping to ease her thirst and her fatigue,' Aldith hissed as soon as they were left alone. 'I will not forget or forgive your accusations. They are made worse by the fact that you tried to blacken my name in front of the lord of the manor.'

'I did not know he was there, listening to our conversation.' Janna wondered how far she could trust Aldith's protestations of innocence. The cook, and everyone else, claimed that her mother had taken no food or drink on her return to the manor house. Aldith's cordial was the only clue to her mother's death that Janna could find, yet the midwife's anger and dismay seemed genuine.

'You are a silly, impudent girl. I understand that your mother's death has upset you, but you do your case no good by making these rash accusations.' Aldith leaned closer, so close that their noses almost touched. 'You would do well to follow my lord's advice. Go home. Do not meddle in what you don't understand.' Cradling the jar with its liquid contents closer to her breast, she stepped away from Janna and followed Robert's footsteps to the bedchamber, casting a triumphant look behind her as she went.

'How much of your cordial did my mother drink?' Janna called after her.

'We shared the whole jug!' Aldith disappeared from Janna's view.

The whole jug? It was true Aldith was proud of her mint cordial, and rightly so. Janna had once tasted some herself, when the midwife had paid her mother in kind for a soothing cream. It was to Aldith's credit that she'd made no secret of the fact that she'd met Eadgyth on her way to the manor house, or that she'd given her the cordial to drink. Even if Aldith was lying about sharing the cordial with her mother, Eadgyth knew its taste. If she'd had any suspicions about it, she would have spat it out and poured the rest of it away. And she would have broadcast her suspicions up at the manor house as soon as she started to feel ill.

Janna felt uncomfortable as her thoughts followed a logical progression. It was kind of the midwife to share her cordial, especially if she was carrying it to sell. And if she was carrying it to sell, she would never have added poison to it. She couldn't know that she would meet her rival, that they would share a drink. It was far too great a risk to carry poisoned cordial when anyone might have stopped her along the road to buy some.

Janna came to the conclusion that she had unjustly accused the midwife – and in Robert's hearing too! She felt a pang of remorse, as well as annoyance that she'd let her suspicions run away with her. Aldith had shown kindness, both to her mother and to her. Now, because of her stupidity, she had one friend less, when friends were what she most needed right now. First Godric, and now Aldith. Soon she would have no friends left at all.

Janna cheered slightly as she remembered the gallant Hugh. And Dame Alice. She had asked Janna to save her baby – but Robert had told her to be gone. It took only an instant for Janna to make a decision. Impatient that she'd already wasted time, she ran down the stairs and set off towards the kitchen to find the garden.

thirteen

JANNA FELT HER spirits revive somewhat as the sunlight warmed her. The sight of a well set her licking her dry lips. Talk of Aldith's cordial had made her thirsty. She pushed the thought aside. A drink would have to wait until her mission was complete. She hurried on past several low buildings and an open shed which housed a cart and a plough. Janna stared about her, fascinated by a way of life so different from her own.

She guessed that the herbs and vegetables might be growing close by the kitchen for easy picking, so hastened towards the line of green trees beyond the stone building. There she found the garden situated in a sunny and protected spot between the kitchen and the timber palisade surrounding the manor house and grounds. Apple, pear and plum trees formed the sides of a screen to provide shelter from the worst of the elements. Within their green bounds Janna found much that was familiar, set out in neat rows for easy identification and picking. She took a quick glance around, envying the variety of vegetables and the space available for their growing. It must be wonderful to have such an abundance of food, she thought, as she eyed the long rows of cabbages, lettuces, leeks, turnips, broad beans, peas and onions. She turned her attention then to the herbs, noting with some pride that there was less variety and they did not look so healthy as the specimens in their own garden. Her garden now, she corrected herself. There was great sadness in the thought, but she took some comfort as she spied the thin, fleshy spikes of bushy ground pine. The fragrant steam from boiling its shoots would aid the baby's breathing. She began to break it off in sections. Would the child survive? Could he survive?

With a heavy heart, Janna recalled her mother's words some years before when, after several miscarriages, one of the village women had finally succeeded in giving birth to a living child only to have the baby die within a few short hours.

'I know not how to explain it,' her mother had said at the time. 'It seems there is some dis-ease which cannot be corrected. The fact that the mother has had such difficulty carrying other babies to term tells me that there is some deep, underlying problem that we do not understand and therefore cannot treat. Mother Nature's way is usually to expel the child before it has a chance to form properly, but in this case it seems that the baby's will to fight kept it alive.' Eadgyth's voice had been troubled as she'd concluded, "Tis better, I am sure, to lose a baby early, before it resembles a living child, than to give birth and watch your son or daughter die in your arms.'

Did this child have the will to keep him alive through these early and dangerous days? A brief vision of her dead cat flashed in front of Janna. The kitten had almost drowned, but his will had kept him alive until his throat had been cut. At least this baby had nothing to fear from a vengeful and rejected suitor.

Janna wondered whether that was really how Godric thought of himself. Here, in the peace of the garden, it seemed absurd to think he would go to such lengths just because she'd told him she wasn't ready to marry.

Janna straightened and looked about for a lavender bush. She knew it grew somewhere in the garden, for her mother had already plundered it. As she plucked the fragrant leaves, her troubled thoughts moved on. Godric's action went against everything she'd observed of him and that had been reported to her by her mother. Kind, decent, courageous. Those were the words she would have used to describe him. True, he had seemed to dislike Alfred. Possibly he even feared him if he believed, like the villagers, that Alfred was the devil. But would he go so far as to kill him, and in such a brutal manner? Janna shook her head. Godric had seemed genuinely shocked and surprised by her accusation. Yet if he was innocent of the charge, who then had killed her cat?

Mindful of the need for haste, Janna scanned the garden for any other herbs that might prove useful. She spied the hoof-shaped leaves of coltsfoot and hurried to pick them, while her mind continued to puzzle over Alfred's death.

Godric had heard a noise that night. Janna remembered now that he'd gone outside and looked around. Could someone else have come out to her cottage and seen Godric embrace and comfort her? Could that someone have waited until he was gone, and then killed her cat? Who would want to do such a thing?

Someone who hated her, who thought of her as a rival, and who perhaps had mistaken Godric for someone else. Someone who carried a knife. Hilde's distorted face, her angry accusations came into Janna's mind. In that moment she realised, with a chilling certainty, that she'd accused an innocent man of a terrible crime.

For a moment she stood still, stricken to the heart. Godric! She had been so wrong about him, so wrong. How could she ever look him in the eye again? How could he ever forgive her?

There was no time to think of it now. Saving the baby was far more important, but Janna resolved that, somehow, she would find a way to apologise to Godric, and try to make amends. She took one last glance about the garden to see if there was horehound, or anything else that might help, and frowned as she noticed some bright blue caps of monkshood. They were growing close to a clump of parsley, a dangerous proximity when their leaves were so similar. Was it there by accident or design? Had someone at the manor discovered that monkshood eased aching joints and the pain of rheumatics when rubbed in with oil, or were the plants prized for a more deadly purpose altogether? Could it even have been a portion of one of these plants that Eadgyth had ingested? She gave them a hurried inspection. Rough scars told her that leaves and stems had been harvested, and quite recently. A cold shiver ran up Janna's spine. She would keep on asking questions, but for now her first and most urgent task was to relieve the child's breathing. In spite of Robert's banishment, she must return to the bedchamber. Janna looked down at the fresh herbs she carried. She had a good reason to be there, as well as Dame Alice's support. Surely no-one could refuse her entry if there was some small chance that she might be able to save the baby's life.

The first person Janna saw as she entered the hall once more was Cecily. The lady was pleading with Robert, who seemed unmoved by her distress. A scowl marred his handsome face as he said something in return. Janna supposed Cecily was in trouble for leaving the house and abandoning her mistress not once but twice, and without even asking permission to go. He broke off abruptly when he noticed Janna, and gestured for Cecily to leave him. Wiping away tears, she hurried into the bedchamber. Janna was left alone to confront the lord of the manor.

Robert scowled at her. 'I told you to go,' he said coldly.

Janna looked up at him, trying to conceal her dislike. Handsome he might be, but it seemed that the power of his position as lord of the manor had turned him into a bully. 'I have picked some sprigs of ground pine, sire.' She bobbed a respectful curtsy, then indicated the handfuls of herbs she carried. 'If you will order these leaves to be boiled, the fragrance of the steam will help your new son breathe more freely.'

'We want no more of your poisons around here.'

'This is not a poison, sire.' Janna choked back her anger with difficulty. 'It's common ground pine, picked from the manor's own herb garden. And these are the leaves of colts-foot. They should be thrown on hot coals; the fumes will clear the congestion in the baby's chest and also aid his breathing. These herbs are not for the baby to swallow. They are utterly harmless.' She recalled the monkshood growing so close to the parsley, and a number of other plants which, if used injudiciously, could cause pain or even death. But Robert was unlikely to have any knowledge of the contents of the kitchen garden, harmful or otherwise, and it was not her place to enlighten him.

'Do not argue with me. I want you to go. Now!' Robert stepped closer to Janna, menacing and forceful. 'No matter what my wife might say, I do not trust you with the care of my newborn son.' He raised a hand to push her towards the flight of steps outside. From the expression on his face, Janna wondered if he would push her right down if she didn't obey him.

A loud cry stayed his hand. At once Robert wheeled and rushed towards the bedchamber. After a moment's hesitation, Janna followed him, still clutching the aromatic herbs.

'My baby!' Dame Alice wept as she held out the limp figure for Janna's inspection. 'Help him! Save him, please!'

But Janna had taken one appalled look at the child, and knew that help was no longer possible. The baby was dead.

'Fetch the priest.' Robert had also taken in the situation at a glance. Now he clicked a finger at Cecily, and jerked his head towards the door. She rushed out, leaving a deathly quiet in the bedchamber.

Janna stepped forward to take the baby but, with a single convulsive movement, Dame Alice snatched him back. Cradling him to her chest, she faced Janna. 'I asked you for help, and you failed me.'

Janna knew that the accusation was spoken in pain, from the desolation of losing a child. Nevertheless, the words cut deep. 'I . . . I am sorry, so sorry, my lady,' she stammered. 'Truly, there was little I could do for him.'

'You've done enough!' Robert's voice was hard-edged with sorrow and anger. 'I've already told you once to get out. I'll have you thrown out if you don't leave now, immediately.'

'No. Wait.' Dame Alice sounded tired to her soul as she said, 'The girl is not to blame. It is God's punishment for my sins that my babies are taken from me.'

Janna kept silent, grateful for the reprieve. Yet she couldn't help wondering why Dame Alice thought God would want to punish her so. Her mother had told Janna that the love of God was everywhere, yet the priest would have everyone believe he was cruel and unforgiving; that the smallest misdemeanour would call down his wrath and that he had no room in his heart for love.

'The girl speaks true,' Aldith affirmed unexpectedly. Janna hadn't noticed her standing at the back of the bedchamber. 'I have seen other babies born and die in like manner, as well as your own, ma dame. In spite of all my physic, there was nothing I or anyone else could do to save them.' She stepped forward and held out her arms. 'Let me take the child,' she said, brisk and matter-of-fact after years of experience. 'Let me prepare your son for burial.'

'No!' Dame Alice's heartbroken cry filled the room.

''Tis better so. There's naught you can do for him now.' Aldith bent and quickly scooped up the baby.

Janna sucked in a breath. If she was going to do it at all, it was better to get it over straight away. 'Mistress Aldith, a while ago I accused you unjustly, and in front of my lord Robert. It was very wrong of me, and I do most humbly beg your pardon.'

Aldith gave a grudging nod. As she bore her small burden away, Robert sent Janna a hostile glance from beneath his bushy eyebrows. 'You accused an innocent woman when it was your mother's own foul concoctions that caused her death, as well as the death of my child,' he said angrily. 'I told you to be gone, and you will do as you are told!'

'But I . . .' Janna searched for the words to defend herself and her mother. She cast a glance of appeal at Dame Alice, willing the lady to speak up for her. But Dame Alice lay still. Tears trickled from her closed eyelids. In her grief, she had no thought for anything other than the loss of her child.

Recognising that this was neither the time nor place, and that anyway she'd probably be wasting her breath if she tried to refute Robert's accusations, Janna bobbed a curtsy and left the bedchamber. Let Robert think she was obeying his command. In fact, Janna had every intention of doing so – but not yet. For the moment, she intended to stay on at the manor and question all those on her list who might have knowledge of the truth behind her mother's death. Aldith was no longer one of the suspects, but that still left Fulk, the priest and Cecily.

Janna started off down the hall in search of them, but had taken only a few paces when she saw the priest swooping towards her. He made the sign of the cross when he saw her, but he said nothing, nor did he check his passage as he rushed on and into the bedchamber. Cecily followed him. Hugh, who had also come in answer to the summons, stopped in front of Janna.

'I understand there is no need for haste, for the baby has died,' he observed.

Janna nodded, hardly able to speak. To her surprise, Hugh took hold of her hand and led her towards a long bench running along the length of one wall. 'Sit down,' he said softly. 'Rest a while. You have endured a great deal these past few days.'

Janna felt tears prick her eyes at the kindness in his tone. She sank onto the bench, conscious all at once of her aching limbs and the pain across her forehead that spoke of too much emotion and anxiety. She had wanted so much to save the baby, had tried her best, but her best just wasn't good enough. She closed her eyes, trying to prevent her tears from spilling. She did not want to cry in front of Hugh.

She heard the bench creak as he sat down beside her; she felt his light touch on her face as he pushed back the hair from her forehead. 'The baby was ailing. You mustn't blame yourself for his death.' He seemed to be reading her mind. He began to run his fingers through her hair, soothing and gentling her. Grateful, she leaned against him and started to relax. If only I could stay like this for ever, she thought, lost in the darkness behind her closed eyelids and held in thrall by the light touch of his fingers. If only I belonged here, if only I was the lady of the manor and Hugh was my dearly loved lord. Lulled by his gentle touch, Janna lapsed into a dream of a life with Hugh. They might take ship and sail away together, sail to the far off lands where the merchant

169

bought all his exotic spices. What sights they would see! What adventures they would have!

And at night, in the marriage bed . . . A great wave of longing and desire washed over Janna; she felt as if she was drowning. It took all her will and all her courage to open her eyes and pull away. Hugh looked down at her, surprised by the abrupt movement.

'Feeling better?' he asked.

'Yes, thank you, sire.' Deeply ashamed of her absurd fantasy, Janna managed to dredge up a shaky smile.

'You look a little happier,' he said, observing her flushed cheeks and the brightness of her eyes.

'You're an excellent physician, Dr Hugh!' Not for anything would Janna confess to him the real reason behind her apparent recovery. Suddenly recalling the differences in their position, she added a hasty, 'I beg your pardon, sire.'

He smiled back at her, seeming to forgive her cheeky remark as he paid her a compliment of his own. 'I am sure your knowledge of the healing powers of herbs far outweighs any small skill I may have.' He surveyed her thoughtfully for a moment. 'And yet you know little of the world outside, I think.'

'You speak true. My mother and I live . . . lived a quiet life together.' Honesty prompted Janna to add, 'But I've had a suitor.'

'And?' His eyebrows lifted in an amused quirk.

'I turned him down.' It wasn't quite true, but it would serve to let Hugh know that she wasn't quite the innocent he took her for.

'I shall take that as a warning, shall I?' Janna couldn't tell if he was mocking her or not. She kept silent, wishing she'd had more practice at this sort of thing.

'A child of the forest, naive and ignorant of the ways of the world, yet able to speak the language of the nobility. In truth you intrigue me, Johanna.'

'I can also write! I can sign my own name,' she flared, resenting his assessment and anxious to impress him.

'Can you indeed?' Janna had the feeling he was laughing at her.

'I may have lived a quiet life, but it doesn't mean I'm incapable of learning about the world should the opportunity come my way,' she said angrily, searching about for something to prove her words. 'After all, I know that our country is at war, and that you support the claim of the Empress Matilda to the throne.'

'What?' Hugh looked momentarily stunned. 'Such talk could get us both into trouble,' he warned. 'I suggest you keep your nose out of my affairs. They are none of your concern.'

'I assure you, my concern is only for your safety,' Janna said hurriedly, embarrassed by his reproof. He'd warned her against upsetting the priest, and now she'd gone and upset him too. To convince him of her good intentions, she decided to pass on the conversation she'd overheard at the alehouse. ''Tis known that you have been seen with my lord Robert of Gloucester, and that he supports the empress against the king. I know not where my lord Robert's allegiance lies, but the Abbess of Wiltune is the greatest landowner in these parts. Her allegiance must surely lie with King Stephen now that he has stripped all land and property from the Bishop of Sarisberie. The king's action is surely too close for our abbess to ignore. I do fear that you might find yourself entrapped, sire.'

Hugh surveyed Janna, looking thoughtful. 'I suspect I may have misjudged you,' he said. 'Thank you for your warning. I will certainly keep it in mind, but I assure you that I come here only to visit my aunt and report on my custodianship of her property.'

'I know also that you visit her quite frequently, and therefore did not need to ask me the way.'

To Janna's intense delight, Hugh looked somewhat discomforted at being caught out. Then he grinned. 'That pretty nose of yours seems to have a way of sniffing out the truth,' he admitted. 'Yes, I see my aunt quite regularly, but I was particularly worried about her on this occasion. I know how hard she takes these failed pregnancies. As for Robert . . .' He checked abruptly. 'And now, Johanna, I must go and comfort Dame Alice, though I wish with all my heart that it had turned out differently, and that comfort wasn't necessary.' He smiled at her, bringing warmth and light to Janna's troubled spirit. 'Wait here in case Dame Alice has further need of you,' he instructed, and walked on through the hall and into the solar.

Janna looked after him, intrigued by the sentence he'd left unfinished. What had he been going to say about Robert?

True, Robert seemed a man given to sudden tempers. In fact, Janna found him rather frightening. So did Cecily, she thought, remembering the scene she'd witnessed. But even if he bullied his servants, he was hardly likely to intimidate a man like Hugh. And he certainly didn't intimidate his wife!

Janna shook her head over the wine that the dame had spilled. What a waste!

She shrugged. The lord of the manor was none of her concern. But Hugh . . . he'd been so kind, so understanding. A dreamy smile stole over her lips as she imagined how her life would be if she and Hugh were married. They would drink wine at every dinner. They would eat roast swan, as well as the king's venison. She would have a different gown for every day of the year, and wear bright jewels of every hue to match. She would ask him to teach her all he knew, so that she could be his equal in every way . . .

A sound disturbed Janna's musing. She blinked, and saw that the priest had come out into the hall.

'You are still here?' He came right up to her. Janna resisted the urge to shrink back against the stone wall.

'Yes. As you see.'

'Where is the baby? I have come to pray for his soul.'

'I do not know. The midwife has taken him.'

'I knew that the baby would not thrive under your care.' The priest sounded as if he'd won a victory. Janna wanted to rip his gloating tongue out of his mouth.

'The baby was ailing ere he was born.' She curled her fists up small to remind herself not to attack the priest. 'It was a miracle he survived even as long as he did.'

'God's miracle – whom you destroyed.'

'I did all in my power to keep him alive – and so did my mother!' Janna retorted.

The priest sighed. 'This won't do, Janna,' he said unexpectedly. 'You are young, and impressionable, and your soul may yet be saved. I must not blame you for your mother's wrongdoing, nor her wrong beliefs, for you have been a dutiful daughter. You have honoured your mother as you were taught, not knowing that your honour was misplaced and your mother not worthy of your love and trust.'

'You are wrong, so wrong!' Janna had taken Hugh's reprimand to heart, but still it took all of her self-control to hold on to her temper. She must try to convince the priest with the sincerity of her words; she would achieve nothing by shouting at him, or attacking him. She took a deep breath. 'My mother was an honourable woman, dedicated to using her skills to cure people of the ills that afflicted them. Surely her skill with healing came as a gift from God?'

The priest opened his mouth to answer, then closed it again. He seemed to be having difficulty finding a response. At last he said, 'I will not hold your mother's deeds against you, nor will I blame you for her bad influence on you. Instead, I will ask you, Janna, to start coming to church once more. Let God see you there, let Him save your soul.'

Janna scowled at him, at a loss for an answer. The priest was wrong about her mother, but her mother had made no secret of her opinion of him and his notion of Christianity. Aldith had called Eadgyth arrogant and proud. It might be that her mother would have done better with the priest if she'd held her tongue. If they had gone regularly to church, the priest might have been more welcoming, might even have celebrated her mother's healing powers instead of damning them.

'I'll think about it,' she muttered. The priest smiled, seeming content that he had saved a soul this day.

'Go to the kitchen,' he said. 'Tell the cook I sent you. Ask her to make up a hot posset for Dame Alice, and bring it up to my lady's bedchamber. And don't interfere, Janna. The cook already knows what to put in it, for I heard Fulk the apothecary instruct her on the matter.'

'What did he ask the cook to do?' Janna asked quickly, wondering if here, at last, was proof of Fulk's guilt.

The priest shrugged. 'I know not, save that the drink was to calm my lady and strengthen her nerves. I, myself, was finishing my dinner and paid no attention to the apothecary's instructions.'

'Master Fulk ordered the posset for my lady at dinner time?'

'Indeed. Your mother was wrath when she arrived back at the manor and saw it. I was in the bedchamber when she tasted the contents, and then ordered it thrown away. Of course, she wanted Dame Alice to sup her own concoction, the mixture that led to her own death.'

'That's not so!' Appalled, Janna stared at the priest. 'Don't you see? It must have been Master Fulk's posset that killed my mother! She tasted it, and then threw it away before it could harm the lady. That is how and why my mother died. The apothecary planned it so, for he hated my mother and resented her influence over Dame Alice. His posset made certain that he got my mother out of his way.'

It was a dreadful thought, made even worse by the realisation that she had taken her mother's place at the lady's bedside. If Fulk had acted to rid himself of her mother, so might he act against this new threat to his professional competence.

'Your grief has warped your judgment,' the priest said sternly. 'Accusing the innocent can never atone for the harm your mother brought upon herself.'

'She did nothing to harm herself – nothing!' She had to convince the priest that she spoke the truth. He was a man of God. He would surely help her in her quest for justice.

Near tears, Janna struggled to find the words to make him understand. But the priest forestalled her. 'I have stretched out my hand in friendship, yet you continue to defy all who would help you find the true path to God's grace. I can do no more for you, Johanna. It is up to you to save your soul, if that's possible.' He brushed past her and returned to the bedchamber.

FOURTEEN

ETERMINED TO PROVE the priest wrong, determined to prove that all those who judged her mother were wrong, Janna wasted no time racing down the stairs to seek out the cook. The woman was busy plucking a goose. Feathers flew in all directions. They were being collected by a thin kitchen maid who wore a sour expression. No doubt the feathers were prized as a stuffing for quilts and pillows for the household, especially the smaller fluffy feathers, but it seemed the maid was taking no pride or pleasure in her work this day.

Janna paused a moment to assemble her thoughts. She must proceed carefully. If she wanted answers to her questions, she would first need to win the cook's friendship and trust. It seemed an impossible task given the start they'd already made. Nevertheless, she had to try.

'What do you want?' The cook turned from the goose she was plucking, and stared suspiciously at Janna. Neither of them could forget the last time they'd met.

Instead of voicing questions and accusations, Janna was learning to proceed more cautiously. 'I beg your pardon for troubling you, mistress, but the priest bade me ask you to make up a posset for Dame Alice, the same posset that Master Fulk ordered for her once before.'

'Why would the priest ask such a thing?'

'He has just come from my lady's chamber to request it,' Janna said carefully. 'Dame Alice is in great need of comfort. She is made distraught by the death of her baby son.' A hiss of indrawn breath told Janna that this was news to the kitchen staff. They stopped working, put down what they were doing and, silent and intent, watched her.

'So the baby has died, no thanks to you and your mother.'

Janna sighed, feeling almost too discouraged to defend herself. 'We did our best, but there was naught we – or anyone else – could have done for him,' she muttered. She was aware of the cook's hostility, but still she had to try. 'Please, mistress,' she pleaded, 'will you do as the priest asks and make one of your special possets for my lady. I feel sure it will do much to calm her.' Perhaps flattery would persuade the cook to do as she was asked.

'Hmmph.' The cook rested her bloody and feather-smeared hands on her hips, and stared at Janna. It was clear from her expression that she wanted Janna gone, but she did not quite have the courage to disobey instructions. So she dipped a scoop into a pot of water hung by a chain over the fire and poured the boiling contents into a mug.

'Pray tell me, what do you use?' Janna pointed to the reddish brown flakes the woman began spooning into the mixture, knowing full well her reply.

'Rose petals.' The cook nipped up a small pinch from another jar. 'Mint,' she said, and cautiously plucked a couple of leaves from a stem standing in a pot of water.

Janna recognised the stinging but useful plant. 'Nettles?' she said.

The cook nodded. 'And honey.' She poured a thin stream of sticky gold into the steaming mug.

She could make a far more efficacious posset herself, Janna thought, but she did not say the words out loud. There was still much to find out and she did not want to antagonise the cook by making suggestions. 'And what do you keep here?' she asked, pointing at a row of jars of similar shape and size to the pot which held the rose petals.

'Sweet marjoram, thyme, poppy seeds, basil, rosemary . . . I grow many herbs for my use.' There was pride in the cook's answer.

'I know that, for I have been out in your garden myself.' Janna recalled the monkshood growing so innocently beside the parsley, and another question sprang to her lips. 'Do you add parsley to your mix?' she asked innocently.

'No. It has no place in this.' The cook gave the steaming mug a vigorous stir.

Janna hesitated. Keeping her tone carefully respectful, she asked, 'I noticed plants of monkshood growing in your garden. Do you include it in your potions, mistress?'

'No! 'Tis a deadly poison!'

'Yet it has its uses for all that.'

The cook stopped stirring and gave Janna a sharp look. 'It is your mother who brews poisons, not me,' she hissed, 'and I will not be accused and insulted by the likes of you.'

Fearing another attack with the broom, Janna stepped hastily out of the cook's reach. 'I meant no harm by my question,' she said quickly. 'I meant only that monkshood has good use as a rubbing oil for aches and pains.'

'I know well the uses for monkshood for Master Fulk himself has instructed me. Now get out of my kitchen! I will take the infusion to my lady myself.' The cook walked out of the door, the mug clutched carefully in her two hands. As soon as she was safely out of sight, Janna began a careful inspection of the herbs and potions ranged along the kitchen shelves.

'And what do you think you're doing?' The sour scullery maid looked up from chasing errant feathers.

Janna ignored the question, continuing to open stoppers and sniff the contents of the jars, occasionally taking an experimental taste. To her relief, neither the maids nor any of the scullions seemed to have the courage to either restrain her or drag her out of the kitchen. Instead, they stood about, still staring at her.

'What are you seeking, mistress?' Janna glanced up and saw it was the maid who had once spoken up in support of her mother. She was young, and seemed sympathetic.

'Many of these spices are new to me. I am interested in their properties.' Janna wished the cook was more co-operative. It would make her task so much easier. This mixture smelled sweet, another a little spicy; there was no rancid stink or taste of monkshood. She would have to ask the question outright.

'I need monkshood to ease my lady's aching joints,' she improvised swiftly. 'Have you any rubbing oil made up, or should I pick it fresh and make the concoction myself?'

'There be some growing out in the garden. You said you'd seen it,' the sour-faced maid pointed out.

'Master Fulk made up a mixture. You could ask him if there's any left.' The young maid giggled suddenly. 'My lord went out riding last week and fell off his horse. He blamed the horse for taking fright and bolting under him but the groom says the fault lies with my lord Robert, who has a heavy hand with the whip and who is not the fine horseman he believes himself to be. Certain it was that my lord complained of a sore back, and was in a foul temper from the pain.' The maid pulled a face. 'We all kept out of his way. We always do, if we can.'

'So Master Fulk has a mixture?' While entertained by the maid's observations regarding her master, Janna was far more interested in the apothecary.

'I saw him make it up myself,' the maid said proudly. 'He ground the root and mixed it with oil and mustard seeds. He warned my lord not to ingest any part of it. He was most careful about warning all of us, miss. And my lord was grateful, for he says that it eased the pain. I know all this for he made Master Fulk show him where the plant grows, and he bade me come too, so that I can make up the rubbing oil should any in the household have aches and pains in want of treatment in the future.' The maid brightened, visibly swelling with self-importance. 'I can make up the mixture now, if you wish?'

'No, do not trouble yourself,' Janna said quickly. 'If Master Fulk has none left, I shall make it myself.' It was hard to hide her elation. Here, at last, was proof of Fulk's guilt. A sudden thought dampened her excitement. Was the apothecary still at the manor, or had he already left for Wiltune? She must act quickly if she wished to trap him with this information.

'I thank you for your assistance,' she said, and hurried out.

'The kitchen garden is the other way,' the maid called after her.

'Later.' Janna flapped a hand in acknowledgment, and kept on going. Where was Fulk? She had to find him straight away so that she could lay out her accusations for all to hear.

Janna had supposed that cows, horses, sheep and goats were lodged at the bottom of the manor house, underneath the family's living quarters. Now that she'd seen the numerous sheds scattered about the manor grounds she thought the animals were probably housed elsewhere, which meant that the undercroft must be used for some other purpose. Perhaps it housed the servants? She decided to start her search there, since Fulk had been staying at the manor house. She opened the door and peered about. The several partitions with straw pallets and wall pegs told her she'd guessed correctly. A number of huge chests indicated the room was also used for storage. The room was cold and ill-lit, having only high and narrow slits for windows. Empty casks and barrels stood about, waiting for the rich rewards of the harvest. There was no sign of Fulk, nor of anyone who might know his whereabouts. She went back outside, ran up the stairs and into the hall.

'Have you seen Master Fulk? I must speak with him.' Janna addressed her question to Aldith, who was the only person present.

'He is with my lady. Robert insisted that he come and take care of her, for she is in sore distress. Wait!' Aldith caught hold of Janna's arm and held her fast. 'You cannot go in there, Janna. Not now. At Dame Alice's request, I have put the baby into his cradle so that she and her husband and their little boy may say their farewells. The priest is with them, and so are other members of the household. You cannot interrupt them. In fact, you would be well advised to do as my lord Robert instructed, and leave the manor.'

'No, I can't. Not yet.'

Recognising she would have to be patient, Janna stopped resisting Aldith's grasp. 'I am truly sorry for what I said to you. Will you forgive me?'

Aldith cast her eyes upwards, and clicked her tongue. 'I understand that you are distraught after your mother's death, but you must be more careful, Janna.'

Aldith sounded just like Eadgyth! Janna gave her a forlorn smile. 'You've been very kind to me,' she observed. 'Why?'

'We will need to get along together if we are to exchange information and work side by side.'

Janna nodded thoughtfully. What Aldith said was true enough, although it might never come to pass. 'You warned me about Master Fulk.' She was bursting to share her discovery. 'I have now found proof that he poisoned my mother!'

'Take care what you say!' Shocked, Aldith shook a warning finger in front of Janna's face. 'You cannot go around accusing him – you cannot accuse anyone, unless you have very strong proof indeed of guilt.'

'Listen to what I have learned.' Janna moved a stool close to Aldith and sat down. She lowered her voice, so that anyone coming into the room would not be able to hear their conversation. 'I have seen monkshood growing freely in the manor's kitchen garden. Fulk used the roots in a rubbing oil to treat my lord Robert's aches and pains! He knows that it is poisonous, for he warned my lord about its properties. And he has it growing right here, close to his hand. But that's not all. He ordered a hot posset to be made for Dame Alice.' Janna paused so that the full import of her words might sink in. 'I have found out, and from the priest himself, that my mother tasted the posset just before she died!'

She beamed in triumph, sure that Aldith would follow her line of reasoning.

'So?' Aldith shifted her stool slightly away as if to distance herself from Janna's suspicions.

'So it's obvious, isn't it! Fulk offered a partnership in his shop at Wiltune to my mother and she went along with it until she'd been received by Dame Alice. After that, she sent him off, leaving no-one in any doubt as to her low opinion of him. She ingratiated herself with the lady, and sullied the apothecary's professional reputation at the same time. No wonder he hated her and feared her influence. No wonder he wished her gone! And he had the ways and means to make his wish come true. A few drops of the rubbing oil in the posset and . . .' Janna clicked her fingers, indicating the rest.

Aldith's round O of a mouth told Janna that Fulk's proposition was news to the midwife. She sniffed then and her face settled into angry lines. 'I know how rude and outspoken your mother could be. Small wonder if Master Fulk wished her harm.'

'She didn't deserve to die for telling the truth!' Janna contradicted sharply. What could she say to convince Aldith that the apothecary should be brought to justice for her mother's death? If she could bring the midwife around to her way of thinking, Aldith might join her in persuading Robert of Babestoche to either try the apothecary in his manorial court, or refer the case to the shire reeve. There might be a chance of justice for her mother after all.

'There is a flaw in your reasoning,' the midwife pointed out. 'Fulk couldn't know that your mother would taste a posset meant for Dame Alice. He would never take such a risk with ma dame's life.'

'Oh.' Janna's high hopes instantly deflated as she recognised the truth of Aldith's words. Then she perked up. 'Perhaps Fulk carried the poison about with him, waiting for just this sort of opportunity.' Sure now that she had the truth, she beamed in triumph at Aldith. 'He could even have flattered my mother. He could have asked her to taste the mixture and give him her opinion on it.'

'If that is so, then others will have heard him ask it. Someone may even have seen him adding the oil to the mixture.' Aldith put a restraining hand on Janna's arm once more. 'Before you accuse anyone, let's ask the tiring women exactly what happened in Dame Alice's bedchamber.'

'I'll ask Mistress Cecily.' Knowing Cecily's secret, Janna felt sure the tiring woman would have watched Eadgyth carefully on her arrival at the manor for signs of betrayal. If Fulk had said or done anything untoward, Cecily would surely have noticed.

She tapped a foot, impatient for action.

'My lord Robert asked you to leave. You are not welcome here.' Aldith hesitated. 'Go back to your cottage, Janna. I can talk to the tiring women and report their words to you, if you would like me to do so.'

Was Aldith just being kind, or was her true purpose to get Janna out of the manor and out of her way? Janna had no way of knowing. She felt ashamed of her suspicions, but she knew anyway that this was a task that she alone must fulfil, for only she knew the right questions to ask, and only she had the courage to ask them.

'It's true my lord Robert told me to go,' she admitted, 'but Dame Alice's nephew has asked me to wait here. As I can't serve two masters, I would rather serve myself. In truth, I can't rest until I know who was responsible for my mother's death. I want justice, Mistress Aldith. So I thank you for your offer, but it would be unfair to involve you in this business, especially if Fulk succeeds in turning all the household against me.'

The midwife nodded, seeming relieved to be rid of the responsibility. Nevertheless, she sounded a note of warning. 'I understand you're looking for someone to blame, but you must tread carefully, Janna! Fulk is an important man in Wiltune. Many hold him in high regard. If you accuse him of poisoning your mother, do you really think anyone will take your word against his?'

'They must, if I have proof.' In spite of her brave words, Janna acknowledged the dangerous path she had chosen. Yet she knew also that she could not give up her search for the truth.

FIFTEEN

JANNA AND ALDITH sat on in silence, each busy with her own thoughts. Janna's eyes began to droop with tiredness, until the sound of a door opening jerked her back to the peril she was facing. To her relief, there was no sign of the lord of the manor. Cecily had emerged. She was on her own, and her steps checked when she saw them waiting. For a moment Janna thought she might retreat, but she set off once more, hurrying on down the hall towards the door.

Janna jumped to her feet. Now was her best chance to prove Fulk's guilt, if only the tiring woman had seen what must have happened and was brave enough to bear witness against him.

'Mistress Cecily, please wait! May I ask you something?'

Cecily's steps slowed to a stop. Reluctantly, she turned.

'The priest told me that the doctor ordered a hot posset to be made up for Dame Alice and that my mother tasted it.' Janna rushed into speech as soon as she had Cecily's attention.

Cecily nodded slowly. ''Tis true. Master Fulk brought the posset to Dame Alice's bedchamber.'

'Did he say what was in it?'

'Nettles and mint among other things. It wasn't the first time he'd ordered it for Dame Alice. He boasted that it was a marvellous tonic, and that it would restore my lady to health far quicker than any mixtures your mother might give her.'

With difficulty, Janna bit back a sharp retort. 'So my mother wasn't with Dame Alice when the apothecary brought in the posset?' She had to get all the facts, even if they didn't take her in the direction she'd planned.

'No, but she came in only a few moments later. She demanded to know what was in the mixture, but Master Fulk wouldn't tell her. So your mother seized the cup and tasted its contents. We were all greatly scandalised, for she never asked Dame Alice's permission to do so.'

Brushing aside Cecily's regard for etiquette, Janna asked, 'Did Dame Alice also taste the posset?'

'No. She said it was too hot to drink, and set it aside to cool.'

Janna felt a surge of excitement. Keeping her voice calm with difficulty, she asked the most important question. 'Cecily, did Master Fulk add anything to the posset after my mother entered the room?'

'No, I don't think so.' She screwed up her delicate features in concentration. 'No, I'm sure not.'

Janna tried to hide her disappointment. 'Did he perhaps ask my mother to try the posset?'

'No, indeed. In fact, he tried to prevent her from taking up the cup. The posset was for Dame Alice to drink, not your mother!'

Janna and Aldith exchanged glances. Aldith shook her head in warning, but Janna could not give up now. 'Did my mother say anything about the posset, about its taste perhaps?' There was an edge of desperation in her question.

Unexpectedly, Cecily grinned. 'She was extremely rude about it. She took a few sips and then poured the rest of it out of the window. When Master Fulk complained, she told him she'd brought a far better tonic for Dame Alice, and while rose petals, nettles, mint and honey might make a sweet concoction, to her certain knowledge they had never cured anything more serious than a mild stomach ache!'

Rose petals, nettles, mint and honey. Janna closed her eyes, acknowledging that it could not be the posset that had killed her mother. Eadgyth would certainly have warned Dame Alice that it contained monkshood if she'd detected its presence. She should have thought of that before.

'That is where I am bound now,' Cecily said. 'Fulk has ordered me to fetch another posset from the cook, although methinks it may do more to relieve ma dame's stomach than her low spirits if what your mother said was true.' She shook her head. 'My poor lady,' she said softly. 'She is in such distress, I think she would do better to drink the wine that has come from Normandy. At least that would dull her senses; it could even bring her the comfort of sleep.'

Janna remembered how the lady had sent the goblet tumbling to the floor. 'Does Dame Alice not drink wine?'

'She does, but she says this latest shipment is tainted. I think she does exaggerate, for the wine tastes very fine to me.'

'I have only ever tasted dandelion and nettle wine,' Janna confessed. A picture came into her mind of Robert and his household sitting down to dine, and the array of fine food and fine wines they would consume. The hollow in her stomach reminded her how little she herself had eaten recently, and how poor and basic were the meals she shared with her mother. With difficulty she brought her mind back to the questions she still wanted to ask. Cecily might have demolished the case against Fulk, but there was a lot more that she could tell.

'I must go,' Cecily said quickly. 'Dame Alice is waiting for her posset.'

'I'll come with you.' Janna fell into step beside her before she could refuse. In silence, they descended the stairs leading to the grounds of the manor. 'Can you tell me what else passed between my mother and Master Fulk after she poured the posset away. Did she by any chance taste any other of his concoctions?' she asked, once they were outside.

'No, she did not. She told him to leave the bedchamber. He would not go and began a loud argument, but Dame Alice insisted that he leave them all in peace. Of course, he returned as soon as he heard your mother was taken ill, but . . .'

'Did he offer her any physic then?' It was possible her mother had taken ill, and then Fulk had seen to it that she never recovered, Janna thought. Her hopes were dashed as Cecily again shook her head.

Not Fulk, then. It seemed he must be in the clear after all. Disappointed, she cast her mind about for others who might have wished her mother harm. She remembered then her conversation with the priest. He'd dismissed her suspicions of Fulk, but how clear was his own conscience? The priest had told her he'd been in the bedchamber and had witnessed the scene between her mother and Fulk. If the priest had fallen for the merchant's patter in the marketplace, he too would have access to a phial of oil and could have used it to poison the posset. It would explain his anger and dismay when he heard her accuse Fulk of the very same crime! She turned to Cecily. 'What about the priest?' she asked. 'Did he touch the posset at any time?'

'No.'

'Or offer my mother anything to eat or drink?'

'No.' Cecily gave a sudden giggle. 'He kept as far away from your mother as possible. I think he was frightened of her. She had an answer for everything he said. She always managed to silence him.'

Janna felt a sharp pang of remembrance. 'An ignorant bigot,' Eadgyth had called the priest, after their hasty exit from his church. 'Because he hates women, he would have us believe that Christ did too.' Eadgyth would have enjoyed giving him a taste of her sharp tongue. Could she have angered him enough to kill her?

Even if she had, it seemed he did not have the opportunity to put wishes into action. Not the priest then, and not Fulk. That meant Janna would have to consider more carefully the time leading up to her mother's arrival at the manor house. In this, Cecily held the key.

She put out a hand to detain the tiring lady, and drew her into the shade of a barn. 'My mother had a visitor in the morning before she died,' she said carefully. Cecily said nothing, but Janna noticed her hands clench and unclench at her side. 'The visit was a great secret.' Janna continued. 'I knew it must be someone very special for I was not allowed to stay and help my mother.'

Cecily's face had paled. She was biting her lips, but still

she said nothing. Janna waited a few moments, then said patiently, 'You were gone from the manor when you were supposed to be resting. You were gone at the time my mother expected her visitor.' Cecily averted her face and did not answer. Janna sighed. 'It was you, wasn't it?' she said, going on before Cecily had a chance to deny it: 'I know, from the herbs I was sent to gather, that you were with child and that you came to my mother for help.'

Cecily jerked upright. Her face was anguished as she gasped, 'You must not tell anyone of this. It's too dangerous.'

'Why? Why is it dangerous?'

'Because . . . because I am unwed, and in Dame Alice's employ. If she knew, she would send me away. I have nowhere else to go.'

Janna wondered who the father was, that he could leave a young girl to face her disgrace alone. Some lowly servant or farmhand, perhaps, who would not dare brave the wrath of the lord of the manor? She had a sudden vision of Hugh supporting Cecily at Eadgyth's graveside. How solicitous he had been over her health; how protective were his arms about her waist as he helped her mount and led her away. Hugh might care about Cecily, but he would not want his aunt to know that he'd got her tiring woman into trouble. Janna felt suddenly faint but, with an effort, brought her reeling senses under control.

'I understand. Forgive me for distressing you, mistress, but I need to ask you more questions about my mother. You see, I had thought she must have taken some poison at the manor house to cause her death, but I see now that I was mistaken. I believe my mother must have taken some food or drink, imbibed some poison somehow, even before she came to the manor house.' Janna watched Cecily carefully, curious to observe her reaction.

The tiring woman was still pale with the shock of having her secret uncovered. Was she also fearful that Janna might discover an even more dreadful secret: that she herself had made sure of the *wortwyf's* silence? Janna liked Cecily, and felt deeply sorry for her, but she knew she couldn't allow her sympathy to blind her to the fact that Cecily had lied once and might well do so again.

'You were with my mother on the morning of her death,' she said carefully. 'Did you see her eat or drink anything while you were at the cottage?'

'No.' Cecily thought for a moment. 'No,' she said again.

'You didn't take anything to her?'

Cecily bridled. 'Of course I did! I gave her a gift in return for her labour and skill.'

Janna nodded. That was only to be expected. 'But you didn't share any food or drink with her?'

'No. I took only the potion your mother made for me.' Cecily shuddered, and tears came into her eyes as she relived what had happened. 'I thought I was like to die. I had such cramps. I was in such pain. I was also in great distress of mind. Your mother was very kind to me. She warned me how it would be, and bade me rest in the cottage so that she could take care of me until the worst of it had passed. But I was in haste to be gone, lest my absence be noted and remarked upon, and so I didn't tarry long.'

'Did my mother go back to the manor with you? Were you with her when she met Mistress Aldith?'

'No!' Cecily shook her head. 'I went on my own. I'd told everyone I was ill and needed to rest, and I crept in hoping my absence hadn't been noticed.' A watery smile gleamed momentarily. 'It seems I was not careful enough, however.'

'So they know you were absent, but no-one from the manor knows where you really were or the purpose of your absence?'

'No.' Cecily seized hold of Janna's hand. 'You must not speak of this to anyone, anyone at all,' she begged. 'Should Dame Alice come to hear of it, I would lose my position here along with my livelihood. Promise me you will keep silent, even if your mother could not.'

'My mother kept her promise to you,' Janna said at once. 'It was only after my lord Hugh spoke of your absence from the manor, and I saw how ill you looked, and how you tried to care for my mother when she lay dying, that I thought her visitor might have been you. Even so, I was not sure. You could have denied it. I might even have believed you.'

Cecily tipped her head on one side, assessing Janna with a thoughtful stare. 'I think you see and know a lot more than any of us realise,' she observed. 'You certainly ask enough questions!'

Janna smiled, taking Cecily's words as a compliment. Yet it was no time for smiling, she realised. Cecily had utterly demolished her carefully constructed case against Fulk and against the priest, and was well on the way to clearing her own name. She might have to start her investigation all over again. 'Can you tell me anything, anything at all, about your visit to my mother that might have led to her death?' she asked.

Tears came into Cecily's eyes once more. 'For certes your mother was in good health and good spirits when I left her.

She was going to make up a new elixir for the baby, and she told me she'd see how I fared when she got back to the manor house.' She began to weep, knuckling her fists into her eyes like a small child as she tried to conceal her distress. 'It was such a long walk back to the manor, I truly thought I was the one who was going to die.'

Janna put her hand on Cecily's arm to steady her. 'I am sorry you had to bear that alone. It must have been hard for you.' She was touched by Cecily's grief, knowing that it reflected an anguish of mind and spirit even more than the memory of her physical discomfort. She had seen the effect of her mother's potion on other young women who had come to her in secrecy. It could be no easy thing to cross the Church's teaching and take the life of a child. Janna felt great sympathy for this lonely young woman. 'You have my silence, I give you my word on it,' she promised.

Cecily carefully wiped away her tears, gave a mournful sniff, and walked off in the direction of the kitchen. Janna watched her go. All her instincts told her that she could trust Cecily, yet the tiring woman had given her no proof that she was innocent, nor could she. She and Eadgyth had been alone in the cottage. Anything might have taken place between them. All Janna knew for certain was that her mother did not die by her own hand.

The manor seemed hushed and still, drowsy in the mid-afternoon sun. It was past dinner-time and Janna's stomach growled with hunger. She debated going home, back to the cottage, for her questions were all done. Her spirits drooped at the thought. She could not give up, not yet.

Surely the answers must lie here, at the manor house,

where her mother had spent her last hours. If only she knew who to speak to, and where to look! While she pondered her next move, Janna walked to the well. She could slake her thirst, if not her hunger.

The cool water refreshed her. She sat down on a bench beside the well, and closed her eyes, the better to focus on the events surrounding her mother's death. Lifting her face to the sun, she felt its warmth enter her body, giving new life and hope to her exhausted spirit.

The sound of a warning cry interrupted her musing. She opened her eyes, and saw an elderly woman and a little boy coming towards her. The child ran ahead, ignoring his nurse's shout to slow down. He was all smiles as he raced up to Janna.

'My name is Hamo,' he announced. 'What's your name?'

'Janna.' The child had the look of his mother along with the dark Norman colouring of both his parents. He was only six or seven now, but he would grow up to be a heart-breaker, Janna thought.

'Who are you?' Hamo eyed Janna's coarsely woven kirtle and rough boots curiously. Her appearance seemed not to faze him, however, for he remained smiling and friendly as he asked, 'Are you a friend of my mother and father? Or my cousin Hugh?'

'None of them.'

'Then why are you here?'

'I came to help your baby brother. I tried to make him better.' Janna found it hard to tell a lie or even to soften the truth under the direct and trusting gaze of the child.

'My brother died. There's only me left now,' he answered matter-of-factly.

'I know. I am sorry for it.'

Hamo studied her. 'It's just as well,' he said candidly. 'My brother would have to be a soldier and go to war or enter the church for a living, for all my mother's property and wealth will be mine when she dies. I am the first-born son, you see.'

'What about your father? Will you inherit his lands and wealth too?'

'No, he's got nothing to leave anyone. All this belongs to my mother.'

Janna stared at Hamo in amazement. She had paid homage to Robert of Babestoche, as was his due as lord of the manor. Yet it seemed he had married well, far better than he might have expected, in fact. Still, it made no odds whose wealth it was, except perhaps to this precocious child and any future siblings he might have. On reflection, Janna concluded this was unlikely given the lady's sad history. It seemed Hamo's inheritance was safe. She wished him joy of it.

Hamo's nurse had caught up with him and now she gave him a reproving glance. 'You will not indulge in idle chatter with servants,' she said sternly.

'I want Janna to play ball with me.' Hamo looked quite unrepentant.

'You do not play ball while you are in mourning for your brother.'

'How can I feel sad about my brother when I didn't even know him?'

'You will do what is expected of you.'

'But I want to play ball.' Hamo stamped his foot.

''Tis too late now. I will play ball with you tomorrow.' The nurse cast a glance towards the sun, perhaps praying for nightfall. The fiery orb was past its zenith, was edging down to the west, tinting fluffy lambswool clouds with a rim of bright gold. Janna judged that there was still plenty of time for a game of ball. She winked at Hamo and he, delighted, grinned back at her.

'I don't want to play ball with you,' he told the nurse. 'You're too old. You never catch it and you won't run after it either.' He turned to Janna. 'Will you play ball with me?' he pleaded.

She glanced at the nurse, seeking permission. The woman shrugged, clearly unwilling to take responsibility for an activity she deemed unseemly. Yet Janna thought she might be quite pleased to have a break from her demanding charge for a while. The woman was getting on in years. Truly, she looked utterly exhausted.

'Do you have a ball?' she asked Hamo, wondering if a Norman child would also play with a pig's bladder stuffed with straw, as the street urchins did.

'Yes!' With a squeal of excitement he dashed off to find it, leaving Janna confronting his nurse.

'I am sorry,' she said softly. 'I am sure the boy truly appreciates your company and is grateful for your care of him.'

'He is too bright for his own good.' The nurse looked sour. Janna felt sorry for Hamo. Surely brightness was to be encouraged rather than frowned upon? But he would escape his nurse soon enough, for in only a few years he would likely be sent away to another manor house, or perhaps a lord's castle or even the abbey. He would learn to read and write, how to fight and how to serve the king. Janna envied Hamo for the wealth and freedom that would let him do exactly as he pleased in the future.

'Catch!' Hamo had returned, and now he threw a ball at her, its flight swift and true and finding its mark hard against her belly.

'Oof!' Winded, Janna fumbled to catch it, but the ball fell at her feet. It was made of leather and, by the sound of the rattle inside, it was stuffed with dried peas or beans. It was round enough to fly through the air and to roll a distance should she miss catching it. She would have to watch it more carefully next time.

'Catch!' she cried in turn as she copied his motion and sent the ball flying back to Hamo.

He caught it, and in one movement sent it hurtling back to her. It was a little high and Janna had to jump for it. She missed, and the ball went flying onwards. With a chuckle, she picked up her skirt and chased it.

'Catch!' Her throw was clumsy, and the ball went off to one side. Quick as a flash, Hamo went after it, diving to catch it before it hit the ground.

'Well done!' Janna clapped her hands together, and Hamo looked pleased. Janna thought he might not get too many compliments, especially not from his crabby nurse. He didn't let this one turn his head though, sending the ball straight and true towards Janna once more.

Again she fumbled and missed, and again she had to chase it. She bent to pick up the ball. A pair of boots planted themselves in front of her. Panting and out of breath, she straightened. Her gaze moved upwards and she found herself staring into a smiling face and dancing eyes.

Hugh.

SIXTEEN

JANNA BLUSHED AS she hastily tried to straighten her kirtle and smooth her hair. What must he think of her, rushing about like a street urchin? This thought was followed hard by another: Hugh already knew what she was. Why should a ball game with a child make any difference to his opinion of her?

'I thought I'd come and keep my cousin company for a while, but I see he's in good company already.' Without asking permission, Hugh took the ball from Janna and threw it back to Hamo. 'Catch!' he cried.

With a squeal of excitement, Hamo leapt into the air and caught the ball with both hands.

'Well done!' Hugh exchanged an amused glance with Janna as they both clapped the boy's efforts. Hamo smiled, suddenly shy. He put the ball behind his back, and began to scuff the earth beneath his feet.

'Don't you want to play any more?' Hugh challenged him.

A great beaming smile spread over Hamo's face. 'Yes!' And before Hugh could change his mind, the ball sped like an arrow towards him. Deftly, Hugh caught it and returned it, while Janna retreated to safety. The ball seemed to have become a deadly missile in the hands of Hamo and Hugh. As she watched the two exchange banter while each tried to out-throw the other, she reflected on how lonely the boy's life must be here at the manor, with only a crotchety old nurse to care for him. The company of a cousin must seem like a gift to him.

As Hugh's company was a gift to her, Janna acknowledged. Now she was seeing a side of him she had not expected. He was showing the heart of the child he once was, evidenced by the loud crow of glee he uttered when he threw a carefully angled ball just a little too high and Hamo missed it. The child scampered after it, seemingly unperturbed until he sent back a return, so low and so fast that Hugh fumbled and dropped the ball. Now it was Hamo's turn to chuckle and taunt Hugh for the butterfingers that had let the ball slip through his grasp.

Janna joined in their laughter, and was surprised. She'd thought she'd never feel happy again. It was reassuring to think that life could go on and that joy was still possible.

She watched the two together, man and boy, united in their enjoyment of their game. Hamo had a mother and father, but what about Hugh? It seemed he had no lands of his own, for he'd told her he'd come to make a report on his custodianship of Dame Alice's property. Janna surveyed him thoughtfully. Was Dame Alice his only living kin, and was Hamo all that kept Hugh from a large inheritance? Certain it was that with so much at stake, Hugh would desire his aunt's good opinion above everything, and would do all in his power to keep it, even if it meant keeping his relationship with Cecily a secret. There came into Janna's mind then the question she most dreaded: how far would he go to keep their secret safe? Yet there were no grounds for suspecting him for, on his own admission, Eadgyth was already dying by the time he and Robert were summoned to the bed-chamber. She was jumping to conclusions about Hugh and Cecily, conclusions that might be utterly false, Janna warned herself, finding comfort in the notion.

A sudden howl interrupted her reverie. She looked up to see Hugh sprinting towards Hamo, who was clutching the side of his face and trying not to cry. Suddenly the lethal missile-thrower was but a little boy again. The red welt on the side of his face spoke of what had happened even as Hugh broke into an apology.

'It's my fault,' he said. 'I'm sorry, Hamo. I shouldn't have thrown the ball so hard. After all, you're just a child.' A forlorn hiccup greeted this tactless observation. Ignoring the outraged clucking of the nurse, Janna pulled a reproachful face at Hugh over Hamo's head and enfolded the boy into her arms to comfort him.

'Of course, you're so big for your age, and you throw the ball so well, it's not surprising I thought you were a lot older than you really are,' Hugh added hastily, doing his best to retrieve the situation.

'Everyone says I'm big for my age.' Hamo broke away from Janna and squared his shoulders as he faced Hugh. 'I've been riding with the groom and practising with my own sword every day so that I shall grow up to be a fine soldier like you.'

'I expect you'll be a far greater soldier than I'll ever be,' said Hugh, and earned a watery smile for the compliment.

'I knew this would end in tears,' the nurse muttered darkly, and tried to take hold of her charge. Hamo backed away and hid behind Hugh.

'Would you like to come with me to the kitchen garden, Hamo?' Janna asked. 'We'll crush a comfrey root to soothe that sore swelling on your face where the ball hit you.'

He nodded, and slipped his hand into hers. As they began to walk towards the garden, Hugh fell into step beside them. Wearing a frown of disapproval, the nurse followed.

'How is Dame Alice faring, my lord?' Janna broke the companionable silence that had fallen between them.

'We have left her to rest.'

'And Mistress Cecily?' Janna watched Hugh closely for any sign that she meant more to him than merely being his aunt's tiring woman. 'Is she now recovered from whatever ailed her?'

'She's doing well enough,' Hugh said casually, seeming not at all troubled by the question. Instead, there was warmth and concern in his voice as he asked, 'And what of you, Johanna? How do you fare, with so much to burden you?'

The sudden thunder of hoof beats prevented Janna from having to answer. Hugh quickly scooped up Hamo and sprang aside to safety. Janna looked up at the horseman, and felt a shaft of anxiety as she recognised the lord of the manor. For one fearful moment she thought Robert was going to run her down. She leapt out of his path, landing awkwardly and wrenching her ankle as she did so. Robert jerked on the reins, forcing his horse to a sudden standstill. His eyes were hard and angry as he stared down at her. 'Why are you still here? I told you to go home before you do any more harm, and I'll thank you to do as you're told.' His glance flicked from Janna to her companion. Ignoring the child clasped in Hugh's arms, he said, 'Make sure the girl leaves the manor at once.' He dug his heels viciously into the horse's flank. Startled, it reared and then took off at speed.

Behind Robert, riding more decorously, came the priest. He nodded at Hugh and Hamo, but could not hide his displeasure at the sight of Hugh's companion. Compressing his lips, he followed Robert out through the gate.

Hugh put Hamo down when he judged it was safe to do so. The boy looked indignant. 'I'm not a baby, you know!'

'I know, Hamo, but I wasn't sure your father had noticed you. I didn't want him to run you down.' There was a steely glint in Hugh's eye as he looked after Robert and the priest, but his expression softened as his glance shifted to Janna. He seemed to be making an effort to hold himself in check. Janna wondered if he was working out how best to follow Robert's orders to get rid of her. She decided to help him out.

'My lord,' she said, 'I must go home, as I've been told.'

'No. Stay and find a balm for Hamo's cheek, I pray you.' Hugh gave a rueful laugh. 'I fear I will feel the lash of his mother's tongue for hurting him, but at least I will be able to say we did what we could to ease the pain.'

Janna nodded, encouraged by his confidence that she would be able to help. Child of the forest she may be, but she was not so ignorant as he might suppose. 'Where do my lord Robert and the priest go so late in the afternoon?'

'The priest has gone to make arrangements for the baby's

interment and to instruct the villagers to attend a requiem mass for the child's soul. My aunt wishes it.'

'And my lord Robert?'

Hugh shrugged. 'Perhaps he needs to report the baby's death to the shire reeve.'

'Why does he hate me so?'

'Who? Robert, or the priest? Or the shire reeve?'

'My lord Robert. My mother and I did all we could to help Dame Alice and her infant son. Dame Alice understands that and is grateful, but my lord Robert has turned against me.'

Hugh was silent for a moment. 'He blames you for his son's death,' he admitted at last.

'But I . . . but we . . .'

Hugh held up his hand to silence her protest. 'I know,' he said simply. 'I know.'

Once in the garden, Janna looked about for the hairy leaves and stalks of comfrey. She was certain such a useful plant would be cultivated here and she soon found it, and in some quantity. She dug down, seeking the spread of roots below. She broke off a portion of thick root, and showed it to Hamo.

'Erk!' he said. Black on the outside, it was white within and full of a glutinous juice.

'It'll help, I promise.' Janna applied the cool jelly-like mixture to the boy's smarting cheek, then turned to his nurse.

'Take these roots and some leaves from the comfrey, and ask the cook to boil them up. When the water has cooled, bathe Hamo's bruise with the decoction. It will soothe his skin and help to bring down the swelling.'

The nurse gave a reluctant nod.

'See to it,' Hugh said sharply. She bobbed a curtsy then and set to picking some leaves. He turned to Janna. 'You have your mother's skill with herbs, I see.'

'She taught me all she knew – and she knew a great deal.'

'Where and how did she gain her knowledge?'

'I know not,' Janna confessed sadly. 'She would not speak about her past.' Fearing Hugh's pity or, even worse, his judgment, she added quickly, 'I must go now, sire. I want to be home before it gets dark.'

'You could stay here tonight, at the manor.' Janna flashed a sidelong glance at Hugh, questioning his motives. 'In case my aunt has need of you,' he added.

'You heard my lord Robert. He bade me go, and I must obey him, sire.'

'Then I will take you home, and fetch the palfrey while I am there.' Hugh swerved off towards the barns, closely followed by Hamo, who still clutched the gummy root to the side of his face. 'Go with your nurse, Hamo.' He bent down and gently pushed the child in the direction of the kitchen. 'We'll play ball again tomorrow,' he promised, to speed Hamo on his way.

Reluctantly, and with many a backward glance, Hamo did as he was told. 'Come.' Hugh beckoned Janna and, together, they went to reclaim his large destrier from a long wattle and daub shed. The horse blew softly from a stall at the far end. Janna looked about her as Hugh saddled the horse. Above her head was a trapdoor. Wisps of hay beneath suggested that the space above was a storage house through winter, while saddles and bridles and empty stalls told the use of the space below.

Janna marvelled that the manor should have all these separate buildings just for livestock and storage. For people too, she thought, as she noticed several straw pallets and a hook on which hung a rough smock and breeches. Serfs must also sleep here, those who had no cottage or shelter of their own. They would be out in the fields now, tending the crops, weeding, digging ditches and getting ready for hay-making. It was early summer, and the grass in the meadows would soon be tall enough to cut.

Hugh led the destrier out into the fading sunlight. This time, he placed Janna in front of him, sitting as decorously as any highborn lady. His arm came around her for support, and she leaned back against him as the horse proceeded on its slow journey across the downs. She was close enough to smell Hugh: a faint odour of sweat mingled with leather and horse. It was masculine, unfamiliar, exciting – and very unsettling.

The ride seemed to last for ever, yet was over far too quickly. Hugh dismounted then reached up and put his hands around Janna's waist. He swung her down from the saddle but kept hold of her, standing close. Janna trembled, and closed her eyes.

His kiss was light and fleeting, but Janna thought there was warmth there too. She resisted the urge to cling to him, to kiss him back. Her heart was pounding so hard she thought it might burst right out of her chest. She took a step away, hoping that this small distance might keep her safe from him. 'Thank you,' she murmured.

'For the kiss, or for bringing you home?' His voice was cool, amused. He seemed not to feel the turmoil of emotion that had so unsettled her. The realisation strengthened Janna and gave her the courage to give him a light reply in turn.

'I thank you for bringing me home, for it was kind of you to take the trouble. I feel sure kisses can be no trouble to you, for you must have bestowed kisses aplenty in your life, and to far more purpose than merely seducing a . . . a naive and ignorant child of the forest!' A vision of Cecily's tear-stained face flashed before her. She took another step away from him.

Hugh laughed. 'I have already admitted that I misjudged you, Johanna – but now you misjudge me! I always kiss to a purpose, but I only bestow kisses where they are wanted.'

Now Janna wished she'd kept silent. She had no knowledge that he wished to seduce her! What must he think of her presumption? 'I beg your pardon, sire,' she muttered.

'Sshh.' He put a finger across her lips. 'I understand,' he murmured.

There was a moment's silence while Janna became aware of the dark forest, silent at her back, and the green fields spread before her, rolling down to the river and to Berford. She felt as if she was standing on a lonely precipice. She had no protection against Hugh should she fall, no protection for a heart that was in danger of being stolen – save the memory of Cecily's sorrow and disgrace. She stood straighter and rubbed her mouth. It tingled where his lips had touched it. She longed for Hugh and feared him in equal measure.

Perhaps he understood something of the storm of feelings that threatened to overwhelm her, for he moved away to untie the palfrey and bring it back to where the destrier waited. He remounted, then touched two fingers to his head in a casual salute. 'Good night, Johanna,' he said, and turned the horses towards Babestoche.

SEVENTEEN

THE COTTAGE FELT cold and unwelcoming, and very, very silent. Tears came into Janna's eyes as she thought how different it would be if Eadgyth was home. The thought of what Eadgyth would say if she knew how Janna felt about Hugh helped to brace her and give her courage. 'Turnip head.' That's what Eadgyth would call her, what she called Fulk and anyone else who got too puffed up with self-importance.

'Turnip head,' Janna repeated silently as she set about milking the goats and foraging for their food. But keeping busy could not disguise the fact that all her efforts to find the person responsible for poisoning her mother had failed.

She remembered that Cecily had said she'd brought a gift. A flicker of interest stirred Janna into action. Where was it? Now she thought about it, she certainly couldn't remember seeing anything unfamiliar about the place. She walked inside. She'd already searched through her mother's medicaments; now she turned her attention to the rest of the small cottage. Her search didn't take long. There was nothing to be found. Could Cecily have lied about bringing a gift?

Or had she perhaps brought a cake, or something to drink with poison in it?

Surely her mother would have kept such a thing to share with her daughter. They always shared everything. Janna looked about, searching for what she might have missed. But there was nothing there that she did not recognise. Nothing.

Too agitated to rest, she walked outside again and paced about the garden, pulling weeds from among her herbs and nipping off dead leaves and flowers, creating order where her mind could find none. Why hadn't she thought to question Cecily about her gift? A moment's reflection told Janna that, if guilty, the tiring woman would have lied. If innocent – the gift would still be in the cottage, waiting to be found.

Janna busied herself with tasks until it was too dark to see. Weary now, she came inside. Her agitated thoughts continued to weave webs in her mind yet she knew she could take the matter no further until she had another chance to speak to Cecily.

She took up flint and tinder to light the fire, then stopped dead as a thought occurred to her. If Cecily had stopped her mother's tongue to protect her secret, she might well take the same action against Janna! She would have to be careful dealing with the tiring woman – very careful.

With a fire burning and an extra light coming from a peeled rush soaked in fat, Janna began to feel a little more confident. The hollow feeling in her stomach returned, and she realised suddenly that she was ravenous. She took up a knife and unlatched the door. She peered out, fearful of what, or who, might be lurking outside. Cecily wasn't the only one who might wish her harm.

All seemed quiet. No Cecily, or Hilde, or even a wild boar. Janna felt a crushing sadness as she recalled her angry accusation. Godric had risked everything to save her, and had then suffered her insults at the graveside. He was a kind and decent man, and she owed him an apology. Could he, would he, ever forgive her for thinking such ill of him?

She bent to dig out some reddish purple carrots for the pot, adding a leek and some beans plus a couple of sprigs of marjoram. The herb would calm her troubled thoughts, as well as adding extra flavour to the pottage. The hens clucked around her. 'Go and lay some eggs,' she told them as she searched the empty coop.

Once inside, she emptied the jug of water into the large cooking pot and hung it over the fire to boil. She gave the vegetables a careful wash before slicing them up. She threw them into the pot to cook, along with a handful of oats to thicken the stock. She should save the goats' milk to make cheese, she knew, but she mixed a little in with some flour to bake another cake on the griddle.

Pottage might not suit the lord and lady of the manor, but to Janna the hot food resembled a feast and she savoured every morsel of it. She set the pot aside and, with the ache of hunger eased, she blew out the rush light and lay down on the straw pallet to sleep.

Tomorrow, she thought, I shall talk to Cecily again, and see if I can trap her into admitting what really happened between her and my mother. And I'll tidy the cottage and sort through my mother's possessions. A shaft of sorrow lanced Janna's heart at the thought. To banish it, she kept on compiling a list of things to do. It hadn't rained for some days; the soil where she'd dug out the carrots had felt very dry. She must fill some buckets from the dew pond to keep her garden alive and thriving. The floor rushes needed changing. She must go down to the river to cut some more. Resolutely, Janna added chores to her list. She must make cheese, and also more wax candles, perfumed creams, and balms and ointments to sell at the market. She must pick some more herbs and hang them to dry. She must . . .

A sudden noise set her upright, ears straining to hear, eyes straining to make sense of the ghostly flickers of fire-light cast by the dying embers in the centre of the room. Was that someone standing in the corner, watching her? Her heart thundered in fright. She stayed still, waiting for the phantom to move, to betray its real and living presence. She could hear breathing, loud rasping breaths that spoke of terror. It took Janna some moments to realise that the breaths were her own.

Now she heard a voice calling her, the name unmistake-able. 'Janna!' Who could be visiting her at this time of the night? She bounded out of bed and pulled on her kirtle and boots.

'Janna! Come outside!' The command was followed by a furious knocking, so loud Janna thought the door might come down. It was a woman's voice calling her, but she could not place it. Was someone in trouble? With some reluctance, Janna pushed the door open and stepped outside.

A group of villagers faced her, the leader bearing a flaming torch held high so that his face was illuminated. With a shock of recognition, she saw that it was Wulfgar, the miller. He shook his fist at her, his face grim and determined.

'What do you want?' With an effort, she kept her voice steady. Sweat pricked her skin in the cool night air. She thought of the knife still lying on the table, and wished she'd remembered to snatch it up before opening the door. Alone and unprotected, she faced the villagers.

'Murderess! Child killer!' Janna peered into the darkness behind the lighted flare, able now to identify the voice. Hilde, the miller's wife. She stepped out in front of her husband and shook her fist at Janna. Her face, savage and sneering, was lit by the flaring light from the torch. The rest of her was thrown into shadowed relief. With her swollen body and wild gestures, she looked like a huge and grotesque ogre.

'Why do you say such things when you know they're not true?' Janna held her ground, determined to make Hilde explain her spiteful words.

'Everyone says you poisoned the baby up at the manor. You took the life of a young and innocent child!'

'Who says so?' It took all of Janna's courage not to flee inside and close the door on the group. She could see the hate in Hilde's face, a hate which must be shared by all or they would not have come knocking at her door. What was their purpose?

Once again, Janna remembered Eadgyth's warning. 'Never turn your back on a wild animal. Never let it see that you are afraid.' But these were people – not animals! Yet, like sheep, they seemed to be following Hilde's lead without question. Should she treat them like animals? Yes, if it ensured her safety!

'Who says that I am a child killer?' she demanded again, her voice loud to cover her fear.

'The priest says so!' An angry murmuring followed Hilde's reply.

'What reason does he give for these lies?'

'You gave the baby a potion of your own concocting – and he died.'

'My lord Robert and Dame Alice know that is not true.'

'Fulk the apothecary told the priest that it was so.'

'My lord Robert and Dame Alice know that I did all I could to save their child.'

'Both the priest and Robert of Babestoche say that the baby died because of the poisoned physic you gave him.'

'The baby died because he was too weak to live.'

'Your mother died from drinking her own poisonous brew. And now you have poisoned the lord Robert's new-born son.'

'I gave him no poison! My mother's elixirs have helped save the lives of your own children.' Janna spread her hands out in appeal. Surely some among this small group must know that she was innocent, must be grateful for the healing she and her mother had given in the past? She looked at their faces in the flickering torchlight, trying to recognise who was there. Her heart quaked as she saw the anger and ill-will reflected by them all. Aldith was not among them, she noted. Nor was Godric. It was a relief that they were not here to accuse her, yet she would have given anything for a friendly face, for some support against these vile accusations.

'Your mother's death was a just reward for her godless ways!' Ulf swaggered forward, a baby in his arms and the rest of his children straggling along behind him. It seemed he no longer thought of Janna as a potential wife, for he continued,

'Just so should you pay for the death of a child with your own death.' He spat at Janna. The glob of mucus landed an ant's width from her toes. Alarmed, she jumped back out of his reach. He leered at her, his eyes hot and hungry, but Janna sensed that there was fear in them too.

Acutely aware of the peril she faced, Janna spread out her hands in appeal once more. 'I swear to you, I did not harm the baby. Nor did my mother. She was skilled with herbs, you all know that for you have all been helped by her in the past.'

'She was a godless woman. Her death is a punishment for her godless ways!'

'She was a good woman. And she believed in God as much as any of you.'

'Why then would the priest not bury her in the church-yard? And why does he say that you, too, are damned?' The miller came forward to stand beside his wife and Ulf. They were so close Janna could hear their breath, read the hostil-ity in their eyes, and see the flecks of spittle around Ulf's mouth. She would have retreated, but the door behind her was closed and there was nowhere else for her to turn.

'The priest is ignorant. He does not understand.' It was not, perhaps, the best thing to say in the circumstances, Janna realised, as she heard the hissing intake of breath. Better to change the subject, and quickly. 'Why are you here? What do you want with me?'

Now they watched her, silent and still. They were waiting for something to happen, just as she herself was waiting. Her heart raced harder; her breaths came short and shallow in her breast. She wiped her damp hands down her kirtle.

'Why don't you go home?' she pleaded. 'I've heard your accusations. There is no more for you to do here.'

Hilde grabbed the flaming torch from her husband and stepped closer, so close Janna could feel the hot breath from the flare. Her eyes were dark holes in her angry face. 'You've killed a child. You've murdered an innocent babe! You're a godless woman whoring after other women's husbands. We don't want you here. You've got to go.'

Janna felt a burning anger as she faced Hilde, yet she knew she should not speak of what lay between them. She had to stay silent for her own sake. She turned to the other villagers. 'I cannot go anywhere. I live here. This is my home,' she said, pleading for understanding.

'Go, and take that devil black cat of yours with you!' The miller's mouth contorted as he gathered saliva. He spat at Janna with a fine accuracy. With a shudder of revulsion, Janna wiped the mucus off her face, understanding that his action represented payback for the kiss she'd so painfully terminated.

'My cat is like any other creature that lives and dies,' she said coldly. 'My cat once lived, but now it is dead.' She looked at Hilde.

'I saw the devil on our way up here, I swear I did,' said Ulf.

'I saw the cat too,' Hilde chimed in eagerly. 'It was playing in the shadows. Did you not see it?' She turned to the other villagers for confirmation.

Janna sucked in a sharp breath. 'The cat is dead!' she insisted, remembering Godric's warning about shape-shifting. She would not give them a further reason to accuse her.

'Then truly the cat is the devil, for I swear I saw it just moments ago.' Hilde smiled as an uneasy muttering broke out behind her back.

Janna knew a moment of pure, wild rage. 'Do you carry a knife with you tonight, mistress?' she hissed. 'Would you use it on me as you used it on my cat?' She turned to face the villagers, feeling sick as she tried to defend herself against their ignorance, and the hate and fear in their hearts. 'My cat is dead. It was killed by Mistress Hilde,' she said. 'She came to my cottage in the night and saw me with the villein, Godric.' Now she addressed Wulfgar directly. 'She thought she was following you, she thought you were with me. To punish me, she slit my cat's throat and tied it to a tree! She also threatened to use her knife on me if she saw you with me again. Pray tell me, who is the murderess here?' She stepped forward and thrust her face close to Wulfgar. 'Be careful,' she warned. 'Be very careful whose bed you lie on, lest your wife next uses her knife on you or your mistress!'

Taking advantage of the stunned silence that followed her words, Janna turned to the villagers. 'My home is here, far from the village. I will not trouble you, nor do you need to trouble me. Please go away.' Not daring to turn her back on them, she felt behind her for the door latch. She watched them steadily all the while, for she sensed that if she turned her back they would attack her like the cowardly animals they were. Yet she sensed also that she must get away from them, for the longer she stayed to argue with them the more angry and determined they would become. She could only hope that, if she was not there to provoke them, their tempers would cool and their senses return along with the light of morning.

Janna snicked the latch, pushed the door open and, in a quick movement, stepped back and slammed the door shut once more. For safety, she dragged her mother's heavy chair against it. For added protection she donned her girdle, then slipped the knife inside her purse. If they came for her, she would be ready. She collapsed onto a stool then, breathless and trembling as she waited to see what the villagers would do next.

A low muttering came from outside, a buzzing like a swarm of bees. A voice was raised, and quickly hushed. The words had been indistinguishable. Janna wondered if Hilde was being taken to task for her actions. A man laughed then, the sound drifting off into silence.

It was quiet outside now, too quiet. Surely she should hear their footsteps, the sounds of crunching leaves, snapping twigs as they returned to Berford? The silence made Janna uneasy. Were they still outside?

Smoke. Smoke and the thin crackling snap of burning wood. She stood up to inspect the fire in the centre of the room. A thin plume coiled upwards from a log which, even as she watched, crumbled and fell away into ash.

Janna settled back down on the stool and tried to calm her frightened spirit, but a new worry came to her mind. How would she manage if she could not trade her skill and knowledge of herbs in return for the goods she needed to live? With the memory of Wulfgar came the realisation that, because of his crazed wife, she would have to grind her own corn in the future. It was an extra task added to a burden already too heavy to bear. She drew a deep breath, weary beyond endurance.

Smoke. Janna looked at the dying fire. The crackling sounds were louder, the smell was stronger. Tendrils of smoke were seeping through small cracks in the mud and straw daub that sealed the wooden frame of the cottage. Aghast, Janna noticed flickers of light as flames began to lick and burn through timber. The cottage was on fire, and she was trapped inside.

EIGHTEEN

'GOD ROT YOUR souls!' Janna shouted, hoping the villagers were still outside to hear the curse. She hated them with all her heart. What had she ever done to make them turn against her like this? But now was not the time for curses and questioning. The cottage was on fire, the flames all around her. She must act, and quickly, or she would be burned alive.

She pounced on the heavy chair and dragged it away from the door. The door was alight now, and the surrounding walls with it. Janna felt terror as she realised she was surrounded by a ring of fire. She must make haste to save what she could! She quickly cast about for Eadgyth's precious weighing scales, but the room was filling fast with smoke, making it hard to see. The smoke stung her eyes and tore at her throat. She began to cough. The sound was growing louder, crackling and roaring as the fire took hold. Hungry tongues of flame closed in on her, licking up the wooden cottage and its contents.

Janna put her hand over her nose and mouth to try to filter the choking smoke that billowed around the room. No time to save anything, she must flee for her life. But where was the door? She peered about, trying to find her direction from the furniture in the room, but her eyes were watering and the smoke was too thick to make out anything at all. In panic, she stretched out a hand then blindly stepped forward. Her boot jarred against a heavy object. She touched it, felt its shape. The chair! She'd moved it to the right of the door, but the door itself was burning. In sudden hope, she turned to the window. It was too small; she would never fit through.

Janna knew that if she didn't get out right now, she would die. She cast about in search of the pot of vegetable soup. Her hands were shaking so badly she fumbled, missed, then at last managed to pull the pot off the hook. She dashed the contents over herself then untied her purse and girdle and ripped the wet kirtle off over her head. Girdle and purse she tied around her waist, then she bundled her kirtle around her hands to protect them.

The smoke was suffocating, she couldn't breathe. The rushes had caught alight now; fiery rivulets snaked across the ground towards her. She had to go. Janna sucked in a quick breath to summon up her courage. Using her bound hands as a battering ram, she ran at the door, shoved it open and raced through. The scorching breath of the flames stung her as she passed, and then she was out and running for her life. The air smelt suddenly cool and fresh. She was safe. She doubled over, coughing and choking, whooping for breath as she tried to suck in enough air to feed her starved lungs.

She smelt the stink of burning hair; her scalp smarted and stung. Her hair was on fire! Shivering with shock and fright, she shook her hands free of the kirtle and wrapped it tight around her head in a desperate effort to smother her flaming halo. Then she looked through the trees at the incandescent pyre that was once her home. She began to retch. She heaved up her dinner in painful, agonised gasps, retching until her stomach was empty and sore.

The spasms passed at last. Janna straightened and looked about her. Despair crushed her as she watched the fire destroying what was left of her life, everything she knew and everything she had shared with her mother.

The animals! Without giving herself time to think about her own safety, Janna ran around the side of the burning cottage to the pen which housed the goats and hens. She could hear an anxious bleating as she came closer, and felt an over-whelming relief that the goats were still alive. 'Get out, get out!' she urged, as she unsnicked the catch that kept the gate closed.

Too fearful to move, they stayed huddled together. 'Shoo!' Janna ran at them, forcing them to move apart. The hens cackled and ran about, dangerously close to being trampled by the frightened goats. 'Shoo!' Janna's voice shrilled high with fright. She flailed her arms to scare them into action, and at last the goats ran through the opening and out into the garden, followed by the hens. 'Shoo!' she shouted again, urging them towards the forest and freedom. As soon as she was sure they were on the move, she raced ahead and into the sheltering trees. A greater fear filled her now. The villagers wanted her dead! She dived into a bushy thicket and rolled flat onto the ground, trying all at once to become invisible. After a few moments, during which she gathered what last remnants of courage she had left, she raised her head and peered cautiously about.

The cottage still burned fiercely, the fire casting its light in a wide arc. Janna watched the scene intently, alert for any movement or sound that would betray the presence of the villagers. How delighted they must be by the success of their mission to drive her away, and by their power over her. Her eyes smarted from the heat and smoke, her skin burned where the fire had scorched her. She blinked hard and stifled a sob as she continued to watch. There was no sound of voices, no sign of human life, no witnesses to the destruction of her home, her life. Like the cowardly dogs they were, the villagers had fled.

Sparks broke free of the blaze and floated through the air. Fire fairies, Janna thought fancifully, until she noticed that a stray spark had alighted on a clump of leaves close to where she was sitting. The leaves were smouldering, could easily flare out of control. Janna jumped up and stamped on them, extinguishing the danger. But the smoking vegetation had awakened her to the hazard she faced. It would be stupid, she thought, to save herself from a burning cottage only to die in a forest fire instead.

She could not seek the safety of the fields in case the villagers were still about. Instead, she forced her trembling legs to run deeper into the forest, ducking branches and bushes, tripping over flints and into unexpected hollows, pushing her way past brambles that caught her tunic and scratched her skin, until she reached a wide clearing. Believing herself safe at last, she collapsed onto a patch of grass.

The burning cottage had set the sky alight. The fiery glow shone above the trees. There was no escaping the horror of her loss. Numbly, Janna kept watching as the leaping flames gradually sank lower. It came to her that she was still clad only in her short tunic. She untied the girdle and purse at her waist, then unfastened the damp and singed kirtle which she'd wound around her head. She shook it out and put it on, her fingers catching in holes where the fire had burnt it right through. Even though it was in rags, it would give some protection to her bare arms and legs, she thought, as she secured her girdle once more.

Janna had cried all the tears she could cry. Now she just felt achingly empty and sad. She stood stock-still while she assessed her situation. She had no way of earning her keep in the future. She was an orphan. There were no family or friends to help her; indeed, the villagers hated her enough to destroy the only thing she had left: her home with all its memories. Janna clenched her hands, feeling another emotion that at first she could not identify. Its intensity filled her with a white heat so strong it drove out all fear and loneliness. It was rage, she realised, an anger that blazed as hot and blinding as the sun. Impulse bade her run down to the village and demand justice. She might still have some support there; not everyone had come out to the forest tonight. Caution told her that it might only have been fear that kept the other villagers away, and that they might not be on her side if forced to take a stand. Janna knew she hadn't imagined the hatred that had prompted those who had fired her cottage. They hadn't cared that she might burn along with it.

She hesitated, at a loss what to do next. Finally, she came to the conclusion that it would be better, for the moment, if everyone thought she was dead. Let the villagers think they had succeeded in their purpose. It was the only way to stop them coming after her again.

With that decision behind her, Janna was faced with a new question. Until she could find some way of bringing the villagers to justice, and her mother's killer along with them, she had to find shelter. Where could she go? South to the sea? No, she wanted to put the protection of the forest between her and the villagers. She could not go east to Wiltune, for she was known there. Nor should she go west. From what Godric had told her, she'd never find the ancient way through the forest that would lead her to safety. North, then? There was a track right across to Wicheford, she'd heard, but she'd never gone so far as that before. She would be walking into the unknown. With this realisation came a thought to reassure Janna: if she knew no-one it would mean that no-one knew her. She would be able to beg for bread and shelter in safety.

Undecided, she hesitated. She was so tired! Her body hurt, and her spirit was weary to death. She was surrounded by the dense, secret fastness of the forest. It was dark enough for shelter, but too dark for venturing into the unknown. Tonight, then, she would hide here. Perhaps her path would seem clearer in the morning.

Wearily, Janna fashioned a nest of soft grass and leaves beneath the comforting branches of a spreading beech, and sank down. Although the night was cool and her thoughts were in turmoil, exhaustion claimed her. Almost instantly, she fell asleep.

The melodious warbling of blackbirds brought Janna suddenly wide awake. She sat up with a jerk, puzzled by the leafy roof above her head. Her heart did a somersault as she recalled why she was sleeping out under the trees. A shudder shook her body. She felt cold and she was wet. It must have rained at some time during the night. Alone and vulnerable, Janna rested her elbows on her knees and buried her head in her hands. She couldn't stay here. She had to think, to make some sort of plan for the future.

Something felt different. Cautiously, she touched her head and felt stubble, all that was left of her burnt hair. Yet not all of her hair was gone, she discovered, as she continued to explore her scorched and tender scalp with careful fingers. She still had a few long locks where sparks hadn't fallen. She shed her wet kirtle to examine her arms and legs. Bright pink streaked her skin where fire and brambles had branded her. She looked down at her kirtle. The front was burnt so badly it was beginning to disintegrate. As she dressed, she comforted herself with the thought that at least there was no-one about to see through the holes in her kirtle. She knew her first task must be to find something else to wear. She could not make her journey dressed like this.

She stood up, and limped slowly to the edge of the forest. A faint glow lightened the sky to the east, heralding the dawn of a new day. Common sense told Janna that she should leave straight away, before anyone was up and about to see her. Yet all her instincts bade her go back to the cottage one last time. Like a wounded animal, she needed to return to her lair.

It made sense to go back and look around, she reasoned. There might be something left that she could salvage, some balm to heal her burnt and smarting skin, maybe even something to replace her ruined kirtle. At the least, she could wash away the ravages of the fire from her skin.

She looked about her, assessing the chances of discovery. The sky was dark and shrouded in cloud. It was early enough for most people to be still abed. No-one would have had time yet to walk to the cottage to survey their handiwork – if they had the courage to come at all.

There was a hint of rain in the air, a fine sifting that kept Janna shivering in the cool early morning. The rain had been enough to dampen the fire, she realised, as she hurried towards the blackened ruin, all that was left of her home. In fact, the rain was providential, for it had probably prevented the fire from spreading through the forest itself. If only it had rained sooner, she thought, some part of the cottage and their life within might well have been saved! As it was, the stench of charred remains hung acrid in the air.

Janna went first to their herb garden in the hope that something might have survived after all. Burnt bones and charred feathers lay among the ashy remains. Laet, Janna thought sadly. In the race for food, and everything else, the little hen had always come last. She raised her glance from the devastating scene. 'Nellie! Gruff!' she called. There were no answering bleats, but Janna took comfort from the fact that there was no sign of burnt goats in her garden either. They must be happily foraging in the forest. Soon enough someone would find them and take them home.

The hives had burnt through, leaking precious honey onto the ground. 'I'm so sorry,' Janna told the bees, although she knew that none could be left alive to hear her. They would not have survived the heat and smoke. Feeling empty and despairing, she walked on through the herb garden. The fire had taken everything, leaving only mounds of ash and black stalks to bear witness to a lifetime of toil. There was nothing left to salvage, no warm milk or eggs to fill her empty aching belly, no sweet herbs or honey to ease the hurt, no balm to replace a shattered life.

Desolate with grief, Janna wandered slowly on through the damp, charred mess to inspect the remains of the cottage and its contents. Their precious chest, which had contained a change of clothing and some warmer wear for winter, had burnt right through. Their meagre bits of furniture: the table, stools, her mother's carefully made chair and cushions were all reduced to ash. So were the bunches of dried herbs, the sachets of powders and pills. Clay saucers and jars had crashed to the ground when the shelf had burned through. While most were smashed, a few pots had survived the fall and their contents remained intact. Yet all the medicaments in the world could not cure the pain in her heart, Janna thought, as she inspected these few pitiful remnants. She kept on searching through the debris, and found the hard flint and small piece of steel. Among the devastation of fire, the means to start it had been saved! With a wry smile, she secreted them in her purse. Should she need to keep warm, should she be lucky enough to find something to cook, being able to light a fire would come in handy.

She crouched down among the ruins of the cottage. Carefully, she began to sift through soggy, blackened fragments, the remnants of her life. Mostly they fell apart as she handled them. Some were recognisable: shards of jugs that had shattered in the heat; a tin basin, warped and buckled and now unusable. A faint gleam caught Janna's eye. Eadgyth's scales! Eagerly, she uncovered them. They were blackened by the fire and twisted beyond repair. Heartsore, she left them lying and turned her attention to the iron cooking pot. It lay beside its chain and hook. Janna peered inside the pot and was delighted to find scraps of charred vegetables stuck to the bottom. She ate them. They tasted foul, but she was hungry and besides, she had no notion of where she might find her next meal.

A rough patch of newly turned earth caught her attention. It looked as though someone had dug a hole and then covered it over. Puzzled, Janna stared down at it, mentally picturing the cottage and its contents. The straw pallet she shared with her mother had completely burnt away, but this was where it had once rested. Could her mother, the keeper of secrets, have hidden something of her past under their mattress? Janna's breath came faster at the thought. She pulled the knife out of her purse and began to dig into the earth. It was already softened from the rain, and loosened easily. Encouraged, Janna's pace quickened. The earth flew in handfuls about her as she dug deeper.

The blade hit something hard, jarring her hand. Cautiously now, Janna felt around the object and then carefully lifted it. A small tin box with a clasp. It was not locked.

Janna's hands shook as she lifted the lid. The first thing she saw was a silver ring brooch studded with multi-coloured gemstones. She gasped with pleasure and surprise. Why hadn't her mother ever shown this to her? She turned it over, and frowned at the inscription engraved on the back.

It meant nothing to her. Carefully, she set the brooch aside. Underneath it was a piece of parchment. She picked it up and unfolded it. It was covered with writing. Janna stared at the symbols on the page, wishing she could read.

Where had her mother come by these things, and why had she hidden them? It was all very strange. A distant memory came to Janna. She was very young, just learning to talk. She was standing outside the cottage. Eadgyth had a stick in her hand, and was tracing letters into soft sand with it. 'See, Janna,' she said, 'see how you write your name. JOHANNA.' As she said the letters, she pointed to the symbols scratched into the sand and sounded them out.

'Johanna,' Janna had repeated obediently. She had picked up the stick then and tried to copy her mother's writing. But it had proved difficult and she had grown bored with it, and thrown the stick down and started to cry. Her mother had been patient with her. She had done nothing further that day, but some months later she had tried again, and then again, encouraging Janna to write and write and write the letters of her name so that now she could do it without trouble, without even having to think about it.

Janna had spoken the truth when she'd told Hugh she could write her name, but that was all she could write. Her mother had never taught her how to read, or to write anything else. Why? Janna frowned at the writing on the parchment, trying to make it out. She could see a J and there was an N, and some Os and an A and another A – but they were none of them joined together in a pattern that she recognised, and they had strange symbols in between that she did not know at all. If her mother knew the letters of her name, surely she must have known some other letters too. If she could read and write, why did she not teach her daughter all her skills, instead of only the skills of healing?

Janna gave an exasperated sigh as she stared into the distance and once more pondered the secrets her mother had kept hidden from her. Her mother had kept her so innocent – and so ignorant. Eadgyth had protected her by telling her nothing, and by trying to marry her off as soon as possible to whoever might prove suitable. Janna wished rather that her mother had told her the truth and trusted her judgment. Instead, by willing her to an early marriage and a lifetime of drudgery, her mother had cheated her of her heritage and her future, whatever that might have been.

Yet nothing had worked out as her mother had planned. In fact, with her mother dead and her home gone, Janna was free to go wherever she wished and have the adventures for which she'd always longed. So why, instead of feeling excited about the challenge ahead, did she now feel so lonely and bereft?

After a few moments' thought, it came to Janna that she belonged here, that her home and her life with her mother were all she knew. Without warning, they had been snatched from her, and as yet she had no idea what might take their place. But no matter where she went or what adventures lay ahead, no-one could ever replace Eadgyth in her life. Janna was sure that, in her own way, her mother had loved her and wanted to protect her, to save her from making the same mistake that had shattered her own life. Even so, she'd called her 'Johanna' as she lay dying. Their argument must have cut deep indeed. If only she could have got to her mother in time to make up their quarrel. Tears of grief and loss came into Janna's eyes. She dashed them away. It was too late for regrets, too late for an apology. She was on her own now, and must make the best of things.

Janna turned her attention once more to the parchment. Was it a message from someone? She kept looking at the symbols, trying to fathom what they all meant. A word at the end caught her eye. Familiar letters, but not quite enough of them. J. O. H. N. She sounded them out as her mother had taught her to sound out the letters of her own name. Joe-han? No, that wasn't right, there was no A between the H and N. Juh oh huh hn? Juh-hin? Joh-hin? John?

John! It seemed to Janna that everything in the world stopped still. John! She recalled Cecily's words as she told Janna of Eadgyth's dying moments. 'Actually, I thought Eadgyth was calling for John, but when I questioned who he was, one of the tiring women told me your name. Your real name.'

Johanna. John. In her dying moments, her mother had called for John. Her thoughts had not been with her daughter but with . . . who? The man she'd always loved? Was John her father? Had she, Johanna, taken his name?

Yes! Janna had never thought before to ask why her mother, a Saxon woman, had given her a Norman name. Now she had the answer: her father must be a Norman, and of noble rank if Aldith was to be believed. No wonder her mother could speak the language of the Normans. Janna was grateful that this, at least, was something her mother had taught her. With a growl of frustration, she caught up the parchment and studied it once more. If only she could read this letter from her father to her mother, so much of the past might be explained. But the symbols told her nothing. They could have been the footprints of spiders for all the sense they made.

Janna carefully refolded the precious parchment and laid it in her lap. She felt as though a great burden had been lifted from her shoulders, the burden of guilt. Her mother had forgiven her for their argument after all.

She looked inside the box to see what else Eadgyth had hidden from her.

A gold ring, large and heavy. It had an embossed design on its face instead of the sorts of sparkling gems which adorned Dame Alice's hand. A man's ring, then? She studied the design. It depicted a swan, but was it only a swan or did that long neck and body form the letter J? Above the swan, on one side, were two beasts with tails, the likes of which Janna had never seen. On the other side was a crown which she thought must denote the man's allegiance to the king. Frowning, she considered the matter and came to the conclusion that the king must have been Henry, for Stephen had usurped the throne during Janna's own lifetime. She certainly could not recall any man of their acquaintance who knew her mother well enough or was wealthy enough to give such a keepsake. The J, if it was a J, seemed to suggest that it had been another present from her father. Janna carefully repacked the casket and set it aside. With mounting excitement, she peered into the hole to see what else she could find. It was empty, save for a glass bottle.

Taking great care, understanding its value and fragility, she lifted it out. Did it have some special significance? Could it once have belonged to her father?

She turned the bottle in her hands, admiring the beauty of the green glass. If only it could speak to her, what secrets it might tell! Janna frowned as she tried to puzzle out why her mother had buried such a precious object when she could have traded it for something more useful. Its appearance seemed oddly familiar. She was sure she'd seen something like this before.

A scene flashed before Janna: Robert of Babestoche, pouring wine into a goblet for his wife. The bottle had looked exactly like this one. Had this bottle come from Robert's own household? Or did all bottles look alike?

For certes, Robert would never have made a present of a bottle of wine to Eadgyth – but Cecily might! Was this Cecily's missing gift? From what Janna had seen of Cecily's circumstances, it seemed unlikely that the tiring woman could have had such a costly gift to give. Unless she had stolen the bottle of wine, someone must have given it to her. Hugh? Was this a gift for Cecily, or his payment to the *wortwyf* for taking care of Cecily's problem? Janna squeezed her eyes shut against the image of Hugh with his arm around Cecily's waist, his tender care of her at the graveside. If Hugh really was the father of Cecily's unborn babe, it was a matter between the two of them, she told herself firmly.

She unstopped the bottle, eager to try her first taste of wine. To her amazement, it was empty. How so, when her mother had had no time to drink any of it? Janna cradled the bottle on her lap as she struggled to solve this new puzzle. If her mother had drunk all of the wine straight away, she would have been far too unsteady to follow Cecily to the manor and minister to Dame Alice. Cecily had not said that her mother was drunk when she arrived. Ill, yes, but not drunk. What, then, had happened to the wine? And why had her mother hidden the empty bottle?

Janna sighed. While her mother's life had been a mystery, her death seemed to have uncovered even more secrets. The real question was: where to start looking for answers?

NINETEEN

ALTHOUGH CONSCIOUS THAT time was passing, Janna sat on amidst the ruins of the cottage. Random thoughts, a jumble of impressions, ran through her head. Somewhere in the events of the past few days lay the answer to her mother's death, she felt sure of it. It was just a matter of fitting all the pieces together.

She looked down at the bottle in her lap. In case a few drops of wine remained, she picked it up and tilted it to her mouth, hoping for a taste to satisfy her curiosity. A few drops moistened her tongue and she held them there, smacking her lips as she tasted the precious liquid. Her brow creased in thought. Unless wine tasted exactly like water, this was water! But the moisture was certainly proof beyond doubt that this was a recent gift, rather than an old token kept as a memento of her father.

It must have come as a gift from Cecily, there was no other explanation. Janna closed her eyes, and tried to imagine the last few hours of her mother's life. Cecily had come knocking on the door, and had handed over her gift. In return, her mother had given Cecily the foul-tasting mixture that would bring on her menstruation. Cecily would surely have stayed

238

for a little while, long enough to listen to Eadgyth's instructions and to take the mixture, but she had not lingered long enough to share a sup of wine. She would have mentioned it else, but instead she'd told of her great hurry to get straight back to the manor before her absence was noted.

So Eadgyth must have drunk the wine by herself, and washed out the bottle afterwards. This in itself seemed surprising to Janna, for she and her mother always shared whatever they had. A bottle of wine would have been a rare treat! Surely she would have kept some of it to drink with her daughter.

Janna had to face the fact that her mother had finished the wine without her. She had rinsed out the bottle and then gone to the manor house to see Dame Alice.

No, that couldn't be true, for Aldith would have noticed that her mother was feeling the effects of too much wine and would have remarked on it. It didn't make sense. Nothing made sense. Janna stroked the cold glass bottle, wishing it could speak its secrets. If her mother hadn't drunk all the wine by herself, someone must have shared it with her. Not Aldith. She would have mentioned it, she would have been jealous of the gift. As it was, Aldith had been kind enough to share her own cordial because her mother had said she was thirsty. If she'd just drunk a whole bottle of wine, she wouldn't have been thirsty – unless she was feeling the effects of poison!

Was the wine poisoned? Was that how her mother had come to die?

Startled, Janna sprang to her feet and began to pace about, trying to keep up with her agitated thoughts.

Her mother could not have drunk the whole bottle by herself; the poison would have killed her long before she got to the manor house. So perhaps Eadgyth had tried just a sip or two, meaning to share the rest of it with Janna later on. Not liking the taste, or maybe thinking the wine was tainted, she'd thrown it out and washed the bottle, then hidden it so as to protect Cecily's identity as she'd promised. She had certainly not drunk enough of the wine to suspect that monkshood had been added to the mixture, for she would have prepared a brew and taken steps to combat the poison if that was so.

Janna gnawed on her top lip as she contemplated where her thoughts were taking her. If her mother had taken only a sip, it would explain why the poison had taken some time to work its dark mischief. It would also explain why her mother had not suspected anything until its symptoms had become fully manifest. The problem was that Janna no longer had any proof of her suspicions, for the wine was now tipped out and gone.

Sudden and shocking, a picture of her dead cat flashed into her mind. So much blood, both under the animal and elsewhere. She had wondered about that patch of blood so far from the animal's body. Now she understood how she'd misread the scene. Not blood at all, but the stain of red wine, the stain left after her mother had poured the contents of the bottle away.

Janna paced silently for a few moments, pondering Cecily's role in Eadgyth's murder. Who had added poison to the bottle of wine? Cecily, who was so anxious to protect her secret she would go even to these lengths? Or was it her lover? Was it Hugh?

It was Dame Alice who owned everything, not Robert of Babestoche. And Hamo was in line to inherit it all. As Dame

Alice's nephew, Hugh would need to look for better prospects for marriage than his aunt's tiring woman if he was to make his way in the world. Soon enough, Hamo would be old enough to come into his inheritance, to claim for his own the manor at Babestoche, as well as the manor now managed by Hugh. By then, Hugh must have married, and married well. For certes he could not afford news of a dalliance with Cecily, and a baby as proof of it, to come to the ears of either his aunt or his future wife. To what lengths would he go to keep that secret?

Hugh – or Cecily? Or were they in it together? Janna remembered the tiring woman's tears of guilt and grief. She remembered also that Cecily had tried to care for Eadgyth as she lay dying, and had braved the priest's wrath to watch her interred. She found it hard to believe a cold-blooded killer could be capable of such kindness as Cecily had shown. Nevertheless, Cecily hadn't hesitated to lie when it suited her. She had to be careful, Janna thought. She'd made wrong judgments in the past, but if she got it wrong this time, her own death might follow. She could not afford to be careless.

Fear lay at the heart of all that had happened, she understood that now. It was because of fear that Eadgyth had died. It was fear that might drive the killer to strike again. The key to the puzzle was Cecily and her unnamed lover. Was it Hugh? With all her heart, Janna wanted to believe the best about the man who had been so kind to her. But she knew she could not afford to let her heart rule her head. The poison had not got into the bottle by accident. Someone had put it there, someone who would stop at nothing to keep

Cecily's secret safe. She held the bottle close to her eyes and looked through the thick glass, trying to put her whirling thoughts into order. It was how the world seemed to her right now, she realised, as she squinted at the distorted shapes that were the ruins of her home. If the bottle could only speak, it would tell her what she needed to know: the name of its owner.

The bottle stayed mute, but other voices spoke in Janna's mind. She'd been focused on who had the means, the motive and the opportunity for murder, but there was something else she needed to take into consideration in order to solve the mystery: the telltale gestures, the actions that revealed more than the speaker realised. Her heart quaked as she understood that there was someone else at the manor, someone who might have an even more urgent reason than Hugh to keep Cecily's secret.

She lowered the bottle. Tendrils of fear twined and knotted in her stomach. If her guess was right, not only did the killer want her dead, but he thought he'd already succeeded. Janna knew that her safety depended on his continuing to believe that. She was in the most deadly danger. The last thing she wanted to do was go to the manor house, yet she knew she must, one last time. She had to speak to Cecily. For her own sake, and for her mother, she had to find out the truth. If she was right, it would mean that Cecily was in far more danger even than Janna. If she was wrong, and Cecily and her lover were in this together, then Janna herself would be walking into a trap – a trap that could end only in death.

All Janna wanted was to flee to safety, but not if her safety was bought at the price of Cecily's life. Not for anything would she have Cecily's death on her conscience. So she must go, quickly, for there was no time to lose.

First, though, she would have to find something else to wear. She looked down at her kirtle, stained from her night among the bushes and shredded from the fire. It would draw curious eyes and curious comments and she could not afford either, yet every other garment she owned had been destroyed.

Her tattered kirtle woke Janna to the danger she faced if anyone came looking for her. The villagers had also wanted her dead. They must all think that they had succeeded. She bent down and picked up her mother's treasures, and hurried into the sheltering depths of the forest. Once safely concealed behind a large beech, she set down the box and bottle, and sat beside them to plan how she might find a change of clothes.

'Janna!' The sound was like the howl of a wolf, a wild cry of desolation. With a gasp of fear, Janna flattened herself behind the tree and peeped cautiously around it. Godric was on his way up the hill. Had he seen her? He seemed to be looking her way. 'Janna!' he shouted again, and turned in a slow circle to scan first the green downs and then the cottage and the forest.

Janna pressed closer to the sheltering tree. Truly, Godric looked awful, she thought. His beard and hair seemed even more unkempt than usual; his eyes were red-rimmed from lack of sleep. Or something else. He scrubbed his face against his sleeve as he peered about. Surely he could not be crying?

Janna longed to go to him. She had so misjudged Godric, she desperately wanted to beg his forgiveness. Shame kept her hidden, and also caution. It would be for the best if everyone thought she was dead – or if not dead, driven out and gone from her home. She tried to console herself with the thought that she and Godric hardly knew each other. He would forget her as soon as some other comely young woman crossed his path, someone more deserving of his love, someone who would give him babies and make him happy. Someone who wasn't an outcast: hated, feared, and driven even to death.

Janna blinked back tears of self-pity, desolation and loss, and continued to watch from her hiding place. All Godric's concentration was now focused on the blackened ruins of the cottage ahead. He walked among the debris, just as she had walked earlier. Like Janna he was looking for something. He lingered for some moments beside the remains of the animal pen, carefully sifting through charred fragments of bones and feathers, before moving on into the devastated remains of the cottage. There, he began a systematic search. He bent down time and again, now to move a blackened beam, now to sift through a pile of ash. There were no bones for him to find, but she might have left footprints. She pressed closer to the tree, trying to become invisible.

Whatever Godric was looking for, he seemed pleased not to find it for at the end of his inspection he stood up and looked about him. It seemed to Janna that he stood taller; he seemed straighter, more confident. Suddenly, she heard her name again.

'Janna!' His voice rang out loud and clear, startling a pair of blackbirds. They squawked and fluttered their wings at the sound.

Janna pressed her hand hard against her mouth to stop herself from answering him. Godric must know now that she hadn't died in the fire. She was touched by the change in him, but reason told her there was no future for them, either in friendship or anything else. Godric was tied to the manor. He was not free to go wherever he chose, whereas she needed to flee the wrath of the villagers as well as the murderous intentions of those who feared her knowledge up at the manor. She *had* to leave, had to go as fast and as far from this place as possible. A glance at her kirtle confirmed her decision. She didn't want Godric to see her in rags, with her hair all burnt; she didn't want this to be his last memory of her. So she stayed hidden, and listened while he began to search through the forest, all the while shouting her name. He was coming closer to her hiding place. Silent as a snake, she wriggled into a dense cover of leafy bushes and tall grass close to the shielding beech, stifling a cry as bare skin touched a patch of stinging nettles. She stayed hidden and listened to him search.

Godric's cries grew fainter; she could no longer hear the crunch of leaves, the crackle of twigs under his boots. In the silence, birds began to chitter and sing once more. At last, when she was sure he had gone, Janna slid out from her cover. She straightened cautiously and looked about her. There was no sign of Godric, and no sound of him either. For the moment she was safe.

She was also thirsty, so thirsty! She hurried to the dewpond and cupped her hands into the water, splashing silver droplets as she drank. The ruffled surface gave her an idea, but she kept cupping her hands to drink until her thirst was slaked. She wiped her tattered sleeve across her mouth then, and waited until the water had stilled. Then she looked down at her glassy reflection.

She looked a fright! Carefully, she washed the smut and ash from her face and hands, then dipped her whole head into the pond to cleanse her sore, soot-blackened scalp. With water streaming down her face, blinding her, she raised a hand and fingered the long wet hanks of hair among the singed stubble. She had no cap or veil to hide the bare patches on her scalp. She would have to cut her hair so that it was all of one length. To leave it as it was invited ridicule and comment. She would be noticed wherever she went.

She drew the knife from her purse. Pressing her lips together to contain her distress, for she had been proud of her long, blonde locks, she began to hack into them. As she cut, she remembered the admiration in Hugh's dark eyes when first they'd met. He would not look at her again, not after this!

''Tis better so,' Janna reminded herself, for her safety depended on the fact that everyone, save one, must believe her dead. She stared at her reflection in the dewpond, at the drying blonde wisps that fluffed around her head like the halo of a saint. No chance now of anyone's admiration – not when she looked like a youth!

Could she pass herself off as a young man? She pondered the thought. It pleased her greatly. People would have less chance of recognising her if they thought she was a boy. As a young girl, alone and defenceless, she would always be at risk. As a boy she could move freely. She would also be much safer in disguise, especially up at the manor where at least one person had even more at stake than the villagers in wanting her dead.

Janna gathered up the incriminating bits of hair and hurried back into the forest to bury them. She must leave no sign of her activities for Godric, or anyone else, to suspect what she was about. She looked down at her kirtle. She needed men's garments, but she could not use the few pennies she had from her sales at Wiltune market to trade, for that would show her intention to the world. What was she to do? Janna came to the reluctant conclusion that she would have to steal some clothes to fit her new identity. She remembered then the horse barn up at the manor house. Inside, on a peg, hung a smock and breeches, no doubt some poor serf's Sunday best, kept for church and special occasions. She would take them. She'd never stolen anything in her life, and baulked at the thought of starting now, but she had no choice. Without proper attire she could go nowhere. Dressed as a boy, she would be free to roam wherever she chose.

She would rather have gone to the manor under cover of night, but she knew there was no more time to lose. She would not be able to take the usual path across the fields, for she would be seen and recognised. Instead, she would have go through the forest to get there.

Janna knew she had no chance of finding the ancient Roman road that Godric had told her about, but she didn't have to go that far into the forest to be safe from prying eyes. She could stay close to the tree line, away from wolves and wild boar. As soon as she'd talked to Cecily she could make her escape, for the longer she delayed, the more peril she faced, both at the manor house and from the villagers.

Godric would tell them that she had survived the fire. They would come looking for her again, for they could not risk her witness against them for their night's treachery and their destruction of abbey property.

She walked back to her hiding place and pulled out the box and bottle. She didn't want to carry them with her, for they were awkward to hold. Yet she must keep the bottle; she needed it to confront Cecily. What about the box? Janna opened it once more and stared at its contents, feeling a frisson of excitement as she picked up the ring. It was a link with her father, she felt certain of it. She slipped it on her middle finger, imagining the hand of her father, the finger that had once worn this ring.

It was far too large for her own finger. As she tilted her hand, it slid off. Janna tried it next on her thumb, but it looked ridiculous there. Finally, she unlaced her purse and placed the ring inside, adding to it the precious piece of parchment and the ring brooch with its strange inscription. Then she knelt and buried the empty box under the bushy screen. It was time to go. She steeled herself to take a last look at the remains of her home. Resolutely fighting tears, she whispered goodbye to her childhood, and to her mother. She had planted rosemary on Eadgyth's grave and had promised to remember her. She had vowed to seek the truth, and make whoever was responsible for her mother's death pay with their own life. Now that Janna understood so much of what had happened, she began to understand also that vengeance was impossible. She was alone and an outcast, now more than ever before. She had not the power to bring anyone to justice.

It was a bitter realisation, made worse by the knowledge that she must flee the village. Her mother's grave would stay untended, probably even defiled by those who would take out their fear and hatred on the dead if they could not take it out on the living.

Janna thought about the ring and parchment in her purse. A glimpse of hope lifted her spirits slightly. She wasn't quite alone, and she might not be utterly powerless either, she realised. Aldith had described her father as wealthy and important; he could even be a Norman nobleman. Should she try to find him? Would he welcome her? Those questions were less important than the central question: if she could find him, could she convince him to act on Eadgyth's behalf? Could she convince him to come back to Babestoche Manor and bring to justice those responsible for Eadgyth's death?

She had to try. Janna vowed to herself that as soon as she'd finished her business at the manor, she would go in search of her father. No matter how long it took, she would do all in her power to find him. Although she had to leave her home and everything that was familiar to her, she resolved that, in time, her journey would lead her home again. By then, she would have changed. No longer an outcast, a powerless victim, she would have the authority of her father behind her and everything would be different.

Janna knew not where her father might be, did not even know which direction she should take. She could only start the journey, and hope that she might find guidance along the way. First, though, she must take her chances at the manor and hope that her wits were enough to save her from the danger that awaited her there.

She set off along the edge of the forest in the direction of Babestoche. Her hopes and her future were bound in the contents of her purse. She wondered if dreams and these small clues would be enough, and just where they might lead her.

TWENTY

I T WAS AFTER noon by the time Janna left the last portion of forest cover and stealthily made her way down to the manor through a field full of sheep. They stared at her with incurious eyes as she hurried past them.

Now a new problem presented itself. Would someone be guarding the gate during the daylight hours? What might she say to the gatekeeper should her way be barred? An urgent message from the shire reeve for the lord of the manor? No, the reeve would not entrust an important message to any other than one of his deputies. He would certainly not give instructions to a serf. She thought anew. Could she be in need of urgent assistance? No again, for why should anyone care about her welfare or what became of her? Janna sighed. It would be too bad if, after all this, she was not allowed in.

As she approached the manor, Janna was still undecided how to talk her way past the gatekeeper. To her great relief her luck seemed to have returned, at least in part, for the great gate was raised, while the gatekeeper seemed far more interested in his dinner than in a bedraggled young woman. Janna scuttled past, with her arms folded across her breast to hide the worst of the burns in her kirtle. Keeping her head down, hoping to avoid recognition, she hurried on to the shed Hugh's horse had been kept in, where the smock and breeches had hung. Hopefully, it would still be deserted save for the lone horse.

Once safely inside, Janna stopped still and held her breath, listening for sounds, be they animal or human. Soft scuffling and rustling told of the presence of mice and rats, perhaps even a cat. Janna felt a moment's sympathy for the cat's quarry. She knew, only too well, how it felt to be hunted. No soft neighs to greet her this time, or even the chink of a bridle. It seemed safe to swiftly strip off her kirtle, unhook the smock and pull it on. It was stiff with dirt and sweat and smelled strange. It was also far too big for her. She stuffed her kirtle down her front, to conceal it and also to change her shape, and tied her girdle underneath her new and enlarged stomach both to keep it in place and to hitch up the smock so that it wasn't quite so long. No matter that her purse still dangled from the girdle; so too did men hang objects about their person.

The clink of coins gave Janna an idea. She took out a silver penny and dropped it under the hook where the smock had hung. It would be noticed when the villein searched for his missing clothes. Janna felt sure that he would keep it without telling anyone of his good fortune, save his family perhaps, for he might spend it to their benefit. With her conscience somewhat eased, she pulled off her boots, then unhooked the breeches and pulled them up. They immediately fell down in folds around her ankles. Janna looked more closely and discovered a cord through the waistband to keep them up and in place. She pleated back the rough homespun and tied the cord tight. The legs were far too long for her. After a moment's thought she rolled up the bottom of each leg so that she could walk without tripping over. It felt strange to be wearing a man's breeches. Janna kicked out, marvelling at her new freedom of movement. She could stride out now; she could even straddle a horse and ride it without showing ankles and legs. It seemed that there were other, less obvious, advantages to changing her sex!

She stepped back into her boots while she pondered the next problem: how to approach Cecily. Dressed as she was, she could not march boldly up the stairs of the manor house and demand admittance. Some other trick was called for. That she must leave the shed was certain. Cecily would not come to her so she must go to Cecily, and find a way for them to meet in privacy and safety. After a moment's thought, Janna decided the best approach was through the kitchen. She was about to leave the barn when a gorget with a pointed hood caught her eye. She snatched down the short cloak and put it around her shoulders, then pulled the hood down over her face. It was meant for winter wear, but it would shield her from prying eyes. Thus clad in her new garments, Janna strode out of the barn to practise her new identity.

Before braving the cook, Janna went first to the garden to seek lily or mallow to give balm to the burns that still stung her scalp and limbs. As she searched for what she needed, a scullion came out to pick vegetables for the evening meal. The girl stopped short in surprise when she noticed Janna. Giving her no chance to speak, or to raise the alarm, Janna hurried into speech.

'Begging your pardon,' she said, her voice deliberately low both as a disguise for her own voice and in an attempt to mimic the speech of a boy, 'I've come with an urgent message for Mistress Cecily. Is she here? Is she well?'

'Yes. Yes, she is here.' The scullion looked surprised. She tried to peer under the hood for a better look at the messenger.

Janna's worst fear was over. She took a quick breath, feeling relief that she had not come too late. 'I have no knowledge of the household. Will you take the message to Mistress Cecily for me?'

'Who is it from?' The servant continued to stare suspiciously at Janna. Janna tipped her head down. The hood fell lower, now covering most of her face.

'From . . .' She was about to say a name, but suddenly understood the danger she courted if she'd calculated wrong, or if her message went astray. 'From someone who would not give me his name,' she amended quickly. 'He saw me about the manor and bade me ask Mistress Cecily to come out and meet him. My instructions were to find an excuse to seek her out and speak to her alone, so that no-one else might hear what I say. Can you do that for me?'

'For certes, when I go to make up the fire in Dame Alice's bedchamber. Where does he say they should meet? And when?' There was a smile of anticipation on the scullion's face. It was clear she suspected an assignation and took great delight from the notion.

'In . . . in the shed over there.' Janna pointed so that there could be no misunderstanding between them.

'The barn where my lord Hugh stables his horse?'

Janna nodded quickly. 'Yes, indeed,' she agreed. 'Ask Mistress Cecily to come just as soon as she can get away. Tell her to make sure no-one sees her leave.' Janna was happy to fuel the girl's feverish imagination. It seemed more likely that the message would get through if the scullion had romance on her mind.

'Go to it,' she urged, conscious of time passing. There was no time to waste, for soon enough the workers would return from the fields. Yet the maid lingered, perhaps hoping to hear more.

'Hurry!' Janna snapped.

As soon as the girl was out of sight, Janna collected what she needed to heal her burnt skin. She went back to the barn to wait for Cecily, and to treat her wounds while she waited.

The juices from the roots and cool leaves soothed her skin, but nothing could soothe Janna's mind. She felt her nerves grow taut as time passed. Where was Cecily? Had the scullion not delivered her message after all? What if the girl had taken fright and instead had given the message to Dame Alice or, even worse, Hugh or Robert?

The barn was dark. She'd closed the door to give herself privacy while she applied the salve to her burns. Perhaps the closed door had made Cecily think that whoever waited for her had now gone? Janna was about to open it when she heard the clink of the latch.

She hastily snatched up the gorget that she'd thrown aside in order to minister to her hurts, and pulled the hood down over her face.

The door creaked open. A woman's form stood in silhouette against the brightness of the open doorway. With a swift movement, the woman pulled the door to, and stood still. 'Are you here?' she asked softly.

Janna knew a moment's triumph. The scullion had delivered the message, and Cecily had come. This meeting must answer everything, for there was much to tell and much to discover. She was sure, now, that she knew the truth behind her mother's death, but it would place her in the greatest danger if she'd got it wrong. In the silence she heard Cecily call again.

'Is anyone here?'

Janna made a movement towards her. Cecily heard, and whirled around. 'Have you changed your mind? Please, *please* tell me that . . .' She stopped short. Her hand flew to her mouth as if to block further speech. Her eyes, startled and uncomprehending, examined Janna.

Janna pushed back her hood, then took off the gorget. Cecily showed no recognition but kept on staring.

'It's Janna,' Janna said helpfully.

Now Cecily started as if she had seen a ghost. 'You!' she whispered. 'I thought you were dead.'

'I'm not.' Then, as Cecily shrank back in obvious fear, Janna offered her an arm. 'I'm real enough. Give me a pinch,' she invited.

Cecily reached out and nipped fabric and skin together with a tentative touch. Then she gave Janna a shaky smile. 'You seem real. Yet we were told that your cottage has burned to the ground, and that you are dead and buried.'

'I'm not – but only you are to know that,' Janna warned.

'I don't understand.' Cecily inspected Janna with wide eyes. 'The priest has just come to tell us that you died in a fire.'

256

'Did he say that he, my lord Robert, and the villagers all blame me for the baby's death and that's why my cottage was set alight, with me in it?'

'No!' Horrified, Cecily stared at Janna. 'The fire was an accident!'

'Like my mother's death was an accident?'

Cecily flushed. 'The reeve told the priest a stray spark from your fire must have set the floor rushes alight.'

'And I'm telling you that it was the villagers who set fire to my cottage. I know, because I was there! They accused me of killing the baby and told me to leave. Who do you think could have incited them to take action against me?'

'I can't say,' Cecily whispered. 'All I know is that Robert went with the priest to report the baby's death to the shire reeve, and to make preparations for a requiem mass. Robert said the priest told the villagers that you had given the baby a physic shortly before he died. He was concerned for your safety, he said, because the villagers were exceedingly agitated and alarmed when they heard what had happened. He assured us he'd done his best to calm them and allay their fears.'

'Lies. All lies,' Janna said fiercely. 'Robert of Babestoche incited them to rise against me. They would not dare to disobey him.'

'Why would he do such a thing?' Cecily drew away from Janna, refusing to be associated with such disloyalty.

'He had his reasons.' Now that she'd planted the thought in Cecily's mind, Janna changed the subject. 'You said that I was dead – and buried. Who told you that?' she asked.

'The priest. He had it from the shire reeve. It seems a villein, Godric, reported the fire. He told the reeve that he found your

body among the burnt remains of the cottage, and that he has
buried you in the forest. He refused to say where, nor would
he show the reeve the site. When the reeve remonstrated with
him, Godric told him that he did not trust the priest to give
you a proper burial, not after the way the priest had treated
your mother. The reeve has threatened to take action against
him, and the priest is so offended he has ordered Godric to
live on bread and water until he confesses. But Godric will tell
them only that he has buried you close to the home you loved,
so that you might rest in peace.' Cecily looked at Janna in
wonderment. 'Why would he say that when you are still alive?'

'I don't know.' But Janna did. It seemed that in spite of
everything, Godric was still protecting her. She said a silent
thank you, wishing she could say it to him in person.

He must have talked to the villagers, suspected their part
in this and realised that her safety depended on his lie. There
could be no other reason for it. 'What else did the priest tell
you?' she asked.

'That's all I know.'

'Not quite all. Tell me about Robert of Babestoche. Why is
he so hostile towards me, do you think?'

'He . . . he believes you are responsible for the death of his
baby son. He is afraid you will go on to do more harm if
someone doesn't prevent you.'

'Knowing all that you know about me and my mother, can
you truly believe that?' It was another seed to take root and
grow in Cecily's mind. Not giving the tiring woman time to
answer, Janna hurried on. 'You gave my mother a bottle
of wine in return for her help.' It was a statement, not a
question, but Cecily nodded in confirmation.

'Yes,' she said proudly. 'It was the finest gift I had to give.' She showed no signs of guilty knowledge, Janna thought. Cecily couldn't know that Eadgyth would hide the bottle. She might well think that Janna herself had shared the wine with her mother. Surely this pointed to Cecily's innocence.

'Where did the wine come from? Who gave it to you?' Janna felt a twinge of doubt when Cecily didn't immediately reply. Had the tiring woman stolen it after all?

Cecily heaved a mournful sigh. 'It . . . it was a gift from my lover,' she admitted reluctantly.

'A gift to you? Or was it for you to give to my mother?'

'It was a gift to me.' Cecily gave a forlorn sniff. 'My lover was exceeding wrath when I told him I had given it away, even after I explained the reason for it. I told him I had naught else to give your mother, but that I must bring a gift in return for her help. After all, I did it for both our sakes.'

Janna knew a moment's triumph. It was followed instantly by black anger and bitter grief. Yet she must not betray how she felt, for nothing was proven yet. There was still much to find out. 'Did you taste any of the wine before you gave it to my mother?'

'No, of course not! It was a gift.' Cecily looked indignant. 'Why do you ask these questions? I didn't want to give the wine away. That bottle was the finest thing I owned.' Her protest sounded wholly convincing to Janna.

It was time, now, to make Cecily answer the question that Janna should have asked her right at the very beginning. 'Tell me then, who is your lover?' she asked softly. She steeled herself to listen to Cecily's reply. What if she'd read the situation all wrong? What if, after all, Hugh's kindness and flattery had meant absolutely nothing?

'I cannot tell you that!' An obstinate scowl marred Cecily's fine features.

'I need to know. Believe me, it's very important. If you won't answer that, then tell me who you were expecting to meet when you got my message?'

The tiring woman stayed silent.

'Is this your usual meeting place?'

Cecily swallowed hard, but kept mute.

'You were expecting to meet your lover, weren't you! You were expecting to meet . . .'

Hugh, whose livelihood depended on his aunt's good opinion?

Or Robert, who stood to lose everything if Dame Alice discovered the truth?

'Robert of Babestoche.' Janna held her breath.

A shocked gasp was her only answer. Cecily glanced towards the door as if planning to escape. Janna's muscles tightened in anticipation of the need to stop her, should she try to flee. 'Tell me who you were expecting to meet here, Cecily!' she demanded.

No reply. In the silence, Janna heard soft scufflings, rustlings as tiny creatures went about their business. 'Listen,' she snapped, losing patience at last. 'I've risked everything to come and see you. Just answer my question. Or nod if I've got it right. You and my lord Robert have had an affair, yes?'

Cecily gave a reluctant nod. Janna felt her muscles relax. She began to breathe again.

'You told my lord you were expecting his child?'

This time the nod was accompanied by tears. Cecily buried her face in her hands.

'I know that what I did was wrong,' she said, 'but his kind words and compliments persuaded me that he cared for me, that he loved me. I know he does not love Dame Alice, for he spends little time in her company and much time seeking his pleasure elsewhere. I thought, when he wooed me, that he meant his loving words. I was wrong.' Her voice shook with desolation. 'When I told him I was with child, I expected him to rejoice at the news. Our own child, an expression of our love.' Unconsciously, Cecily's hands moved to stroke her stomach, to cradle the unborn baby that was no more. Tears coursed down her cheeks unheeded. 'Instead of welcoming a child to bless our union and seal our love, he was exceeding wrath with me. He bade me tell no-one of my condition.'

Now that she had started, the words gushed out in a flood. Cecily was finding relief in unburdening herself. 'While I waited for him to speak of love, he told me instead that I would have to leave, go somewhere safe, and that he himself would make the plans for it. I understood then that, while Robert takes his pleasure elsewhere, he will do nothing to upset Dame Alice or cause her to turn against him. He warned me that she must never find out about our liaison for, if she did, she would cast me out of the manor and I would have nowhere to go!' A tinge of bitterness crept into her tone. 'I suspect he fears that Dame Alice might take similar action against him as well. He greatly fears her wrath for she holds everything in her own right, as an inheritance from her family. Robert was but her steward before she married him.'

Fear. Cecily's words confirmed what Janna had suspected lay behind all that had happened. Fear of being found out. Fear of losing the comfort and privilege to which Robert had become accustomed.

Cecily raised a tear-stained face to Janna. 'I know now that what was between us is over. I was only ever a passing fancy for Robert, but I do not wish to leave Dame Alice and my home here. I know I have wronged ma dame, but she has been kind to me. She is the only family I have.'

Janna put a comforting arm around Cecily as she started to cry once more. Cecily's hopes and dreams were already shattered, but there was more to come. This final betrayal would likely destroy her altogether. Janna could only hope that Cecily was stronger than she looked. She searched for the words to break the news as gently as she could.

'You said the wine was a gift from Robert. What did he say when he gave it to you?'

'He said I looked ill. He said that he was worried about me. He bade me keep the wine for my own, and drink it down for it would give me strength and make me well again.' Cecily tossed her head. 'I know now that his only concern was to keep my condition a secret until he could send me away.'

'Was the bottle sealed when he gave it to you?'

'No, it was not.' Cecily looked faintly puzzled.

'Because it was not sealed, did you perhaps add anything to the wine before you gave it to my mother, special herbs perhaps, or maybe some honey to make it more palatable?' This was Cecily's final test, although Janna was already sure she knew the answer.

'No, there was no need. The wine of Normandy is very fine, whatever Dame Alice might say about it.'

A sudden vision rose before Janna: Robert pouring wine for Dame Alice. She had knocked the goblet from his hands, claiming that the wine was tainted. Before trying to poison his mistress, had Robert first tried to poison his wife? Janna tried to calm her agitation. She must not speak of it, at least not yet.

'This was not a fine wine,' she said softly. She put her hand on Cecily's arm to steady her. 'The wine that Robert gave you was mixed with monkshood. The poison was meant for you, Cecily.'

'No!' Cecily's howl of distress echoed around the empty barn.

'Robert meant *you* to drink the wine,' Janna said steadily. 'That was how he planned for you to leave Babestoche Manor. He knew his secret would be safe if you were dead.'

'No!' Cecily cried again, her voice catching in her throat. 'You are mistaken, Janna. Your grief over your mother's death will not let you believe that it was one of her own potions that poisoned her.'

Janna wondered if Cecily really believed that, or if she was merely trying to protect Robert, and herself, from the truth. She walked over to an empty barrel and reached inside to find the bottle she had secreted there. She held it out to Cecily for her inspection. 'This is the bottle that you gave to my mother, is it not? She took a sip or two, but she poured the rest away, recognising, I think, that there was something wrong with it. You told me that my mother called for a monk as she lay dying. You were wrong. She was trying to tell you that the wine was poisoned and that the poison was monkshood. She was trying to warn you that Robert wants you dead.'

'No! I don't believe you. Surely you are wrong!' The statement was uttered without conviction. The seeds that Janna had planted were now in full bloom.

'We never drank wine, my mother and I. Not being familiar with its taste, she would not have known at first that there was anything wrong with it. And so she drank enough to kill her,' Janna persisted. 'It seems that Dame Alice was more fortunate.'

'What do you mean?' Cecily looked puzzled as she tried to work out the apparent change of subject.

'You told me she said that the wine was tainted. I, myself, saw her knock to the floor the wine Robert poured for her.'

Cecily's face paled as she came to understand the full import of Janna's words. She reached out and took the bottle from her hands, and turned it over and over as if to fathom the secret it held. 'This was my gift from Robert,' she whispered, 'and yes, I defied him, I broke my promise of silence. I thought it was safe to do so. I thought if I could go to him afterwards and tell him that the danger had passed, he might relent and let me stay. Instead he berated me for going to your mother, even though I promised him that I'd never uttered his name with a single breath, and that no-one could connect my plight with him.'

Janna remembered the scene she'd witnessed between them in the hall. In truth, Cecily had been pleading to stay on at the manor. But instead of chastising her for leaving without permission, as Janna had supposed, Robert was in a rage because she'd involved Eadgyth in their affair. 'You have every reason to fear my lord Robert,' she warned. 'He lies behind everything that has happened. You see, he heard me ask Aldith if there was monkshood in the cordial she shared with my mother. After your confession, he knew exactly how and why my mother died, and he also knows that I do not believe she died by her own hand. To protect himself, he discredited me and did all in his power to stop me talking about my suspicions. That's why he incited the villagers to frighten me away and to burn my cottage. I'm sure he was delighted to learn that I'd died in the fire!'

'How could I have so misjudged him!' Cecily thrust the bottle back into Janna's hands.

Janna thought of the other young women who had visited her mother for the same reason as Cecily. 'You are not the first to be gulled by flattery and kindness,' she said, hiding a wry smile as she thought of Hugh.

'And because of it, your mother now lies dead.' Cecily shuddered. 'I am so sorry, Janna. Truly, I would rather have died in her place than bring her harm and cause you this grief. Yet I acted in all innocence, please, *please* believe that.'

'I do believe you. And I don't hold you responsible for my mother's death. The blame lies full square with my lord Robert, who has shown that he will stop at nothing to save his own skin.'

'How did you know he was my lover? How did you come to suspect him?'

'My lord Hugh told me how distressed Robert was when my mother took ill and he was summoned to Dame Alice's bedchamber. He thought it was because Robert expected to find Dame Alice at death's door, but I think it was the shock of seeing you alive and well when he thought he had silenced you for ever.'

In her distress, Cecily was tearing at the kerchief in her hand, ripping it into shreds. Janna felt deeply sorry for her, but she had come here to convince Cecily of the danger she faced if she stayed on at the manor. 'I thought nothing of it at the time,' Janna continued, determined that Cecily should know and understand everything. 'It was only when I added it to everything else that had happened, including the scene I witnessed between you and Robert and the subsequent action he has taken against me, that I understood who was behind all this.' No need to mention Hugh's name, she thought, feeling suddenly light-hearted that, for once, caution had kept her out of trouble.

'There were others I suspected guilty before I thought of my lord Robert,' she admitted, not wanting Cecily to get entirely the wrong idea about her powers of deduction. 'Aldith the midwife, the priest and Fulk the apothecary – they all had good reason to want my mother dead, and the means to bring it about. When I began to ask questions, I was forced to rule them all out for one reason or another, until only Robert was left. The kitchen maid confirmed that he knows where monkshood grows in the garden and is fully aware of how dangerous it is. His motive was to silence you, and he had the perfect opportunity to do it, except you gave his gift away and my mother died instead.'

Tears came into Janna's eyes. She hurriedly turned away so that Cecily would not see them. 'I must go,' she said. 'It's not safe for me to stay here. It's not safe for you either, mistress. You must leave this place, and quickly, before Robert tries once again to silence you.'

There was no response. Cecily was staring blindly at the bottle that had caused so much harm. Janna set it down on the earthen floor, and wiped her hands. 'You must flee,' she said again. 'You've escaped death for the moment, but you'll always be a threat to Robert while you stay here.'

'I doubt he'll try anything against me now,' Cecily said tiredly. 'The baby is lost so that danger is over. No-one would believe me if I was to speak out against him. He must think the secret of the wine is also safe, for the only witnesses were you and your mother. So far as he knows, his secret has gone to the grave with you.'

Janna shook her head. 'Even if you could be sure of your safety, mistress, it would surely be better for you to leave, to start a new life away from this place with its sad memories. Do you not have some kin you could go to, who would give you shelter and look after you?'

'I have no-one save Dame Alice. My father was her tenant, and she took me in when he died. I was only a child, but she was very kind to me.' Cecily's lips quivered. 'I have betrayed her kindness, I know, but I will not do so again, nor will I let any harm befall her.' She squared her shoulders and faced Janna. 'From now on, I will taste my lady's wine before she drinks it. Ma dame will not find it tainted again.'

Janna gave a reluctant nod. She respected Cecily's desire to make amends, but still she felt deep concern for the tiring woman. 'Just as I have assumed a new identity, so can you too.' She grasped Cecily's hand. 'Come away with me,' she urged. 'Come away to safety.'

'No.' New courage and conviction shone in Cecily's eyes. Janna understood that she would not be persuaded to run. She released Cecily's hand and stepped away. 'Then I beg you, for your own sake, to be careful,' she said. 'And for the safety of both of us, please keep your knowledge that I am alive to yourself, for Robert would have me dead – and you too, if it assures his safety.'

Cecily nodded sadly. 'I will keep a careful watch,' she said, adding, 'but it is not only Dame Alice who keeps me here. I fear what might become of me, should I leave. I have not your courage, Janna.'

Janna was startled by the admission. She gave a short laugh. 'It is not courage that accompanies my journey, it is hope. Besides, I have lost my home and all here wish me dead. I have no choice but to leave. But you, mistress, have more courage than you know.' And you will need it, she added silently. It would be hard for Cecily to face Dame Alice with the knowledge of her betrayal, but even harder to face Robert knowing that he had wanted her dead.

Cecily smiled faintly. 'I have an old kirtle that would fit you better than those grubby articles you wear. It would certainly suit you better! If you will but wait here, I can fetch it for you.'

'No.' Janna put out a hand to detain her. 'I am content with what I have.' It was not quite true. Her skin was beginning to itch; creatures seemed to have taken up residence in the dirty, sweat-stained smock and breeches she wore. The thought of a fine clean gown to wear was tempting beyond belief, but Janna was content with her new identity if not her clothes, and the clothes would wash. 'Do not trouble yourself about me, mistress,' she said. 'I am leaving now. You will not hear from me again.' She hoped that was not true, but her secret wish to return with her father and bring Robert to justice was not something Janna was prepared to share with Cecily. Noticing the tiring woman's obvious bewilderment, she explained further. 'Henceforth I mean to live as a youth, to have a youth's freedom as well as the safety of a new identity. Pray keep my secret if you value my life.'

'I will, I swear it.'

Janna thought she could trust the promise, for to reveal the secret would add greatly to the danger Cecily herself faced. 'Goodbye.' She wanted to wish Cecily luck and give her a hug, yet she was conscious of the differences in their station. Cecily had no such inhibitions, however. She threw her arms around Janna in a close embrace.

'May God go with you,' she said. 'I promise that your secret is safe with me.'

'In return, you must promise me that you will be careful. Don't trust Robert, don't trust him at all.'

'I promise.' Cecily released Janna. 'I am truly sorry about your mother,' she whispered. 'I will always wish that I had drunk that wine myself.'

Janna tried to say something, to comfort Cecily's troubled conscience, but she could not find the words. She swallowed over the large lump forming in her throat, and instead pressed Cecily's hand.

Cecily returned the pressure briefly. 'I must go before I am missed,' she said, and pushed open the door. Janna watched her walk away, and hoped that she would fare well and keep safe. She wished that she'd been able to change Cecily's mind. It would have been so good to have a friend, someone in whom to confide and to share things. Cecily had been kind to her. So had Godric and Hugh. Janna felt a great sadness as she realised she might never see any of them again. With an effort she shook off her melancholy. It was time for her to leave, and quickly, before the serfs returned with the beasts. She took a last look around the barn, reluctant to leave this illusion of shelter and safety.

The sight of the empty peg where once the smock and breeches had hung made her pause. So, too, did the empty bottle standing on the floor. She should find somewhere to hide all the evidence that might put her in danger, and Cecily too. About to pick up the bottle, a further thought stopped Janna. She left the bottle standing and picked up the silver coin instead. She placed it in her purse then pulled out the flint and steel she had secreted there. There was a way to hide everything and, at the same time, punish Robert of Babestoche for the harm he'd done. She might not be able to bring him to justice – not yet – but she had the means to pay him back in kind, just a little. She would do so, and gladly.

Safe in the shelter of the forest, Janna looked back at the leaping flames of the burning barn. They cast a great glow against the darkening sky, a golden glow the colour of revenge but also the colour of hope and of promise for the future. With a smile on her face, and courage in her heart, Janna turned and began to walk north through the trees.

Janna
Mysteries
BOOK TWO

Rue
FOR
Repentance

FELICITY PULMAN

RANDOM HOUSE AUSTRALIA

PROLOGUE

THE SCRAWNY, MUD-stained youth froze in his tracks. Someone was coming! He quickly snatched up the snare he'd been about to set, and slipped it down the front of his tunic. Should he be seen, he must seem innocent – but he would do all in his power to avoid being seen for it could mean the difference between his life or death.

Nervous, needing a hiding place, he scanned the forest. A sheltering screen of holly bushes nearby was his best, his only option. He raced towards them and, wincing, eased himself between the prickly leaves, trying not to shake or disturb them in any way, or make any sound that might betray his presence. Once safely inside his thorny cover, he peeped out to see who was on his trail.

Sometimes a guide came through the forest, leading a band of pilgrims, or perhaps a cleric or a nobleman, to safety. When that happened, laughter and chatter usually accompanied their passage, for the travellers would have permission to be in the forest and would be passing through on legitimate business. But this traveller moved silently, and therefore must be alone.

If it was the forester who pursued him, he was in deadly danger. Gravelinges was a royal forest and the king's forester patrolled it regularly to protect it from poachers, to make sure that there were always deer and wild boar for the king and his barons to hunt, as well as hares, rabbits and even fat doves. Anyone caught red-handed would be hauled to the forest court, where justice was summary and swift: if your life was not forfeit, at the very least your hands could be cut off, so Edwin had heard.

Edwin looked down at his hands. They were dirty but not blood-stained, at least not so far as he could see. To make sure, he wiped them across a patch of damp grass, then turned them over and wiped them again. He inspected them carefully. Cleaner now, but it was perfectly possible that there might still be blood under his fingernails, for he had killed and eaten while hiding out in the forest. Rabbits, hares and squirrels, voles, mice and birds – anything to fill his empty, aching belly and keep him alive just a little longer. He felt about him for a small twig and quickly began to scrape it under his cracked and broken nails in a vain effort to lift out the ingrained dirt. All the while he listened as the traveller came closer.

If not the forester, then who? The servants of his liege lord? Edwin's heart sank further as he pondered the possibility that he might have been traced here to the forest. Even now, he might be walking into a trap. He cowered lower in the prickly holly, trying to make himself invisible.

The walker was a youth, and he was alone. Even better, he seemed unarmed. Edwin cautiously eased some leaves aside so he could see the boy more clearly. His eyes narrowed in calculation as he weighed up the choice of staying hidden and taking his chances, or jumping the youth and catching

2

him by surprise. Whether he was here on legitimate business or was an outlaw, the boy might have something worth stealing. He might even have brought food and ale along for the journey. Edwin's mouth watered at the thought.

A fallen tree lay close behind him. Edwin reached out and quietly raised a branch that had broken away, testing its strength and weight. It would do. He had the advantage of surprise. A well-placed blow . . .

Edwin smiled to himself. His muscles tensed. Poised, ready to spring, something yet made him hesitate. He watched as the unsuspecting youth passed close to the holly bushes. The boy looked about him, his face open to scrutiny. 'Who's there?' he cried.

Edwin's eyes widened in surprise. His fingers relaxed their firm grip on the dead branch and his smile broadened. He settled deeper into his prickly hiding place to wait, to watch, and to make quite sure.

ONE

THE FIRST THING she needed, Janna decided, as she followed the faint trail that snaked through the forest, was to find a pool or stream to wash out her filthy clothes. Her lip curled in disgust as she looked down at the peasant's smock and breeches she wore. Men's garments, stolen from a barn at Babestoche Manor. Not only were they far too big for her, they were stained with sweat and dirt. In fact, they stank. She raised her arm to take a surreptitious sniff under her armpit, and nearly fainted from the powerful odour released by her action. Even worse than the smell was the fact that she was itchy all over. Something, or lots of little somethings, was living in her clothes. Janna felt her skin crawl. She longed to scratch her arms, her legs, her body, but she knew scratching would make the itches much worse. Better by far to find somewhere she could strip off and wash herself as well as the garments she wore. Even her eyebrows itched, while her scalp tickled with crawling creatures, real or imaginary.

If the dashing lord Hugh could only see her now! Janna shook her head as she tried to imagine his reaction. There had been admiration in his eyes when he'd looked at her in the past. Admiration, and perhaps something even more than that. But now . . .

Forget it! Forget him, she told herself sternly. Hugh thought she'd died in the fire that had consumed her cottage. Almost everyone thought she had died. Only two people knew she was still alive, but Janna trusted them not to betray her. It was better for her to be gone from sight. Safer. Meanwhile these clothes, these filthy garments, were part of her disguise, and she would have to endure them.

She quickened her pace. She knew not her destination, knew only that she was heading north in a desperate attempt to flee from those who had burned her home and who wanted to harm her. She had heard that this trail went north through the forest of Gravelinges to Wicheford on the other side. Her journey would not end there, but it would put the barrier of the forest between her and all those whom she had once thought of as friends. The thought of their treachery cast a dark shadow across Janna's heart.

The great canopy of branches high above turned the forest into a cool, green dimness. Only a few rays from the setting sun pierced the leafy shield, pebbling the path with coins of gold. Bright spongy moss coated tree roots, while sticky-footed ivy clung to dead and living trees alike, encasing them in ruffled coats of green. The soft groans and murmurs of wood pigeons gave way to an alarmed rattle of wings as they flew from Janna's approach. She felt as if she was walking through an enchanted wonderland, yet loneliness and sorrow walked beside her, step by step.

She scanned the silent forest for signs of water, and licked dry lips. She'd been walking for a long time. How much further did she have to go? Everyone knew that Gravelinges was enormous, but how big was enormous? Could she walk through the forest before nightfall, or was she already running out of time? She had no way of knowing where she was. Huge beech and oak trees towered above her, silent watchers in the dark forest, interspersed with birch, ash and hazel too, their summer green brighter than the dark patch of holly ahead. Janna shivered. The forest was a dangerous place to be, especially at night, when it became the demesne of wolves and other fierce creatures.

Her footsteps quickened, but then slowed again almost immediately. The trail was barely discernible in the dim light. She was further through the forest than she'd ever gone before, and could not rely on familiar landmarks to guide her. Janna was afraid that, in her hurry, she might misread her way, might become truly lost.

A faint rustle ahead froze her to a sudden stillness. Her heart thumped with fright. Slowly, her gaze sifted the landscape. There was a tall thicket of weeds in an open space ahead, which might give shelter to anything from a rabbit or deer to an outlaw. She watched for shaking leaves, for any signs of movement, but all was still now. Her gaze moved to the clump of holly bushes and then on and over the flat leafy cover spread beneath several huge oak trees.

Nothing moved. Janna turned slowly in a full circle, watching and listening. Then she took a few steps forward, pressing her feet carefully on grass and weeds so as not to make a noise, for she sensed now that she was not alone.

A silvery trilling set her heart leaping with fear. A pale yellow-grey wood warbler, flushed from cover, flew upwards.

7

She felt the stir of air from its flight on her cheek. Sweat prickled her shoulder blades. 'Who's there?' she cried, her voice high and wavering with fright. Too late, she recalled that she was wearing a man's clothes. 'Is anyone there?' she tried again, striving for a deeper tone.

Silence. Janna's ears stretched to hear a noise that wasn't her own. She could feel eyes watching her every move. She whirled abruptly, hoping to catch – what? Something animal – or human?

Janna swallowed hard, feeling again the sweat of fear as she recalled the last time she'd been lost in Gravelinges in the dark. She'd stumbled across the path of a wild boar. In her panic to escape she'd run in a circle around it, enraging it to such a degree that it had charged and charged again. If Godric hadn't been out poaching that night . . .

Godric. Janna's mind skittered hastily away from the image of the sturdy villein. She didn't want to think of Godric right now. He lay too heavily on her conscience for comfort.

No noise, no movement, save for the frightened thudding of her heart. Janna forced her legs to move once more, taking one reluctant step after another while she assessed her predicament. Wild animals didn't only come out at night, she reasoned, but if it was a wild animal stalking her now it would not trouble to conceal the noise of its passage. Which meant that the watcher must be human.

Perhaps it was the king's forester? Her mouth twisted in a grimace. She had only her feminine wiles to talk her way around the fact that she was trespassing in the royal forest, and she doubted they would be enough to save her – especially dressed as she was now! But if the forester was following her, surely he would have shown himself, would have challenged her just as soon as he noticed her?

Not the forester then. Could it even be Godric, who sometimes came through the forest on legitimate business, guiding people through to safety? Briefly, desperately, Janna wished that it might be Godric. In spite of feeling deeply ashamed, she longed to see him, longed for the comfort of his familiar presence. But she dared not call out again, for it was more likely that the silent watcher was an outlaw. Janna had heard frightening stories of those who fled the king's justice. They hid in forests and preyed on travellers, seizing whatever they might find and showing no mercy to any who would prevent them.

Icy fear pricked up her spine. God rot it, she thought, wishing she was safely home in her cottage with her mother and Alfred, her cat. She drew in a deep breath to steady herself. Her home, and those she loved, were gone, all gone. She was alone out here, with no kith or kin to comfort her and only her knife for protection. She drew it out of its sheath and, feeling slightly braver with a weapon in her hand, she began to walk on.

Her way became more open, the tree cover now quite sparse. Janna realised she was no longer climbing. She seemed to have reached the high point of the forest, for the open weedy growth ahead lay downhill before being swallowed into darkness under the trees. She walked towards it and looked about. It must be very late for the sun, always slow to disappear in the summer months, was now gone and the light was fading fast from the sky. Even if she hurried, Janna knew she could not get through the forest before nightfall.

Nor could she keep on walking for she would stray off the path. Already it was so faint as to be almost indiscernible. She'd heard tales of travellers who'd been lost in Gravelinges for days, weeks even. If they survived, they were half-mad with fear by the time they were rescued. Whatever else she did, she must not lose her way.

Should she then remain here through the night, and continue in the morning? She looked about her, feeling a shiver of unease. She shouldn't light a fire. Although the flames would bring warmth and a measure of protection from any wild animals that might be lurking nearby, they might also attract the attention of the king's forester. She couldn't risk that. Nor could she risk making a nest of grass out here in the open. If she slept on the ground she would be in danger from any wild creature, animal or human, large or small, that crossed her path. Better, perhaps, to wedge herself up in a tree for the night, she decided. It would be uncomfortable, but she would be in a position to protect herself; she would be safe.

With her knife, Janna drew a large and careful circle around her feet to mark the faint trail she was following, then cut a long staff of hazel and staked it in the centre so that she could see it from a distance. After a moment's thought, she pulled out her old kirtle, which she'd hidden under her smock, and tied it to the top of the stake. She stepped back and surveyed her handiwork. Her kirtle had been burnt to tatters in the fire. It was useless to her, but it made a good beacon. Besides, she no longer needed the disguise of a fat stomach, for anyone who met her from now on would be a stranger to her. Even if, by unlucky chance, she were to come across someone from her past, they shouldn't recognise her either. She was no longer Janna, daughter of the *wortwyf*, the herb wife who had died in mysterious circumstances. She was now a youth called John.

Janna nodded to herself, satisfied. With frequent glances at her home-made marker to prevent herself from roaming too far, she began a careful inspection. She was looking for a tree with a lot of branches to cradle her and keep her fast should she fall asleep and forget to hold on. She also kept a lookout for any sign of water, or even some juicy berries. Her stomach growled with hunger; her throat scratched with thirst. A few pale discs caught her eye. She pounced on the small puffball mushrooms, and inspected them carefully before peeling them and stuffing them into her mouth. They were still white and tender enough to eat raw. Although they'd be better stewed, they brought saliva into her mouth and helped to fill her hollow belly.

Janna tried to ignore her discomfort, ignore too the itches that plagued her, and the tickling, biting midges that swarmed around her face. But she could not ignore the uneasy sense that she was not alone. If the watcher was human, it seemed he was in no hurry to accost her. Perhaps he intended to wait until she fell asleep?

Janna's heart thumped hard and heavy in her chest. She found it difficult to catch her breath. I'll stay awake all night, she promised herself, and gripped her knife more tightly as she searched for a tree with branches reaching down low enough for her to haul herself up. There was a thicket of yew ahead, a dark, dense tangle of knitted branches and spindle leaves. Her mother's voice came into her mind: 'Yews are

11

ancient and sacred trees. The druids built their temples nearby, believing them to be sites of burial and resurrection.' Janna took a step towards them, then stopped as she remembered her mother's warning.

'The fruits and seeds are highly poisonous, so you must be careful, Janna. Stay away from them, if you can. They're otherworld, and they're dangerous.'

The trees rose before her like a solid wall; she could not penetrate their depths. They would make a perfect hiding place. Could she risk it? It wasn't as if she was planning to eat any part of them! Then Janna remembered what else she'd been told: that faeries believed that yews had the power to make them invisible, and used yew to conjure up a darkness in which they might disappear. Janna, too, sought to disappear; she hurried over to them and eased herself into their sheltering arms.

Climbing was so much easier wearing breeches, she realised, as she pulled herself upwards from branch to branch. In fact, just about everything was so much easier for a man than a woman!

When she could no longer see the ground below, she judged she was high enough to be unobserved, and secure enough to defend herself should anyone climb up and attack her. She wedged her body into the interlacing branches, and hooked her arms around them for safety. It was almost completely dark now. She couldn't see anything other than her immediate cover, but she knew her home-made beacon was close enough for her to find in the morning.

With a sigh, she closed her eyes, then quickly snapped them open. She must not go to sleep. She touched the purse at her waist, heard a faint crumple of parchment and the clink of coins. Everything she owned that was of value to her was in her purse, including her journey's purpose: the clues that might lead her to her father.

With the last of the light gone, the night became cold. A light rain began to fall. Janna pulled the hood of the gorget over her head, and huddled deeper into her prickly shelter in a vain effort to stay dry. The rain kept on, soaking through the gorget as well as her smock and breeches. It was too gentle to cleanse the filthy garments or drown the creatures that tormented her with their biting, but it was persistent enough to chill her to the bone. Janna shivered, and debated climbing down from her tree. She was cramped from crouching among the branches. If she walked about, her blood would flow freely once more and she might get warm.

If she wandered about in the dark, she might also get attacked! She would certainly get lost. Janna stayed where she was, and continued to shiver as she listened to the sounds of the forest at night: the haunting call of an owl overhead; the scuffle of a scavenging badger below and, in the distance, the anguished howl of a wolf. Secretive rustles betrayed the hunters; squeaks of distress marked their prey.

The night wore on, black and dismal, all trace of moon and stars hidden behind dense cloud. In spite of her best efforts, Janna's eyes closed. She slept, jerked awake, and slept again.

When she next awoke, the sky was beginning to lighten with dawn, and the birds of the forest were celebrating the birth of a new day with chirps and cheeps, trills of interrogation, whistles, and snatches of songs. Janna rested quietly for a moment, listening to their conversations. But her body felt numb with cold; she was desperate to get down from her tree. Her limbs were cramped and stiff and, as she clambered downwards, she slipped off a rain-slicked branch and crashed through prickly foliage to land with a thump on the ground. She groaned with the pain of it. A brief vision of her home flashed into her mind: the fire warming and lighting the small cottage, the fragrance of dried herbs, hot griddle cakes and rich vegetable pottage, her mother's busy efficiency, and Alfred's welcoming purr . . .

Tears came into Janna's eyes. She felt once more the wrenching grief of her mother's death, an aching sense of loss. There was also the added frustration of knowing that her mother had been on the brink of divulging the secret of her father's identity, a secret Janna could never know now unless she could find out what was in the letter she carried. But for that, she would need to be able to read, and that was something Eadgyth hadn't taught her. Janna thought about the parchment, with its undecipherable marks. Only the name at the end meant anything to her. John. It was her father's name, she was sure of it. She burned with curiosity to know what he had written to her mother. Eadgyth had loved him, she knew that now, yet his words had been enough to make her mother pack up and run, and keep his identity for ever a secret.

Janna came back to the present, becoming aware of her surroundings once more. She choked back a sob. She was lonely and frightened. Yet she knew that somehow she must find the strength to carry on, for she'd made a vow to herself: to seek her unknown father and, with his help, bring the man guilty of the murder of her mother to justice. So she scrubbed the tears from her cheeks with a grubby hand, then eased herself up into a sitting position and carefully massaged the base of her sore spine. She stretched out her legs, rotating first one foot and then another. Satisfied that nothing was broken after her fall, she stood up then, and walked over to the stake she had left as a marker. She pulled it from the ground, removed her bundled kirtle and threw it into the shelter of a clump of bushes. The stake she kept, for it gave her an extra weapon to protect herself, should she need it.

Remembering her sense that she was being watched, she glanced about, searching for signs. A sudden crackle of twigs set her heart leaping into her throat. She backed behind a tree, then realised the noise came from a grazing deer. Fascinated, Janna stood still, watching it. Its belly was swollen, reminding her that the fence month might already have begun, the time when the forest was forbidden to everyone so that the does might drop their fawns and nurture them in safety. She had to get out of the forest as soon as she could.

The doe stepped on delicate feet towards Janna, head bent as it nibbled grass, lulled into a sense of safety by Janna's stillness. She extended a cautious hand towards it. 'Tck, tck, tck,' she called softly. Startled, it jerked its head up and surveyed her with liquid brown eyes. Then it bent its head once more, and resumed feeding. She smiled at it, feeling a sense of peace as she contemplated the creature's innocence and trust.

She tiptoed past it, fighting her reluctance to leave the safety of this open space for the dense forest that lay ahead of her. She must get through the forest today. Not for anything would she spend another night like the one she'd just passed.

She walked on and under the sheltering trees, then stopped, unsure now if she was on a path at all, for the way ahead seemed unmarked and undisturbed. She looked upwards, hoping to determine her direction by the position of the sun, but the forest had closed over her head and the sky was barely visible. Hastily she retraced her steps, and felt relief as she reached the clearing once more. She tilted back her head to find the sun, but dark clouds banked thick across the sky; there was no trace of golden radiance. Even as Janna glanced about, rain began to fall once more, soaking through her already wet clothes. 'Hell's breath,' she muttered miserably, knowing that she would give up almost anything if it would buy her food and shelter. She longed to be free of the forest. Its silence oppressed her.

To stand still was to give in to despair. Janna began to prowl around the open space, trying to bring life to her chilled feet and limbs. She looked down at her leaking boots, wishing she had wooden pattens to protect them. While she paced about, she pondered what to do. Finally, she shrugged. She couldn't follow the path home, for she had no home any more nor was there anyone in the village willing to give her shelter. It seemed she had no choice but to try to find her way through the forest. She walked back to where she'd left the trail, but there was no sign of it now. Fear almost paralysed her. It took all her strength not to open her mouth and scream for help in the hope that someone, anyone, be he forester or outlaw, would come to her aid.

She curled her hands into fists, feeling her nails dig into her palm. The pain helped to calm her. Breathe, she thought, remembering Eadgyth's instructions to a panicky patient.

She took a slow, deep breath, feeling time pass as the cold air sucked through her nostrils and down into her chest. Slowly, she expelled her breath through her mouth, blowing it out in a thin stream. It looked like smoke from a fire in the chill morning.

After several more breaths, and feeling slightly calmer, she looked about her, seeking signs. But there were none. 'Just keep going along the edge of the clearing,' she told herself. 'The path must be here somewhere. Have patience, and you'll find it.'

Step by cautious step, she began to circle the open space. A new thought alarmed her now. How would she be able to tell the difference between the track she'd come from and the track that would lead her to where she wanted to go?

Without warning, her foot slipped from under her and she slid down through layers of leaves, down into icy cold water. It sucked up around her, filling her boots and making her gasp for breath. Speechless with shock, Janna flailed about until she found her footing. She realised then that in fact the water came only to her thighs.

She looked about her at the great, leaf-filled depression in which she stood, and decided that she must have fallen into a large and ancient dewpond. She tried to step out, but slimy mud, formed from the detritus of the centuries, held her boots fast. Janna stood on one foot and leaned on her staff to help her balance while she wriggled her other foot until she'd managed to work her boot free. She took off the boot and threw it to safety, then cautiously lowered her bare foot to the bottom of the pond. She shuddered as it sank deep through the icy slime. She wriggled her booted foot, tugging hard until the sucking mud released it. A second boot joined its companion on the leafy bank. With a gasp of fear, Janna suddenly snatched up her purse and opened it, belatedly understanding the danger if the precious parchment inside had got wet.

The outside of the purse was damp, but its contents were dry. Janna released her breath, uttering a quiet 'thank you' to whoever might be listening. She flung the staff onto dry ground, and untied her girdle. Purse and girdle followed the staff and boots to safety. Time now to attend to her greatest need: water! She scooped twigs and leaves out of her way, bent her head and began to drink, relishing the icy wetness in her dry mouth and parched throat. She drank until she could drink no more, but now another idea had come into her mind. She was already wet and uncomfortable. She had nothing to lose save the family of biting creatures that inhabited the garments she wore. With a quick glance around her to make sure that she was alone, she gingerly lowered her body deeper into the water. Anchoring herself in the freezing mud, she stripped off the stolen gorget and smock, untied her breeches, and gave them all a good scrub before dressing herself once more. The gorget came last, but the hood clung cold and wet around her head and water dripped into her eyes. She took it off and cast it out onto the grass.

Remembering the itches, she ducked her head under and massaged her fingers through her hair, giving it a thorough rinse in the freezing water. She could feel the strangeness of its short stubble, all that was left after the ravages of the fire and her efforts to trim it short with her knife. At last, when she was satisfied that every little creature must be drowned, she felt her way towards the rim of earth that circled the large leafy basin. A memory teased her mind. Godric had told her about the ancient road built through the forest by the Romans. Could this dewpond have been fashioned to provide water for the soldiers and merchants who had once traversed this land?

Something sharp pierced Janna's foot, and she cried aloud, forgetting for the moment her need for secrecy. She raised her foot above the water, and frowned as she inspected it. The tender skin of her instep was cut and bleeding. What could have been so sharp that it had pierced her skin like that? Not a flint, surely, but a sword perhaps, or a dagger? Janna knew that such things were sometimes found in water. She'd heard that it was once a custom for the ancients to throw their weapons into rivers and pools in order to propitiate the gods and seek good fortune. Coming across a pool in a huge forest such as this must in itself have seemed like good fortune to the old ones. They might well have shown their gratitude with costly gifts.

She took a deep breath and ducked down, carefully feeling through the icy mud for something sharp. Her own knife was quite small, no match for a wild animal or an outlaw. The staff she'd found was better than nothing, but with a real weapon in her hand she would feel much, much safer.

Janna's lungs were bursting. She shot upwards and gasped for air, greedily sucking it in. Her teeth chattering, she was tempted, so tempted, to get out of the pool. Instead, she forced herself to take another deep breath and duck down into the darkness. She groped about in the slimy mud. Nothing. She surfaced once more, her whole body shaking with cold. One last time, she promised herself, and filled her lungs with air.

This time her search was rewarded. Janna felt the blade's sharpness bite into her hand. She snatched it back, then cautiously stretched out her fingers, feeling inch by careful inch until at last she touched the blade again. Her chest was on fire. She was desperate to take a breath but she stayed down, carefully patting along the flat of the blade until she came to the solid shape of its hilt. She closed both hands around it and tugged, feeling the sword slide free. She shot up, breaking the surface with a triumphant whoosh of escaping air. She breathed deeply, savouring the air's freshness, and looked down at the muddy object in her hands.

It was longer than a dagger, but shorter than the swords worn by noblemen such as the lord Hugh. Part of the hilt was broken off, but there was enough left for her small hand to grasp the weapon. She swished it around in the water, carefully breaking off lumps of caked mud and grit and rinsing it clean. The blade was rusty, its sheen dulled from its long immersion in the water. But it was sharp enough to inflict a grievous wound, Janna realised, as she gingerly put her foot to the ground and limped out of the dew pond.

Wiping her injured foot clean, she eased it into her boot. She put on her other boot, picked up the gorget and looked about for her purse and girdle. There was no sign of them. Janna frowned and looked more carefully, unable to understand the significance of their disappearance. Where could they be?

Panic constricted her chest. She began to search frantically, thinking she must have misread the direction in which
she'd thrown them. Perhaps they'd slid beneath a bush or
got buried somewhere in long grass and bracken? She
scoured the clearing, widening the area of her search to poke
into banks of tall nettles and patches of flowering weeds,
although she knew in her heart that she'd not mistaken the
direction. They had gone. Someone must have been there all
along, watching her, waiting for just this opportunity to steal
from her the only clues she had that might lead her to her
father.

TWO

J ANNA BOWED HER head as a wave of grief and loss swept over her. She had so little, yet even this had been taken from her. A few silver pennies – yes, they might be of use to a desperate vagabond, as might the ring and brooch if he could trade them. But, for Janna, the real value of the contents of her purse lay in the parchment she'd carried, the letter she'd found from her unknown father. She was sure the letter was the key to everything, if only she could read it. Would an outlaw be able to read? Janna doubted it. He'd surely keep the other things, but would he perhaps throw away the letter, thinking it worthless?

A faint glimmer of hope lifted Janna's spirits. If she could only follow in the thief's footsteps, perhaps she might find the parchment discarded along the track. She looked about her once more, this time seeking the shelter nearest to where she'd cast her boots from the pond. The thief must have hidden somewhere while he watched her and waited to pounce. He might well have left some signs of his passage.

A dense thicket of hazel stood close by. Gripping the sword tight in her hand, she headed towards it. She examined the trees carefully, as well as the ground surrounding them, in case there were any signs to be seen: a thread snagged on a withy perhaps, or bruised and broken herbage. Her search was rewarded by the sight of a footprint indented in a patch of soft earth. Another print followed, leading away from the thicket. Janna stepped forward in the same direction, alert for any further clues to point her way.

Several times she thought she'd come to a dead end, but she trusted her instincts and kept on, following the most obvious route through the trees. Although she constantly checked the ground around her, there was no sign of her father's letter. But scuffed moss, a broken twig, some flattened grass or herbs, a sliver of snagged bark all helped to point the way. She placed her feet lightly, carefully, while words repeated in her mind like a prayer: 'Please let him throw away the parchment. Please let me find my father's letter.'

She found herself now in a dense patch of the forest, hazel and holly hedged by a wall of prickly brambles. There seemed no way through. Baffled, Janna stopped and looked around her. Then she stepped forward for a more careful inspection. Every instinct told her she was close to her quarry, but the brambles barred her way. Or did they? Here they were bent one way, there another, cunningly plaited to disguise a thin and twisting passage through. Quiet as a hunting owl, Janna eased herself to the left then to the right, pushing deeper into the prickly heart of the brambles, until suddenly a small clearing opened before her. She walked into it, then hastily slid sideways behind the trunk of a large beech for concealment. She could see the thief clearly. She gripped the sword tighter and watched him.

He was sitting with his back to her. Janna saw a faint glimmer of light as he held the gold ring up high to inspect it. Her other treasures lay on the ground in front of him. Clearly, he was gloating over his day's work.

A wave of rage coursed through her, as fierce, as white hot as the blazing sun. Without thought, she launched herself towards him, arm raised and sword at the ready to strike him flat with the blade and, if necessary, run him through. How dare he take her treasures, how dare he!

Swift and silent as she was, still the young man heard her and jerked upright to face her. His upraised arm deflected the sword's blow. The blade missed the side of his head and hit him flat against the wrist instead. He grunted with pain but was still able to grab her wrist and wrench the sword from her grasp, flinging it safely out of range. Enraged, Janna swung back her foot and kicked out, aiming for his groin, hoping to cripple him with pain. But she was too slow and he read her mind. Just as her foot came forward, he released her and jumped nimbly out of her way after giving her a shove so that she lost her balance and fell. Before he had time to flee, she launched herself at his ankles and tugged, pulling him down on top of her. She rolled free and raked his face with her nails. 'Devil's spawn!' she gritted through her teeth. She began to pummel him with her fists. 'Dog's droppings! Pond slime!'

She kept up the attack, feeling proud of the fact that she was getting the better of the rogue, until she realised he was making no effort to defend himself. Instead, he'd curled into a ball to present the smallest target to her flailing arms and fists.

'You can stop hitting me, mistress. I won't harm you,' he muttered. As she understood the import of his words, shock stopped Janna mid-blow. Wide-eyed, she jumped to her feet and snatched up the sword, ready now to grab her treasures and run.

'H-how did you know I was a girl?' she stammered.

His face reddened slightly. He grinned at her, but did not answer. Janna felt her own face redden as she worked out how he'd managed to fathom her secret. 'You watched me bathe, you . . . you bastard, damn you to hell!' She closed her eyes as she remembered how she'd stripped off and washed both herself and her clothes. Mortified, she lashed out once more.

He took a hasty step out of her reach. 'I turned my back to you as soon as I realised what you were. Who you are!' he protested.

Janna wondered whether she could believe him. It was certain that he'd seen enough to know the truth! She comforted herself with the thought that mostly she'd crouched down in the water to wash, and that she'd both undressed and dressed in the pond. She remembered then the rustles she'd heard the night before, her sense that she was being watched. She eyed the youth warily. He hadn't harmed her – not yet. But that didn't mean he might not try in the future.

'Why are you wearing men's clothes anyway?' he asked, his grin returning as he commented, 'Certes they don't become you, nor do they fit you very well!'

'They do well enough.' To prove her words, Janna tugged on the cord holding her breeches in place to tighten it, then hitched the breeches higher so she no longer trampled the fabric underfoot. 'And don't change the subject either!' she flashed, recalling the reason she had followed him. She bent and snatched up the ring which the young man had let fall in the surprise of the attack, and hastily shoved it into the purse that lay on the ground nearby, hearing the comforting crump of parchment as she did so. The brooch and silver coins had also been dumped on the grass. They swiftly followed the ring to safety. Janna straightened then, and subjected the thief to a defiant glare, ready to spring at him once more to protect what was rightfully hers.

He held up his hands in a gesture of peace. 'I'm sorry,' he muttered. 'I . . . I have nothing save the clothes I am wearing. I was going to use what I stole from you to travel somewhere safe, to find shelter and buy food. But I won't try again, I promise.'

'Why are you here in the forest?' Janna demanded, not in the least mollified by his explanation. 'What are you hiding from?'

'Why are *you* here?' He turned the question back on her. 'What are *you* hiding from?'

Janna was silenced, but only for a moment. 'I asked first,' she muttered.

A grin stole over his face once more. 'I'll make a bargain with you. I'll tell you my story if you'll tell me yours,' he said. He waited for her grudging nod before continuing. 'I am on the run from my lord. He's a cruel man, cruel as the devil. He beat me.' The youth touched his dirty face. Janna saw a jagged scar on his chin, and winced in sympathy.

'I ran away 'cos I decided I'd rather live as an outlaw than stay at the mercy of that swine,' the youth continued. 'I've been hiding here in the forest ever since, catching whatever I may to eat, and drinking water from that pool you fell into.'

'How long have you been here?' Janna strove to keep any hint of warmth from her voice, lest he believe she might take pity on him and share with him her treasures.

'I don't know the time in days exactly, but I reached the forest as the trees were just coming into bud from their winter sleep. I think it must be mid-summer now?'

Janna nodded. 'Close enough. The fence-month may well have started already. You must certainly leave the forest as soon as possible, as must I.'

'Why?'

''Tis the time when the does give birth to their fawns. The forest is forbidden to all at that time so that mothers and their babies are not disturbed. 'Tis a dangerous time to hide here, for the forester will be on constant watch to protect the king's deer for the hunting season to come.'

The young man nodded thoughtfully. 'I'll have to take my chances. I can't leave until the seasons turn full circle.'

'Why?' Now it was Janna's turn to ask the question.

'If I can stay hidden for a year and a day, I shall have earned my freedom from my lord.' He grinned ruefully. 'That's if I can stay alive for that long.'

In spite of her best efforts, Janna felt some sympathy for the ruffian. His story touched her. So, too, did the realisation that, although he'd stolen her purse, he'd made no effort to harm her, or keep her goods once she'd tracked him down. She, too, had stolen something: the clothes she wore, and from a poor peasant who could ill-afford to lose them. She was in no position to judge what anyone might do when pushed to the limit of need. 'What will you do after a year and a day?' she asked.

The young man shrugged. 'I would like to become an apprentice, to learn a trade, but I have not the money for that. So I will do anything at all that might help me earn my bread and keep.'

'No-one will give you work and shelter once they know you're a runaway serf,' Janna pointed out.

'They will if they think I've come from Wales. That's what I'll tell them. They won't care who my lord was, so long as I show willing and work hard.' The youth flexed his muscles. 'I am strong,' he boasted, 'and I can turn my hand to anything I'm asked to do. I'll have no trouble finding someone to take me in, I promise you.'

Janna nodded thoughtfully, while her mind ticked over in a tumble of ideas. If she helped him, so too might he help her. She held out her hand. 'My name is Johanna, but I'm known as Janna,' she said. 'I, too, am in hiding. That's why I'm dressed like this. I call myself "John", for he was my father – a man of wealth and importance,' she added proudly.

The youth nodded. He relaxed his wary stance, sprawling back against the grass. 'My name is Edwin.'

'If you come from Wales, shouldn't you should call yourself by a Welsh name? Hoel or Gwyn, something like that?'

'Edwin, Hoel, it makes no matter so long as they believe I'm a free man from across the border.' He shrugged, and patted the grass beside him. 'Sit down,' he invited. 'I won't hurt you.'

Not taking any chances, Janna hooked the purse onto her girdle, and tied the girdle firmly around her waist. Then she sat down as she was bid, sword close at hand, keeping a careful distance from Edwin.

28

'So where are you bound? And why are you hiding?' he prompted.

Janna took a deep breath, hardly knowing where her story should start. With the fact that her cottage was burnt to the ground and she was homeless? Or a few days before then, when the nightmare first began?

'I am Janna, daughter of Eadgyth the *wortwyf*,' she said. 'My mother used her knowledge of herbs to heal the sick. Just a few days ago, she was called on to physic the lady of Babestoche Manor, Dame Alice, and her newborn babe.' She paused, debating whether or not she should tell Edwin how her mother had also looked after Cecily, one of Dame Alice's tiring women, and how Eadgyth had drunk the poisoned wine that was meant for Cecily.

'My mother taught me all she knew, but she is dead,' Janna continued, choosing her words carefully. 'She died in mysterious circumstances, and I have sworn to avenge her death and bring the culprit to justice. But I need my father's help for this. Although I know who caused my mother's death, I cannot accuse the man for he is all-powerful whereas I am but a humble outcast. So now I'm going in search of my father.' She patted the purse at her waist. 'My mother never told me who he was, but I hope that this letter and these pieces of jewellery will help me find him.'

'No wonder you took after me in such a fury!' Edwin gave her a rueful smile. 'I'm sorry,' he said again, adding, 'But why do you dress like a youth and travel in such secrecy?'

Janna sighed. 'The man responsible for my mother's death turned the villagers against me. They burned my cottage to the ground, thinking I was in it. It is safer for me if everyone thinks I died in the blaze, but just in case anyone sees me . . .' She swept a hand down her body, indicating the clothes she wore.

Edwin's lips pursed in a silent whistle. He regarded Janna thoughtfully for a moment. 'It seems to me that, if we can't stay here in the forest, we should journey together. We might be able to help each other,' he ventured.

Janna nodded in agreement. 'Your lord searches for a lone runaway, while you understood what I was quickly enough.' She slid a sideways glance at him, and he reddened once more.

'Yea, well I was in a . . . a position to see more of you than most,' he said, shame-faced.

'Than any man has ever seen before,' Janna said tartly. 'Had you not seen what you saw, would you say I could pass for a youth?'

He looked her fully in the face now. He was taller than her, and Janna noticed that he was also a little older than her own sixteen years. His face was comely rather than handsome, and he had an attractive smile. She noticed the scratches on his dirty brown cheek, freshly made and dappled with beads of blood. She, too, had left her mark on Edwin. 'You should wash those scratches,' she said. 'I'll find some herbs that will help them heal.' She felt sympathy for the mistreated youth, but she would not say sorry; she wasn't quite ready to forgive him yet.

He nodded his thanks. 'You dress like a man,' he said then, 'but you walk and talk like a girl.' He jumped to his feet, put a hand on his hip and took a few mincing steps.

Janna was surprised into laughter. 'I do not!' she protested.

'You laugh like one, too.'

Janna gurgled into silence. 'I can't dress like a girl,' she pointed out, making her voice purposely deep. 'These clothes I'm wearing are all that I own.'

'That's better,' he approved. 'And if you walk like so . . .' He began to stride about, his arms loose and swinging freely by his side. Janna scrambled up and began to copy him, walking first beside him and then in front, so that he could watch her.

'Like this?' she asked.

He grinned at her. 'You fight like a girl, too.' He gently touched his scratched face with his dirty hand.

Janna kept silent, refusing to feel guilty for protecting what was rightfully her own.

'If you're going to live as a boy, you'll need to learn how to defend yourself in a fight. You haven't the strength to fight fair, but your instinct was right.' Edwin patted his groin. 'A hard kick here will cripple your attacker and give you time to run like the devil himself. But you were too slow. I knew exactly what you had in mind.' He forked two fingers and, before Janna had a chance to react, he stabbed them towards her eyes. 'You could also try to blind your opponent like this, or . . .' Edwin's fingers closed together. 'You can use your hand to break his nose, or his neck.' His hand became a blade as he chopped up towards Janna's nostrils and then sideways at her throat. She felt the side of his fingers slam hard against her skin, and swallowed involuntarily.

'Hit hard, hard as you can. And be quick, you have to take your enemy by surprise,' Edwin continued. 'But what will you do if he comes from behind you?' Giving Janna no time to reply, he ducked behind her and grabbed her, pinning her arms to her side and holding her close to his chest. With a startled cry, she tried to fight him off. 'What will you do then?' he whispered. His breath blew warm against her ear. She felt a deadly fear as she realised she was powerless in his grasp.

Still he held her, while she struggled uselessly in his grip. He gave a small huff of amusement and continued to hold her tight. The sound enraged Janna and she increased her efforts, but to the same end. She could not get away from him.

'You stamp down on my foot. Hard,' he told her. As Janna's knee came up he released her suddenly, and skipped away out of danger. 'Don't signal your actions,' he warned. 'And don't give your enemy any chance to escape.'

Janna nodded slowly. Suddenly, she sprang towards him. Her fingers stopped a hair's breadth from his eyes.

'Yea, that's it. Now go practise on someone else!'

Janna scowled at him. Her heart was still racing after the fright he'd given her. Unrepentant, he grinned back. 'You'll do, John – so long as you remember who and what you are!'

'I'll remember.' She squeezed her fingers together and tried a few practice chops at the air, pretending that she was aiming at an opponent's neck. And his nose. Her fingers formed into a V to stab at unseen eyes. For good measure, she stamped down hard on an imaginary foot.

Edwin craned his head back to look up through the green veil of leaves. 'There's not enough sunlight to tell which direction we should walk in,' he said. 'Do you know the way through the forest?'

'No.' Janna's face fell. 'I lost the path at that clearing by the pool.' She looked about her. 'I have no idea where we are now.'

'We're at the place I've made my home.' He jerked a thumb behind him. Looking past him, Janna noticed a small shelter fashioned from branches and stuffed with mud and leaves. Longer branches were laid on top of the primitive walls to form a rough roof; they were covered with a layer of reeds for extra protection. She had to look hard to see the shelter, for it was almost indistinguishable from the surrounding forest. It would give Edwin some cover from rain, but was too small for anyone to live in any comfort. Nearby was a small circle of blackened flints, with three branches meeting at a point above the space in the middle. Janna realised she was looking at Edwin's fireplace.

'What do you do for food? Do you have any?' she asked, suddenly ravenous.

Edwin shuffled his feet, looking shifty. 'I trap small creatures with this,' he admitted, pulling a snare of plaited fibres from the front of his tunic. 'I cook them and eat them.'

Janna felt juices seep into her mouth. 'I'm so hungry,' she said. 'Do you have anything we can eat now?'

'No.' He smiled slightly. 'I could offer you some water, but I saw you drink your fill in the pool.'

'You have water? And something to cook in?' Janna's gaze flicked around the forest floor, settling on several plants of interest to her.

Edwin nodded.

'Then light the fire,' Janna instructed. 'Before we go anywhere, I'll make us a pottage of herbs to fill our bellies for the journey.'

'We can't, not in daylight! The smoke will betray us.' Edwin cast a nervous glance about him.

Janna hesitated. Her stomach growled with hunger. She was famished. 'Let's risk it,' she said. 'The forester is probably miles away, and even if he does see the smoke we'll be gone before he can track its source.' Not giving Edwin a chance to protest, she drew out her knife and hurried towards a clump of nettles. She kept an eye on Edwin's movements as she plucked the nettles by the stem and carefully cut away the stinging leaves. A patch of chickweed drew her on, and she harvested a handful of green shoots before moving over to gather some dandelions and a snippet of wild garlic to add flavour. Although her treasures were safe in her purse, she still wasn't sure how far she could trust the young outlaw. It was true that they might be able to help each other; nevertheless, Janna reminded herself to be wary, to stay on guard just in case she'd misread his intentions. So she watched him.

His boast had not been an idle one, she thought, as she recalled how powerless she'd been in his grip. In a fair fight between them, he would be the winner. He was taller, and he had a wiry strength that became evident as he wrestled with a dead branch to break it up for kindling. The fire laid and the tinder struck to light it, he poured some water from a crudely fashioned jug into a small iron pot and hooked it over the flames to boil.

Reassured that they had a common purpose, Janna ventured further, looking for mushrooms to add bulk to the brew. She couldn't find any more puffballs, but a few oyster mushrooms fanned out from a rotting tree stump and she gathered those, along with some late white mushrooms that nestled in an open grassy patch. She inspected them carefully for insects and to make sure they were truly an edible variety and not any poisonous look-alike. Satisfied that they were sound, and that she'd gathered enough to satisfy their hunger, she searched now for a bird's nest. Some eggs, or even some berries, would make a welcome addition to this most basic of broths. The nests were empty and berries still unripe, but she espied something even better. Janna smiled with antici-pated pleasure as she hurried towards the big white splats of lacy elderflowers peeping through the green cover. She held up the front of her smock like an apron, and dropped in what she'd already gathered, then cut several elderflowers to add to her collection, finally circling back towards the fire-place. The pot hung over the fire, steam rising in the cold air, but there was no sign of Edwin. He had vanished.

With a sinking feeling, she looked about for him. 'Edwin?' she called softly, remembering to keep her voice pitched low. 'Where are you?'

There was no response. 'All the more for me, then,' Janna muttered, trying to keep up her spirits. Carefully laying aside the elderflowers, she threw the mushrooms and plants into the pot and, shivering, stepped closer to the fire to warm herself and dry her clothes. All sympathy for the outlaw had gone along with his disappearance. Beaten by his lord indeed, she thought, as she recalled the scar on his chin. Got that in a free fight more like, probably while he was trying to steal from someone else!

A slight rustle set her fumbling for her knife. She whirled around, frantically trying to recall the moves Edwin had taught her. The eyes. The nose. The neck. The foot.

As she saw who it was, she relaxed. Wearing a proud grin, Edwin strode forward and dangled a limp furry form in front of her nose.

'Erk! What's that?' Janna jumped backwards.

'A leveret.' He set down the hare and pulled out his knife.

'But it's only a baby!' Janna protested.

'That's right. I found it lying in a clump of grass.' Edwin looked down at his prize. 'It must have been ailing or I wouldn't have caught it.' He began to strip the fur from the small body.

Janna shuddered, but she didn't stop him when he threw the leveret into the broth. He peered in after it, and sniffed suspiciously. 'That's poisonous.' He pointed at one of the mushrooms.

'No, it's not.'

'I don't eat fungus. It can kill you.'

'I know. You have to be careful. But that's a white mushroom, and there are also some oyster mushrooms. They're quite safe.'

Edwin looked at Janna. 'How do I know you're not trying to poison me?' he muttered.

'You don't,' Janna said cheerfully, 'but you don't have to eat them if you don't want. I'm hungry enough for both of us.' She offered him an elderflower. 'Have one.' She stuffed the sweet lacy flower into her mouth and chewed it with relish.

Edwin took a cautious bite, looking dubious. Then he licked his lips in appreciation, and quickly scoffed up the rest. It seemed he'd decided to trust her after all. Janna smiled to herself, and picked up another flower.

They ate the pottage with their fingers, taking pleasure from the hot food. It went some way to settling the ache of hunger in their stomachs. Even the hare was shared between them, although Janna tried to close her mind against what she was eating as she picked the flesh from the small bones.

'A feast fit for King Stephen himself,' Edwin commented, and licked his fingers. Janna pulled a face at him. If Edwin really believed that, he must be truly deluded. But his ready grin showed her that, even if he'd never attended a banquet, his imagination was every bit as vivid as her own.

'Are you ready to leave now?' he asked, when every last morsel was finally eaten. He stood up, and looked about for the jug and the pot that had held their meal.

'You should first break up your shelter,' Janna suggested, 'just in case the forester comes this way.'

'He won't. I've never seen him anywhere near here.' But Edwin began to dismantle the branches that had made up his home. Eager to be gone, Janna lent a helping hand by throwing away the flints that marked the fireplace, and scuffing the scorched earth inside the circle to disguise it.

She picked up a last lump of flint and clay, but it flaked and began to crumble in her hand. It slipped from her grasp so Janna gave it a kick instead. The clod fell apart under the impact of her boot. She was about to walk away when she realised that there was something twisted and misshapen in its centre. With quickening interest, she crouched down to examine the remains more carefully.

It was a small figurine, fashioned from pale clay and baked hard as iron. Janna jumped up and fetched the jug that Edwin had put by. There was still some water in the bottom, and she poured it carefully over the figurine, wiping away the last clods of earth that disfigured it. A mother holding a child came to life in her hands. Janna caught her breath as their features washed clearer. Was this Jesus with the Virgin Mary? Or was this something much, much older? She looked at the little statue, tracing the lines of the mother's face, the tenderness of her expression as she looked down at her child. A lump came into Janna's throat as she thought of her own mother. She stole a quick glance at Edwin. He was still busy pulling his shelter apart and hadn't noticed. Janna opened her purse and placed the figurine carefully inside. It was ancient and precious but, even more important to Janna, holding it had brought some comfort, some ease to her own aching, lonely heart.

'Now are you ready?' Edwin demanded as he walked over to her and picked up the sword. He handed Janna the staff she had carried, and raised an enquiring eyebrow.

'That's my sword. I found it,' Janna said indignantly.

'Do you know how to use a sword?' He made no effort to hand it over.

'Do you?' she challenged, and snatched it from him.

'Some of us villeins used to practise our fighting skills against each other. We'd talk of cracking our lord over the head to pay him back for all the beatings he gave us. But we had no swords to practise with, only stout sticks.'

'Then here's a stout stick for you.' Janna handed over her staff, then stepped aside and waited for him to pick up the pot and jug. 'Where did you get those?' She pointed at them.

He looked away and didn't reply, instead setting off towards the clearing. Janna didn't need to be told that he'd probably stolen them. But who was she to judge, when they might well have made the difference to his survival, she thought, as she began to walk after him, consciously imitating the easy swing of his stride.

'We need to make up some story to tell, once we come to a village or town.' She addressed her remark to his back. 'If we're going to be Welsh, perhaps we should call ourselves something other than Edwin and John.'

'It's too hard. Complicated. What if we forget and don't answer when people talk to us?' Edwin threw the question over his shoulder without checking his stride.

Janna thought for a moment. 'Could our mother have been Saxon, wed to a Welshman?'

'Good idea. It might also explain why we don't speak as the Welsh do.' Edwin turned, flashing his easy smile at her. Janna found herself smiling back at him. She began to relax, rolling her shoulders to ease tight muscles. The past few days had taken their toll.

'And where are we bound?' Edwin asked.

Janna shook her head. 'I don't know,' she confessed. 'I can't read my father's letter, so I don't know where to start looking for him.'

'What about Winchestre?'

'Why there? What about London?'

'Winchestre is the royal city where the Treasury is kept. If the king isn't in Winchestre, people will know where he's gone.' He looked back to make sure she understood him. Seeing her look of incomprehension, he continued impatiently, 'You said your father was wealthy and important. If you don't know where your father's manor is, surely your best hope is to find him through the king?'

Excitement blazed across Janna's face. 'I didn't think of that!' She touched the purse hanging from her girdle, feeling the shape of the folded parchment through the rough woven fabric. Winchestre! It was worth a try. It was an added comfort that Edwin seemed to be trying to help her. But she couldn't afford to lower her guard, she reminded herself. He'd been living wild in the forest, putting his own interests before anything else. She must take care never to come between him and his freedom when they came to a town or village, for she might well pay too high a price if she was careless.

CHREE

'O you know the road to royal Winchestre?' Janna asked, as they came once more to the forest clearing where she'd spent the night.

'No. Do you?'

Janna shook her head. 'But once we reach a village we'll look for someone who knows the way.'

'First we have to get through to the other side of the forest. Which way should we go?' Edwin asked, coming back to a more basic question.

Janna shook her head once more. 'I was hoping you knew how to find the path,' she said. 'I don't even know which direction I've come from.'

Edwin laughed. 'You came from over there,' he said, and pointed.

'Then we must keep walking this way.' Janna pointed in the opposite direction.

As they skirted the shallow dew pond, a smile twitched Janna's mouth. Reaching out, she gave Edwin a hard push.

'Hey!' he yelled as he slid down into the icy water.

'You saw me having a wash, so now it's my turn!' Janna retorted, and began to laugh as she noticed Edwin's horrified expression. 'Go on,' she encouraged. 'If you clean up the scratches on your cheek, I'll find some herbs to help them heal.'

'But I don't want to be clean!' Edwin protested. 'I put the mud on my face and clothes so I can blend into the shadows when the forester comes along.'

'Oh.' That made sense to Janna. 'But we're walking out of the forest now, so you won't need to hide for too much longer,' she pointed out. 'If you're really dirty, people will notice you, and they'll talk about us. You'd better clean yourself up, Edwin.' She flashed a wicked grin. 'I'll wash your back, if you like?'

'You'll turn around, and not look again until I say so,' he contradicted firmly.

Smiling, Janna complied.

'So what will you do when we get to Winchestre?' Edwin asked. Soft splashings told Janna that he was profitably occupied.

'I'll ask around, see if anyone can help me find my father.' Ready to fulfil her promise to Edwin, Janna began to wander about, keeping a lookout for pink flowering betony, mallow, strong-smelling yarrow, or the creamy flowers of wood sanicle.

'You need to find someone who can read,' Edwin pointed out.

The thought of a stranger reading her father's letter made Janna uneasy. Her mother had gone to such lengths to protect the secret of her birth. She risked setting her father against her for all time if private, maybe even dangerous, information about his liaison with Janna's mother became known to others.

'I just thought of something else,' Edwin continued. 'Does your father support the king or his cousin Matilda in their battle over the crown?'

'I know not,' Janna admitted. She spied the bright yellow flowers of ragwort and stopped to pluck some sprigs, wrinkling her nose at the strong smell from the bruised leaves. But it made for a good cleanser and healer, as did the hairy Herb Robert growing nearby.

'If he is of fighting age, your father may not be in Winchestre at all,' Edwin warned. 'Not only does King Stephen wage war against his cousin and her half-brother, Robert of Gloucester, but he's also having to fight his barons, to keep them under control. They're using this time of unrest to grab more land, they're becoming too powerful. Maybe your father is one of them, Ja . . . John?'

Janna straightened slowly, feeling discouraged as the difficulties of her search became apparent to her. 'I have to start looking somewhere. Winchestre seems as good a place as any.' She stayed silent for a few moments, lost in thought. Coming back to the present with a start, she asked, 'How do you know all this if you've been hiding here in Gravelinges?'

'I follow the travellers, I listen to them talking.'

'Just like you followed me?'

Edwin suddenly stopped splashing. 'Yes,' he admitted after a pause. 'I was desperate, you see. I planned to surprise you, to fell you with a blow and rob you of whatever you carried. Then I suspected you might actually be a girl. I was curious, and so I stayed hidden to see who you were and what you did.'

'And last night?'

'I kept watch over you.' The splashing started up again.

Janna gave a snort of disbelief. She raised her voice so as to be heard over the noise of the youth's ablutions. 'You were hoping I'd fall out of that tree and break my neck, so you could rob me without blame!'

'No!' he protested. 'I wondered why you were in the forest by yourself. That's all.'

Janna wondered how far she could trust him. 'Hurry up,' she said gruffly. 'I certainly don't want to spend another night out here.' With you. The words remained unsaid, but she didn't care if Edwin understood her true meaning.

Yet in spite of everything, her lips curved into a smile as he said cheerfully, 'You've only had one night in the forest. I've had days, weeks, *months* out here! I was even beginning to talk to the trees and the birds and the animals. Imagine!'

Janna could. After all, she used to talk to the hens and goats she and her mother kept on their small plot of land. Even the bees in their hives used to get a daily update on what was happening in their lives. She could quite understand how a lonely youth might find comfort in pouring out his troubles to something that would neither judge him nor give him a harsh reply. In fact, she fancied Edwin might have had little in the way of warmth and companionship even before he came into the forest.

'You've heard all about me, but you haven't told me much about yourself,' Janna commented, as he emerged from the pool. His skin was clean now, and the marks from her nails showed clearly. Janna pulled a regretful face over the damage she'd done.

'Phwoar!' Edwin's nose wrinkled in disgust as he smelled

the ragwort. But he stood quietly until Janna had finished spreading the astringent juice over the scratches on his cheek. He was shivering in his wet clothes.

'Why don't you take off your tunic and squeeze out the water?' she suggested.

He nodded, and did as he was bid. Janna drew breath in a shocked gasp. His back was marked and criss-crossed with scars from old beatings. Some were still not quite healed and looked red and painful. 'Come here,' she said. She made Edwin bend over so she could examine the wounds more closely. With a gentle touch, she used the remains of the ragwort to cleanse the worst of them. 'I'm not surprised you ran away,' she said, as he pulled on his tunic once more.

'Like I said, he was a vicious old devil.' Edwin began to step around the clearing, examining it carefully for signs of the path they should follow.

'So where does this vicious old devil live? Where have you come from?' Janna prompted, curious to know more.

'He has a manor near Tantone in Somer Shire. I walked for many miles, for it was in my mind to seek work in Winchestre, or even in London. Then I became lost in this forest. I decided to hide here until my time was up for by then I'd realised that my lord had sent his servants in pursuit of me.'

'Why did he do that? Why did he bother?' Janna didn't mean to disparage Edwin, but she was genuinely curious to know the answer. Certain it was that a lord would pursue a missing serf, but the chase would not last long, especially if the serf was as poor and as lowly as Edwin appeared to be.

'He is miserly as well as vicious. He guards what is his and holds on to it far beyond reason. Everyone on his manor has cause to hate and fear him, for everyone has been called to account for some act of carelessness, some slight or misdeed, some imagined oversight. We have all been punished, even when we were not guilty. Walter of Crice will not listen to any explanation or any excuse but takes the whip to all, even to his own wife and children, so it is said. In truth, I think he goes out of his way to find reason for punishment, for he seems happy only when he's causing misery for someone else.'

Janna was silenced by the bleak picture he painted. Yet her imagination couldn't leave it alone; she was sure he hadn't told her the full story. 'Were you accused of something? Is that what made you run away?' she persisted.

Edwin looked up abruptly, abandoning his search for the path. A wash of colour swept over his face. 'My lord's favourite steed went missing, and I was held to blame for it.' His voice was harsh, bitter with hatred as he made the confession.

Was that guilt or indignation that stained his countenance? 'And did you steal his horse?' Although Janna kept her voice carefully neutral, both of them knew that Edwin was guilty of one theft at least.

'Of course I did not!' he flashed. 'Do you see it here? I would have kept it if I'd stolen it! And I would have ridden to the far end of the kingdom to escape that devil.' He cast his eyes downward, his face set in sullen lines as he began to search once more for any faint signs of a way out of the forest.

Janna berated herself for asking such a stupid question. Yet the thought still troubled her: what if the horse had gone lame? Edwin might well have had to abandon it somewhere. 'If you didn't take it, then who did?' she asked, anxious to understand.

Edwin shrugged. 'I don't know. It was a fine beast, any man might covet it. All I know is that my lord will not rest until he reclaims it – which means he will not rest until he finds me. There it is!'

Bewildered by his unexpected admission, Janna cast about for signs of the horse, then realised that Edwin was pointing at a faint mark in the grass. Ready to forgive him, and forgive herself for her lack of trust, Janna flashed him a grateful grin. 'Well done!' she said, and gave him a whack across the back, instantly regretting the action as she recalled the deep cuts she'd just treated.

'Ow!' he protested loudly.

'Isn't that the sort of thing men do to each other?'

'Who goes there in the king's royal forest?' A loud shout startled Janna into silence. They stared at each other, momentarily numb with fear. Then, putting a warning finger to his mouth to caution silence, Edwin grabbed Janna's hand and began to run, pulling her with him along the trail he'd found. Janna sprinted beside him, hoping she could trust Edwin to find the way. Even in her fear of being overtaken by the forester, she revelled in the freedom of movement the breeches gave her as her legs pumped up and down, pounding downhill through the trees.

'Stop! In the name of the king, I bid you stand and give me your names and your reason for trespass in the king's royal forest.' The voice was uneven, somewhat breathless. The forester was chasing them. Edwin tugged harder on

Janna's hand, and she kept on running. Both of them knew that there'd be no mercy shown if they were to stop and meekly surrender.

They ran on, stumbling into hollows and tripping over rough flints hidden among the tangled, weedy undergrowth. They let go, needing their hands to protect themselves from the brambles that snagged their clothes, whipped their faces and tore at their skin. A long strand of sticky goosegrass wrapped around Janna's ankle; she yanked her foot free and, panicking now, put on a burst of speed to catch up with Edwin. The sounds of pursuit were louder but she was tiring. A pain cut into her side, sharp as the sword she carried. *Aelfshot.* The Saxons believed this sudden stab was caused by darts shot by elves, but Janna knew she felt it only when she'd run too far and for too long without rest. 'You go on,' she panted hoarsely as Edwin turned to check her progress. 'I'll find a tree to climb.'

'No!' He stopped and grabbed hold of her. 'My safety lies with you, just as yours lies with me. We're in this together. Quick!' Instead of heading deeper into the trees he hauled her towards an opening in the forest. Janna had no choice but to follow him, and saw the sense of his action when he dived headfirst into a patch of tall weeds. At once he was hidden from sight, and Janna wasted no time going in after him, although she felt exposed and vulnerable away from the shelter of the trees. Bracken and tall herbs formed part of their shield, but so too did stinging nettles and prickling thistles, and Janna had to fold her lips hard together to stop herself crying out. She lay still, listening to the pounding of her heart and the heavy rasp of her own panting breaths.

She pressed her lips tighter to stifle the sound, while the thudding footsteps of their pursuer came closer.

'Come back!' he shouted as he passed close beside them. 'I know you can hear me. Come back here at once!'

They stayed silent, even when a blackbird alighted nearby to forage for a juicy worm. It took one startled glance at them and squawked loudly before taking off to find a less menacing hunting ground. All sound from the forester ceased. Janna couldn't see him, but she could sense him waiting, and watching. She prayed that they, too, were invisible, and that Edwin would keep still until all danger had passed. For herself, she was too frightened even to blink. Any movement, the slightest sound, might give the forester the clue he needed to find them.

Time passed. Janna felt as if she'd been lying hidden for an eternity. She desperately wanted to poke her head up, to see where the forester was and what he was doing, but she lay silent beside Edwin instead and waited for the danger to pass. Her heartbeats had begun to quieten, her breathing had returned to normal by the time the forester eventually set off. They could hear the diminishing sounds of his voice calling out in the hope that he would be heeded and obeyed.

More time passed. The pressure of Edwin's hand on her arm confirmed the need for stillness and silence, lest the forester be waiting down the track to trap them when they showed themselves. She became aware of Edwin trembling beside her. She thought at first that he was fearful, until the shudders grew stronger and she realised he was shivering with cold in his wet clothes. 'We should go on now, before you freeze to death,' she breathed softly into his ear.

He nodded and cautiously raised his head above the cover of the weeds. Once he'd made sure the forester was really gone, he stood up and began to run on the spot, rubbing his arms to get the blood flowing through his body. Janna nodded in approval but, seeing the warning finger come to his mouth once more, she didn't say anything. Instead, she extracted her sword from the weedy growth, then jabbed a thumb towards where they'd left the path. On receiving his nod she set off, trying to place her feet quietly upon grass so that no crackling leaves or twigs might betray them, ready at an instant to melt into concealing undergrowth. Suddenly, she became aware that she couldn't hear Edwin. Had he run off and left her? Alarmed, she spun around, and was reassured to see him pacing silently behind her. He grinned at her. She flashed a smile in reply, feeling a little guilty that she'd doubted him.

The trail was wider now, and more distinct. It was becoming well-trodden, just like the beginning of the trail on the other side of Gravelinges. It, too, must be used by farmers in autumn, some of whom, for a fee, were allowed to bring their pigs into the forest to eat the beechmast. With a sudden lift of her spirits, Janna assumed they must be coming close to Wicheford, and safety.

'Stay where you are!' A triumphant cry punctured her confidence and set her pulse leaping with fright. Her first thought was to hide, but even as she searched desperately for cover, the forester sprang out onto the path to confront them. She stepped backwards, cannoning into Edwin. He shouldered her aside and, with one almighty shove, sent the forester staggering to the ground.

'Run!' he shouted.

At least we've had a chance to rest, Janna thought, as she sprinted beside him. She felt proud that she could keep pace with Edwin even though she was a girl, but she knew she would also tire more quickly. Still she ran valiantly, following the trail down through the trees, through gloomy shadows under leafy canopies where every bush and thicket seemed to conceal a threat to their safety, and through open weedy clearings where she felt even more vulnerable to the hunt.

'Stop!' The cry sounded behind them. The forester was in pursuit once more. Janna forced her aching limbs to pump harder, sucked breath deep into her burning lungs. To be caught by the forester was bad enough. To be caught after striking him to the ground and running away would invite a punishment too dreadful to contemplate. Flight was the only answer, their only hope of salvation. Fear added a burst of speed to Janna's feet.

They ran on. Janna felt now as though she'd passed into a new dimension, a place where her body no longer seemed part of her consciousness. Her chest rose and fell with her breaths; her feet flashed briefly in front of her, left, right, left, right as they sped onwards, but she felt nothing past the desperate need to escape. She sensed Edwin check slightly and matched her stride to his, looking past him to see for herself what had given him pause. Only a narrow fringe of forest separated them now from water meadows and a river lying ahead. Behind them, the forester kept shouting, but in front of them danger also lay, in the form of a mounted man. By the stillness of his stance, and the direction of his gaze, Janna understood that he'd already spied them and that trying to hide from him was futile. Nor could they turn back. And so they kept on running, while he spurred his horse to meet them. They came together at the edge of the forest.

'What frightens you? What do you run from?' In spite of his handsome mount and the elegance of his tunic, the man spoke in the Saxon language. The realisation gave Janna the courage to answer truthfully.

'We're running from the king's forester.' She kept the sword hidden behind her back, knowing that the man would suspect the worst if he saw it. His expression hardened. Janna wondered if she'd misjudged him. The king's forest laws were popular with no-one save those of his favourites who'd been granted hunting rights in the royal forests. The Saxons especially had reason to hate and resent the edict set in place by William the Bastard, who had conquered their country and killed their king. Forced off their own lands, forced to work for their hated enemies, thegns and villeins alike were also prevented by forest law from cutting wood to build their homes, or trapping wild creatures to fill their empty bellies. Was this man on their side, or was he only speaking their language?

'Take shelter in there. Hurry!' The man pointed at a long, timbered shed nearby. It was so close to the forest edge Janna hadn't noticed it before.

'Thank you,' she breathed, even as Edwin pushed her towards it.

The door had hardly closed behind them when they heard a cheerful shout. 'Master Roger! What brings you through the forest in such a hurry?' This time, the man spoke the language of the Normans, but Janna had been taught to speak it by her mother and she understood his words. Edwin, however, tensed.

'He's trapped us here like rats, and now he's going to hand us over to the forester,' he hissed into Janna's ear.

'No, he's not. Sssh. Let me listen.' Janna bent and put her ear close to a space in the wooden palings. She heard the jingle of the bridle as their rescuer dismounted to talk to the forester.

'Where are they, Serlo? Two youths? You must have seen them.' The forester also spoke in Norman French now. His voice was rough with fatigue; he struggled to catch his breath. The chase had taken its toll.

'I've seen no youths. Are you sure they came this way?'

A short silence confirmed that the man's shrewd question had hit home. Just as Janna eased a sigh of relief, the forester said petulantly, 'They were following the trail through the forest. They must have run past you.'

'Do you doubt my word?' Their rescuer sounded angry now.

'No, no. I'm just surprised you haven't seen them.'

'If they realised you were after them, they might still be hiding in the forest. Did you have them in your sights all the while?'

'I did not!' The forester's voice was sharp, accusing, as he continued, 'One of the ruffians struck me such a blow that I fell to the ground. By the time I got after them, they had disappeared from my view. I was sure they were coming this way and so I made haste to follow them even though I can scarce move from the pain of the attack.'

Janna stiffened, sure that the forester's lie would make their rescuer think twice about his chivalrous action. While Serlo might be prepared to save villeins fleeing from a harsh and unjust law, he wouldn't harbour anyone who'd resort to violence to escape from a king's man. She peered through the crack, in time to see the forester rubbing his head, an aggrieved expression on his face. Hardly daring to breathe, she waited through a long silence as their rescuer weighed the pros and cons of confessing his lie or continuing to shelter a pair of dangerous villains.

'What are they saying? Do you understand any of it?' Edwin whispered nervously.

'Yes. Sssh.' Janna clamped a hand over his mouth and leaned closer to the gap between the wooden stakes, straining to hear whatever might be said.

'. . . but if I see them, I'll be sure to keep hold of them and send word to you.' Janna felt slightly cheered as she understood what Serlo was saying. He had hold of them already, but hadn't spoken of them to the forester. That must mean he was prepared to let them go free, once the danger had passed. She released Edwin, and put her eye to the crack, trying to see what the forester would do next. Fear slammed into her with the force of a body blow as she found herself staring directly into his eyes. Had he seen her? Did he know someone was hiding inside the shed? She dare not blink lest she betray their presence.

'What are you . . .?' Edwin subsided into silence as Janna gave him a hard jab in the ribs. Her eyes stayed fixed on the forester, who continued to stare at her. Moments passed. Hours. Months. Years. And then the forester turned to Serlo and asked, 'What's in the shed over there?'

'Nothing now, Master Roger.' Their rescuer gave a shrug. 'It's a winter shelter for my sheep, to keep them out of snow and flood, but the time for that has passed now. See how well my flock is doing. We shall have a goodly stock of wool to sell at the fair this year, and a bountiful harvest too if the weather stays kind.' There was pride in Serlo's voice as with one hand he grasped the forester and drew him around, while with his other hand he indicated a flock of white-faced sheep, grazing peacefully under the watchful eye of their shepherd. The generous sweep of his hand encompassed all the fields beyond the river: dark, ploughed earth lying fallow, golden barley and ripening wheat. Janna felt a great warmth towards him as she understood how successfully he'd managed to deflect the forester's attention from the sheepfold and their suspected whereabouts. Serlo kept a grip on the forester's arm and, still talking, led him away, following the green wall of trees at the edge of the forest.

Once she judged they were safely out of earshot, Janna whispered an explanation of what had transpired to Edwin, including the forester's version of how he was attacked.

'I gave him a shove and he fell over,' Edwin protested. 'I didn't mean to hurt him, I just wanted to buy us some time.'

'I'm sure you didn't hurt him. There was no sign of any mark on him, but that didn't stop him trying to make a greater cause against us. Lucky for us, his ruse didn't work.'

'So what do we do now?' Edwin asked, restless and anxious to be gone.

'Nothing, for the moment. I don't know where Serlo's taken the forester. They may still be close enough to see us if we leave. And where would we go? We can't cross the river in daylight, and we can't really go back to the forest either, not if the forester is still about. I suggest we stay here until nightfall, and make our escape then.'

Edwin grunted uneasily. 'Serlo? Is that his name? He thinks I hit the forester. He thinks we're dangerous. He may want to hand us over to the sheriff instead, and claim a reward for his trouble.' He shook his head. 'I think we should leave now.'

'It's not safe. At least, not yet. Let's wait a while,' Janna insisted.

Edwin huffed a sigh. 'It's all very well for you to say "wait". You're not the one on the run. You didn't thump the forester. You're not suspected of stealing a horse either.'

'You can go if you want to, but I'm staying here.' Janna sat down. To underscore her words, she shifted around so that her back rested against the timbered frame of the shed. She stretched her legs out in front of her, and closed her eyes. Just for safety, she casually folded her hands over her purse. If Edwin decided to make a move, it would not be with any of her belongings – at least, not without a fight.

'You still don't trust me, do you?' His voice was amused. Janna felt embarrassed that he'd read her mind so easily. Or was it shame for doubting him? Uncertain now, she recalled how he'd taken her hand, matching his speed to hers as he pulled her along. He hadn't run away to save himself. Instead, he'd helped her hide from the forester.

'No, I don't trust you,' she said truthfully, pushing aside her uneasy conscience.

'I've already apologised for stealing your purse. It's safer for both of us if we stay together, but we have to trust and even like each other if we want people to believe that we're brothers.'

'Stay together? I thought you were leaving right now?' Janna opened her eyes to study him.

'No. Not yet. You're right. It's not safe. We'll go as soon as it gets dark.' He stretched out beside her.

'Go where? We still don't know the way to Winchestre.'

'Sssh. I hear voices. I think they're coming back.'

The voices grew louder. Janna tensed, waiting for betrayal, but the voices passed, becoming softer until there was silence once more. Just as they started to relax, the door of the shed flung open with a sudden crash. A tall figure blocked the light, and blocked all chance of their escape. It was the horseman, Serlo. They scrambled to their feet to face him.

Serlo was in his mid-years, his freckled face burnished red by the sun and topped with a shock of red hair. From his commanding air and confident speech, Janna guessed he must be the lord of this manor. A quick inspection confirmed her guess: his tunic was made of good linen and decorated with a border of embroidery. His boots, although mud-spattered, were made of fine leather. 'Now,' he said threateningly, 'you'd better tell me what really happened in the forest.' He planted his hands on his hips and puffed out his chest. 'Tell me the truth, for you can be sure I'll beat it out of you if I suspect either one of you is lying.'

Janna was thankful then that she'd understood his conversation with the forester, and that she'd repeated it to Edwin. They might otherwise have tried to bluff their way out of trouble, and would have earned themselves a beating for it. But how much of the truth should they tell? She stole a quick glance at Edwin, then looked away. One of them had to say something. It had better be her, for Edwin had far too much to lose. She would speak for both of them – and in as low a voice as possible!

'We thank you kindly, sire, for hiding us from the forester,' Janna began, thinking it wise to flatter their rescuer as well as show themselves humble and well-mannered, so that he might think twice before believing all that the forester had said of them. As an added precaution, she addressed him in the Saxon tongue, not wanting him to know that she'd heard, and understood, his conversation with the forester.

Serlo grunted acknowledgement, all the while looking them over as if to assess their worth. He frowned as he took in Edwin's damp and tattered appearance, his half-starved, wild air. His attention moved then to Janna. She quickly looked away, not wanting to show her full face to him lest she betray her real identity. Instead, she studied the earthen floor intently as she launched into explanation. 'We are two brothers from beyond the Welsh marches, sire, come to seek employment wherever we may find it.'

'Has your lord given you permission to leave his manor?' Their rescuer eyed them suspiciously.

'We . . . we are not tied to anyone, sire.' Janna's thoughts raced as she tried to come up with something to satisfy the man's curiosity. 'Our father was Welsh, a craftsman, but he died when we were just babes. Our mother found a living . . .' Janna flushed as the man's eyes narrowed in calculation, '. . . working in an alehouse.' If the man believed her mother was a whore, he might well think her daughter one too! Except she wasn't a daughter, she reminded herself.

'My name is John,' she said hastily, 'and my brother is called Edwin.'

'You do not speak like a Welshman, John.'

Janna felt a flash of triumph that he'd not seen through her disguise. 'Our mother was of Saxon stock, sire, and sick with wanting her home and her kin around her.' She was rewarded by the brief flash of sympathy in his eyes. But he was not yet done with them.

'One of you struck the forester. Which of you was it?'

Janna glanced at Edwin. As she opened her mouth to defend him, he said, 'It was me, my lord. I gave the forester a hard push, to give us time to get away from him. He fell to his knees, but I didn't hurt him. I didn't strike him either.'

'I should put you in to the sheriff for such an act.' Yet a faint smile curled the man's lips upwards.

Emboldened, Janna asked, 'Will you allow us to leave now, sire? If the forester is gone and it is safe?'

'No.' The smile grew broader as the man shook his head.

'No?' Janna's voice skidded dangerously high. Her heart beat fast with fright. Did he mean, after all, to give them over to the sheriff?

'There is much to be done on the manor, and I am short of labour, especially as half the villeins are struck down with some poxy disease. You may stay a while, and repay your debt to me by doing their work for them.' He was no longer smiling. Janna knew that even though his words were couched as an offer, he expected to be obeyed. She glanced at Edwin, uncertain what to say or do. To her surprise, he nodded acceptance.

'Good,' the man said briskly. 'My name is Serlo, and I am

the reeve of this manor.' Janna felt a moment's surprise that she'd so misjudged his position here. But Serlo was still speaking. 'You will follow my commands and work in return for your bread and lodging until I no longer have need of you. Do not cross me for I will raise the hue and cry should you try to leave.'

Janna's heart sank. She fingered the shape of the small statue in her purse, the mother hunched so protectively over her child. It gave her the courage to ask the question. 'How long will you keep us here, Master Serlo?'

'What does it matter? You said you were in search of work. I am offering it.'

Janna wondered how to convey to him the urgency of her quest to find her father, without giving too much away. As she struggled to find the words, Edwin forestalled her.

'We are grateful for your kindness, Master Serlo. Be sure that we will pay our debt to you in full.'

'Come with me.' Mounting his horse, Serlo beckoned them to follow behind. Janna cast a glance at the sword she'd salvaged from the pond, now lying half hidden behind a rough wooden feed trough. Edwin caught her glance and shook his head. He started off after Serlo and, after a moment's thought, Janna stowed the sword out of sight, along with Edwin's jug and pot, then scurried after the pair. Serlo had said that the shed stood empty through the summer. The sword should be safe enough for the moment, but she would come back for it once they were given permission to leave.

It was a long walk over the marshy ground of the water meadows. Mud and dung stuck to Janna's boots and she again wished she had a pair of wooden pattens to protect them from all the muck. Serlo led them across the river and up to the manor house. He bade them wait while he entered the yard and dismounted to fetch some implements. To Janna he handed a heavy wooden mallet; to Edwin a pair of long-handled sticks, with a Y-fork on one and a small sickle blade on the other. Once more he mounted, and walked them on and up into the fields beyond. Some of the ploughed fallow land was studded with fat horned sheep and their long-tailed lambs. They nibbled at new shoots of weeds and grass, and dropped the dung that would be spread to make the soil more fertile for the next cycle of planting. The earth was dark, marked with patches of white chalk and studded with flints that glinted in the watery sunlight. Scarlet poppies turned their faces to the sky, bright splashes of colour among the green wheat growing nearby. Looking more closely, Janna could also see an abundance of prickly purple thistles, red deadnettles, charlock, dock and hairy pink corncockle. The flowers made a pretty picture, but Janna knew they would spread and choke the wheat if left unchecked.

Weeding fields and spreading dung was back-breaking work. It was normally done by the villeins of the manor in return for a small plot of land and shelter for their families, yet these fields seemed almost deserted. She wondered how Serlo could be so careless of his lord's property, and why his lord let him get away with it. Then she remembered the poxy disease, and understood why the reeve was forcing their service to his cause. She became aware that he was talking to them, throwing words carelessly over his shoulder as he rode along. She hurried to catch up with him and Edwin. To her dismay, the reeve's words confirmed her fears.

'I'm behind with everything here because of this cursed pox. The sheep are still to be washed and shorn and the hay to be cut, just as soon as we get some sunshine. There are new ditches to dig, and hedges to repair around the growing corn. But you can begin by weeding the corn, and breaking up clods and picking large flints from the fallow fields, anything that might get in the way of the plough. You can also spread the sheep's mundungus to make next season's crops grow better. While you are here, you will sleep with the servants in the hall and break your fast with them. Mistress Tova, the cook, will give you food and ale to take out into the fields for your dinner and supper. I don't want to see you back at the manor until it's dark. I am out around the manor farm every day in my lord's absence, so make sure I'll be keeping an eye on you and how hard you are working.'

Janna groaned inwardly. With the sun rising early, and the summer light fading late from the sky, it made for a long day's labour. She cheered herself with the thought that at least they'd be meeting new people, any of whom might know the way to Winchestre. Their service here could not last for ever; sooner or later they would be given permission to leave.

Edwin gave her a hard nudge. 'What?' she asked, startled out of her reverie. He began to walk with exaggerated strides, swinging his arms manfully by his side. Puzzled, Janna stared at him, then became aware that Serlo was watching them both and frowning with suspicion. Suddenly catching on, she squared her shoulders and lengthened her stride. 'He's only young,' Edwin called, as he drew nearer to Serlo, 'but he's strong.' He jerked a thumb towards Janna. 'He's a good worker, you'll see.'

Another grunt met this observation, but Serlo turned then and set his horse for home. Edwin flashed a grin at Janna and she pulled a rueful face at him. It was so easy to forget her new disguise. So easy, and so dangerous.

FOUR

AFTER A FEW days out in the fields, Janna ached all over. Her fingers were torn and bruised from picking up sharp flints and hacking into thistles, while her back felt bent out of shape from bending over to beat out hard clods of earth with the heavy mallet. In her nose was the stink of sheep dung. Although she'd washed her hands and feet in the river before coming in for the night, she could still smell it.

She stretched out on her straw pallet, trying to find ease for her tired body and her unquiet mind. To stop herself from the misery of recalling her past life with her mother in their small cot at the edge of Gravelinges forest, which always brought with it the slow burn of anger at the injustice of what had happened to her, Janna thought instead about Urk and what had happened that day while she was out culling weeds.

Urk was by far the oldest of the group of children who had been sent into the fields to scare away the crows, rooks and other scavengers that swooped down to eat the ripening corn. The youngest, aged three or four, banged drums and shouted. The older children carried slingshots, and it was a matter of competition and pride between them who could fell the most birds. Behind the children came Urk's mother, cutting weeds and keeping an eye on the youngsters to remind them of their purpose should their natural high spirits lead them astray.

Urk was tall and heavyset, and slow by nature. He reminded Janna of a scruffy hen she'd owned, which she'd called 'Laet' because it was always last to get to the feed. The hen would not have survived if Janna had not fed it separately. Janna suspected that Urk's mother might also give her oldest son special treatment. Yet he was a merry lad, with a sweet smile and a willing nature. He was also the most accurate of them all when it came to using the slingshot. This day he'd had the misfortune to bring down a dove in front of Serlo, and had his ears severely boxed as a result. Janna cringed as she remembered how Mistress Wulfrun had pleaded on her son's behalf.

'He doesn't understand what he's done wrong, Master Serlo. Please don't punish him so.'

'It was eating the wheat, Master Serlo,' Urk chimed in. 'You told us to kill all the birds who ate the grain.'

Serlo glowered at the unfortunate boy, then gave him another clip across the ear. 'Doves are for my lord's sport, not yours,' he shouted, as if the boy was deaf rather than slow. 'Don't you dare kill another – don't ever touch the doves again, or I'll take your slingshot from you and you'll never get it back!'

Urk's lip quivered; he looked on the verge of tears. 'And no more playing with fire either!' Serlo turned on his heel and marched off.

Mistress Wulfrun placed her arm around her son and gave

him a hug. 'Don't take it to heart,' she comforted him. 'Master Serlo doesn't mean it.'

Feeling sorry for the boy, Janna bent once more to her task. Suddenly, she found Mistress Wulfrun beside her, with Urk a pace behind. 'Master Serlo is usually more patient with him,' the woman confided, as she stooped to cut weeds. She glanced at Urk. 'And you don't play with fire, do you, son?'

'No.' Urk stood still, watching them. Janna wondered if he was too afraid now to use his slingshot.

'He woke up one night when he was small,' Mistress Wulfrun explained further. 'We were all asleep but he wanted to go outside. I think he was just curious to have a look around the manor in the moonlight. He had the good sense to take a rush light so he could see his way, but when he walked into the byre a cow mooed and frightened him. He dropped the light into a pile of hay, and the byre caught on fire. He didn't do it on purpose – and there was no harm to the animals,' she added quickly, forestalling Janna's question. 'But my son got such a fright he started screaming. Everyone came running. The animals were led to safety, but the byre burned to the ground.' She looked at Urk, concern scoring deep lines across her pleasant, homely face. 'Of course, he shouldn't have gone near the manor, and my lord was very good about it, very understanding. But Serlo was angry, I think because he feels responsible for everything that takes place here. He is usually fair in his dealings with us, but it seems he has neither forgotten the fire nor forgiven my boy.' She looked at Janna. 'I can't be with him all the time. Will you also keep watch over him out in the fields, John, when I'm not here?' she pleaded.

'Of course I will, mistress.' Janna didn't know what else to say to comfort the woman or her son, but she wished now that she'd thought of something, anything, to ease the situation, to make Urk feel better about himself, and his mother less worried about him. She yawned, and shifted about on the straw pallet, trying to compose herself for sleep, but her bed was prickly and her whole body ached. Contributing to her unease was the company she kept. All Janna's life there had been only her mother and, later, the cat Alfred in their cottage. Now she was expected to sleep in the hall with all the servants of the manor, most of them men and boys. Edwin had set their pallets into a corner, away from the crowd around the fireplace. He'd put Janna next to the wall, keeping himself between her and the others. She was grateful for his protection, but even so she lay awake, unaccustomed to the night noises, the sighs and murmurs, the cries of nightmares, and the odours of farts and sweaty clothes and dirty feet.

When at last she fell asleep, her dreams were full of endless fields spread before her. She stooped over them, with the smell of animal excrement in her nose and the knowledge that her tasks would never be done. And so it seemed still when she woke to yet another grey dawn and the realisation that a new day lay before her, and one after that, and then another and another. She groaned softly. Hot tears stung her eyes.

'What's wrong?' Edwin stirred beside her.

'Nothing.' Janna was conscious of the servants nearby, any one of whom might be wide enough awake to carry the tale to Serlo if she confessed to Edwin how sad and desperate she felt. She wiped her eyes on the back of her sleeve, and tried not to sniffle.

Edwin seemed to understand. 'My body is one big ache, and my arms feel like they're on fire,' he muttered, as he stood up and squared his shoulders to face the day.

'At least our bellies will soon be full!' Janna felt a little more cheerful as she stored her straw pallet in an alcove off the hall. She looked about, but there was no sign of the bread and ale with which they normally broke their fast. The table stood bare, and Janna's stomach rumbled with hunger. Beckoning Edwin to follow her, she hurried down the stairs and on towards a stone building nearby. There might be other pickings waiting for them in the kitchen, a scrap of bacon perhaps, or even a pasty. Saliva flooded Janna's mouth at the thought, and her steps quickened.

She loved going into the kitchen. It was a source of wonder to her that anywhere could hold such an abundance of food. She took a deep sniff, anticipating the delicious smells of meat roasting on a spit over the fire, newly baked bread, the rich aromas of a bubbling pottage, the spicy fragrance of herbs. Instead, she smelt a sharp and acrid stink. A young maid stood at the large table in the centre of the room, chopping onions and weeping over her task.

Janna sniffed again and realised that it wasn't onions she could smell, but smoke and burnt offerings. Bewildered, she looked around for the cook, but there was no sign of Mistress Tova, only Serlo and the kitchen servants. Hands on hips and face red with anger, Serlo was berating one of the skivvies. Feeling sorry for the boy, yet reluctant to attract the reeve's attention, Janna stopped abruptly. Edwin crashed into her. 'What are you . . .?' His words died on his lips as he took in the situation. But it was too late. Serlo had seen them. Tilting her chin in assumed bravado, Janna waited for him to address them.

'The cook has gone and got the pox now. She's all over spots,' he said, by way of explanation. 'And no-one seems to know anything about baking bread.' He flung out a hand towards some flat, blackened rounds which must once have been small loaves.

'I can bake griddle cakes, Master Serlo,' Janna said quickly, keen to lend a helping hand and, if possible, get the young boy out of trouble. She noticed the flare of surprise in his eyes as he turned to face her and realised, with a sinking heart, that she'd have done much better to hold her tongue. 'My . . . our mother taught me how,' she added, sneaking an anxious glance at Edwin as she did so.

'Hmph,' Serlo grunted. He cast a glance around the kitchen, at the silent kitchen hands and lowly skivvies huddled near the door, waiting only a chance to disappear from view. His glance settled on a young woman, and he reddened slightly. 'Hasn't your mother taught you how to cook, Gytha?' he demanded, in a softer tone than he'd used with the boy.

'No, Master Serlo, she has not.' The girl tossed her long dark ringlets. Janna waited for an explanation or an excuse for her lack of skill, but none came.

Curious, and rather impressed by Gytha's impertinence, for Janna judged the girl a little younger than herself, she leaned slightly to one side for a better view. Gytha was beautiful, she decided, with a pang of envy and of pain as she mourned her own lost locks, and her rough disguise. Evidently Gytha was the cook's daughter, yet she wasn't often in the kitchen for Janna hadn't seen her there before. Now, she faced Serlo with pride, secure in her own beauty and a position that seemed equal to Serlo's own.

He's smitten with her. Janna's lips curved upwards into a smile as she understood his sudden fluster. But he was well in command of his emotions when he turned his hard gaze back on Janna. 'Make some griddle cakes then, John, quick as you can. There's much work to be done.' With a last suspicious glance at Janna, he hurried out.

'I'll help you.' The beauty moved towards Janna with a friendly smile. 'I wouldn't admit it to him,' she jerked her head in the direction of the disappearing reeve, 'but my father taught my mother the arts of the kitchen while he was alive, so she was able to keep his position here after he died. In turn, she has taught me all she knows. I can cook, and cook well, but I will not be a skivvy to the likes of Serlo. I have set my sights much higher than the reeve.' A dreamy smile tugged at the corners of her mouth.

'You will cook for the lord of the manor when he returns?'

'No, indeed. I shall do more, much more for my lord than cook for him.'

Could Gytha really mean what she was saying? Even as she scolded herself for her nosiness, Janna's insatiable curiosity prompted her to probe further. 'You are my lord's mistress?'

'Certainly not!'

'I beg your pardon,' Janna apologised hastily. 'What I meant to ask is: are you betrothed to him?'

'Not yet.' A calculating expression briefly marred the young girl's beauty. 'But it's only a matter of time before he recognises that our destiny lies together.' Head tilted to one side, she studied Janna. 'You're new here, aren't you, John?'

'Yes.' Janna answered without thinking. 'Yes,' she said again on a deeper note, hoping the girl hadn't seen through her disguise.

'My name's Gytha,' she said, and took Janna's hand. 'Come on, I'll show you where everything is kept. It'll be a blessing if you can do the cooking while my mother is ill. Not for anything would I have Serlo tramping around after me, breathing down my neck and telling me what to do.'

Yet you have no hesitation in shifting the burden onto my shoulders, Janna thought. With a wry smile, she acknowledged that she would far rather slave in the kitchen all day than break her back out in the fields.

She rinsed her hands, and began to rub fat into the flour, noticing how fine and white it was compared to the gritty brown flour which was all she and her mother had been able to afford. She poured some goat's milk into the mixture, hiding a smile as Edwin sidled over. He edged closer to Gytha, looking hopeful. Gytha fluttered her eyelashes and gave him a demure smile.

'This is my older brother, Edwin,' Janna said, amused. Gytha might have designs on the lord of the manor, but it seemed she couldn't help flirting with any marriageable prospect around. 'What ails your mother and the villeins, mistress?' she asked. It was possible she might know of a preparation that could help them.

'They burn with fever and they're covered in itchy spots. They are too sick to leave their beds.' Gytha looked genuinely concerned now, and Janna could understand why. She'd seen the ravages of this disease before, how it could scar skin and destroy hearing and sight, and even kill if taken badly enough. No wonder Gytha looked frightened. She obviously had ambition for her future, an ambition dependent on her youthful beauty.

'You should stay away from your mother. I hope it's not too late,' Janna advised. 'Once one gets the disease, most everyone else around and about will get it too.' She hung a flat tray over the kitchen fire and waited for it to heat.

'Put some eggs with that.' Gytha whisked into a larder and came out with several eggs cupped in her hand. Trying not to look too impressed by such riches, Janna cracked them open and spilled the contents into the bowl. Once the eggs were beaten into the milk and flour, she ladled the mixture in small dollops onto the tray. Her stomach growled with hunger. She fought to restrain herself from peeling off the cakes and stuffing them straight into her mouth.

'My mother looks so ill. The spots plague her so she can't stop scratching.' Gytha seemed genuinely wretched now. 'I wish I could do something to help her.'

Janna thought of the potions she and her mother had made when a similar disease had struck down a number of villeins in a hamlet near their own. 'If you wish, I can brew a decoction for the fever and make up a lotion to soothe the itchy spots,' she promised, adding quickly, 'but you must help me first. These cakes are almost ready. Perhaps you could fetch the ale and take it up to the hall?'

'And what would a youth like you know about fevers and lotions?' Serlo's voice made Janna jump. She hadn't heard him return. She cast a nervous glance behind her. 'Our mother was a . . . a healer,' she stammered, thinking it safest to keep as close as possible to the truth. 'But she also worked in an alehouse,' she added hurriedly, as she recalled what she'd first told Serlo.

'She was a very skilful healer, Master Serlo,' Edwin cut in swiftly, anxious to take the reeve's attention off Janna. 'People came from all over to see her when they had a pain or a disease.' He couldn't possibly know that for a fact, Janna thought, but even if he was making it up, he was actually speaking the truth.

'Then let your brother do the cooking, and you can see about making my villeins well again,' Serlo told him. 'The sooner they can go about their tasks, the sooner you can both leave the manor farm.'

'I . . . I have not my brother's talent for healing,' Edwin stuttered. 'I can't cook neither.' He brightened as he thought how to embroider the tale. 'In fact, our mother always said that young John here was by far the more skilled when it came to indoor work such as this. I am more use out in the fields.' He raised an arm and flexed the muscle to make his point.

'Then you can work alone in the fields today. Your brother will stay here and brew his concoctions to make my people well again.' Serlo gave them a curt nod, and stepped back to watch their final preparations. Even though most of his attention was reserved for Gytha, Janna could understand how the proud beauty sought to avoid him. Such close proximity to Serlo was making her nervous, and that in turn made her clumsy. Janna stifled a cry as her wet, greasy fingers slid off a bowl and it crashed into pieces on the floor. Scarlet with shame, she kept her head bent as Serlo berated her for her carelessness. Her gratitude towards the reeve was waning; she was beginning to wonder if they might have been wiser to take their chances with the forester.

Once they'd all broken their fast, the men left to go about their work while Gytha returned to the kitchen to supervise the servants over preparations for their dinner at midday. Janna made her excuses, and escaped out to the kitchen garden to seek the herbs she needed to bring relief to the cook and the manor's villeins. She was pleased to recognise several plants her mother had grown in their own garden. She plucked some feverfew, intending to add it to a syrup with mint and valerian to help dull the pain and cool the fever. She continued to browse among the herbs, searching for marigold, septfoil, elecampane or mallow. Roots, flowers or leaves could be useful in a potion to expel the poison or a lotion to cool and soothe the itchy spots.

Harvesting the herbs, smelling their fragrance, reminded Janna of the last time she'd collected herbs for healing. She'd been in the manor's kitchen garden at Babestoche, and there was a child's life at stake. She sighed. The past was behind her, she reminded herself. Her own mother was dead, and so was Dame Alice's baby. He had been ailing from the start. She would wager that not even King Stephen's own physician could have kept him alive. Still, for the sake of Dame Alice, she wished she could have saved the child. If her mother had only acknowledged that Janna was growing to adulthood, and had trained her to administer to the sick instead of merely letting her prepare and make up the potions for them, it would have helped Janna so much in the dark days following Eadgyth's death. It would have helped Janna now. Miserably she acknowledged that because of Eadgyth's lack of trust, she had not the knowledge or experience to properly diagnose the true causes of illness, nor her mother's skill when it came to binding wounds, setting broken bones, or even administering a healing massage. But she had watched her mother on many an occasion, and for now that would have to do.

Clutching her handful of herbs, she hurried back into the kitchen. A quick glance told her that Serlo had left off interfering, and that Gytha was now supervising the plucking of fowls, the gutting of herrings and the dicing of vegetables that they – or someone – would be eating for dinner. Janna resolved that if any of it came her way, she'd keep half for Edwin. She'd seen his hunger as he ate the griddle cakes she'd prepared, how every last crumb had been wolfed down. In spite of his strength he was too thin, but regular food would soon restore him to full health and vigour. Perhaps, then, he might have a chance with the lovely Gytha?

Ignoring the activity going on around her, Janna carefully washed her hands and the herbs she had collected, just as her mother had always done. Then, with Eadgyth's instructions whispering through her mind, she set about preparing what was needed to help the sick. She had only Gytha and Serlo's description of the disease to go on, but even so she was almost certain that she had seen its like before. She knew how to make the preparations that would give ease, even if she wasn't sure she could cure the pox. Of course, prayers and holy relics might also help – for certes the priests would think so – but so far as Janna was concerned, she had little knowledge of such things and the patients must look to that sort of cure for themselves.

She hung a pot of water to boil over the fire, moving to one side a dish of savoury pottage to make room for it. 'This won't take long,' she told Gytha, when the young woman protested. She added leaves and roots to the steaming water. Leaving the decoction to simmer, she began a survey of the kitchen, bemused at the array of spices she had not encountered before, and the abundance of corn, fruits and vegetables stored in huge barrels and baskets in the larder. A hock of ham hung beside the fireplace, being cured in the smoke from the fire. She took a deep breath, inhaling the rich and potent mix. Bread and vegetable pottage had been their staple diet, but she and her mother had often known great hunger at this time of the year, after what little grain that remained had grown mouldy and the new wheat was still too green to harvest.

She prowled around the kitchen while she waited, testing and sniffing the spices. Some she remembered from her encounter with the spice merchant at the market at Wiltune. She wished now that she'd asked their purpose. At the time they had seemed so far out of her reach, she'd been reluctant to bother him with too many questions. Still, she could taste and sample to satisfy her curiosity now, and this Janna proceeded to do, enjoying the unexpected heat of some, the elusive fragrance and piquancy of others. She could see how they might add flavour to meat, vegetables and puddings. She itched to try them out.

'Pray, take me to see your mother, Mistress Gytha,' she said, once her medicaments were ready. 'I shall try to ease her discomfort.'

The cook and her daughter did not share the servants' sleeping quarters upstairs in the hall of the manor house, but had a separate cot of their own, set close behind the kitchen. Janna had come to know the cook in the mornings when she and Edwin broke their fast and waited to collect their dinner. She was a disapproving, thin-faced woman whose tongue had been sharpened on the misfortunes of others. But she was a sorry sight now, Janna thought, as Gytha pushed open the door and led the way into their cottage.

Mistress Tova lay on a straw pallet. She looked flushed and uncomfortable. Her hair lay in lank strands on her forehead, and her restless fingers scratched first at her face and then at her arm.

'Don't scratch!' Janna said quickly. 'The sores will become full of pus and take much longer to heal.'

The cook's gaze moved from her daughter to Janna, who came forward then so that she might see her patient more clearly. With a conscious effort, she made her voice deeper. 'I beg your pardon for speaking sharply, mistress.' She was about to curtsy but remembered in time to catch herself and bobbed awkwardly instead. 'I am here to help you. My mother was a healer, and she taught me something of her craft. I've made up an infusion for you to drink. It will dull the pain and cool your fever. There's also a lotion to bathe your skin. It will soothe those itches and help the spots to heal. You must not scratch them or you will be left with scars afterwards.' She held up a phial and a jar of lotion, so that the cook could see what she carried.

The woman nodded, even managing a faint smile. 'I would be glad of some comfort, John, for in truth I think my head is about to burst. And my skin feels as if it's been branded by the devil's own fire.'

Janna was somewhat relieved to hear the cook's words. Her mother's patients had described their symptoms in similar fashion. As she set about ministering to Mistress Tova, the woman gave her daughter a sharp glance. 'Get back to the kitchen, Gytha, and make sure you prepare a goodly feast, just in case my lord returns today. John can minister to my needs.'

Gytha ducked her head in obedience and vanished outside, leaving Janna alone with the cook. Janna kept her head bent, for Mistress Tova's sharp eyes and avid tongue seemed to miss nothing.

'You are very young,' she said now. 'You have not even a hint of a beard.'

Janna cleared her throat. 'I may be young, but I am strong, mistress,' she said, fending off any implied criticism.

'And skilled too, it seems.' The cook sniffed the draught that Janna handed to her. 'Pray tell me what is in this? I'd like to know how you have prepared it, for it is usually my task to minister to any who might fall ill here on my lord's demesne.'

As Janna detailed what she had used and her method of preparation, the cook nodded approvingly. Her eyes were alight with interest. After a first suspicious sip, she drank the

78

mixture down. 'And how did you prepare this?' she asked, when Janna unstoppered the cooling salve she had made.

'Septfoil?' she queried, interrupting Janna's recitation.

'It's sometimes called tormentil.' Using a small piece of cloth to keep her fingers free of contact with the sores, Janna began to dab the lotion onto the cook's skin.

The cook was silent for a few moments. 'You have a wide knowledge,' she commented.

'My mother was very skilled at healing. She wanted me to learn her craft and so she taught me what she knew.' It was the truth.

'And your brother? Does he have the knowledge too?'

'He has no aptitude for healing. He . . . he likes working outdoors, tilling the earth and caring for the animals.' Janna hoped that was true of Edwin.

The cook grunted. 'Master Serlo will keep him up to the mark. He is a hard taskmaster, but a fair one, you'll find. Do as he tells you and he's kindly enough. Go against him, and you'll live to regret it. He tends the manor farm as if it was his own and he expects the same from all of us. Indeed this is his life, for he has no family to think about. My lord is fortunate he has Serlo to look after everything in his absence.'

'Master Serlo has indeed been kind to us,' Janna acknowledged. She continued to dab the cooling lotion onto the cook's face and arms.

The cook gave a quiet moan as the liquid touched several spots she'd scratched raw. 'Am I hurting you, mistress?' Janna asked.

'No, indeed.' Mistress Tova gave Janna a watery smile. 'I am grateful for your aid and comfort.'

'If you will remove your kirtle . . .' Janna remembered her new identity just in time. 'You could also use this lotion on your stomach and back. I will leave it here with you.'

'Thank you.' The cook nodded gratefully.

'And I will mix up some more medicaments, and visit you again tomorrow.' Janna moved towards the door.

'I am sure Master Serlo would be very grateful if you could also attend those villeins who are too sick to work, John. There is so much to be done, and too few hands now to do it. I know the reeve is anxious, for my lord is expected home soon. He will want to give a good accounting of his steward-ship during my lord's absence.'

'I will do what I can to make them all well,' Janna promised. Curiosity prompted her to probe further. 'You have a very beautiful daughter, mistress. I pray that she will not contract your disease.'

'As do I,' the cook said promptly. 'My daughter is of an age to wed, and I have great hopes of a good match for her. In fact, Master Serlo has already spoken to me. He would be a good catch for Gytha. I have urged her to consider his offer, but . . .' She hesitated. Pride overcame prudence. 'I believe my lord is also attracted to Gytha and I know she cares for him. If he was to suggest that they wed . . .' The cook smiled at the thought.

'Then I hope they'll find happiness together,' Janna murmured. 'God keep you, mistress. I'll call in tomorrow.' Smiling to herself over the high hopes of the cook and her daughter even while wondering if they were deluding them-selves, she opened the door and let herself out of the cottage.

ϜIVE

THE NEXT FEW weeks were busy for Janna. She physicked her patients and so found her way around the manor farm and the hamlet outside the manor gate where dwelt those villeins who gave service and goods to their lord in exchange for land to tend and somewhere to live. Urk and his mother she'd already met, but Janna now came to know everyone else in that small community, husbands and wives, sons and daughters. At first they were watchful, suspicious of this young stranger, this boy who claimed to possess the power to heal their hurts and lessen their misery. They asked instead for Mistress Tova, and Janna had to explain over and over again that the cook herself was struck with the pox and confined to her bed. But at Serlo's urging, and as they themselves began to feel the benefit of Janna's healing salves and lotions, they came to accept her, and welcomed her into their homes.

For Janna, this was something new. She didn't know much about living in a close community, for she and her mother had always dwelt alone at the edge of the forest. Janna found she enjoyed the villeins' friendship and their appreciation. Tending the sick also gave her new confidence that her years of watching Eadgyth so closely might count for something after all. With practice, she might yet come to possess her mother's skills with healing. It was a source of pride to Janna that Mistress Tova made a good recovery, with only a few scars to show where the spots had been. Gytha escaped unscathed. Others were not so lucky and bore the scars of their misfortune, but it was a consolation that no-one died.

As soon as they were well enough, the villeins returned to work in their own fields, although their time was restricted by Serlo, who insisted they also catch up on tasks on the lord's lands that they'd neglected while they were ill. Rainy days postponed haymaking so, instead, Edwin and Janna continued to cut weeds, dig ditches and repair the hedges that protected the fields of corn from hungry animals. Whenever she could, Janna fled to the kitchen garden to tend the plants and herbs that grew there, but the days were long and the work was always hard.

Janna had reasoned that the sooner the villeins were back on their feet and out working in the fields, the sooner she and Edwin would be free to leave. Yet Serlo continued to find work for them to do and made sure they kept busy. He seemed determined that they would repay their full dues for his silence. He rode around the manor and kept an eye on everyone and everything. He always knew exactly what was going on and what needed to be done. Janna had come to admire and respect the reeve for his good care and husbandry of the manor, even while she grumbled over the toll paid by her body. Yet she was aware too that she was growing stronger and more able as the weeks went by, and she gloried in the fresh air, exercise and freedom that her new life afforded her.

Of the lord of the manor there was still no sign, although Gytha was forever preening herself in case he returned unexpectedly.

'He's much older than me, but not so old as Serlo,' Gytha confided on one occasion, when Janna found her admiring her reflection in the still waters of a small duck pond. 'He has at least twenty-five years.' She puckered her lips to blow a kiss to herself.

'And he has not spoken of marriage?'

'He wishes first to make his way in the world.' Gytha tossed her head. Janna could see that she was out of sympathy with her lord's ambition.

'Why should he wish to do that?' Janna spread out her hands to encompass the fields stretching before them. 'Surely this fine demesne brings him in a good income?'

'It is not his to inherit.' Gytha sounded resentful. 'It's not fair! My lord works so hard, he aims to make this the finest manor farm in the shire, but his cousin will take it all when he comes of age. My lord will be left with nothing!'

Janna nodded in understanding. It was becoming the custom for the first born to inherit everything, which made life very difficult for those sons who came after. They had few options other than to enter the king's service and hope to earn bounty in battle, or else go into the church. A third option, and the best from their point of view, was to marry a woman with a dowry and lands of her own. Looking at Gytha, Janna felt sorry for the young beauty. She might have her hopes pinned on the lord of the manor, but unless he was either blind in love or very stupid, he would be looking to wed someone far more suited to his ambition than the cook's daughter.

'When you grow up you should try to be just like him, young John. He's such a man to admire. He's very brave, and very handsome. He's the handsomest man I've ever seen,' Gytha gushed.

Janna wondered just how many men Gytha knew that she could make the comparison with such confidence. 'When does he return?' she asked, thinking that perhaps even now he might be off scouting marriageable prospects.

'We expected him long before this.' Gytha scowled. 'He went to visit his family, but the country is in such unrest he might have been summoned by the king to his castle in Sarisberie. It's not so far from here. Or he might have gone on to Winchestre.'

Janna's ears pricked up. 'Do you know the road to Winchestre?' she asked quickly.

'No, I do not.' Gytha pouted, her mind fixed on her own problems rather than Janna's question. 'Really, there is no reason for him to be anywhere but here,' she groused. 'While there's fighting between the king and his barons, who keep changing their allegiance in the hope that it might profit them, none of the trouble comes anywhere near here. As for the empress's claim to the crown, my lord told us there was a council of peace between Stephen's queen and Matilda's half-brother, the Earl of Gloucester, at the end of May. It was arranged by Bishop Henry, the king's brother, who hopes to bring about a reconciliation between the king and his cousin.'

This was welcome news to Janna. 'Pray God he succeeds, for all our sakes,' she said.

Gytha nodded absent-mindedly. 'Perhaps my lord is still with his family,' she said, coming back to the topic that most interested her. 'Perhaps even now he is arguing his right to keep this demesne. Oh!' She clasped Janna's hand in sudden hope. 'Pray that he succeeds, John, so that our future here together may be assured.'

Janna wondered whether to sound a note of caution, but decided it was none of her business. 'I hope your wish may come true, mistress,' she said, and gently removed her hand from Gytha's grasp. She did not wish to become involved in the young woman's schemes.

It was not so easy, however, to keep herself detached from the villeins and the servants of the household for, having come to know them all as she ministered to their needs, she was popular and much sought after as a result of her kindness and skill. She stood in the kitchen early one morning, waiting for the cook to pack up their dinner and half-listening to Mistress Tova's gossip. Janna had taken special care to stay on friendly terms with her, for it meant that she and Edwin might gain extra meat, or a piece of fowl, or a stale pastry or some fruit along with their bread and ale for the day. Their hard work out in the fields meant that they were always hungry, so Janna was happy to put in extra time and care in return for extra food.

'Of course, that girl would look at anyone who wore breeches.' The cook's lips tucked down with disapproval as she continued in her petulant whine. 'Only yesterday, I saw her walk past him. She pretended to stumble, and kicked aside her kirtle so that she could show off her bare legs. I've seen the way she looks at him! One of these days, you mark my words, that girl will –'

'Who do you mean?' Janna was already tired of the cook's spiteful gossip; her long nose seemed made for poking into where it wasn't wanted. Besides, Janna was keen to be out in the fields for, in spite of the hard work ahead, she thought the day might bring some sunshine, a change from the spitting rain that had plagued them these past few weeks.

'Bertha, of course. Haven't you been listening to me?'

'Yes indeed, mistress, of course I have,' Janna said hastily, anxious not to get on the wrong side of this woman who seemed to wield almost as much power within the household as Serlo did in his master's demesne.

'You must warn your brother about her.' Mistress Tova clicked her tongue vigorously. 'He's handsome enough, I grant you, but he shouldn't encourage her. No good will come of it, you'll see. She'll break his heart before she's done, for she's a flighty girl and besides, she has her sights set much higher than Edwin.' There was an extra note of sourness in the cook's voice. Janna wondered if she considered Bertha a rival to Gytha's chances with the lord of the manor. Her suspicions were confirmed as the woman continued her gripe. 'Not that she'll get anywhere with my lord. A keen eye for a pretty girl my lord might have, but he's not for the likes of Bertha.'

Janna nodded agreement, even while wondering how the cook could show so little common sense when it came to her own daughter. Yet she had some sympathy for Gytha, and also for Bertha, as she remembered her own dealings with the handsome Hugh, a Norman nobleman, whom she'd met at Babestoche Manor while she was trying to save the life of Dame Alice's newborn son. He'd been so kind to her after her mother had died. She was also quite sure she hadn't misread the admiration in his eyes when he'd looked at her. But Hugh, too, had his way to make in the world. Janna knew that he was not for her, although his kisses had shaken her heart and soul, shaken everything she'd thought and believed in. How easy it would have been to love him, even knowing that it could lead only to disaster! She shook his image out of her mind. Hugh belonged to her past life and besides, she was a youth now, and so would not attract the eye of any man, be he as highborn as Hugh, or as lowly as Godric, who had protected her so bravely.

She turned her face away so that the housekeeper wouldn't notice her sadness. The voice continued, relentless as a midge in summer. 'Young as you are, John, you should also guard yourself against Bertha's wiles. I tell you, that Bertha will set her cap at anyone. Young or old, it matters not.'

Janna wondered if the cook realised she was contradicting herself, but was too weary to question it. Instead, she pondered what the luckless Bertha had done to attract so much spite and ire. Bertha was the carpenter's daughter. She was slightly older than Janna, and while she was no beauty, she had a pleasant countenance and always had a friendly word for everyone. Perhaps it was her popularity that soured the old biddy. It was a popularity that her own daughter did not share because of her airs and graces and her deliberate efforts to keep herself apart. Perhaps others on the manor also resented the favouritism shown to Gytha by Serlo, for servants and villeins alike worked every hour of daylight while it seemed that Gytha could please herself what she did. She was seldom in the kitchen, preferring instead to sit beside the well in the yard, or under a sheltering tree, where all might view her dainty stitching and admire her efforts at embroidery.

'. . . but you'll see him soon enough.'

'Who?' Janna realised her mistake as soon as the question left her mouth.

The housekeeper pursed her lips. 'If you are not bothered to listen to me, you'll have to stay ignorant, John,' she said. 'Besides, I haven't all day to stand here gossiping.' As if it was all Janna's fault.

'I beg your pardon, mistress,' she said meekly, and made her escape before the housekeeper relented enough to regale her with another half-hour of malice.

'You'll see him soon enough.' The cook's words piqued Janna's curiosity as she left the manor and trudged up to the fields beyond.

'Is someone coming to the manor today?' she asked Edwin, in case his intelligence was better than hers.

'Maybe the lord. He's supposed to be here for the hay-making. It's late, but they'll start cutting the grass as soon as this rain stops.' Edwin looked worried. 'I hope he won't ask too many questions about us.'

'Who is he?' Janna was surprised to realise that after all this time, she didn't even know whose manor they were on.

Serlo held such firm control over everything, she'd almost forgotten the manor belonged to someone else.

Edwin shrugged. 'Don't know his name. Don't care, so long as he doesn't find out who we really are.'

'I hear he's quite young and very handsome, although to hear Gytha tell it you'd think he was as ancient as God.'

Edwin laughed. 'He might be as handsome as the devil himself, but it can't matter to you. You're a youth, remember?'

'Oh, he'd be far too busy to look at me, even if I were a girl,' Janna said cheerfully. 'I'm told he has his eye on Gytha, and that Bertha has her eye on him.'

'What?' Edwin swung around to confront Janna. He took a savage swipe at a patch of deadnettles.

'It was just idle gossip. You know what Mistress Tova is like.' Janna felt uncomfortable, remembering now how Edwin had sidled up to Gytha when he first saw her.

'She's a wicked old crone,' Edwin muttered. Turning his back on Janna, he began to hack into thistles as if his life depended on eliminating every single one.

With a sigh, Janna looked about her. No matter how many thistles they cut, there were always more to find; she was beginning to think the harvest would be more bountiful if they reaped thistles rather than corn!

Although they used a pair of long-handled sticks to cull the tall, prickly weeds, Janna's hands were scratched and sore. She could feel the sting of their spikes through her smock and breeches whenever she came too close. She hated them! Now, she turned her back on them and, instead, began to cut into a clump of hairy pink corncockle.

In the new freedom her tunic and breeches provided her, she'd almost forgotten how it felt to be constrained in a long kirtle. Her past life was beginning to seem more and more like a dream, and yet her quest nagged at her conscience: she needed to find her father. She wanted justice for her mother's death. Finally, she gave voice to her thoughts.

'If Master Serlo won't give us permission to leave the manor, we must ask the lord if we may go.'

'Master Serlo needs our help with haymaking. He told me so only yesterday.'

'You work too hard, that's the trouble.' Janna paused a moment to survey Edwin's efforts as, seemingly tirelessly, he slashed through the spiky thistles. 'If we were both of us as useless as Gytha, he'd get rid of us tomorrow. Today, even.' She bit her lip as she remembered the distress she'd already caused Edwin. She wished she'd held her tongue.

'Gytha has other uses so far as Master Serlo is concerned,' Edwin said dryly.

'True enough.' Janna felt slightly reassured that Edwin had come to realise he was wasting his time on Gytha. She decided to jolly him along. 'And what is this I hear about Mistress Bertha showing off her legs to you?'

'Who told you that?'

'Do you need to ask?' Janna continued before Edwin had a chance to respond. 'I'm meant to warn you that she's a flirt, a flighty girl, and that she'll break your heart.'

'Mistress Bertha cares nothing for me, whatever Mistress Tova might think!' Edwin's voice was gruff with embarrassment.

Janna looked at him. Edwin's wild, half-starved look was gone; he was filling out, becoming a man. Janna had seen how some of the young women looked at him when he passed by, although he never stopped long to talk with them, to tease them or flirt with them as they obviously wished he would.

'You might not stand a chance with Gytha, but I reckon you could have your pick of anyone else if you weren't so shy,' she observed.

Edwin flushed. 'Look at me!' he countered angrily. 'I'm a fugitive from my lord's demesne. How can I woo a maid when I have nothing to offer her, nothing at all?'

'That'll change when you've waited out your year and a day,' Janna comforted him.

'Yea, it will. But only if we can get to Winchestre, and if I can find work to earn my keep.'

'Then we might as well get started,' Janna said cheerily. 'You won't mind if I ask the lord's permission to leave?'

'I'd rather stay until we're told to go,' Edwin countered. 'Serlo is a good reeve, far better than my own lord, and we have food and shelter here. Trust me, it's much more comfortable living here than living wild in field and forest, having to scavenge and steal to stay alive. Besides, Serlo saved us from the forester. We owe him for that.'

'We've already worked hard enough to repay him a hundredfold,' Janna grumbled.

'It's safer for me to stay here, tucked out of sight.' Edwin thought a moment. 'It's not as though you have any real plan to find your father. A few weeks more can't make any difference either way.'

Janna gave a grudging nod, accepting the truth of Edwin's words.

'Besides, I hear there's to be a great feast after haymaking is done, with much ale and merrymaking. You wouldn't want to miss that, would you, even if it means you'll have to ask a maiden to dance with you?'

Janna threw back her head and laughed at the thought. As she brought her attention back to the task in hand, her gaze sharpened and she straightened abruptly to look ahead. Her heart skipped a beat. She felt light-headed with shock.

That sleek, black destrier! She could swear she'd seen the horse before. She'd even been on its back, riding in front with Hugh sitting behind her, his arms around her to keep her safe. So close they'd been, she had wished the ride might last for ever. She squinted her eyes against the light, trying to see the rider more clearly.

He was clean shaven, with brown, shoulder-length hair. A green cloak almost covered his long tunic. She looked into his dark eyes.

Yes, it was, it truly was! Her legs folded under her and she collapsed onto the ground, faint and giddy with fear. She bent her head to her knees, knowing that the rush of blood would make her feel better. More than anything, though, she needed to hide her face. Hugh thought she was dead, burned in the fire along with her cottage. It was safest for Janna if everyone thought that.

'What is it? What's the matter?' She heard Edwin's anxious voice through the heavy pounding of her heart.

'Hide me, Edwin! Stand in front of me.' Janna didn't raise her head. 'That's my lord Hugh coming our way. What's he doing here?'

There was silence as Edwin surveyed the figure coming towards them. 'I noticed him before,' he commented then. 'He's come from the forest, and he rides alone. He must know the way, or there'd be a guide with him else.'

'I suspect he knows the way very well.' Through her own fear and confusion, Janna had found the answer to her question. 'I suspect he's done the journey through the forest many times.' She remembered how Gytha had talked about her lord and how he managed the manor on behalf of his family, and wondered why she hadn't made the connection before. How could she have been so stupid! Hugh himself had told her that he was visiting his aunt to report on his custodianship of her property, while Hamo, Hugh's cousin, had boasted that in time, he would inherit everything. 'The lord Hugh has been away visiting his aunt at Babestoche, which is on the other side of this forest,' she said slowly. 'Dame Alice must own this manor farm, for Hugh is her nephew and Gytha has told me he's in charge here until his cousin comes of age. Oh, Edwin!' Her voice shook as she looked up at him. 'This is the worst possible place we could have chosen to come for shelter!'

'Have courage,' he murmured, as he bent and sliced into a patch of nettles. 'You are a youth now, remember, and the lord comes very near to us. You'd better get back to work or he'll certainly stop and give you a piece of his mind.'

Conscious that it was good advice, Janna scrambled to her feet and began to hack into a patch of yellow-flowering charlock, deliberately turning her back on the oncoming horseman. All her senses were strained as she listened to the sound of the horse's hooves and the jingle of its bridle. In spite of herself, a slow blush mounted her cheeks.

'God be with you,' Hugh's cheery voice rang out.

'God be with you, sire,' Janna mumbled in reply. She didn't turn around, but heard Edwin's voice echo her own greeting. To her horror, the sounds had stopped, which meant that the horse had too. She risked a quick glance behind her, not wanting to turn around but wondering if it would be considered rude to ignore Hugh and keep on working.

'You are strangers to my manor, are you not?' Hugh sounded puzzled. Janna waited, her heart thudding, for Edwin to reply.

'We are, my lord. Your reeve, Master Serlo, gave us shelter in return for our labour. He has asked us to stay and help with the haymaking.'

'Which is very late.' Hugh cast his eyes skyward, assessing the chances of the sunshine continuing.

'There has been much illness as well as bad weather, sire,' Edwin hastened to explain.

Watching from under lowered lids, Janna saw Hugh nod silently. 'Who are you? What are your names?' he asked.

'I am Edwin, and this is my brother, John.'

Janna turned to Hugh. She ducked her head in obeisance and kept it bent to avoid his gaze.

'And where are you from? Do you have permission from your liege lord to leave his manor?'

As Edwin launched into an explanation, Janna turned to attack a patch of thistles.

'Your young brother seems determined to earn his keep,' Hugh interrupted, sounding amused. Janna did not dare to look at him.

'He's young, sire, but he's a good worker. Our mother always said that young John here was never at rest until all was done and proper.'

Edwin sounded so convincing! Janna stifled a giggle.

'I can see your mother was right. I'll have a word with Serlo when I find him. Maybe you can stay on to help with the harvest too. There is always a need for good and willing workers.' The jingle of the bridle told Janna that Hugh was on the move once more. Only when the sounds had faded into the distance did she dare to raise her head and look about her.

'There, you heard him! He wants us to stay.' Edwin sounded wistful. 'I'd like that, John, I really would.'

'Don't even think about it!' Janna said furiously. 'Didn't you listen when I told you that the villagers set fire to my cottage, with me in it? It's too dangerous for me to stay here!'

'You didn't tell me he had anything to do with it.' Edwin jerked his head in the direction of the dwindling figure of Hugh.

'No, but . . . but . . .' Janna couldn't tell Edwin that it was Hugh's uncle by marriage, Robert of Babestoche, who had incited the villagers to rise against her. If Hugh found out who she really was, it would only be a matter of time before Dame Alice and Robert found out too. Janna had managed to escape with her life once; she didn't intend to take any further chances.

'But . . . but what?' Edwin raised an enquiring eyebrow.

'He was part of it. Hugh, I mean,' Janna muttered. 'It's not safe for me to stay here.' Even as she said the words, she knew that she wanted to stay, just to be near Hugh. Being so close to him again had utterly unnerved her. In spite of her short hair and villein's garb, she longed to show herself as she really was, and tell him the truth: that she was alive, that she had escaped the fire that was meant to destroy her and her cottage. Then she remembered Gytha, and the light died in her eyes. It seemed that Hugh had a weakness for pretty serving girls and also the glib tongue to convince them that they were special in his eyes. 'We have to leave. We must,' she insisted.

'We can't. Not without Serlo's permission.'

'He can't stop us if he doesn't see us go.' Janna wondered why Edwin was being so obstinate.

'He can raise the hue and cry after us with the forester and with the sheriff. I've done enough running away, Ja . . . John. Please, let's stay here as long as we can.'

Janna was silent, torn between wanting to help Edwin and to protect herself.

'We probably won't see him again,' Edwin urged. 'He'll be far too busy and important to bother with the likes of us. Our dealings are with Master Serlo, not him. Besides, he doesn't suspect a thing. In fact, he thinks well of you for being such a hard worker!'

Janna gave a grudging nod, acknowledging the truth of Edwin's argument. 'Then you must speak for me, protect me from him,' she conceded, adding fiercely, 'but only until our time is up! Then I'm going to Winchestre, whether you come with me or not.' She bent to slash at the hated weeds once more.

SIX

AFTER HER unexpected encounter with Hugh, Janna spent as little time in the hall as possible in case he came in and found her there. She broke her fast at speed and, while Edwin waited about afterwards for Hugh or Serlo to give the villeins on week work their orders for the day, she would hurry to the kitchen and wait for Mistress Tova to pack up dinner and supper in a sack for those who had no land to provide for themselves. Listening to Mistress Tova meant that Janna was well up on the doings of the manor, and the gossip that was attached to them.

Not everything was going smoothly and Mistress Tova had plenty to say about that too. A fox had got into the henhouse one night. The rumpus had woken the servants sleeping in the hall, and they'd rushed down to investigate, but several hens had already been savaged and killed. The maid in charge of feeding them and collecting their eggs had been in a lot of trouble, although she tearfully repeated over and over again that she was sure, positive, absolutely certain that she'd shut the coop tight for the night.

Next, a young lamb had been found dead. The sheep had all been washed prior to shearing. They'd been put back in their fold but the lamb was found some distance away, although the shepherd said he'd counted them and had stayed guard in his little hut all night. The lamb's carcass was cut and bloody. It was certain that no natural illness or weakness had killed it, while the shepherd swore no wolf could have carried it off either. He, too, had felt the sharp edge of Serlo's tongue.

On another occasion, cows managed to escape from their byre and plunged through a hedge into a field of ripening wheat. Before the hayward could sound the alarm, their hooves and their appetites had destroyed a large portion of new grain, which meant there would be less for the harvest and therefore less to tide everyone over through winter and the hungry months before the next harvest.

What intrigued Janna most was her suspicion that the incidents had been planned, and for a purpose. Walking past the henhouse on the day after the hens had been savaged, she'd noticed a small bunch of rue beside the gate of their run. It had seemed odd at the time, so odd that she'd paid close attention when she found another bunch of rue near the sheepfold after the slaughter of the lamb. Was the herb dropped by accident, or had the perpetrator regretted his act of violence after the event? Was this his way of saying he was sorry? No-one seemed to think anything of it, but Janna couldn't believe in happenstance. Perhaps to the others the rue was just a useful herb, but she understood its special significance. 'Rue is for repentance,' Eadgyth had told her. 'Rue stands for regret.' The bunches of rue must surely mean that these things had happened for a reason. But what could that be?

The question had niggled her so that, after the cows went wandering, Janna searched for rue near the byre. It had taken some finding, for by then the animals had been found and herded back. The ground around about was muddy and the herbs had been trampled underfoot, but Janna found enough scraps to know that a bunch of rue had been picked and placed there.

No accident then, but for a purpose. Who was responsible, and why? Janna had a growing suspicion that she knew the answer to the first question, and possibly even the second. She resolved to keep watch, and wait until she had some grounds for accusation. Meantime, she hoped with all her heart that her suspicions were wrong. She became aware that Mistress Tova was still talking.

'There have been too many accidents since my lord Hugh's return. This sort of thing never happens while Master Serlo's in charge.' Mistress Tova gave Janna a long and meaningful glance, before adding hastily, 'Of course, Gytha is delighted to have my lord back at the manor again, but even so . . .'

Janna stopped herself from defending Hugh, not wanting to betray any special interest in him to the gossiping cook. But she couldn't help worrying about it, for although Serlo had questioned everyone after the incident with the cows, no-one seemed to have any knowledge of how they might have escaped the byre, nor any intention of revealing the secret if they had. The cowherd seemed blameless; his family could vouch for his presence in their midst at the time the animals must have gone astray. Someone else was therefore responsible, and Serlo was making every effort to find the culprit. Janna was quite sure that the reeve suspected her and Edwin, being the newest arrivals on the manor farm. He'd certainly questioned them for a long time.

Janna's thoughts went back to that interview, and how uncomfortable she'd felt under Serlo's accusing gaze as he'd made them recount where they'd been and what they'd been doing. He had a nasty rash on his hand, Janna remembered, and she'd sought to divert his attention by offering a healing salve. But he'd brushed her concern aside, clearly determined not to be deflected from his purpose: someone was going to be held responsible for the destruction; someone was going to get the blame. Yet at the end he'd made no accusations, but instead had ordered every villein out into the field to plant peas, beans and vetches, so that there might be something to eat in place of what had been destroyed.

'Of course, you and Edwin are newly come to the manor.' Mistress Tova's voice broke into Janna's thoughts. She didn't have to say anything else for Janna to know what she was thinking.

'Edwin and I aren't responsible for any of these accidents. We know nothing about them!' Janna hoped that her denial would be believed, and also passed on with the rest of the gossip that Mistress Tova shared around so freely.

The cook looked thoughtful. 'No-one wants to think the worst of you, John, not when you were so good about curing us of the pox. No.' She went quiet for a moment, as if wondering how far she could trust Janna with her suspicions. 'No,' she continued, 'it seems that we're just having a run of bad luck.' She tied up the sack of food and thrust it towards Janna. 'I've put in a small meat pie for your dinner,' she said generously, and Janna beamed her thanks.

The sun had finally come out, the long days had settled into sunshine, and haymaking had started at last. Hugh was present for the ceremony that marked its beginning, when at dawn the hayward tied a bunch of flowering grasses to his scythe and crossed himself in prayer before making the first cut. Janna had stayed as far away from Hugh as she could, mingling with the villeins as they followed the hayward in a line through the water meadows, scything the long grass that would keep the animals from starvation during the lean winter months when the meadows were flooded. When she next looked around for Hugh, he had gone. She smiled with relief, her smile returned by the women and children who followed behind them. Their task was to spread the grass out to dry, and turn it so that it bleached to a pale gold in the hot summer sun. The sweetness of cut grass, and the fragrant herbs that were felled with it, scented the air.

All able-bodied villeins, plus their wives and children, were expected to take part in this boon work for their lord, just as they were pressed into service at other busy times on the farming calendar. Their reward, at the end of each day of haymaking, was to take home as much hay as they could carry on their scythes. Only when all the grass was cut, dried, bundled and stored would they be released from their extra days of labour. While this caused some grumbles, they mostly worked with a will so that they could finish the task and get back to tending their own fields.

After the fuss about the straying cows, there'd been no further incidents. Janna had begun to convince herself that the culprit was truly repentant, and that they could all rest easy now. So she was happy and quite unsuspecting as, sack of food under her arm, she walked past the stables on her way down to the water meadows for the day's haymaking. The sound of Hugh's voice stopped her. After a quick look around the yard to check that no-one was watching, she sidled over to the door and peered around it. Hugh was in a stall with his destrier, swearing loudly as he inspected its hoof. Janna knew an instant of alarm, but then calmed her fears with the thought that horses often went lame and that this must just be happenstance. As she watched, Hugh removed a loose shoe and then carefully extracted an iron nail from the horse's hoof, swearing profusely all the while.

To allay her suspicions, Janna inspected both sides of the stable door, looking for any telltale sign. It was bare of everything but the latch. She felt a rush of relief until she realised that what she sought and feared to find was lying on the ground in front of the door: the aromatic silvery green leaves and small yellow flowers of rue, half-hidden under her boot.

Janna snatched them up. This was proof, if proof was needed, that this was no coincidence. All these so-called 'accidents' had been planned deliberately. As she hurried through the water meadows, she cast the sprigs of rue into the long grass to hide them. Who could be responsible? One by one, she went through everyone she knew, trying to find a possible culprit.

It was a puzzle. While many of them might have the opportunity to carry out these acts, there was only one person she could think of who had any reason to do such things. From everything she'd heard and witnessed, Hugh was a good overlord, kind and fair, while Serlo was respected and trusted by everyone. Why should anyone want to harm either man, or his reputation, or the manor farm itself, at least anyone other than a child?

Urk. Everything pointed to him. He was free to come and go. No-one paid much attention to him, or took him seriously. And he, alone of anyone she knew, had a reason to cause trouble and then repent his actions.

Although she'd tried to keep her promise to Mistress Wulfrun, it was impossible to watch Urk all the time. Janna was sure the boy brooded over his punishment at the hands of Serlo and that he might well want to hit back at the reeve. The posies of rue seemed to confirm his regret afterwards for what he had done. Janna wondered whether she should warn Urk's mother, yet she didn't want to cause the woman even more grief and worry. Instead, she resolved to double her watch over Urk, and also to warn him that she knew what he was doing and counsel him over the consequences. She must make him realise that, if he was caught, retribution would be horrible both for himself and for his family.

Pleased to have formulated a plan of action, Janna skipped a few steps and then, after checking that no-one was about, she tried a couple of cartwheels, copying the actions of some children she'd seen larking about. She'd been dying to have a go and, to her satisfaction, she almost succeeded. She had another try and then another. A bit wobbly, she decided, but she was sure she'd improve with practice. She strode on, feeling happy, healthy and almost content. She was used to the labour now, and revelled in the growing strength in her muscles and her freedom to run, to shout, even to turn cartwheels and do anything else a boy might do. She smiled to herself, and hurried on to join Edwin and the others who were busy forking up the dry grass and stacking it into bundles. Urk was among the group. He was almost as tall as Janna, and far stronger and quicker. He gave her a smile. It was the perfect opportunity, and Janna took it.

'Are you very angry with Master Serlo, Urk?' she asked, moving closer to him so that they could talk without being heard.

'No. I'm scared of him.'

It was true. Janna had seen him cower away and try to hide whenever Serlo came near. 'I wonder, did you hurt that baby lamb we found the other day? The one that was all bloody and lying out in the field?'

'No! I like baby lambs.' Urk's lips set in a straight line, and he forked the hay with renewed vigour.

'Do you know who hurt it?' she pressed.

'No.' Urk shook his head without slackening his pace. 'It's not right to kill baby lambs.'

'No, it isn't,' Janna agreed, feeling rather at a loss. 'What about the cows that got into the field?' she tried. 'Do you know who let them out of the byre?'

The boy shook his head, not bothering to answer.

'Or the hens? Do you know how the fox got into their coop?'

'No.' Urk kept on forking up hay.

'What about my lord's horse? Was it you who hammered the nail into its hoof?' Janna pressed.

'No!' He stopped and turned to her then. 'I'm scared of horses. They're too big.'

'None of those things was an accident,' Janna said. 'Someone did them on purpose. Someone who wants to cause trouble to Master Serlo and the lord Hugh. Do you know who that could be, Urk?'

He lowered his head and began to kick out at the green stubble left from the newly cut grass.

'It's all right to tell me if you know anything about it,' Janna urged. 'I won't tell anyone else what you did, I promise, just so long as you stop.'

'But I didn't do anything!'

'If Gabriel says he didn't do it, then he didn't do it.' Mistress Wulfrun materialised on the other side of Janna. 'I know what you're thinking, John, but he's a truthful boy. I've never known him tell a lie, even when he's got in trouble for it.'

'Gabriel?' Janna asked, confused.

'We call him Gabriel,' Mistress Wulfrun explained. 'He may not be the brightest star in the sky, but he's kind and loving, and he has such a sweet smile we believe he's been touched by God's own hand.'

Urk smiled at Janna, as if in proof of his mother's faith in him. 'I didn't do none of those things,' he said, softly but firmly.

Janna wondered whether she could believe him and his fond mother. 'I hope that's true,' she said, 'because you can be sure that when Master Serlo finds out who was responsible, that person will get such a beating he may be half-killed.' She read the fear on Urk's face and was briefly repentant, yet she'd spoken only the truth. If Urk's conscience was clear, then Serlo couldn't touch him or his family. Meantime she had delivered her warning. It was all she could do.

In spite of Urk having the only reason she could think of to do these things, she found that she believed he'd told her the truth. But if not Urk, then who? Edwin? It hardly seemed likely when he was so keen to stay on at the manor, and was so grateful to Serlo for giving them food and shelter. Yet Janna had formed the impression lately that Edwin was keeping something hidden from her, some sort of secret. She hadn't thought much about it, for although the two of them had become firm friends, she thought of him only as a friend and no more than that. She certainly didn't expect him to confess every little thing to her. But where once he'd been always at her side, now he was sometimes missing, gone about some errand of his own. To kill a lamb? To lame a horse?

No! Janna shook her head, unable to imagine Edwin doing any of those things. Besides, he seemed happy enough. He certainly didn't seem to be harbouring the sort of hatred and spite that must lie behind acts of this sort.

What most worried Janna was the thought of what disaster might happen next. If someone was causing problems for a reason, he'd be unlikely to stop until his purpose was achieved. What could that purpose be? If she could only find that out, she might be able to put a stop to these so-called 'accidents', which, in turn, would help ensure her and Edwin's safety.

Questions continued to bedevil her as the villeins prepared to enjoy medale, the drinking festivity to celebrate the end of haymaking. The grass had been cut and dried, and collected into stacks with thatched covers to protect it through the winter rains, or carted off to be stored in the barn. For the moment, their task was done, although Serlo had already warned that sheep-shearing and harvesting were next and that he expected them to stay on and help. She took comfort from the notion that he couldn't suspect them of causing the problems – unless it was at Hugh's urging that he wanted them to stay.

It was with a sense of anticipation that she followed Edwin up to the manor hall on the night of the celebration. Mistress Tova, Gytha and the rest of the kitchen servants had been busy. Trestle tables were set up to form a large square and were laden ready for the feast. Wooden platters were piled high with food, with brimming pitchers of honey mead and ale set beside them.

'This'll do me,' Edwin said cheerfully, as he surveyed the spread. 'You can have the leftovers.' He patted his stomach and gave Janna a wolfish grin.

Janna laughed, but her mirth vanished as she looked beyond Edwin and saw Hugh standing beside Serlo at a table raised up on a platform. He was surveying the crowd below.

'I have to go,' she muttered, and swung around.

'You can't miss out on medale!' Edwin caught her arm and dragged her back, looking horrified at the thought.

'But he's here! My lord Hugh is here!'

'So what? Why are you so afraid of him? What makes you think he'll even remember you?'

It was a fair question, Janna acknowledged, and one she couldn't answer unless she told Edwin how kind Hugh had been to her after her mother died; how they'd played ball with his cousin, Hamo; and how he'd taken her home on the back of his destrier afterwards. And then he'd kissed her! She blushed at the memory.

'Stay,' Edwin urged now. 'He thinks you're my brother. He doesn't know who you really are. Don't let him spoil the feast for you.'

Janna risked another glance in Hugh's direction, her heart jolting painfully as she noticed who else was standing beside him. Gytha. She wore a new gown for the occasion, home-spun but with a greenish tinge that became her dark locks and creamy complexion, and added a bewitching green tint to her hazel eyes. Hugh sat down at the high table, accompanied by Serlo and several others. After he'd said grace, Gytha began to serve him, bending over so that she could smile into his eyes.

Janna stood still, swept by a tide of pure envy. She wanted to flee, to hide from the sight, yet a painful curiosity bid her stay, to watch the interplay between them so she would know for sure whether the girl's trust in Hugh's intentions was well-founded or misplaced.

'See?' Edwin nudged Janna, unwittingly adding to her distress as he said, 'You don't need to worry that he'll notice you. He has eyes only for Gytha.'

'As she has for him,' Janna said bitterly, wondering how Edwin could sound so cheerful. 'Don't you mind?'

'About Gytha? No, why should I?'

So Edwin was over his infatuation with the cook's daughter. Good, Janna thought. She must work on him anew to get him to leave the manor with her. She might feel sorry for Gytha if the girl's high hopes for Hugh came to naught, but she'd feel even sorrier for herself if Hugh defied common sense and became betrothed to the young girl. It seemed flight was her only choice if she was ever to know peace of mind. She sat down beside Edwin, but she found now that she'd lost all appetite and could only look without interest at the mound of food he'd piled on the trenchers of bread in front of them.

'Do you mind if I sit with you two?' Without waiting for a reply, Bertha took a seat on Edwin's other side, flashing a cheerful smile at Janna as she did so. The two of them set about wolfing down huge portions of fish, fowl and mutton, but Janna felt too sick to eat. Instead, she picked up her cup of ale and drained it, then sneaked a glance at Hugh and Gytha.

It was clear that the girl was doing all in her power to woo him. Janna wondered if it was only wishful thinking that made her question whether Hugh was quite so enamoured with the serving wench as she was with him. She knew Hugh to be courteous, and so he was now, bending his head to listen to something Gytha was saying. Yet his gaze roved the room until he caught sight of Janna. She blinked and looked quickly away, while her face flamed scarlet. His glance had been questioning; he was frowning at her. Had she done something wrong? Worse, did he suspect that she or Edwin might be behind the laming of his horse and the other disasters that had befallen the manor? Janna wanted to leap up, to go to him and protest her innocence. With an effort, she stayed seated and tried to look as if she was enjoying herself. She sneaked another look, to find Hugh still watching her. Her heart thudded painfully, her chest felt too tight to breathe. She cast about for a chance to escape, but knew there was none. She would not be able to leave the hall until after the lord had arisen from the table and retired to his solar. It would be unforgivably rude to do so. In case Hugh was still watching, she poured herself another mug of ale and quaffed it down, trying to look as unconcerned and as boyish as possible.

'You should eat something, John,' Bertha urged, and held out a portion of fat hen in her fingers. 'You'll never grow as tall and strong as your brother, else.' She smiled at Janna.

Distracted from her dark thoughts, Janna felt a flash of amusement as she took the food from Bertha's fingers. 'Thank you,' she said, wondering if the cook's sour gossip had some truth in it. Was Bertha indeed flirting with her as well as with Edwin – and everyone else who wore breeches, if Mistress Tova was to be believed? Janna ate the fowl, her appetite reviving somewhat as she savoured the delicacy, so that she continued then to help herself from the trencher.

'Are your family here tonight, mistress?' she asked Bertha, seeking to distract herself from the scene being played out at the high table.

'Yes, indeed.' Bertha waved an arm towards the tables opposite. 'That's my father and mother, and my two sisters sit next to them. Not for anything would any of us miss this feast.' With an expression of bliss on her face, she began to tear the flesh off a chicken bone with her teeth.

Janna had met one of Bertha's sisters when she'd taken medicaments to cure her of the pox. Now she looked with interest at the rest of Bertha's family.

'Bertha's little sister wants to meet you, John,' Edwin told her, with a sly smile. 'She thinks you're very handsome. Perhaps you might like to dance with her later?' .

Janna choked on a piece of fish, and began to cough. Edwin thumped her on the back. Scarlet in the face, she quaffed down some ale. 'Fish bone,' she spluttered, by way of explanation.

Bertha smiled in ready sympathy. 'I had an uncle who choked to death on a fish bone,' she said, and embarked on a long story, giving Janna a chance to recover her equilibrium.

Only when every last morsel was eaten were the tables cleared away and stacked. Now I can leave, Janna thought, but Hugh still stayed seated at the high table, gazing serenely at the scene in front of him. Gytha leaned over him to pour wine into his goblet, her arm against his, her breast almost brushing his cheek. Janna clenched her hands and turned away, knowing she was trapped for the while.

Several villeins stood together at one side of the hall. Janna recognised the shepherd with his pipe, then noticed that the others also carried musical instruments. Occasionally she'd heard someone playing a tune in the marketplace; sometimes people sang words to the music, or even danced around. Janna hadn't paid them much mind. Her mother only ever hummed a tune when she thought she was alone and no-one was listening. Janna thought there must be something shameful about it because Eadgyth had been so angry when Janna had asked if she would teach her the song. Music had never been part of Janna's life, so she could hardly contain a gasp of surprised pleasure now as, with one accord, the villeins turned to the eager crowd gathering around them and began to play.

The shepherd held his pipe to his mouth and blew through the holes in it, dancing his fingers up and down to produce the sounds. One of the villeins struck a small drum, setting up a rhythm for the dancers, who were now swirling around in pairs, stamping their feet in time to the beat, and shrieking with delight. The third member of the party held a wooden bowl with a long neck along which several strings were tied. His fingers plucked and stroked the strings so that his sounds and the sounds from the pipe spoke to each other, sometimes blending together and sometimes taking turns to create different sounds altogether. Janna listened, enchanted, while her feet tapped in time to the rhythm.

'John? I would have a word with you.'

Hugh's voice dragged Janna from her reverie. She gave a start of surprise, and looked anxiously for Edwin and Bertha to save her. But they had joined the throng of dancers and she sat alone.

She leapt to her feet and bobbed her head. 'Sire,' she murmured, remembering to keep her voice deep. She did not dare look at Hugh. Instead, she moved closer to a shadowy recess where the light from the candles scarcely reached.

'I believe I have you to thank for ministering to my workers when they were ill with the pox. I am grateful to you. Serlo tells me we would have been even further behind with everything but for your cures.' Janna felt her hand seized. Something round and cold was pressed into it. Hugh released her hand and she looked to see what he had given her. A dull glint told her what it was: a silver penny! She thrust it into her purse.

'Thank you, sire,' she stammered, glancing quickly up at him before looking away again.

'I have a horse gone lame – a nail awry in a loose shoe. Will you see if you can do aught to help? Arrow is in pain, and I fear he may become crippled if the wound festers.'

'Yes, sire. Of course I'll do all I can.' Janna's heart lurched at the thought of ministering to Hugh's destrier under his watchful gaze. She kept her head bent.

'Come to the stables tomorrow, after you have broken your fast. I'll wait for you there.'

Janna nodded. 'Sire,' she whispered, wishing that he would go and leave her alone yet wanting him to stay, wanting this moment with him to last for ever.

'You have no need to fear me, John.' Hugh's voice was kindly. But his next action filled Janna with alarm as he reached out and tilted up her chin. She had no choice but to look full at him.

'I thought so,' he murmured, coming closer to peer at her in the shadowy darkness. 'You remind me of a young healer I once knew. Her name was Johanna. Do you know of her, John? Was she perhaps a sister, or a cousin to you?'

'No! No, sire. My brother and I come from Wales.' Janna's voice shook as she told the lie. She longed to confess to Hugh, and to ask if he had kept his promise to her, but she dared not. 'We have no living kin here in England,' she said, in case he still harboured suspicions about her.

'And yet you look so like her,' Hugh mused, adding as if to himself, 'They say Johanna died in a fire.'

And were you sorry to hear that? Janna pressed her lips firmly together so that she could not ask the question, although she longed to know the answer. It was some comfort that Hugh remembered her; she took more comfort from the regret in his voice when he said, 'Johanna had a great gift for healing, and so did her mother. They are much missed at the manor of Babestoche, and in the neighbouring hamlets, for there is no-one now to physic the sick and help the dying.'

'Surely there is a midwife in the village, my lord?' Janna knew he was mistaken about the villagers' regret, but she wondered what had become of Mistress Aldith, one of the few of her mother's acquaintances who had shown her any kindness.

Hugh shrugged. 'Her business is to birth babies, but my aunt has little faith in her, that I know. Whether she can do else, I know not.' His gaze sharpened on Janna's face. 'Where did you learn your healing ways?' he asked.

'From . . . from my mother, sire.' Janna knew she should stick to her story. Others had heard it, and could repeat it to Hugh if he asked. It would increase his suspicion if she told him something different now. 'She was Saxon born, but when she wed my father, she went to live with him in Wales. He died when we were still quite young, but my father had a cot and enough land to keep us so my mother stayed on, for her own family were either dead or gone away.'

'I thought Serlo told me your mother worked in an alehouse?'

'So she did, sire, sometimes, for she had us to help her about our home,' Janna improvised rapidly. 'As soon as he was old enough, my brother tended the fields and planted the corn. He also looked after our sheep and goats, while I helped by growing vegetables for the pot, and herbs for my mother's medicaments. My mother was settled in Wales.

It was her home. And ours, until she died.' Janna knew she was gabbling, but she hoped the wealth of detail might help to convince Hugh. She hated lying to him, hated it, but she knew that her safety depended on it.

'Why, then, did you leave Wales?'

Janna gulped. 'I . . . er . . . my oldest brother has wed. He has taken the land and the cot for his own, so Edwin and I decided to seek a living in Winchestre. We are free born, sire,' she added for good measure.

'This isn't Winchestre,' Hugh commented dryly.

'No. No, sire, it isn't. But we have no money of our own so we are forced to find food and shelter along our way, which we repay with our own labour.'

'Then I wish you both good fortune.' Hugh paused a moment. 'I've watched you and your brother. You are hard workers, and your skill as a healer is also welcome here. You may stay on my manor as long as you wish.'

'Th . . . thank you, sire.' Janna stepped away from Hugh and bowed her head, desperate for him to leave. To be so close and not tell him the truth was a torture to her. When she looked up again, he had returned to his place at the table but he watched her still, his face screwed up into a thoughtful frown. Knowing she must act, and quickly, Janna turned to a young girl standing nearby. She was Bertha's young sister, Janna realised, and she was looking at Janna with a hopeful expression on her face. Without giving herself time to think, Janna grabbed the girl's hand and led her into the throng of laughing, dancing villeins.

Just as she had no notion of music, so Janna didn't know how to dance either. It didn't seem to matter among all the noise and confusion, but still she tried to copy the actions of those around her, clapping her hands and stamping her feet in time to the beat. When the villeins linked arms or whirled their partners around by the waist, so did Janna, and when they formed into a long line and danced around the high table, so did Janna along with Bertha's sister. She hoped Hugh was still watching. She hoped he was satisfied that she was who she claimed to be. But in truth, she thought, as she stole a quick glance at him, it was Gytha who held his attention now, for she held a plate of sweetmeats before him, tempting him both with the delicacies and with her eyes.

Janna looked quickly away and concentrated on following the pattern of the dance. She was just beginning to enjoy herself when a sudden shout sounded above the music. 'Fire!'

At once there was pandemonium. Some began to scream, some froze to the spot with terror, while others pushed past and over them in a desperate effort to get through the door and down the stairs to safety. It took some time for the hall to clear and everyone to realise that the danger lay not in the manor house but outside in the fields.

One of the haystacks was alight. They could see the glow above the palisade of sharpened stakes that fenced the manor house and yard. Cold dread gripped Janna as she listened to new cries of alarm. If the fire moved on and destroyed the other haystacks, the winter fodder would be burned and the animals would starve. Yet everyone milled around, waiting to be told what to do until Hugh shouted out above the hubbub: 'Follow me to the stream!' He raced ahead through the gate, and everyone fell into line behind him.

Janna saw that Hugh had already left instructions with Serlo for he, along with a group of his own, ran towards the shed where all the farming implements were housed. Undecided how best to help, Janna followed the crowd through the gate and up into the field, then stopped to watch. In the light from the flames, she saw that Hugh was now dividing the villeins into two groups, sending some towards the small stream that ran down into the river, and beckoning others to follow him to the flaming haystack. As Serlo and his helpers raced to the stream with leather buckets from the shed, the villeins began to form into a long line, making a chain that led from stream to haystack. At once they began to fill the buckets and pass them from hand to hand up the line. Serlo stayed by the stream to keep the buckets moving, while Hugh took up station beside the haystack to direct the flow of water onto where the flames were fiercest.

Once the contents were thrown, the buckets were thrust at a knot of children waiting nearby. They took turns to race back with the empty buckets to the stream to be refilled. Janna noticed Urk among them, carrying two buckets at a time and racing faster than anyone. Had he been in the hall with everyone else before the haystack caught alight? She couldn't be sure. All her attention had been on Hugh, and then on her dancing partner as she tried to convince Hugh that she was a youth. It was certain that Urk was on the spot now, and doing all he could to help put out the fire – but had he set it in the first place? It seemed unlikely, when he was making such an effort to help now.

Janna looked about. Was anyone missing? Who else might have fired the haystack? She had little doubt that this was no accident, but she was greatly fearful that Urk would be blamed for it. After all, he'd set fire to hay once before. Serlo would surely believe he might do so again.

She stepped closer to scrutinise the chain more carefully. Hugh was beside the burning haystack, his face illuminated in the blaze as he directed the villeins to throw the water where it would be most effective. Serlo was still beside the stream, keeping a watchful eye on the buckets moving up the chain, and also on the children, making sure they ran back to the haystack once they'd handed over the empty buckets to be filled. There was order amid the panic, for everyone knew how vital it was to keep the fire from spreading. Janna's glance narrowed as she tallied off the line of peasants labouring to pass along the heavy buckets without their precious contents being spilled. There was no sign of Edwin. Where was he?

She moved along the line to look for him.

'You! John! Get into the stream and help fill those buckets!' Serlo had seen her, and Janna knew that to disobey would invite his wrath as well as his suspicion. She hastened to do as she was told.

There was barely enough light from the flickering flames to make out the identity of her companions. But Edwin was not here, she was sure of it. She bent to her task, grabbing buckets from the children, sweeping them through the water to fill them, then heaving them up and into a pair of waiting arms. It was back-breaking work, but Janna had been toughened from her weeks in the fields and she knew she felt the strain less than the women who worked beside her. But they carried on without complaint, desperate to save the fodder that would keep their animals alive through winter, with meat on the table for themselves and their families.

'Give me a bucket.' She heard Edwin's voice beside her, and turned on him with a mixture of relief and fury.

'Where have you been?' she hissed.

He hung his head. She thought he looked guilty, and feared the worst. 'What's going on?' She grabbed his arm. 'Did you set fire to the haystack?'

'Of course not.' He wrenched his arm away. He didn't look at Janna but leaned over to fill a bucket as he said, 'I came to help as soon as I realised what was happening.'

'I hope no-one else noticed your absence! Don't you see, Edwin, we are the last to come here so we must be the first they will blame when they come to realise that these are not accidents but deliberate attempts to do harm.'

'Don't be silly! This was an accident, surely.' Edwin handed over a brimming bucket and grabbed another from a waiting child.

'How could it be an accident? Why would a haystack suddenly catch fire in the middle of the night?'

'Sometimes they overheat, especially if the grass is still green. It happens.'

It was true. Janna hadn't thought of that, but in her heart she was sure it hadn't happened that way. 'What about the dead lamb?' she asked. 'That wasn't an accident.'

'A fox? A wolf?'

Janna shook her head. 'A wild animal would have eaten the lamb, not killed it and left it for someone to find. Besides, its wounds were made by a knife, not teeth.'

'Yea, 'tis true.' Edwin's forehead creased into a frown as he thought about it.

'And the cows that got out and the fox that got in. And Hugh's lame horse. Do you really think all those things were accidents?'

'What happened to the horse?' Conscious that Serlo prowled about, watching them, watching everyone, Edwin hastily dipped his bucket into the stream.

His frown deepened as Janna told him what she'd seen and found at the stable. 'These things have all happened since my lord Hugh returned to the manor,' he interrupted her recital. 'It seems he's not as good at managing the farm as his reeve.'

So Mistress Tova was still spreading her poison. This time Janna was determined to defend Hugh. 'That's not true. You can't blame my lord for any of this.'

'I'm only saying what everyone says.'

Janna shook her head. 'These are not accidents, they're deliberate actions by someone wanting to cause harm,' she insisted.

'How can you be so sure?'

'The posies of rue left behind at the scene.'

'Rue?'

'For regret. That's what the old ones say, anyway. I wondered at first if the rogue felt regret for his actions after he'd done the deeds, but now I'm not so sure.' Without meaning to, Janna looked for and found Urk. He was coming their way, a bucket dangling from each fist. In spite of the gravity of the situation, his face creased into its customary cheerful smile as he thrust the buckets at Janna and Edwin.

'He looks happy enough. Maybe it's him,' Edwin commented.

'No, it isn't.' But Janna wasn't as sure as she sounded. 'I wondered if it might be you,' she said, deciding to voice her concerns.

'Me?' Edwin looked astonished. 'Why would I do something like this?' He gestured towards the haystack. 'What have I got to gain?'

The flames were dying at last. Smoke and the stink of wet, burnt hay tainted the air. Janna sighed with relief that the danger was past. 'I don't know. I just don't know anything,' she confessed.

SEVEN

ER WORRIES KEPT Janna wakeful and restless during the night. Her eyes felt puffy and pricked with tiredness when she finally rolled off her pallet and made herself ready to face Hugh. She was sure that she could smell herself, and she longed for a wash, but there was no privacy to be found unless she left the manor farm – and that she couldn't do, not without Serlo's permission. She certainly could not sneak out at night and plunge into the river, for if anyone saw her undressed they would know the truth. So she sighed, and wet her fingers and tried to smooth the singed stubble that covered her head, which was all she could do to make herself presentable. With a catch of alarm, she realised that her hair was growing long again. She patted the knife in its sheath. She must ask Edwin to cut her hair this very night.

With bread and ale consumed, she left Edwin to wait for the cook to assemble their dinner, and to chat to the serving maids while he waited, for he had become a great favourite in the kitchen. Her heart beat hard in fear and excitement as she first gathered soapwort, marsh mallow leaves and woundwort from the kitchen garden, then walked towards the stables clutching her bouquet of herbs.

There was no sign of Hugh, or anyone else other than a young boy. Janna frowned as she looked more closely. The youth was leading a small herd of nanny goats and their young through the yard towards the gate. Even as Janna watched, the boy raised his arm and aimed a pebble at one of the kids. It hit the goat on the rump and it jumped, bleating pitifully as it did so.

'Stop that!' Janna shouted. The boy hardly glanced at her before picking up another, larger stone. This time he aimed for the goat's head. The animal dropped, stunned, and lay in the dirt, kicking feebly.

Without thought, Janna raced towards the boy. Before he could run away, she had caught him, and she boxed his ears hard, packing all her new-found strength into the punch.

'Ow!' he shouted, wriggling and squirming in Janna's grasp. 'Let me go!'

'How dare you!' she panted. 'How dare you harm that little goat!'

'It's for our dinner.' The boy had turned sullen now. 'First finders of a dead animal gets to keep it, so Master Serlo says.'

'I'll wager Master Serlo doesn't say you can go out and kill it first!' Janna kept hold of the lad. She gave him a hard shake.

'There's no-one here to see me, 'cept you. Why should you care? Everyone does it.'

Somehow, Janna doubted it, but she wasn't prepared to debate the point with the lad. 'Then I'll tell Master Serlo what you've done. If everyone is doing it, he won't mind, will he?'

She felt the boy cower against her. He began to tremble with fright. Janna understood why when Hugh's cool voice interrupted them. 'What's happening here, boy? Why are you throwing stones at my goats?'

Janna let the child go. She stayed silent, leaving him to talk his way out of the situation as best he could. All bravado gone, he began to cry.

'Take the goats out and look after them properly, Eadwig,' Hugh said sternly. 'Be sure I will count them when you bring them in tonight. When you get home, tell your father he's to come to the manor house and bring you with him.'

The lad fled, leaving Janna alone with Hugh. She knelt to pick up the herbs she'd dropped when she'd grabbed hold of the goat's tormentor, feeling some relief as she watched the kid rise to its feet and stagger off to find its mother.

'I saw everything that happened,' Hugh said into the silence. 'I was waiting just inside the stable. I heard you shouting at Eadwig. I saw it all, Johanna.'

Janna froze.

'I'm right, aren't I?' Hugh continued softly. 'Your appearance might have changed, but your voice – and your manner – not at all!'

Janna stayed on her knees, not daring to move or say anything. Hugh put his hand underneath her elbow, and yanked her upright. 'I think you owe me an explanation,' he said, and began to propel her towards the stables. 'You can minister to Arrow while you tell me why you burnt your home to the ground and left us all to think that you were dead.'

'I did not burn my home, sire!' Janna was outraged that he could think such a thing.

He cocked his head to one side, studying her. 'The abbess is wrath, for the cottage was her property and now it is

124

destroyed. And Godric, the villein, has told us that you died in the fire and that he has buried you in the forest. Why so many lies, Johanna, and to what purpose?' His voice lost some of its hard edge as he continued more softly, 'Was the fire an accident? You know, because I told you, that Dame Alice agreed to pay heriot to the abbess and mortuary to the priest after the death of your mother. If the fire was an accident, I doubt the abbess would hold you to blame, while the villagers would surely have helped you to rebuild your cottage and given you shelter until that was done. There was no need to flee, or to tell such lies.'

How little you know of the villagers, Janna thought, as bitter memories swelled up in her mind. She did not know what to say to Hugh, and so she stayed silent.

'In truth, I am disappointed,' he said then, as he snicked open the latch and led her into the stable. 'I had thought you more honourable, more courageous. I didn't take you for a coward, Johanna.'

'I am not a coward, sire!' Janna could stay silent no longer.

'And yet you have run from the village, and even disguised yourself as a boy to escape detection.' Hugh stalked on past a line of horses and stopped at Arrow's stall. The destrier blew a gentle greeting as Janna entered. She wondered if he remembered her. She stood awkwardly, uncertain how to make the horse lift his hoof so that she could inspect it. Hugh solved the problem by doing it for her. Janna clicked her tongue, distressed by the ugly wound which already was beginning to fester from the dung and dirt which had worked its way into the cut.

'I need boiling water and something to wrap the hoof,' she

said. 'I'll have to cleanse it first. Then I'll bind these healing herbs against the wound. You must not ride him, sire, or even take him from the stall.' She glanced down at the mud and dung on which the horse stood. 'It would be best if the horse stood on clean rushes for the while,' she added.

Hugh grunted. But he released the horse's hoof, and shouted for a stable lad to fetch what Janna needed. While they waited, he fixed his dark gaze on her once more. 'Who is Edwin? What is he to you?' he asked now.

'He's . . .' Janna was going to claim him still as her brother, but she was sure Hugh would not believe her. She decided to stick as close to the truth as she could. 'I came across him in the forest, sire, in Gravelinges. I was alone, and frightened, and he took care of me. It is true that he comes from Wales and that he has to seek his fortune after his eldest brother inherited both cot and land when his mother died.' Janna kept her fingers crossed behind her back against yet another lie. She hoped Hugh would not doubt her word as she added, 'Please believe me, sire. I did not set fire to the cottage. That was the work of the villagers, and that is why Godric seeks to protect me now.'

'The villagers burnt your home?' Hugh sounded horrified. 'Why would they do such a thing?'

'Because . . .' But even Janna's quick wits could not come up with a convincing enough story, other than telling Hugh the truth: that her mother had drunk the poisoned wine that Robert had given to Cecily, and that he knew Janna had found out his secret, which was why he'd incited the villagers to take action against her. She was sure Hugh would not believe it of his uncle-by-marriage, and so she stayed silent.

'I am sorry you did not bring your troubles to my aunt,' Hugh said, when it became clear that Janna would say no more. 'Dame Alice would have helped you, I am sure of it. She had great respect for your mother's skill, and yours too.'

'I am sorry too, sire,' Janna said softly. 'I was alone and frightened. With no home and no family, it seemed best for me to run away, and so I did.'

'You are safe now.' Hugh gave her a troubled glance. 'There is no need to disguise yourself any longer, Johanna. You could stay here and help Mistress Tova in the kitchen. I know she would be glad of an extra hand. And heaven knows we often have need of a healer for burns, and broken bones, and the pox if it comes again. You could be very useful to me, if you wish to stay.'

'I thank you for your offer, sire. Of course I am happy to help anyone in need of a healer, but I wish to stay as I am – at least as others think I am,' Janna said stiffly. She wanted to tell Hugh he was wrong; that she was no longer safe now that he knew her true identity. More than ever, she and Edwin needed to flee to Winchestre. She must talk to Edwin; they must leave that very night.

'You have nothing to fear from showing yourself as you truly are.' Hugh looked more puzzled than ever. 'In truth, your disguise does not become you.'

Janna felt a painful blush stain her face as she recalled how he'd once looked at her with admiration in his eyes. No more, not ever again. The thought stung. 'I beg you, sire.' She forced herself to look into his eyes, so he could see that she was in earnest. 'Do not allow anyone to punish the villein, Godric, for his lies. He told them for my protection, just as I would ask you, sire, to keep the truth about me to yourself. I . . . I cannot explain to you why my life is in jeopardy, but I beg you to believe it, and keep my secret now if . . . if you care about my safety.'

Hugh stayed silent, still looking troubled.

'Please, sire!' In her desperation to secure his silence, Janna realised she'd grabbed hold of Hugh's arm. Quickly, she released it. 'Please, sire,' she said more quietly. 'I matter to no-one other than those who wish me harm. Please protect me with your silence.'

'Very well.' The promise was given grudgingly. It was clear Hugh was unhappy about the course Janna had urged on him. 'I know that the priest stirred up trouble against your mother, and that he might have influenced some of the villagers because of his refusal to bury her in consecrated ground,' he conceded. 'I have spoken to Dame Alice about the priest but she will not take action against him.' He stopped, and gnawed on his bottom lip. He seemed to be wondering how far he could take Janna into his confidence.

'You must understand that this is a difficult situation,' he said then. 'My aunt . . . married unwisely. Robert was her father's steward, and after her father died he wooed Alice. Being her father's only heir, and with all that property at her disposal, Alice was supposed to petition the king for permission to marry, but she was desperate to have Robert and no other. With a baby on the way, it became urgent to find someone who was prepared to wed them. This priest . . .' He broke off as the stable lad came clattering in, bearing a bucket of hot water and the bandage Janna had requested. But Hugh had said enough for Janna to understand the situation. Anger flamed anew as she reflected how worthless was the dame's husband. First, and to secure his future, he had seduced Dame Alice. Next, and for his own pleasure, he had seduced Cecily, the dame's tiring woman. Janna wondered how many others Robert had seduced – and abandoned – during his marriage.

'I want you to know that I petitioned the Abbess of Wiltune for a requiem mass to be said for your mother's soul, and for your own,' Hugh said now. 'I have to say that she was reluctant at first. It seems she knows something of your mother's past, but I managed to convince her of your worth, and so it was done.' Hugh surveyed Janna, his face grave as he added: 'Obviously a mass for the dead was not necessary on your account. I can only hope that you walk in the grace of God's blessing, and that you will continue to do so.'

'Yes, oh yes, sire, and thank you. From the bottom of my heart, I thank you for your kindness.' So he had kept his promise to her! Janna felt almost giddy with relief.

'Hmph.' Hugh looked as if he needed convincing that he'd done the right thing. 'And what are your plans for the future?'

To go in search of my father, Janna thought. But she wasn't prepared to take Hugh so fully into her confidence. 'To go to Winchestre, sire, to seek employment there.' It was part of the truth.

'With Edwin?'

'With Edwin.' Janna nodded confirmation.

'Why don't the two of you stay on here? I've already told you your worth to me, and Edwin is a good worker.'

'Thank you, sire. You are very kind.' Janna had no intention of accepting his invitation, but she wasn't going to tell

Hugh that she was proposing to run away that very night. Instead, she set to work, crushing the waxy green leaves of soapwort into hot water before bathing the wound. Hugh and the stable lad kept tight hold of the destrier so that it would not move, or kick out at Janna while she worked. She was grateful for the lad's presence, for it made further conversation difficult. Hugh had already given her much to think about, but she needed a quiet time alone to mull over what he had told her. For the moment, she concentrated on her task, feeling the great horse flinch as she set about binding its hoof, wrapping the hank of unspun wool tight to keep the healing herbs in place, and also to prevent any more dirt from entering the wound.

'Clean out this stall,' Hugh ordered, once Janna was finished and the horse was standing firmly on its feet once more. 'Then go and cut some clean rushes to lay on the ground.' As Janna made to do what she was bid, Hugh grasped her arm. 'Not you,' he said, angling his head towards the lad. 'Him.'

'I am capable of doing the work just as well, my lord, and it will go quicker with two of us.'

Janna felt a queer thrill in defying Hugh, and knew a moment's deep satisfaction when he said, with a smile quirking his mouth, 'I can see you haven't changed anything other than your clothes. You are still as independent as you were when you lived with your mother. Very well, then. Do as you wish.'

'Thank you, sire.' With difficulty, Janna kept a smirk of triumph off her face as she seized a besom and began to sweep the dung and dirt into a pile. When she next looked up, Hugh's silhouette blocked the light from the door; the next moment he had disappeared from view.

The stable lad didn't look at her as they worked together to clear Arrow's stall. Janna wondered how much of her conversation with Hugh he had heard. At least enough to let him know that Hugh regarded her so highly he'd arranged a mass to be said for her soul. Had Hugh said her name in his hearing? Janna cast her mind back over their conversation. No. With luck, the boy still thought of her as John. Perhaps he didn't trust her now. If so, she couldn't think of anything to say to make matters right, and so they filled and dumped their bucket loads in silence.

The lad went over to a row of implements then, and selected two scythes. He gave one to Janna. 'To cut the rushes,' he said shortly, and led the way out, heading down towards the river.

Looking up at the fields, Janna noticed the blackened remains of the burnt haystack. With a feeling of dread, she realised what she must do. 'Let's cut the rushes at the stream,' she said, pointing in the direction of the haystack. The stable boy frowned at her, seeming resentful that she was taking charge. 'It means we can carry the load downhill instead of uphill,' Janna pointed out.

He gave a grudging nod and changed direction. Janna followed him, veering off to the haystack as they passed. She bent to examine the ashy remains. The scene and the smell reminded her of the time she'd searched the burnt ruins of her own home, and how her search had uncovered her mother's secret cache with its clues to her father's identity, the clues she could not read and didn't know how to interpret.

Hugh's words came back to Janna. He'd said that the abbess knew something of her mother's past. Janna wondered now if, instead of fleeing in a blind panic, she should first have sought an audience with the abbess. Perhaps it was still possible? It would certainly be worth the risk of being seen by the villagers if the abbess could tell her where to begin her search for the truth about her mother – and her father. Janna pushed the thought aside for consideration later, and began her search.

She knew exactly what she was looking for and she examined everything very carefully, first the ruined remains of the haystack, then widening her search to encompass other haystacks nearby. It didn't take her long to spy it, the leaves a silvery green, the flowers a bright splotch of yellow tucked into the pale straw of a nearby haystack.

Janna snatched out the posy of rue, and ground it to shreds under her boot. Too late, she wondered if she should take Hugh into her confidence, if she should have kept it to show him or even brought him out with her to search the haystacks. Would he have believed her, or had she already stretched his trust too far?

It was too late, now, to think of it or to regret her action. Janna looked towards the stream where the stable lad was already hard at work cutting rushes for Arrow's stall. She hurried to join him. There was no sign of Edwin now, or her dinner either, Janna realised. With haymaking over, shearing had begun. The hurdles had been taken down and the animals were free to graze in the water meadows, but there was no sign of them or their keeper. She wondered where they were folded now, for it was there that shearing would be taking place and where she needed to search for Edwin if she wanted her dinner this day.

Janna was sweating, hot and filthy by the time she and the stable lad had finished cleaning out Arrow's stall and spreading armfuls of clean rushes over the bare earth floor. It seemed to her that the horse stood easier now. She knew Hugh's pride in his sleek black destrier and, having an affinity for all living creatures and in particular this one who had twice borne her on his back, she hoped that the cure was already working, and that the wound would heal without leaving any lasting harm.

With her task over, Janna hurried to the well, keen to slake her thirst. She sank the bucket down, then wound it up again. After splashing cool water over her hands to cleanse them, she cupped them and drank her fill. She was glad to get away from the sullen stable lad, glad to have a few quiet moments alone to think once more about her conversation with Hugh. She was mortified that he had recognised her, and found her out in all her lies, but she also felt an easing of her mind that she no longer had to pretend with him, that he knew the truth, or most of it at least. She hated lies; she hated deceit, and her anger flared anew at the memory of those who had made such a subterfuge necessary.

Her thoughts turned then to the abbess, who knew something about her mother. Hugh had indicated that the abbess thought badly of Eadgyth. She would also think badly of Janna once she found out that Janna was still alive, for she would believe that Janna had fled to escape the consequences once her cot had burned down. Was it worth braving the abbess's wrath in the hope she would relent enough to tell Janna what she knew?

With her thirst quenched, Janna sat for a few moments beside the well to rest and ponder the question, leaning her back against the rough stone wall with a weary sigh. But the shocks of the day were not yet over.

'Hello! My name's Hamo. What's yours?' A child's voice jerked her out of her reverie. She sat upright with a gasp, feeling giddy and disorientated. This had happened once before. Was she dreaming now, or was it happening all over again? She blinked as a little boy's bright face came into focus. She recognised him. Just so had he introduced himself to her at the manor house at Babestoche. She looked about her, recognising her surroundings as Hugh's manor farm, and breathed a faint sigh of relief that her mind wasn't playing tricks on her. But what was Hamo doing here?

He held tight to a piece of rope attached to a mangy dog. All skin and bones, with matted fur, it now limped over to sniff around Janna's toes. She backed away, her alarm increasing as she took in Hamo's companions with a quick glance.

They were just coming through the gate. There was no sign of Hamo's elderly and disapproving nurse. In her place, and still some distance away, came Cecily and . . . Godric? Janna blinked and peered more closely. Yes, there was no mistake. It seemed that Hamo had found himself a new nurse, as well as a guide to bring him through the forest. With an effort, she brought her attention back to the boy's questioning gaze.

'I know you,' he announced firmly, and then more questioningly, 'aren't you . . .?'

'My name is John,' Janna said gruffly, too alarmed by his unexpected arrival to worry about being rude and interrupting the young lord of the manor. Her alarm increased as she noted Cecily's steps quicken to protect her charge. Cecily knew that Janna hadn't died in the fire, but Janna had sworn her to secrecy. Would she keep the secret even now?

And Godric, how could she face him? He had protected her so loyally, but he didn't know the truth for she'd stayed hidden when he came looking for her. She hadn't wanted him to see her, arguing to herself that she couldn't afford to become involved with him, or feel beholden to him, for he was tied to the manor whereas she was free to go – to run for her life, as it turned out. Her decision had seemed sensible at the time but now she could feel only shame at her mean spirit and lack of trust in not showing herself when he'd called her.

'My name is John,' she said again more firmly, and jumped to her feet, desperate to escape before anyone could challenge her identity. She'd forgotten about the dog. Startled by her sudden movement, it sank its teeth into her ankle and hung on, growling. The pain was sharp as a cut from a sword, and Janna stopped with a cry. 'Get your dog off me, Hamo,' she ordered.

'Bones!' Hamo dropped the rope. He tried to prise the dog's teeth apart, but it growled and sank them deeper.

'Be careful! Mind he doesn't bite you,' Janna said, automatically protective.

'Godric will help. He brought us through the forest and he found Bones. He'll know what to do.' And before Janna had a chance to protest, Hamo turned and shouted the villein's name. There was nothing else for Janna to do then, but wait for the shame of discovery.

'Bones! Let go!' Godric arrived in a burst of speed. He hardly looked at Janna. All his attention was on the dog as he bent and firmly prised open its jaw.

Janna felt the teeth withdraw, and wondered if she still had time to make a run for it. But Hamo had grabbed hold of her hand. 'This is John,' he said gravely, holding on tight. She had no choice but to stand still and face Godric.

'Thank you for getting the dog off me,' she said faintly.

His eyes widened. He said nothing, but he went pale. Janna knew she would never forget the look on his face as he studied her intently. Confusion gave way to elation, which immediately darkened into anger and utter rejection. His face closed into a bitter scowl, and he turned away. Cecily had reached them now, and she took in the situation in one quick glance. 'Janna! What are you doing here?'

Godric still said nothing. Janna wanted to find the words to reach him, to make him understand why she'd acted as she had, and to tell him what was in her heart. She tried, but she couldn't think of anything to say that might make the situation any easier. Stricken mute, she looked down at the ground.

'Janna?' Hamo queried.

'There you are, John! I've brought your dinner.' Edwin had come dashing into the yard, and he hailed Janna as soon as he spied her. As he noticed the still tableau beside the well, his footsteps slowed. He held out the sack of food to Janna as he advanced towards them.

With a muttered exclamation, Godric pushed past them all and headed towards the gate, moving at speed. 'Godric! Wait!' Janna said urgently. 'I can explain . . .' But he ignored her plea and increased his pace. The dog took off after him, moving as quickly as its maimed paws would allow.

'Bones! Come back!' Hamo made an effort to grab hold of the rope trailing behind his pet, but Cecily grasped him and hauled him back. 'You must stay with me, Hamo,' she said firmly, and looked at Edwin.

'Who is he?' she asked Janna.

A short silence followed Cecily's question, before Edwin cheerfully gave her his name. 'I am John's elder brother, mistress,' he added by way of explanation, and sketched a bow. Still no-one said anything, Janna because she was incapable of speech and Cecily because she was utterly confused. Edwin's worried glance moved between them both, and then he looked after Godric's disappearing figure. His frown deepened.

Cecily's glance followed his. 'Over here, sire!' She hailed a couple of strangers who were just coming through the gate. Seemingly Godric had guided the men through the forest along with Hamo and Cecily, for one of them put a hand on Godric's arm to restrain him. The other fumbled a coin from his purse but by the time he held it out, Godric had pushed past the pair and was gone.

In answer to Cecily's call they surrendered their mounts, including several heavily laden sumpter horses, to the waiting groom and paused to give instructions. As the groom led the horses away, Janna noticed that one of them had cast a shoe and was walking awkwardly.

'Shearing's started. I have to get back,' Edwin said hurriedly. 'You'd better come too, John, or you'll feel the sharp edge of Serlo's tongue.' He thrust the sack at Janna and disappeared around the side of the barn.

'John? Doesn't he know who you really are?' Cecily turned to Janna to clear up the mystery.

Janna sighed. 'Yes, of course he does. And so does my lord Hugh.' At the mention of Hugh's name, Cecily gave Janna a questioning glance, but she didn't say anything. 'I met Edwin while I was lost in Gravelinges,' Janna continued. 'He . . .' She was about to tell Cecily the truth of what had happened, but stopped herself in time. This was Edwin's secret, not hers, and his safety depended on her keeping it. 'He's from Wales and we're going to seek work in Winchestre,' Janna said instead, wishing there was no need to lie to Cecily, or anyone else. She was sick of telling lies, sick of having to hide the truth. 'We decided to travel together but, by greatest misfortune, we found work and shelter on this farm not knowing that it belongs to the lord Hugh.'

'To Dame Alice,' Cecily corrected Janna.

'But he manages the demesne for his aunt.'

'Yes, that is why we are here.' Cecily nodded thoughtfully. 'After my lord left Babestoche, Hamo fretted so much that Dame Alice decided to let him come here for a short visit.'

'How is ma dame? Is she quite recovered from . . .' Janna wasn't sure how to phrase the question delicately, but Cecily answered readily enough.

'In truth, ma dame still grieves over the death of her infant son. She is low in spirits and in health. She told me it would relieve her mind greatly to think that Hamo is here and happy with my lord Hugh.'

Janna surveyed the tiring woman, thinking it also a shrewd move on Dame Alice's part to remove Cecily from her husband's influence. Too much harm had already resulted from Robert's untoward interest in Cecily. Janna wondered how much Dame Alice suspected about their past liaison.

Cecily caught her hand. 'I know I said I would stay and watch out for ma dame,' she whispered, 'but I had no choice when she asked me to accompany Hamo. His own nurse is too old to make the journey and besides, Dame Alice believes Hamo needs someone closer to his own age to take care of him and amuse him.'

'I shouldn't worry about ma dame's safety,' Janna consoled her. 'That is, unless Robert has turned his affection to another young woman in your household?'

'No.' Cecily gave Janna a rueful smile. 'I think he has learned his lesson – as have I.'

'Then Dame Alice is in no danger. In fact, Robert will be trying to convince her that he has always had her best interests in his heart.'

'Pray God that you are right.' Cecily turned from Janna then, and swept a low curtsy. 'My lord,' she said hastily, greeting the two strangers who were now almost upon them. 'I hope you are not too weary after your journey? If you will come with me, I will take you to meet the lord Hugh, Dame Alice's nephew.' She turned abruptly away from Janna, at a loss to explain her earnest conversation with a lowly farmhand.

Janna came to her rescue. 'I'll see about finding the dog, mistress. And the young lord.'

'Hamo?' Cecily's hand came to her mouth. 'I didn't see him go! Where is he?'

'I'll set off in search of him right now, mistress.'

Leaving Cecily to take care of Hugh's visitors, Janna prepared to search the manor grounds, bringing with her the sack of food that Edwin had thrust at her. She was hungry and so, she was willing to wager, were the dog and its master. If shouting didn't bring them into view, a sack of food well might.

EIGHT

'HAMO! HAMO, WHERE are you?' Janna had searched the kitchen garden and orchard, as well as the undercroft and all the barns, workshops and other buildings that made up the manor's demesne. She'd even gone upstairs to peek unobtrusively into the hall, to make sure that he was not among the throng gathered around Hugh. Gytha was up there, she noted, with an instant pang of envy as she saw the beauty circulating among the guests, pouring wine into goblets and offering platters of food.

Hamo was nowhere to be seen, and Janna was growing anxious. The manor was close to stream and river. Could Hamo swim? She hurried downstairs and peered first into the well. 'Hamo?' she shouted, and listened to her voice echoing downwards. There was no reply. Wasting no time, she rushed out through the gates to check the manor's fish pool, but there was no sign of a child, drowning or otherwise. Janna's anxiety increased as she looked down over the stubbled water meadows to the swiftly flowing river beyond. Although it was quite shallow, the fast current could turn into whirlpools in the deep holes that pockmarked the riverbed. Even more dangerous was the water mill further downriver. Its great wheel churned in a thunder of foam with the force of the water channelled into it. She looked upstream towards the water-logged marsh, which was equally dangerous to a child who couldn't swim. Beyond the river and straight ahead was the solid green wall of the forest of Gravelinges. Might Hamo have crossed the river in safety at the ford, and be on his way home to his mother?

No, she thought, remembering Cecily's words. He'd pined at home; he wanted to visit his cousin Hugh. So why, then, had he run away?

She remembered the lame and mangy dog. Hamo seemed to have adopted it as a pet, and yet it had run after Godric when he left the manor. Had Hamo slipped away to find it? And if so, where might he have gone? She turned in a circle, trying to spot any signs of the boy and his dog. Behind the manor spread the fields, basking gold and green in the hot afternoon sun. The sounds of frightened baaing and bleating gave direction to the shearers, but there was no sign of Godric, or the dog. Would he go straight home? Had Hamo followed them into the forest? She shielded her eyes and peered across the water meadows once more, in case she could see anyone walking towards the forest. The thought of Hamo lost and alone gave her the shudders, until a new horror forced itself into her consciousness. Now she stood, icy cold in spite of the heat, and shaking with dread. Hamo's disappearance. Was this the next disaster to befall Hugh's manor? If so, whoever was behind what was happening must either have had advance warning that the party was arriving today, or have acted on impulse and with lightning speed to take advantage of Hamo's unexpected appearance. How likely was that? Fighting anxiety, Janna cast about for any signs of movement.

A couple of swans, followed by a line of fluffy grey-brown cygnets, paddled majestically upriver, labouring against the current that dragged them down towards the mill. There was no sign of any other living thing either in the water or beside it, but Janna couldn't see very much of the river's path for it was shrouded by trees. She forced herself to stand quietly, to think things through. There was no point in alarming herself needlessly, or rushing about looking in all the wrong places, she decided. Better, surely, to think of the most logical explanation for Hamo's absence: that he'd gone in pursuit of the stray dog, and Godric.

It was a hot day. Godric and his party would have had a long walk through the forest, might even have spent the night there. Neither Godric nor Hamo had taken water from the well to drink, or any food, so they would be thirsty and probably hungry too. Where might Godric or Hamo have gone for refreshment?

The river, Janna decided. Upstream or downstream? She shrugged. She had no idea, but there was no time to waste in indecision, not if she wanted to catch up with the pair.

'Hamo?' she shouted, as she hurried down towards the ford. 'Godric?' If Hamo was with Godric, why had he not brought the boy back to the manor? Her pace increased. If Hamo hadn't found Godric, he could be in the most deadly danger. 'Hamo!' she shouted. 'Where are you?'

A faint cry answered her, and she felt a momentary relief until she realised it was Godric's voice she could hear, not Hamo's. She couldn't see him, but his voice had come from the dense thicket of brambles and trees that lined the river's path upstream.

'Godric!' She broke into a run, the quicker to reach him. 'Hamo's lost,' she bellowed. 'Please, please help me look for him!' She pushed her way through trees and bushes, only to find her way barred by the mangy dog, which snarled and bared his teeth. 'Get out of my way!' Janna was too worried to be afraid. She aimed a kick in the dog's direction, and it backed off, barking furiously. 'Godric!' He'd been up to some illegal fishing, she realised, as she spotted a flash of silver on the river bank behind him.

'Where is he? Where's Hamo?' He'd come running, forgetting to hide the evidence of his poaching in his anxiety over the boy.

'I don't know. I thought he might be looking for you and the dog.'

'Bones.' Godric gave the dog a disgusted glance. 'Look at it! I tried to leave it behind, but the stupid thing kept following me.'

Even though the dog had given her grief, Janna thought Godric was being a little harsh. That the dog was in pain from its paws was evident. The dog had been lawed to conform to the harsh forest laws. Three claws had been cut off to the knuckle on each forepaw so that the cur could not chase after the king's game, but not enough care had been taken. Its paws were bloody, and full of pus. The dog was also half-starved, reasons enough for its antisocial behaviour. But Janna had no time for Bones now. Her anxiety overrode even the awkwardness she felt being face to face with Godric as she quickly explained the situation to him.

'You go on upriver and I'll go down towards the mill,' he said at once. 'Keep calling. If either one of us finds him, we must go in search of the other.' He glanced up at the sun. 'If neither of us finds him by the time the sun touches the tree line over there, we should retrace our steps and meet back here so that we can get back to the manor before it gets too dark to see.'

Janna nodded agreement, greatly relieved that he was prepared to help her search and that there were no recriminations – at least, not yet. 'Hamo!' Godric had already started off, following the river downstream. The dog limped behind him. Janna hastened off towards the marsh, also calling Hamo's name. Along the way, and just to be on the safe side, she quickly kicked Godric's illicit catch back into the river.

She hadn't gone far when she heard a shout. 'He's here!' Immediately she turned and raced downstream in the direction Godric had taken. After a few moments, she saw him. Her body went cold with shock as she saw that he carried the limp and dripping body of Hamo.

Pray he isn't dead, she thought, as she rushed up to Godric and fell into step beside him. He was striding up towards the manor, bearing his burden at the greatest speed he could muster. The boy was blue around the lips, and he hung lifeless in Godric's arms. Janna fought down her rising panic. She couldn't bear the thought that after all, they had come too late to help Hamo. There was a bloody gash across his forehead, but Janna noticed one of his eyelids twitch and felt a huge surge of relief.

She cast her mind back into the past, to a time when she and her mother had passed two villeins arguing over possession of a pig. As they'd passed by on their way to market, the argument had escalated over whose pig it was to sell. Punches were thrown, and finally one of the villeins pushed the other into the river. Hearing his cry, Eadgyth had turned and run back to aid the culprit rescue his victim, but the man was lifeless by the time they managed to get him out of the water. Janna remembered what her mother had done. 'Put Hamo down!' she told Godric.

'We have to get him back to the manor house.' Godric's pace didn't check.

'Put him down! On his stomach.' Janna grabbed hold of Godric's arm and dragged on him to make him do as she asked. 'We have to push the water out of his chest.'

Reluctantly, Godric laid Hamo down on a bed of soft grass. Janna turned his head to one side, then straddled the boy's back and pressed down hard. A gush of water erupted from Hamo's mouth. She lifted his arms to give him a chance to breathe in, then pressed down once more. She kept pushing and lifting until at last the boy began to cough and splutter. He took in a great whoop of air, and began to breathe on his own. But he was incapable of speech, so Janna turned to Godric. 'Where did you find him? What happened to him?'

'He was in the river, lying face down. Drowning.'

'I can see that,' she said impatiently. 'I mean, was anyone else there with him, anyone at all?'

'No.' Godric looked puzzled. 'Only me. If you hadn't sounded the alarm, if we hadn't gone after him, he would have died. It's lucky we found him in time.'

'How did it happen? Can you tell?'

Godric shrugged. 'He must have slipped and fallen into the river.'

'What about that wound on his forehead? Do you think he might first have been hit over the head and then pushed?'

'Why should anyone want to do that?' Godric squatted beside Janna, who had her arm around Hamo now and was helping him to sit up. 'What's going on? Why are you asking me these questions?'

'I can't tell you.' Janna wasn't done yet. She had one final question, but she dreaded hearing the answer.

'Did you notice any rue nearby? I mean a posy picked, not rue growing wild?'

'No. But I wasn't looking for anything like that.' Godric lifted a questioning eyebrow. 'Why should there be a posy of rue lying about?'

'It's for regret. Repentance.'

'I wish you'd explain yourself, Janna.' Godric lifted the boy into his arms once more. 'But I know that you don't care to explain anything to me, anything at all.' His tone was bitter as he strode off in the direction of the manor house, leaving Janna to scurry after him.

A great cry went up as they came inside the gate. It was clear Cecily had confessed to losing Hamo, for everyone came running from all directions to welcome them back. Hugh was at the forefront of the crowd. As Godric made to hand Hamo over to his cousin, Hamo wriggled free. 'I can walk by myself,' he announced with dignity, and bent to pat the mangy dog that had followed them in.

'What happened, Hamo?' Hugh asked the question that Janna most feared.

'Nothing.' The boy looked up, all injured innocence now.

'Tell me!' Hugh folded his arms and waited, hiding his concern with an appearance of exasperation.

'I . . . I wanted to find Bones.' Hamo made to take the dog in his arms but it bared its teeth and whined softly. Hamo backed off.

'I'm afraid the dog followed me when I left the manor, sire,' Godric admitted.

Hamo shot him a grateful glance. 'I saw Godric going towards the river. He didn't know I was following him,' he added, determined that Godric shouldn't get any blame for what had happened. 'When I got there I couldn't see him, or Bones, but I guessed he went downriver and that's where I went. But Godric must have gone the other way.'

Janna waited somewhat anxiously for Hugh to ask why Godric had gone up the river at all instead of crossing the ford and heading for home.

'What happened to you? Why are you so wet?' Fortunately for Godric, Hugh was much more interested in Hamo.

Hamo shrugged. 'I followed the path of the river a little way. I thought Bones might have fallen in but I couldn't see through all the reeds so I came close to the edge to have a look and . . . and I slipped and fell.' He touched the gash across his forehead, and winced when he saw the blood on his fingers. 'I s'pose I must have hit my head.'

It was possible Hamo's admission gave his dignity even more of a battering than his head and clothes had taken in the river, Janna thought. She heaved a deep sigh of relief as his words sank into her understanding. An accident, no more than that. 'Godric saved me.' Hamo looked at Janna. 'And also . . .'

'John,' Janna said firmly, before Hamo could say her name in front of everyone.

'And I thank you for it.' Hugh gave Janna a searching glance, then took Hamo by the hand. 'A hot bath for you, young man. Mistress Cecily!' He beckoned her forward, then turned to Godric. 'I'd like a word with you too,' he said, and hurried off. Godric exchanged an anxious glance with Cecily as they followed Hugh. 'I'll make up an ointment to put on the young lord's cuts and bruises,' Janna called after them, resolving to use some of the ointment to treat her ankle, where the dog's teeth had left their mark. Cecily lifted her hand to show that she'd heard, and kept on going. Ignored and forgotten, the dog trailed them up the stairs and into the hall.

With the drama over, the rest of the crowd began to disperse, the two visitors among them. Janna watched them leave. She wondered who they were and why they were visiting the manor. One was finely dressed. His tunic was richly embroidered and his boots were made of good leather, though scratched and stained with mud and muck. The journey through the forest had left its mark. His companion was more plainly dressed, and walked a pace or two behind his master. She looked about for Edwin to ask him who the lordling was. He was always quick to hear the gossip from the kitchen staff. There was no sign of him, but Gytha was still lingering, and as she caught Janna's glance, she smiled and came over.

'That boy will be in trouble for running away,' she observed, and wrinkled her nose. 'I hope he doesn't expect us to find shelter for that smelly, flea-bitten bag of bones he's found.'

Janna hid a smile. She was quite sure that Hamo had every intention of keeping his pet. She was also quite sure that the boy would prove more than a match for Gytha when it came to getting his own way. 'We have visitors, I see,' she responded.

'Master Siward and his manservant. They go to the great fairs to buy and to sell for their lord, but one of their horses is lame so they must break their journey here for a while.' Gytha shrugged, clearly uninterested.

'And have they travelled far?'

'They come from somewhere in the west.' Gytha yawned, and then brightened as a more interesting subject came into her mind. 'Master Siward paid me a great deal of attention when I served the wine and cakes. I do believe my lord Hugh was quite put out by his interest.' She gave a self-satisfied giggle. Janna wanted to hit her, but turned away instead, telling herself that her jealousy was unworthy. The girl was beautiful, and if Hugh wanted a dalliance with her it was none of Janna's business.

She remembered her promise to Cecily, and turned her steps towards the kitchen garden. Fangs of hunger reminded her that she'd dropped the sack containing her dinner while she'd tried to resuscitate Hamo. Should she go after it? She sighted the angle of the sun slanting across the downs. No, it would take too long. She would just have to go hungry. The thought contributed to Janna's misery as she bent to pluck the herbs she needed for the healing ointment.

She was on her way to the kitchen when Godric found her. 'I was going to leave without seeing you again,' he said curtly, 'but I thought you should know, Janna, that your running away has brought ill to my family, to my manor and to the village. I told a lie to Dame Alice and my liege lord, Robert of Babestoche. I told them that you were dead.'

Janna cast a quick glance around, making sure that no-one could hear their conversation. 'I know, Godric, and I am grateful to you, more grateful than I can say.'

'But I have been sore punished for the lie.' Godric spoke over her thanks. 'The priest has claimed mortuary from me, payment I cannot afford, and –'

'But why? Why claim mortuary from you?'

'Because I said that I had buried you in the forest, and because he claims that we were betrothed. He has taken my best goat in payment, even though the abbess has asked nothing from me. Nor has Dame Alice or anyone else. I told the priest he was mistaken about us, but he will not believe me.' There was such a depth of bitterness in Godric's voice that Janna couldn't bear it.

'I'm so sorry.' She put her hand on Godric's arm, but he shook it off and pulled away from her.

'That's not the worst of it,' he said. 'My mother took ill and died. There was no one to physic her as your mother did last time she had an attack and couldn't breathe properly. By running away, you've left the village without a healer, Janna.'

'I . . . but they drove me out!' Janna spluttered. Surely Godric knew that the villagers had burned her cottage down, that she'd had no choice but to flee?

'Everyone mourns your death.' He spoke sincerely.

'Everyone?' Janna's voice raised in anger. 'The villagers set fire to my cottage, Godric. They didn't care if I burned along with it. That's why I ran away. That's why I didn't dare show myself even to you!'

He glanced sharply at her. 'You should have trusted me,' he muttered.

Janna knew that he was right, but still she tried to justify her actions. 'I had to go! Don't you see, it wasn't safe for me to stay. I thought if I . . . That is, I didn't want . . .'

'. . . to see me. I know. You've already made that quite clear in the past.' Godric's mouth clamped down in a tight, hard line. Without saying goodbye, he turned and strode off towards the gate of the manor.

'I'm sorry about your mother. I'm so sorry, Godric,' Janna called after him. But he walked on, not acknowledging that he'd heard her words, or that he'd forgiven her.

There was still no sign of Edwin when at last, weary and hungry, Janna went to her bed. Although she felt concern, she told herself that Edwin was free to come and go about the manor as he pleased. What crowded into Janna's mind now were the events of the day. So much had happened to trouble and distress her. She felt great anger and impatience that she couldn't explain to Hugh, Godric and Cecily why she'd acted as she had, and great shame as she realised how they must view her now.

'It's not fair!' she muttered rebelliously as she turned and turned again, trying to get comfortable on her prickly straw pallet.

Restless, impatient for action, she lay and listened to the night noises, the snarks and snorts and mumbles of the sleepers. She had planned to leave the manor this very night. In the absence of Edwin, should she now go on her own? Yes, she thought, and half-rose from her bed. She subsided again as more careful thought advised against it. While she wanted most desperately to run away from Hugh, caution told her that she would do better to wait until Edwin could go with her. Alone, she was vulnerable, even if she was dressed as a boy. Edwin's presence, and their fabricated family history, would protect them both.

Janna passed an uneasy night. The faint light that heralded the dawn found her wakeful and anxious to rise. She scrubbed at her face with her hands and smoothed back her hair, feeling again its silky growth since the fire. She slipped quietly from her bed and pulled her knife from its sheath. She tested its edge with a cautious finger, and frowned. Then she remembered the great whetstone outside the blacksmith's shop, left in position for the villeins to sharpen their scythes while haymaking. She was bent over the whetstone with her knife when Bertha walked past, carrying a small sack. Janna greeted her cheerfully.

Bertha stopped short, looking startled. 'What are you doing out here so early, John?' she asked, not returning Janna's greeting.

'Sharpening my knife.' Janna wondered if she could take advantage of Bertha's good nature. 'Are you any good at cutting hair? Will you cut mine?'

Bertha's attention came full onto Janna then. She hesitated. 'Does it have to be done now?'

153

Janna nodded. 'Yes, if you please, mistress.' She didn't want to delay, and the alternative was to cut her hair herself. Without being able to see anything, she knew she'd make an awful job of it.

Bertha sighed. She dropped the sack she was carrying and held out her hand for Janna's knife, while Janna settled herself down on the stone block within easy reach of Bertha's hands.

'How does your family, mistress?' she asked, to make conversation while Bertha set about hacking at her hair. She tried not to wince as snippets fell about her feet, curled round like small golden snails.

'What?'

'Your family. Are they well?' Janna wondered what pre-occupied Bertha, and why she was abroad so early. The sun had not yet arisen. Mist shrouded the cots and turned trees into many-armed ghosts in the pearly light.

'Yes, my family are well, thank you. And you? Are you well?'

'Yes, I thank you.' There seemed no more to say on that topic. What else could they talk about to pass the time? Janna's thoughts turned to the missing Edwin. 'I wonder if you've seen my brother at all, mistress? He was not in his bed last night, and I'm wondering what has become of him?'

'Edwin?' The knife slipped in Bertha's hand, nicking Janna's scalp. Janna stifled a cry. She shifted uneasily on her stone seat, wondering at Bertha's clumsiness. 'No, I haven't seen him,' Bertha continued snappily. 'Why should you think I have?'

'No reason,' Janna said hastily. 'I'm concerned about him, that's all.'

'I expect he'll turn up soon enough. There!' Bertha slapped Janna's shoulders in a hasty dust-up, sending bits of hair scattering in all directions. 'You look like a boy again, John.'

And what did Bertha mean by that last remark, Janna wondered. Had her disguise worn thin, or had Edwin told her the truth about both of them? Was that why she seemed so anxious for Janna to be gone?

No. Janna dismissed the notion. Edwin's truth was too dangerous to be told. She was just imagining the worst.

'Thank you, mistress,' she said. As she walked past the last of the little cottages towards the manor, she looked back, curious to know where Bertha might be going, but the carpenter's daughter had already vanished. Hunger drove Janna on to the kitchen, and also the hope that she might find Edwin there, ravenous after his night out and ready to break his fast. She had to jump sideways to avoid the sharp teeth of Bones, who was tethered nearby, before she could enter the door.

'So there you are,' Mistress Tova greeted her. 'And where is your brother?'

'I know not, mistress. I thought he might be here, having something to eat.'

'I haven't seen him since yesterday afternoon.' The cook poked her long nose into the air, and sniffed.

Janna tried to hide her disquiet by stuffing a hunk of bread into her mouth and chewing vigorously, before washing down the mouthful with a gulp of ale. Once her appetite was satisfied, however, she took the chance to question the rest of the kitchen staff. To her alarm, no-one had seen Edwin.

'Run away and left you to face Serlo alone, most like. I always knew he was no good.' The cook dusted her floured hands down her apron before adding a final word. 'Just wonder what he's taken with him,' she muttered darkly.

'Nothing! He's as honest as I am!' Even as Janna leapt to Edwin's defence she remembered how he'd tried to steal her purse. She also remembered all the lies she and Edwin had told. 'Master Serlo has probably found work for him to do elsewhere about the manor that's keeping him busy,' she said, conscious of the rising tide of heat that coloured her face with shame. Yet she had to defend Edwin, and herself, lest the burning of the haystack was laid upon their shoulders, along with the other disasters that had happened recently.

Mistress Tova sniffed again. 'Master Serlo will keep good watch over your brother. He won't be able to cause any more trouble while the reeve is there.'

Janna knew what she was thinking, what everyone was probably thinking. She was about to tell the cook off for spreading malicious lies, but stopped herself in time. In the past her hasty words had often caused her trouble, but she was learning from bitter experience to put a guard on her tongue, to think before she spoke.

'Master Serlo is a good reeve,' she agreed instead. 'And a good catch for any girl – even if Mistress Gytha doesn't want him for a husband,' she added, hoping to divert the cook from her suspicions.

The cook shot her a sharp glance. Janna tried to look demure, but her eyes twinkled with mischief. ''Tis true,' Mistress Tova acknowledged grudgingly. 'My lord certainly knows Serlo's worth, for he treats him well. Serlo has a good-sized cottage, and he was given the gore acres to cultivate for himself. I've seen the cartloads of goods that Serlo takes to the big fairs, his own bounty as well as my lord's, and good quality, all of it. Fetches a good price too, I'll be bound.' The cook tapped a bony finger against her long nose. 'There'll be no shortage of pretty girls waiting in line when he decides to take a wife. Of course, he'd marry Gytha tomorrow, if she would only have him. I've told her she could do a lot worse for herself than marry Serlo, for once young Hamo comes of age . . .'

She shrugged thin shoulders, leaving unsaid her wish that her daughter would secure her future with the reeve rather than trying to seduce the reeve's master who, at the end of the day, might be left with nothing. Janna wondered whether to encourage the cook to urge her daughter to see sense, but decided it was wiser to keep out of their affairs. Instead, she thanked the cook for the sack of dinner she'd provided, and asked after Hamo.

'Staying in his bed today, at Mistress Cecily's insistence, but there's nothing wrong with his appetite.' The cook's words set Janna's mind at rest that Hamo was none the worse for his ducking. She remembered the tethered dog beside the kitchen door.

'And Bones?' she asked. 'What is to become of the dog?'

The cook scowled, and jerked a floury thumb over her shoulder. 'I'm to give it vittles and water.' Janna saw a bright eye peer hopefully around the doorway at them.

'If the young lord is to keep his pet, then I'd like to put some medicament on its paws,' Janna said. 'Hopefully, the cur's temper will improve once it is out of pain.'

'Get the skivvy to muzzle it,' the cook advised. 'It'll have a piece of your breeches, otherwise.'

Janna laughed. 'I know all about that,' she said cheerfully, and put down the sack of food while she went off to pluck some herbs.

Her hands stank from the juice of ragwort as she brewed a lotion with sanicle to put on the dog's paws. Conscious that time was passing, but feeling slightly guilty that she was getting out of the difficult part of the treatment, she gave some of the astringent mixture to the skivvy with instructions to first cleanse the dog's paws and then wrap them tight to protect them from becoming dirty and infected once more. 'Keep Bones tied up and out of trouble,' she said, adding, 'and get someone to hold the dog's jaw tight so he won't bite you.' Ignoring the skivvy's horrified expression, she gathered up a fresh paste of healing herbs for the big, black destrier that awaited her in the stable.

She was pleased to find no sign of Hugh, while his mount seemed much better. She summoned the surly stable lad to hold up the hoof while she unwound the bandage to check. The wound was healing nicely, and she felt a sense of satisfaction as she washed it with lotion and applied the new paste. Human or animal, it mattered not who or what she treated so long as she could heal them, she thought, as she bound up the horse's hoof once more.

Bright sunshine had burnt away the early morning mist. Janna emerged from the dimness of the stables and stood blinking in the sunlight. Shearing was still underway and she knew she should go down to the fold to help, but for a moment she lingered, enjoying a moment's rest in the warmth of the sun.

A flock of geese disturbed her reverie. Honking and hissing, they swarmed around her. Janna drew back, alarmed by the close proximity of the big birds with their sharp, serrated bills. The harassed goosegirl flapped her arms and shouted at them, doing her best to round them up and drive them on through the manor gate and down into the stubbled water meadows to feast on frogs and grasshoppers. Janna kept quite still until they had moved on before following them through the gate.

Her path to the sheepfold took her past the young goatherd. She was surprised he was still in charge of the little flock but then noticed how subdued he looked. Even if Hugh hadn't taken a switch to the boy, his father probably had. In fact, the boy might have had a beating from both of them. Janna felt a little sorry for the lad. It was clear that he'd learned a hard lesson from it all. She gave him a smile as she walked past, and earned a scowl in return.

Dogs yipped and barked as they circled the sheep penned into the fold. All was chaos and confusion. Frightened lambs and sheep baaed in protest as they were caught and thrown to the ground, while the villeins cursed as they fought to hold them still long enough to bind their feet so that they could be shorn. The shearers also cursed the struggling sheep, and tried not to nick the animals' skin as they clipped the wool with heavy, one-handed shears, for the skin could be used as vellum for writing on and was therefore valuable. Excited children laughed and ran about and got in everyone's way, harried by the irate shepherd who was trying to bring some order to the proceedings. Janna looked around, without much hope, for Edwin, but there was no sign of him.

Undecided what she should do, and whether she had the strength to wrestle even one sheep to the ground, she looked to the shepherd for guidance. He surveyed her with a critical expression, obviously sharing her doubts. 'You, John,' he said. ''Tis said you have the healing touch. Some of my flock have fly sores. They're over there.' He jerked a thumb at a small fold which had been hastily erected out of hurdles roped together. It was packed with shorn and shivering sheep. 'Get one of the children to help you.' He beckoned Urk to come forward. The boy smiled happily at Janna, pleased to be singled out for such an important task.

'Take each sheep out of the pen and bathe the sores with that mixture.' The shepherd waved a hand towards a large wooden trough propped beside the fold. It was full of a yellow liquid. Janna sniffed the air, picking up what she'd missed before among the stink of animal dung and dust: the distinctive stench of ragwort.

She nodded and let herself into the small fold, followed by Urk. Sheep pressed around her, baaing lustily and pushing at her from all sides. Urk grabbed hold of a ewe and marched it out and over to the trough. He looked at Janna, awaiting instructions.

'Well done, Gabriel.' She hastily followed him out of the fold. 'I'll bathe its sores if you'll stay in the pen and bring the sheep out one by one?'

The boy nodded acceptance and handed over his charge. Janna held onto the ewe by its horns. After a moment's thought she picked up the handful of wool that stood next to the trough and dipped it in, wrinkling her nose at the stink as the liquid swirled about. There were a few nicks and smears of blood on the animal's skin. Janna bathed them first to get rid of the flies which were already harassing it. Wincing at the sight of the ulcerated flesh on its nether regions, Janna gave the sores a thorough wash. The stinking ragwort would cleanse them and kill any maggots, but she thought she detected also the aromatic tang of tansy to repel the flies that had caused the problem in the first place.

Urk had been watching and, as Janna finished her ministrations, he dragged another ailing sheep out of the small fold and handed it to Janna in exchange for the ewe.

'You can take that one back to the big pen, then bring me another,' Janna told him. 'And thank you, Gabriel. You're being a great help.'

One by one, the sheep were washed and released into the fold, under the watchful eye of the shepherd, who moved about, supervising his flock. Janna was hot, tired and sweaty by the time the last sheep was bathed. Urk came out of the fold to take the animal from her, but it broke free before he was close enough to clutch hold of it. With the alluring prospect of rich grazing in the water meadows ahead, the ewe bumped past Janna and set off at speed, followed by Urk in hot pursuit.

Knocked off balance, Janna fell against the edge of the wooden trough. It tipped, splashing its contents over her smock and breeches. Janna surveyed the damage in dismay. Her clothes were filthy, and she stank. She saw that Urk had managed to capture the absconding animal and was bringing it back to shut in with all the other sheep. Her task was over. She looked towards the cool, flowing river, and got to her feet.

'By your leave, I'm going to rinse this stinking mixture off my smock,' she told the shepherd. Not giving him a chance to argue, she hurried on down to the water. She untied her girdle and laid it and her purse on the river bank before leaning over to wash the stain from her smock. She sneaked a quick look around to see if anyone was paying attention then leaned further until she overbalanced into the river. The shock of the icy water on her hot skin took her breath away for several long moments. Recollecting her purpose, she began an opportunistic floundering, determined to make the most of this chance to give herself and her clothes a hasty rinse. She also took a long drink of water, relishing its coldness as it slipped down her dry throat. Finally, she regained her footing and emerged from the river. She made her way towards the place she'd dropped her belongings, wringing the water from the front of her smock as she walked.

The last of the sheep were being tied and shorn, while other villeins carried the fleeces back to the manor. There, women were already combing the fleeces smooth with the dried heads of teasels, which were prickly as hedgehogs. The best fleeces would be sold at the annual fair at Wiltune. Janna had been to the fair once, and still remembered the excitement of it all. It was the high mark of the year, both because it was a holy time to commemorate the death of St Edith, but also because merchants and travellers came from miles around to sell their wares.

Revelling in her clean skin and clean clothes, Janna picked up her girdle and purse and tied them safely around her waist.

'Where is your brother, John?'

Janna jumped. She hadn't noticed Serlo's approach. His gaze rested quizzically on her wet smock. She quickly crossed her arms over her chest lest he see the shape of her breasts mounded beneath the fabric. 'He must be working elsewhere about the manor, Master Serlo. Perhaps my lord Hugh has given him a task?' she improvised quickly.

Serlo frowned. 'He should be here, helping with the shearing,' he said.

'And so I shall tell him, just as soon as I see him.' Janna gave an exaggerated shiver. 'I fell into the river and I'm cold. May I have your leave to run in the fields until I am dry?'

With a reluctant nod, Serlo waved her away. Feeling relief, Janna retraced her steps to the sheepfold to retrieve the sack of food, and took off up into the fields. She kept up the pace until she was hidden from his sight by a field of growing wheat. She slowed to a walk and looked about for somewhere to eat her dinner, while she pondered what to do next. Edwin had seemed so keen to stay at the manor. What had happened to change his mind? If he'd run away, why hadn't he asked her to go with him? He knew she wanted to leave, and that it was only his wish to stay that was keeping her here. It didn't make sense. Even if he'd left without her, he could at least have said goodbye.

If Edwin really had gone, she might as well leave too, she concluded. There was certainly no future for her here, in spite of Hugh's kind offer. She sat down in the shade of a patch of brambles, and opened up the sack of food. She munched on some bread and sheep's cheese while she considered what had been happening here on the manor. Years of standing about and watching Eadgyth treat her patients had taught Janna to look, to listen and to learn. As she ate her dinner, she thought through the incidents she'd witnessed, racking her brains to make sense of it all. Was there anything to link the incidents together, other than the posies of rue?

No, there was not, she concluded. Perhaps she should approach the problem from another angle. Why the rue? What was the reasoning behind the incidents?

Janna cast her mind back to everything her mother had told her about the herb. 'It's known as "herb of grace" to Christians, for they believe rue is a symbol of the true repentance that leads to God's grace,' Eadgyth had said. But it was clear to Janna that the culprit repented nothing, for the incidents kept on happening. Not repentance, then. What else had she been told? 'The Romans thought they'd gain a second sight and see visions if they took the herb, but others have used it to curse their enemies.' Eadgyth's eyes had twinkled as she'd continued. 'You can also wear rue for luck, for protection, or as a cure against disease. In fact, daughter, it seems the ancients couldn't quite make up their minds whether the herb should be used for good or ill. For myself, I believe the herb has many good uses, and these I will show you.' And so she had, Janna thought, remembering the many medicaments to which rue could be added.

She sighed. She was no nearer to working out the truth of the matter, but she was sure that something else was going to happen, perhaps worse than all that had gone before. She wondered what the next disaster would be, and felt a shiver of premonition.

Something niggled at the back of Janna's mind; something she'd seen, something important that perhaps could tell her who was responsible. She closed her eyes, the better to recall what she'd seen or heard, but the memory remained elusive.

She was thoughtful as she walked back down to the fold, where the last of the sheep were being sheared. If Edwin was gone, she should leave too. But not now; she couldn't risk Serlo seeing her go. He was already suspicious enough. If she left, it would confirm Serlo's belief that she and Edwin were behind the so-called 'accidents'. They would be pursued, and by the forester too. Janna had no doubt Serlo would carry out his threat to raise the hue and cry. Nor would he willingly let her go if she asked to leave, not when she was one of his suspects; not when it was his intention to get more work out of them in return for his silence. Uneasy and afraid, she wondered if she should make a run for it anyway. Whatever her decision, Janna knew she must wait until nightfall. If there was no sign of Edwin by then, maybe she could sneak out while everyone was snoring. But in which direction should she go?

Janna resolved that whatever she chose to do, she must first find out the way to Winchestre. But as she asked her question, she found herself more confused than ever by the responses.

'Winchestre lies that way.' One shearer stopped clipping to point downstream. 'No, you'll find the road over there,' said another, and jabbed a finger in the opposite direction. 'It's behind us,' said a villein, who was busy making his mark on his own sheep. He took time to poke his thumb back towards the fields.

She would go over the fields and see what lay beyond them, Janna decided, as she picked up an armful of rolled-up fleeces and laboured back to the manor with her burden.

Even if the road took her in the wrong direction, it would lead her away from the manor, and also from Babestoche where Dame Alice and Robert lived. It would lead her to safety. She could always ask about Winchestre along the way, and change direction at a crossroads, if need be.

All these thoughts left Janna's head as, with the day drawing to its weary end, she suddenly heard a bell begin to toll. She recognised the sound. It came from the church at nearby Wicheford and, on Sundays, it summoned the faithful to mass, including those villeins from the manor who felt like making the journey across the downs. But today was not Sunday, and the bell rang on and on, clanging its urgent appeal long past its usual recording of time or occasion. The villeins hurriedly gathered up the last of the fleeces and hastened to the manor to find out the cause of the summons, Janna among them.

'Hamo.' She heard the boy's name mentioned several times as they came closer to the confusion and bustle in the yard. It was said with annoyance, impatience, and also with anxiety. Janna's steps quickened. Surely he couldn't have gone missing again after such a narrow escape last time? But it seemed that he had. A cry of alarm had gone out and everyone was being pressed to search for him. The yard was full of servants and labourers, all milling around and discussing what to do. At their centre, trying to organise the comings and goings, and looking distraught, was Hugh. Janna noticed several unfamiliar faces amid the throng, strangers from neighbouring Wicheford. United in adversity and drawn by a sense of community, they too had come to join in the search for the missing boy.

Hugh raised his voice. 'Hamo was last seen playing with his ball here by the undercroft,' he shouted above the hubbub. 'I want the women and children to search the gardens and all the buildings of the manor. The rest of you will comb the fields and search along the river, up and down. Pay careful attention to the mill, and also the marsh. I, myself, will take a small party into the forest. Although the fence-month has passed, the does will still be guarding their young. Should any of them stray into the fields do not, on any account, do anything to startle or harm them, or the forester will call you to an accounting before the king.' With chopping motions of his hands, he began to divide the villeins into groups, ready to send them off in different directions.

Janna hurried up to him. 'Where is the dog, my lord?' she cried. 'You should also look for Bones.'

Hugh glanced down at her. 'I haven't seen it, have you?' Janna shook her head. Hugh raised his voice once more to shout: 'Look out also for a stray dog.' His face was tight with worry as he continued to issue instructions to the villeins.

'I hope you find him soon, my lord.'

Hugh nodded. Janna stood back, and waited to be told where to go. A sudden thought came into her mind, and she sidled forward once more. A quick glance confirmed her fears and struck dread through her heart. A small posy of rue lay on the doorstep of the undercroft.

NINE

JANNA BENT DOWN and picked up the posy. Her first thought was to show it to Hugh, and tell him what she thought it meant. Her second thought urged caution. The posy, in itself, proved nothing, for all the other posies were either gone or had been destroyed, some by Janna herself. She had nothing, now, to prove that these acts were deliberate and that Hamo had not wandered off by chance. This time he must have been taken, and by someone who wished him harm.

Janna felt sick. She longed to spill out her worries to Hugh, but a question stopped her even as she opened her mouth. Who stood to gain by Hamo's disappearance – perhaps even his death? The answer had been spelled out to her, only too clearly, on her first meeting with Hamo.

'All my mother's property and wealth will be mine when she dies,' he had told her. 'I am the first-born son, you see.'

Hamo, as the first and only surviving child born to Hugh's aunt, Dame Alice, would inherit everything on her death. In the interim, Hugh kept this manor for his aunt, but he would be expected to vacate it once Hamo married. Unless, of course, the child died before then?

Janna swallowed hard. She cast a glance at Hugh, hating what she was thinking yet understanding that she could not deny the truth of his situation. Only Hamo stood between him and a vast inheritance from Dame Alice. All the evidence could easily point to Hugh. These incidents had only started on his return to the manor. He, more than anyone, was free to come and go as he wished; no-one would dare to challenge him. Had he set up a pattern of accidents to convince his aunt that Hamo's disappearance – even his death – while regrettable, was just another accident?

Rue for regret. Repentance. Yes, Hugh might well regret the circumstances that forced him to act in this way. And he might well feel repentance for his actions.

It was still no excuse for murder! Janna continued to watch Hugh direct proceedings, meanwhile berating herself for letting her thoughts run away with her. Hugh murdering Hamo! It was laughable, quite out of the question. She herself had seen his fondness for his cousin when they'd played ball together. And Hamo wouldn't have fretted after Hugh left the manor if his cousin hadn't shown him genuine kindness. Nor did it seem likely that Hugh would have tampered with his own destrier's shoe to lame the horse, for his anger had been apparent and his concern quite real.

No. Janna tried to laugh off her fears. There must be some other explanation. If not Hugh, then who? Edwin? Janna shook her head. His absence might indicate guilt to some, but he'd gone missing before Hamo's disappearance. Unless that was to cover his actions and avert suspicion? Janna remembered that this wasn't the first time Edwin had gone missing. He'd been absent on the night of the medale, when the haystack had caught fire and the villagers had come together to put it out. Had he gone off to fire the haystack, and come back later pretending innocence? Was that what he intended to do now? But that was assuming Hamo had vanished for a reason, perhaps for ever, and she couldn't bear to believe that. She sighed with exasperation. Her imagination was taking her into all sorts of places she didn't want to go.

Where was Edwin? She had to find him in order to clear his name. Yet it was also true Edwin had a bad side to his character, she conceded. After all, he'd tried to steal her property. Janna's hand went automatically to her purse. She heard the coins clink at her touch, and felt the shape of the small statue she had found, the mother clasping her child. Her fear eased slightly, and she smiled at the notion that the statue had brought comfort.

Mother and child. She felt a sudden pang of deep distress as she recalled Dame Alice. The lady was utterly cast down by the death of her newborn babe. She would surely go off her head with grief if her only surviving son also died.

This won't do, Janna told herself sternly. It's too early for despair. Hamo's missing, not dead. And he hasn't been gone for long. She remembered the mangy dog. Hamo must have gone in search of it once more. He would surely soon be found.

By now, everyone had been summoned by the urgent, clamouring bell. Although she'd been ordered to search outside the manor with the men, Janna decided instead to hunt for Bones. Instinct told her that if she could find the dog, she would probably find Hamo too. Regardless of what the rue might mean, it was too great a coincidence that boy and dog should both be missing. So she tried the kitchen first, where she'd last seen Bones. She searched within and without, but there was no sign of dog or boy. She widened her search then, calling as she went, but there was no answering bark or shout for help. It seemed she was right: both of them had vanished. So where had they gone, and with whom?

'You! Boy!' Serlo had his horse on a rein, ready to mount, but now he stopped and beckoned Janna to come to him. His face set in a thunderous frown as he waited for her to draw near. 'Where's your brother?' he barked. From the hostility in his tone, Janna understood that she and Edwin were under suspicion for this too. It took all her courage to face the reeve.

'I don't know where Edwin is, Master Serlo,' she answered politely. She became aware she was still clutching the posy of rue, and hastily secreted it behind her back.

'And the young lord? I don't suppose you know where he is either?'

'No.' Janna hesitated, wondering if she had the nerve. 'But I do know he's not with Edwin,' she added boldly.

'And how would you know that if you don't know where your brother is?'

'I know Edwin, Master Serlo.' Janna hoped that, indeed, she did. 'I know he wouldn't take the boy away for any reason, even in fun.'

Serlo's frown deepened. 'What makes you think there's any reason behind Hamo's disappearance other than that the silly child has wandered away and got lost?' he snapped.

171

Janna kept silent. Hamo was anything but silly. He'd run after his dog and got into trouble for it. While he might go in search of the dog once more, it seemed unlikely he'd go to the river again, or even stray far from the manor unless enticed away by someone he trusted. But she couldn't blame Serlo for trying to put a good face on things. Besides, it was perfectly possible she'd read the situation wrongly. The fact that there was a posy of rue on the steps of the undercroft might not have anything to do with Hamo's disappearance; it might be a sign of something quite different, something relatively minor. Up until now the incidents had caused harm, but they were not too serious for all that. Kidnapping a child, the heir to this manor farm, on the other hand, was a very serious crime indeed.

'Get out and look for Hamo,' Serlo growled. 'I don't want to see you back here before dark. And make sure you bring your brother with you!' With a scowl he mounted his horse and rode out through the gate.

Janna pulled a face at his departing back. 'I'm already looking for Hamo,' she muttered. 'What do you think I'm doing? Walking about for my health?' Nevertheless, she linked up with a group of women who were busy searching through the manor grounds. Although she joined them in calling out Hamo's name, she also called for Bones. But only silence answered their calls.

The bell began to toll again, a low and mournful sound. A shiver ran through Janna as she came to understand its meaning. The sound was to guide the lost child home to safety. It would continue to toll until Hamo was found. And if Hamo didn't come running home, it would mean that he could not; it would mean that he was dead.

Partly following Serlo's instructions, partly to avoid Serlo himself, but mostly because she was worried sick, Janna left the manor grounds to search along the length of the river. She stayed out until it grew too dark to see properly. In twos and threes, the villeins began to return, shaking their heads in hopeless despair as they asked each other for news. Hugh called for resin torches to be fetched. With flames held high to light their way, some of the men streamed out of the gate to continue their search once more, a few on foot and some on horseback to ride further afield. Janna was relieved to see that Serlo was among them. The women and children, meanwhile, went off to their own cots to see about an evening meal and a night's rest.

Not wanting to encounter Mistress Tova's gossiping tongue, or questions about Edwin's whereabouts and sly innuendoes about his reliability, Janna wearily climbed the stairs to the hall and settled down onto her pallet, determined to continue her search as soon as dawn lightened the sky. Momentarily, she wondered what had become of Edwin. But her thoughts soon returned to Hamo. She pictured him falling into the river and being crushed by the mill wheel, or blundering through the forest, lost and frightened, not knowing which way to turn. There were wolves out there, and wild boar. Having no weapon, or anything to defend himself, Hamo would be easy prey.

Janna screwed her eyes tight shut, trying to block out the pictures she'd conjured up. With so many people out looking for him, how could Hamo stay lost – unless someone was determined that he shouldn't be found? She tried to push the thought from her mind but it lay there like a stone, too heavy to shift, too heavy to ignore.

Janna passed a restless night. Nightmares frightened her awake, so that she lay, heart thudding, listening to the snores of the sleepers and, at regular intervals, the lonely sound of the clanging bell. In the end, she fell into a deep sleep and didn't wake until one of the villeins gave her a hard shake. 'You'd best get up, John, if you want time to break your fast,' he said. 'Master Serlo wants us out at first light to look for the young lord.'

Janna hurriedly did as she was bid, but she was still yawning and only half awake as she munched on a chunk of bread and tried to come up with a plan. The first thing, she decided, was to give the undercroft a thorough search, just to satisfy herself that the posy of rue was in no way connected with Hamo's disappearance.

'Where's your brother, John? I want a word with him,' Serlo said sternly. Startled, Janna whirled to face the reeve. She hadn't seen him come in to the hall but, judging from the thunderous frown on his face, he was in a temper and determined to take it out on someone.

'I . . . I know not where Edwin is, Master Serlo,' she confessed miserably, sure now that she would be punished in Edwin's place.

'I judge him responsible for the young lord's disappearance – and you will be suspect too, if you cannot bring

Edwin to account. I'm out of patience with you both, but there's no time to waste on you now. If you don't have Edwin here by nightfall, I'll raise the hue and cry after him. I'll call in the sheriff. Be sure that I'll also urge the forester to tell all he knows. There'll be no place for you to hide after this, John, you or your brother. Just think on that.'

'I swear we know nothing about the young lord's whereabouts, Master Serlo,' Janna said hurriedly. 'But I will go in search of Edwin. And the young lord, if you'll give me leave to go?'

Serlo nodded curtly, and turned away to deal with a group of women who awaited further instructions. Gytha was among them, and in spite of her anxiety Janna felt a twitch of amusement. Serlo couldn't keep his eyes off the girl. All his remarks were addressed to Gytha. She stood before him, hardly responding to his attention, while Serlo watched her as a starving man might watch his last crust disappearing down the mouth of a rival.

Janna turned and walked quickly down the stairs. She had more pressing problems to think about now: was it more important to find Hamo or Edwin? Could they even be together?

Another possible companion for Hamo came into Janna's mind. Urk was older than Hamo, but he was about the same age in his reasoning. Hamo would think nothing of running free on his cousin's property – his own property – while Urk had already shown that he wasn't aware of, or didn't understand, the rules that bound the villeins living on the manor farm. He would be delighted to go searching for Bones, or even play a game with Hamo if the young lord still had his ball with him.

Where might the two of them go? After a moment's reflection, Janna thought it most likely that they'd stay right here within the confines of the manor, where the ground was cleared and suitable for play. In which case they must soon be found. On the chance that they'd strayed further, Janna decided to search for them in the villeins' cots that spread beyond the manor. Not understanding the differences in their station, perhaps Urk had taken his new friend home with him.

She hurried outside the timber palisade, making straight for Mistress Wulfrun's cottage. There was no sign of Urk, or Hamo, but Janna decided to stay and check all the cots while she was there. Most everyone had already joined in the search for Hamo, but Janna alerted a mother who had just been brought to bed with child, and also an elderly and infirm grandmother, and bade them keep a careful watch out for him. The rest of the cots were empty. Remembering her earlier idea, Janna headed back to the manor house. She could hear the villeins' voices calling Hamo's name as they hunted for him up and down the river. If Hamo was there, dead or alive, he would certainly be found.

Several riders flashed past. Janna stared after them. She didn't recognise the horses, but she knew at least one of the horsemen. Hugh. He had donned his green cloak for the journey and it sailed out behind him, given wings by the wind. She wished him a silent 'God speed', pleased he wasn't riding his own destrier, that he was giving the horse's hoof a chance to heal. They must be widening the search, she thought.

Women and children now moved about with a steady purpose, methodically inspecting once again every nook and cranny that might provide shelter for a small boy. The men fanned out beyond the manor walls, some to continue the search up and down river, looking especially at the mill and the great marsh; the rest to walk through the tall corn or search the meadows on either side of the river, and the outskirts of the forest beyond.

Janna wondered if she should go with the men, but investigating the undercroft was on her mind now. She would rather know the real purpose behind Hamo's disappearance. She hoped to set her mind at rest. So she walked into the undercroft below the hall, and began a systematic search for anything, anything at all, that might explain the significance of the posy of rue left lying on the doorstep. What was she looking for? She wished she knew.

She kept her mind and eyes focused on the scene in front of her as she poked about. She was looking for something out of place, or something spoiled, perhaps. Even something missing – but how would she know if that was so? She sorted through the few poor possessions stored by the servants who shared her sleeping quarters in the hall, then moved on to the rest of the undercroft where food and grain were kept. Being the hungry month, the time just before harvest, the sacks of grain were few; most were empty. One of the sacks was ripped and Janna checked it carefully. Precious grain spilled out of it. Mouse droppings confirmed that it was mice rather than a human hand behind the deed.

There were also barrels, and several chests. She tried the lid of one of the chests, but found it locked. So were most of the others, she found, as she tried them all. Only one opened to her touch, but a quick riffle through its contents confirmed that there was only a woollen blanket, worn thin and perforated with moth holes, and some chipped pots and jugs inside it. Nothing in the undercroft appeared to have been tampered with; everything seemed in order. Just to be sure, Janna tapped on each one. 'Hamo?' she called softly, but there was no reply. She didn't know whether to be glad or sorry.

With her inspection over, Janna walked outside and paused for a moment while she worked out where to look next.

She was hot, thirsty and tired. And hungry. There were apples growing on the trees that bordered the kitchen garden. As Janna visualised the juicy fruit, her mouth began to water in anticipation. She hurried towards the fruit trees, hoping that the apples were ripe enough to eat, and that no-one was around to watch her steal one. A movement caught her eye and she stopped, wondering what it could be. It looked like a long brown snake. The frayed end told Janna what she'd seen. Curious now, she traced its source to a large wooden barrel. She peered over, and found Bones cowering behind it.

'Come here!' she ordered. She tugged hard on the rope. The unwilling creature skidded around and came into full view.

'Where's Hamo?' Janna demanded, then felt silly as she realised she was talking to a dog. But so had she talked to the animals she and her mother had kept at their cottage. 'Do you know where he's hiding?' Her words seemed to soothe the dog, for it stopped cringing away and baring its teeth at her and, instead, sat down and looked up at her with pleading eyes. Janna was incensed to see that its paws were still untreated by the kitchen skivvy. She chided herself for passing on the task rather than taking care of it herself.

'Poor old Bones.' She dragged the dog inside the empty kitchen and set about finding it some scraps, hoping to bribe it into good behaviour so that she could put the medicament on its paws. Perhaps the dog knew something about Hamo's disappearance; perhaps it could even lead her to Hamo? First, though, Janna wanted to take care of its wounds so that at least it could walk properly with her when she went searching.

Once the dog was busy chomping its way through a piece of raw meat, Janna poured water into a basin and set about cleansing its front paws. As she suspected, the claws had been cut off without care, and the wounds were dirty and full of pus. The dog growled at her as she probed deeper. 'Have a bone, Bones,' she said, and hurriedly stuffed one of the cook's soup bones into its mouth.

It dropped the bone and began to shiver and whine softly as Janna first cleansed then bound its paws with scraps of wool smeared with the cream she'd made up earlier. It seemed to sense that she was friend not foe. It even managed a feeble wag of its tail when she was done, while it wasted no time getting back to the feast she'd provided. 'You realise I'm going to blame you for stealing this food,' Janna told the dog as she scoffed up a cold meat pasty while she waited for it to finish eating. She was only half-jesting. Mistress Tova would be incensed when she realised what was missing.

Hastily, she drained a mug of ale to slake her thirst. 'Come on,' she said, feeling slightly more cheerful after her repast. She pulled on the dog's leash once more. With a last look of longing at a ham that hung enticingly beside the cooking fire, the dog trotted after Janna, still limping slightly.

Holding on to the rope to keep the dog with her, Janna crossed the river. If Hamo wasn't within the manor walls, neither was Edwin for he, too, would have been found in the search. With Serlo's warning sounding in her ears, she went first to the sheep shed where once they'd taken shelter from the forester. As she'd suspected, it was empty. She peeped behind the rough wooden feeding trough, and felt a great relief when she espied the rusty sword she'd secreted there, along with Edwin's pot and jug. If Edwin had left the manor to go adventuring, he surely would have remembered to take everything with him. Wherever he was, he couldn't be far away. Hunger must surely drive him home, and soon.

A group of peasants beating through the edge of the forest beyond caught Janna's eye. Urk's mother was among them, and Janna hastened to join them. Edwin could take care of himself; it was Hamo who occupied her thoughts now. A quick glance confirmed that Urk was not part of the group. She made a beeline for Mistress Wulfrun, hoping her suspicions might prove correct.

'Mistress,' she greeted her. 'I've been looking for Urk . . . Gabriel. Do you know where he might be?'

Urk's mother nodded. 'He went off with the other children to search the barn,' she muttered, looking worried.

'Was he alone, do you know?'

'No, I told you. He was with the other children.' Mistress Wulfrun shot a suspicious glance at Janna. 'Why do you ask?'

'I wondered if he might have gone somewhere to play ball with a special friend, perhaps?'

'Ball?' Mistress Wulfrun couldn't have looked more confused if Janna had asked whether Urk had grown wings and flown up to the moon.

Janna nodded thoughtfully. Hamo might have the leisure to play ball games, but it seemed that Urk did not.

'And did Gabriel sleep in his bed last night?'

Mistress Wulfrun drew herself up to her full height and glared at Janna. 'He was not out setting fire to a haystack, if that's what you're trying to suggest.'

'No!' Janna was sorry to have offended Urk's mother. She wasn't sure how to put things right. 'It's just that the young lord loves to play with his ball. I wondered if Gabriel had gone off to play a game with him, that's all.'

'Gabriel has no time to play games.' Mistress Wulfrun strode on, calling out Hamo's name as she went. Janna clicked her tongue impatiently as she realised she hadn't had an answer to her question. She left the villeins to their search and went back to the manor, dragging Bones on the rope behind her. The clanging tones of the bell followed her passage. Janna scrutinised the knots of people coming and going, wishing more than anything to recognise Hamo among them. Although several small figures brought her to a heart-thumping halt, closer inspection always revealed them to be some other child. She hurried inside the gate and went looking for Urk and his friends.

Oblivious to the urgency of their task and the real danger to Hamo, the children were having a game, throwing hay about and shrieking with delight. Urk was by far the oldest, but he also seemed to be having the most fun. She drew him aside. 'Have you seen Hamo, Gabriel?' she asked.

He shook his head. 'Hamo's lost,' he said helpfully.

'I know. I wondered if you'd seen him. Did you maybe go somewhere to play ball with him?'

'Ball?' Urk looked just as puzzled as his mother.

'Did you see Hamo today? Do you know where he is?' Janna tried again.

'No. Hamo's lost.' Urk bent down to pat Bones. 'Nice dog.' Bones's tail twitched in acknowledgment.

Janna sighed, feeling discouraged. 'Go on then and look for Hamo,' she said, and gave him a gentle push in the direction of the younger children. Urk ambled off, giving her a bewildered glance as he left. Janna looked up at the sky. The sun had begun to fall towards the earth; it would be dark within a few more hours, and then Serlo would demand an explanation of Edwin's absence. She felt like a watermill in a dry river bed, churning around uselessly and achieving absolutely nothing. She'd been rushing about everywhere, but she still had no answers to give Serlo, and no idea where to find them either. What was she to do? With dragging steps, she went back to join the searchers at the forest's edge.

She looked across the water meadows to the manor beyond, with the small cots of the peasants clinging to its side like ticks to a dog. Behind the manor stretched the cultivated fields, stripes of ripening corn interspersed with patches of dark, fallow earth. A small copse of trees stood to one side, jutting into some of the strips and cutting the field into an awkward shape. From the height and distance of her position, Janna could see now that the copse hid a solid, stone-built cottage.

'Who lives there?' she asked, while beside her, Bones began to whine. 'Sshh.' She smacked his muzzle gently to shut him up so that she could hear Mistress Wulfrun's reply.

'Master Serlo. The cottage and those gore acres around it belong to him.'

Janna gave a long, low whistle as she quickly revised her opinion of the reeve. Mistress Tova had mentioned Serlo's cottage and fields, but Janna hadn't realised the full extent of his holding. Gytha would do well to encourage him, Janna thought now, for her chances of improving her station were far greater with Serlo than they could ever be with Hugh. As Serlo's wife she would have a certain status; she would also become a woman of property. Yet as she mentally compared the two in her mind, she had to admit that in Gytha's position she'd also be hoping for a future with Hugh rather than plighting her troth with Serlo.

With an effort, she dragged her thoughts back to the more pressing matter of the missing boy. 'Has anyone looked in Serlo's cottage for Hamo?' As she spoke, Janna gestured towards it. Bones strained on his leash beside her, still whining.

'Yes, indeed.' Mistress Wulfrun caught hold of Janna's arm. 'Don't think to go searching there, John. Master Serlo will not take kindly to anyone trespassing on his property. Besides, I saw him go in for his dinner at noon. Wherever Hamo may be, you can be sure he's not there.'

Janna nodded, accepting that the woman was giving her good advice. 'You know the manor farm better than I do, mistress,' she said. 'Where do you think Hamo might be?'

'I wish I knew.' The woman scratched her nose, looking thoughtful. 'They say my lord Hugh has gone to break the bad news to Dame Alice, but in his absence Master Serlo will continue the search until the boy is found. Conscientious as he is, he knows every rock and tree on the manor farm. Wherever Hamo is, alive or dead, Master Serlo will find him.'

'Then let us pray that Master Serlo finds Hamo alive!' The alternative was too horrible to contemplate. As Janna walked on, calling Hamo's name in the silences left between the clanging tones of the bell, she wondered how Cecily was faring and what she was doing. Newly in charge of Hamo and wanting only the best for Dame Alice, she must be beside herself with anxiety. And self-blame. How had Hamo managed to escape Cecily yet again? It was something she should have thought to ask right from the start.

Janna turned abruptly and hurried back to the manor, tugging Bones, who continued to bark and pull on his rope to get free.

Janna was just crossing the yard when she saw Cecily vanish through the line of pear and apple trees that hedged the kitchen garden. At once she followed, curious to find out what Hamo's new nurse sought there. But it seemed that Cecily had merely escaped to find some privacy, for Janna found her sitting hunched under a pear tree, weeping as if her heart would break. Her head was buried in her lap and her arms were wrapped around to muffle the sounds she was making. She didn't hear Janna approach.

'Cecily.' Janna put an arm around her shoulders to comfort her. At Janna's touch, the tiring woman leapt in fright and shied away. 'Oh, it's you, Janna,' she said then, and subsided onto the ground once more. She wiped her eyes on her sleeve, and gave a mournful sniff. 'What am I going to do?' she burst out. 'My lord Hugh has gone to tell Dame Alice that Hamo is missing. Ma dame will never forgive me if harm has come to him. I'll never forgive myself. Oh, Janna, I have caused such trouble to my lady and her kin!' She burst into a storm of weeping once more. This time she didn't pull away when she felt Janna's embrace, but leaned into Janna and wept even harder.

No wonder Cecily was hurting, Janna thought. She had loved Robert once, loved him enough to forget all honour, and all loyalty and gratitude to Dame Alice, Robert's wife. That he'd proved so base, so unworthy of her sacrifice, must double both her sadness and her shame. And now there was the added blame of the disappearance of Dame Alice's beloved only child. There was nothing Janna could say to ease Cecily's pain or make things right for her. All she could do, all anyone could do, was look for Hamo and pray that he'd be found before it was too late.

Janna continued to hold Cecily, patting her arm as she did so. 'Hush,' she said at last, offering what little comfort she could. 'Everyone's out searching for Hamo. I'm sure he'll be found soon.' She wasn't sure, but she wasn't prepared to give up hope either. 'Maybe we can put our heads together, and see if we can make some sense of all this?'

Cecily nodded, and gave a forlorn sniff. Encouraged, Janna asked, 'When did you last see Hamo, Cecily? How did he come to run away?'

'I know not.' Cecily gave her eyes a fierce scrub on her sleeve, and sniffed again. 'I was called away to the kitchen to speak to the cook about Hamo's meals. I asked him to come with me but he didn't want to, and so I left him playing with his ball.'

Janna reflected, with bleak amusement, that Hamo's new nurse didn't yet have his measure. Telling, not asking, would be far more effective if she wanted the child to obey her. She remembered what Hugh had said. 'He was playing by the undercroft?'

'Yes. He was throwing his ball at the wall and trying to catch it. Actually, he's very good at it.'

Having played ball with Hamo herself, Janna knew just how accurate was his aim, and how skilful his catching. She also knew that Hamo loved to play ball and realised she could hardly blame Cecily if the boy resisted her efforts to drag him away.

'How long were you gone?' she asked.

'Only long enough for the cook to show me what she had in her stores, and for me to give her some directions regarding Hamo's likes and dislikes. She was willing enough to listen and to learn, there was no argument there. But when I came out again and looked for Hamo, he was nowhere to be seen. I swear to you,' Cecily clutched Janna's arm in agitation, 'I was not gone for long. Moments only!' She began to cry once more.

'Was the dog with Hamo while he was playing with his ball?' It was a chance question, but Cecily's answer reinforced Janna's certainty that the two were linked together somehow.

'No,' she said. 'We'd been looking for the dog everywhere. Hamo couldn't find it. He was very upset.' She looked down at Bones, now sitting placidly beside Janna. 'Where did you find it?' She brightened momentarily. 'Maybe Hamo . . .?' Her voice trailed off as Janna shook her head.

'Bones was here, in the kitchen garden,' she said. 'There was no sign of Hamo.'

'But Hamo and I looked here just before he disappeared. Bones wasn't here then.'

'I saw the dog outside the kitchen when I broke my fast yesterday, but I didn't see him after that until I went looking for Hamo earlier today, and found the dog cowering behind those barrels over there. He seemed very frightened, I don't know why.' It was something to think about later, but for now she was anxious to question Cecily further. If Hugh was somehow implicated in Hamo's disappearance, then Janna vowed to find it out. 'Tell me about my lord Hugh. Where does he go? Does he spend much time with you in the hall and in the solar?'

Cecily frowned at Janna, and remained silent.

'Mistress Gytha is very attractive, is she not?' Janna prompted, hoping to goad Cecily into speaking by throwing in a snippet of kitchen gossip. 'I know she cares for my lord. I wondered if he might spend time dallying with her?'

'Gytha?' Cecily's eyes widened. Too late, Janna remembered that at one time she'd wondered if Cecily herself was enamoured with Hugh. She wasn't then, but perhaps that, too, had changed in the time Janna had been gone. Janna wished she could undo her question.

'Gytha?' Cecily echoed again. She gave a short laugh. 'I think my lord might wish to do better for himself than the cook's daughter.'

Although Cecily's words echoed what Janna herself had

thought, still she couldn't help feeling sadness at being reminded that if Gytha was beneath Hugh's attention, she herself must come even lower. Then she remembered the purpose of her questions. If Hugh was guilty, as she feared, he could have no place in her heart, none at all.

'I doubt that my lord has spent much time with Gytha or any other pretty woman who might take his fancy, for he has been very busy since his return.' Cecily's voice broke into Janna's thoughts. 'He goes out every day to inspect the fields, and see what's to be done about the manor, and make sure that all is as it should be. He's told me of his concern that the manor isn't more productive. I believe there have also been several unfortunate accidents recently. Although my lord Hugh pays tribute to Master Serlo, whom he says is an excellent reeve, I suspect his main aim is to convince his aunt of his own good stewardship, and to stay in her favour so that she will let him keep the manor for himself after young Hamo comes of age.'

So Hugh could have gone anywhere and everywhere, with no-one to check on his movements. Janna knew she could push Cecily no further. It was clear she had little real knowledge of how Hugh passed his days. But she might yet have some useful knowledge for Janna.

'Who are the visitors that travelled with you through the forest? Where are they bound?' she asked, feeling sure Cecily would have taken more interest in them than Gytha, and that she'd be able to give a better answer. It might be, she thought hopefully, that the travellers could tell her the way to Winchestre. They might even be going there themselves. If that was the case, maybe she could follow them.

A sudden memory troubled her. Edwin had been present when the travellers arrived – and he'd been missing ever since. Had he already interrogated them about Winchestre? Was that why he'd vanished? Or had he disappeared for another reason entirely? She became aware that Cecily was watching her, eyes narrowed in suspicion.

'You're always asking questions,' Cecily observed, 'and always to a purpose. What's on your mind, Janna?'

Janna was tempted to trust Cecily with her plans but knew that she should not, for she could do nothing nor go anywhere until Hamo was found. 'Nothing in particular is on my mind,' she lied. 'I'm just trying to work out who Hamo might be with, or where he might be. I'm trying to help, mistress.'

'I doubt Hamo's gone anywhere with the visitors.' Cecily thought for a moment. 'In fact, I know he hasn't, for I saw them with Serlo, taking part in the search.' Her voice shook; she fought for control.

'Who are they? Where are they from?' Janna asked again. It seemed unlikely that strangers could be responsible for Hamo's disappearance for they would have no reason to wish the boy harm, nor would they have the local knowledge to keep him hidden. Yet their identity was of interest to her, for in that might lie the answer to another disappearance and a solution to at least one of the mysteries that plagued her.

'They come from near Tantone. I think 'tis in the next shire from ours.'

Tantone. Janna nodded as her suspicion was confirmed. 'Why have they come here?' she asked carefully.

'They stopped to break their journey because one of their horses is lame. Their destination is Winchestre and they plan to be there in time for the annual fair of St Giles.' Cecily sounded troubled as she added, 'But I think there might be another purpose to their travels. I heard them ask my lord Hugh if he'd seen or given shelter to any outlaws over the past few months.'

'Outlaws?' Janna's voice squeaked upwards in horror at the realisation that Edwin's secret must be known to Hugh. With an effort, she tried to control her agitation. 'What did my lord tell them?'

'He asked if the outlaw was travelling on his own. When Master Siward said "yes", my lord replied that he had not come across any man travelling alone. Oh!' Cecily caught her breath. 'Is that . . . is he Edwin? Is Edwin him?'

Janna was sorry, now, that she'd questioned Cecily. She was sure the tiring woman would not have worked it out if she hadn't prompted her to it. But it was too late, now, to take back her words. She nodded.

'Oh, Janna!' Cecily clutched her arm, her own woes forgotten at this new threat. 'We might have been murdered in our beds!'

'Nonsense!' Janna could understand Edwin's disappearance now, but she wished he was here to argue his cause and state his innocence. More than anything, she was grateful to Hugh for keeping both her secret and Edwin's. She felt mean and unworthy when she remembered her suspicions about him, yet she knew she must not trust him unless and until she could prove him innocent of any knowledge of Hamo's disappearance.

190

'If my lord Hugh has kept Edwin's secret, and mine, I beg you to do the same,' she pleaded. 'Besides, Edwin has left the manor. I think those men have frightened him away.' For all she knew, it was true.

'Thank goodness for that.' Cecily breathed a soft sigh of relief. She climbed to her feet, and stretched out her hand to Janna to pull her up. 'I must get back,' she said, and looked suddenly awkward. 'Janna, I hate to see you as you are. I wish you –'

'It's all right. I don't mind.' Janna brushed dust and grass seeds from her breeches. 'You go on ahead. You shouldn't be seen with me. It might cause talk.'

Cecily hesitated. 'Go on.' Janna gave her a push. 'I'll follow you.'

A mournful tolling spoke the message that Hamo still wasn't found as the villeins returned to the manor, the women and children parting from their menfolk at the gate to make their way back to their own cots. Janna could see the leaping flames of smoking torches. The men had returned only to fetch them so they might continue the search. She could hear Serlo's voice bellowing out above the confusion, and she lingered a little longer, watching as the lighted flares streamed out and disappeared beyond the manor walls. She noticed that the forester had joined the search, and shrank back into the shadows. She must make sure to keep out of his way if he was still around in the morning.

The bell commenced its mournful tolling once more, calling out to the lost boy, summoning him home.

A wave of desolation swept over Janna. She was sure now that Hamo was not lost, but had been taken by someone and hidden somewhere. If he was lost, or had met with some misadventure, he would have been found. Could that mean that he was still alive? Janna took some comfort from the thought, even while she struggled against naming the only man who could wish Hamo harm.

Yet Hugh was absent from the manor. He had gone to fetch Dame Alice, which meant that there was no-one here to take care of Hamo while he was held captive. Perhaps, then, the boy must be dead after all?

No! Janna pushed the thought away from her. She couldn't give in to despair. She wouldn't!

Something else was bothering Janna now. Intent on clearing it up, she set off after the tiring woman, walking with long free strides. Cecily had said that Hamo was playing ball against the manor wall when she'd been called away to the kitchen to talk to the cook. Who had called her away? And where was Hamo's ball?

Cecily was about to climb the stairs up to the hall. She'd stopped to pluck an armful of flowers from the garden, perhaps to brighten the chamber in time for Dame Alice's arrival or perhaps just to cheer herself up. Janna had almost caught up to her when a sudden roar stopped them both.

'John!' Before Janna could move, could run, Serlo was upon her. He grabbed hold of her smock in one big hand, and began shaking her as a dog would a rat.

'Stop it! Stop that!' Cecily said sharply, and bent to calm Bones, who'd begun to bark hysterically.

Serlo gave her one startled glance. 'He is a thief, just as his brother is a thief!' He gave Janna another hard shake. Janna

192

jerked her chin at Cecily, trying to tell her to go away and leave them. But Cecily stayed. 'What evidence do you have for such an accusation, Master Serlo?' she asked calmly.

'A length of fine woollen cloth is missing from a storage chest in the undercroft.' Serlo kept tight hold of Janna. 'Two silver goblets are also missing.' He thrust his face into Janna's, scowling ferociously. 'Where are they?'

TEN

Janna's first feeling was overwhelming relief. The posy of rue must have been to mark a theft, not the taking of Hamo. In spite of her situation, she felt almost light-hearted.

'I know nothing of these articles,' she said steadily, pitching her voice louder to be heard above the noise Bones was making. The dog had tried to sink its teeth into Serlo's ankle, and had received a kick for its efforts. Now it kept a wary distance, but it continued to bark and growl at the reeve. 'I have no possessions for you to search,' Janna continued, 'but I warrant that no matter where you look, you will find nothing to link either me or Edwin to the missing objects.' The storage chests had been locked, she remembered now. Whoever had the key must surely be responsible for the thefts. She opened her mouth to voice her thoughts, and quickly closed it again. It could only increase Serlo's suspicion if she confirmed she'd already investigated the chests.

'What about your thieving brother?' Serlo gave her another shake. 'I gave you until nightfall to find him – and the young lord. Where are they? What do you know of them?'

'Nothing, Master Serlo. I don't know where they are. I wish I did.'

'There, Master Serlo,' Cecily said, 'You have your answer. She knows nothing.'

Janna closed her eyes and groaned inwardly. Had Serlo noticed Cecily's slip? If so, he gave no sign of it.

'You will stay here under lock and key until your brother returns,' he said sternly.

And if he doesn't return? Janna dared not ask the question.

'Master Serlo, may I suggest you consult my lord Hugh before locking up this . . . this youth,' Cecily said quickly, trying to make up for her mistake.

The reeve frowned at the tiring woman, seemingly puzzled by her intervention. 'With respect, ma dame, this matter does not concern my lord or you,' he said coldly.

Cecily looked at him with dislike. 'Nevertheless, I will put this matter before my lord as soon as he returns with Dame Alice,' she said firmly.

In spite of her precarious situation, Janna's mouth twitched up in a smile. It seemed the tiring woman had some iron in her spirit in spite of her fragile appearance.

Her smile vanished as she heard Serlo's reply. 'And I will keep this villein safe under lock and key until that time'.

Despite Cecily's continued protests, he dragged Janna across the yard and pushed her into the barn. His shove sent her flying into the darkness. She fell against a pile of hay, feeling the hard ground graze her knees through the rough fabric of her breeches. She heard the snick of the latch as it came down to hold the door fast, and then a frantic howling. Bones was shut outside, and not happy.

'You'll be sorry for this!' Cecily's threat came loud and clear through the wattle and daub walls of the barn, and so

did her next words: 'Come on, Bones, you come with me.'
The sounds of whining faded into the distance. Janna kept
silent. She didn't know if Serlo was still outside, but she
knew that calling out wouldn't change his mind. She would
not demean herself further in his eyes.

It was pitch black inside the barn. Janna couldn't see at
all. She scrambled to her feet and stretched out her hands,
ready to explore her prison. But the barn was crammed full
of hay and she quickly found there was nowhere to go. She
sat down to consider her situation. While she hoped that
Hugh wouldn't suspect her of theft, it was perfectly possible
that he would lay the blame on Edwin. Thanks to the
travellers, Hugh now knew Edwin's circumstances. Janna
was the only one who could speak up for him and try to
clear his name. In all conscience she wondered if she could
or should, when Edwin had been so quick to help himself
to Janna's own possessions.

A sudden realisation brought a hot wave of shame to
Janna's cheeks. She was ready to believe the worst about
Hugh's intentions towards his young cousin, while expecting
him to believe the best about her. But, whatever he thought,
she knew she couldn't count on him to interfere with Serlo's
decision. It was really up to her to help herself. Meanwhile
there was Hamo to consider. As she was not going anywhere
soon, she might instead ponder where the child might be.

Try as Janna would, she could think of no place that
hadn't already been searched. Her thoughts took a different
tack. Was she making too much of Hugh's relationship to
Hamo? Did the theft prove that no-one wished Hamo any
harm? While Janna tried to tell herself that the child had

merely run away once more in search of his dog, and that he'd become lost, she was filled with dread that he was lying somewhere, bound and gagged, or even worse, already dead.

She shook her head, trying to dismiss her fear. Worry over Hamo was taking her nowhere. Once again, at the back of her mind, came the thought that she knew something, had seen something that might shed some light on Hamo's disappearance. She sat quietly, trying to free her mind of all her worries so that the missing memory might take their place. But nothing came to her. The knot of anxiety tightened in her stomach. She was trapped here and, if Serlo kept his word, she would face the forester, and maybe even the sheriff, in the morning. Face them alone, without Edwin.

Suddenly angry, she pounded her fist into the hay. It wasn't fair that he'd run off without a word, leaving her to face this mess on her own. Where could he be? Once he'd recognised the travellers, would he have hurried off to Winchestre on his own, not knowing that the travellers themselves planned to go there? It seemed unlikely. Edwin knew she wanted to go to Winchestre. He would have told her his plans; he would have taken her with him because his own safe passage lay with her and with their story.

He must be lying low then, waiting for the travellers to leave so that he could safely show his face again. The forest? Was he hiding there once more? It was possible. Even so, Janna found it hard to believe that he would not have got word to her somehow. Who else could he trust if not his travelling companion?

A name came into Janna's mind, and she frowned and sat straighter as she recalled Edwin's earlier disappearances. She hugged her knees to her chest and rested her forehead against them as she began to sort out the arguments both for and against the one person to whom Edwin might turn for help, and trust with his safety. She found that she could think of no arguments against; everything confirmed her new suspicion.

She jumped up, anxious now for action. She had to get out of here, she had to go and find Edwin. She looked about her, realising that her eyes had become accustomed to the darkness. A thin sliver of twilight filtered between the overhanging thatched roof and the top of the sturdy wooden walls, faintly illuminating the contents of the barn. She peered at the hay piled behind her and then, with quickening interest, at the solid shapes of farming implements stacked beside the stout door that shut her in.

She hurried to inspect them, hoping to find a sturdy axe to hack her way through, but there were only some curved sickles, which were the wrong shape for an attack on something as solid as the door. She turned next to a wooden plough with its iron cutting parts. She felt the coulter and share carefully, but they were fixed firmly into place and no good for her purpose anyway. She looked to see what else might be helpful, and saw several flails for threshing corn once the harvest was in.

Janna picked up the long shaft of a jointed flail, and jiggled it experimentally. Yes, it might work. It was certainly worth a try. If Serlo meant to keep her locked up, he should have given more thought to his choice of prison. He certainly should not have underestimated her need to escape! She tucked the flail under her arm and began to climb the pile of hay, sneezing ferociously as dust swirled and eddied around her. Her foot slipped; Janna grabbed a handful of hay to save herself. It came away in her grasp and she crashed down into a heap on the hard ground. Hampered by the flail, she tried again, scrambling up and slipping down just as she'd almost reached the top of the stack. Once more she tried, and once more after that. She was utterly determined that Serlo would not find her here in the morning. At last she managed to reach the thin crack of light that marked the division between the wall and the thatched roof. Janna knew she had to hurry for, once the sun set, the villeins would all go to bed rather than waste a precious rush light. Before that happened, there was someone she needed to see, and much for her to do.

She pulled the flail from under her armpit, and thrust the long handle into the thin crack between wall and thatch. Using all her force, she began to push against reeds and straw, levering the stick up and down so that they began to loosen. She sneezed and sneezed again as dust, spiders and earwigs sprinkled down onto her hair and shoulders, but she kept on working until she had dislodged enough thatch to form a small hole. A quick slide down the hay to the farming implements, and this time she climbed with a sickle in her hand, hooking it through the hay to give her extra purchase on her way up again.

The small curved blade cut away the loose reeds one by one until there was a hole large enough to wriggle through. Wasting no time, Janna dived halfway through and peered out into the night.

A quick glance was all she needed. Plunging to the ground head-first would only achieve a broken neck. She wriggled backwards until her feet rested once more on the piled-up hay, and turned around. Balancing on her elbows and stomach, this time she thrust her feet first through the hole she'd made. She eased herself through, pushing until she could hold on no longer. With a cry, quickly stifled, she fell to the ground, landing awkwardly so that an ankle twisted painfully beneath the weight of her body.

At least she was free! Janna stood up carefully, and took a cautious step on her sprained ankle. She sucked in a breath at the sharp pain and quickly shifted her weight to rest on her other foot. What she needed was a stout stick to lean on. She peered anxiously into the dusky darkness, half-expecting Serlo to pounce on her once more. But everyone who was not out on the search had gone indoors for supper and to bed. Keeping to the shadows, Janna left the manor and hobbled towards the carpenter's cottage as fast as her sore ankle would carry her.

She knocked on the door. It was opened by Bertha herself. Janna watched her closely, looking for any signs she might have missed when she'd questioned her once before. 'I give you good night, mistress,' she said in a friendly fashion.

'God be with you.' Bertha looked out past Janna's shoulder, scanning the track that gave access to the villeins' cots. 'What are you doing here?' she asked curiously, bringing her attention back to Janna.

'I'm looking for Edwin.'

'Why should you think I know where he is?' A scowl masked Bertha's pleasant features. Janna wondered if she was going to have the door slammed shut in her face. She quickly leaned against it to prevent the possibility.

'Several reasons,' she said cheerfully. 'I always thought Edwin was shy with girls. I also know he kept away from them because, with no home and no prospects, he has nothing to offer a wife. He told me so himself. But now I'm not so sure.' She peered at Bertha in the pale light of the rising moon. 'You're in love with him, aren't you?'

'Why should you think so?' Bertha cast a quick glance over her shoulder, perhaps to check on her family's where-abouts. She stepped outside the cottage, forcing Janna to move away from the door.

'Because you came over and sat with Edwin and me instead of with your family at medale.' Janna noticed Bertha hadn't denied the claim. It gave her the confidence to continue. 'Because Edwin knew that your sister wanted to dance with me, which meant that he must have met your family already. Because he wasn't around when the haystack was fired and we were trying to put out the blaze. Was he off dallying with you, mistress?'

Bertha's lips clamped firmly together. Janna waited for her denial, but it still didn't come. 'Also,' Janna continued, wondering if she was being rash, building too much into Bertha's parting remark after she'd cut her hair, but deciding to take the chance anyway. 'You know who – or what – I really am. Edwin would not have told you that unless he trusted you.'

Silence greeted Janna's remarks.

'If it's any help, I think Edwin cares for you too, mistress,' Janna continued, remembering how angry Edwin had been when she'd passed on the cook's gossip concerning Bertha. She'd misread the situation at the time, thinking he was upset about Gytha. But she was quite sure she was on the right track now. 'You were carrying a small sack when I asked you to cut my hair. That was food for Edwin, wasn't it? You're hiding him somewhere.'

Still Bertha remained silent. Janna began to lose patience with her. 'You can trust me,' she snapped. 'Edwin does. We're in this together, you know.'

Bertha blinked. She opened her mouth to speak, and closed it again, looking undecided. Janna decided to help her out. 'Do you know that Edwin and I are being blamed for the theft of some woollen cloth and two silver goblets? Have you seen any such things, mistress?'

'No.' Bertha licked dry lips. 'No, of course not!'

'Then it would be good if Edwin came out of hiding to speak his innocence. As it is, I've been locked up in a barn for the theft.'

Now Bertha looked thoroughly bewildered. 'But I escaped,' Janna explained, continuing earnestly, 'Mistress, if you know where Edwin is, and if you value truth and justice, I beg you to take me to him now.'

Still Bertha hesitated. Janna itched to give her a push, just to get her moving. She restrained herself with difficulty. 'Did Edwin tell you about the visitors to the manor?' she asked instead, wondering just how much he had taken Bertha into his confidence. She was fearful that she might be jeopardising his safety with her question, but she also needed something to convince Bertha to help her.

It was some relief when Bertha nodded slowly. Janna decided to put her mind at rest if it would help her cause. 'It is true that the travellers look for Edwin, but that is not their main purpose for being here. They are on their way to trade goods at the fair in Winchestre, and have only delayed their visit while their horse is lame. And they are also helping in the search for Hamo.' The thought diverted Janna for a moment. 'You don't know where Hamo is, do you?'

'No.' This time the answer came bold and clear.

'No. Well, I am sorry for that. But we can both reassure Edwin concerning the travellers, for they have asked the lord Hugh about him, but he has kept our secret.'

Now Bertha looked startled. Janna smiled grimly to herself. 'Please,' she begged. 'Please, mistress, tell me where Edwin is, for my sake and for his.'

Reluctantly, Bertha stepped aside, and beckoned Janna to come in.

'He's here?' Janna could hardly believe it.

Bertha nodded. She put a finger to her lips, warning Janna to silence, then led her through the carpenter's workshop and into the room beyond. While Janna greeted Bertha's surprised family, Bertha picked up a bucket of slops containing vegetable peelings and assorted greens, and a small sack of grain. She walked on through to a pen adjoining their cottage. In it were a pig and three small piglets, two goats and several hens. They crowded around Bertha as she walked in, clamouring to be fed, but she pushed past them and walked on to a small thatched cover at the back of the pen. A pile of wood was set under the thatch out of the weather. Janna's confusion grew.

'Edwin?' Bertha called softly.

He peered around the wood pile with a cheerful grin, which quickly turned to a frown of concern when he noticed that Bertha had company.

'Have you been here all the time?' Janna asked, astonished.

'No,' Bertha answered for Edwin. 'He told me he was leaving the manor, and he showed me where he'd be – up a tree in the forest. You were right, John – Janna – I brought food to him there. But when Hamo went missing, I knew Edwin was in danger of being found, and so I went to fetch him as soon as it grew dark.'

'I watched you all go out to search for the boy.' Edwin's tone was regretful as he added, 'I wanted to help look for him too, but I dared not come out of hiding, for the travellers were part of the search party. You know who they are? You know why I had to run?'

'Yes, I know,' Janna reassured him.

'And the boy? Hamo? He is still not found?'

'No.' The bell began to ring out its lonely message once more, confirming that the search continued. Edwin's words reassured Janna that he really knew nothing about Hamo's disappearance. But that left the problem of the missing length of woollen cloth and the silver goblets. 'Some things have been stolen from the storage chests in the undercroft,' she said now. 'What do you know about it, Edwin? And don't lie to me, either. You stole my purse from me, I haven't forgotten that.' A shocked gasp, quickly suppressed, told Janna that Edwin hadn't been entirely honest with Bertha.

'I don't know nothing about stealing goods from the undercroft,' Edwin blustered, angry that Janna had shown him in a bad light. 'What's missing? And why should you think I had anything to do with it? I haven't even been at the manor, I've been up a tree!'

'Sshh, keep your voices down,' Bertha warned. 'I'll leave

you two to argue while I feed the animals.'

Watching Bertha empty the bucket of greens and slops, and throw grain to the hens, hearing the clucking, grunting and bleating as the animals fought one another to get to the food first, reminded Janna of her own chores when she'd lived with her mother. She felt a sharp pang of sadness. Their lives had been hard, but she'd been happy enough. She felt so much older now; she'd lost her childhood innocence the day her mother had died and she'd come face to face with evil. She would never be the same again.

Janna shook off her dark thoughts with an effort. While Bertha squatted to milk the goats, Janna began to tell Edwin what had been happening in his absence. Bertha joined in, ranging herself on Edwin's side until Janna was convinced that they knew nothing about either the stolen property or the missing Hamo. They continued then to confer in low voices, with Janna trying to persuade Edwin to show himself while he and Bertha fiercely resisted all her arguments.

'You've turned me into an a fugitive!' Janna said hotly, when she saw he would not be persuaded.

'You were a fugitive when I met you,' Edwin reminded her.

It was true. But that fact didn't help Janna now. 'I'm supposed to be locked up in the barn. I'm certainly not going back there! But I can't leave the manor either, not while Hamo is still missing. What am I to do?'

'You can stay here with me,' Edwin offered.

Janna moved over to investigate the small space between the fence of woven wattle and the woodpile. It was barely large enough to hide Edwin.

'I s'pose you could stay here,' Bertha said reluctantly. 'The animals are my responsibility. No-one else comes out here but me. And my father, when he needs more wood, but Edwin knows to stay hidden unless he hears my voice.'

'No, I thank you. I'll find somewhere else to hide.' Janna screwed up her face in concentration. Where could she go, and what could she do to help find Hamo? 'I wish I knew whether he was lost or taken!' she burst out.

'Taken? Who?' Both Edwin and Bertha turned to Janna in confusion.

'Hamo.' She pondered a moment, wondering if she could take them into her confidence. Yes, she decided. Three heads might be better than one at working out this puzzle. Besides, Bertha had lived here all her life, she might well know something from the past to help make sense of the present. 'I wish I knew whether Hamo's disappearance was connected in any way with what else has been happening here,' she said carefully, and began to tell them about the sprigs of rue that were left each time to mark the scene of the so-called 'accident'.

Talking about it helped to get the sequence of events clear in her mind, she found.

'I thought Hamo's disappearance was yet another "accident" when I found the posy of rue beside the door of the undercroft,' she said, 'but when Serlo accused me – us – of stealing the woollen cloth and goblets, I thought I must be mistaken, and that the rue was left to mark that instead. But now I'm not so sure.'

'Why? What have the accidents and Hamo going missing got to do with each other, then?' Bertha frowned at Janna.

'I wish I knew,' Janna said again. 'It's just that after I found the rue, I decided to search the barn myself to see if it meant anything. Serlo claims that the missing articles came from some wooden chests stored there, but I know they were all locked when I looked at them.' She frowned, worried that she already knew the answer to the question she was about to ask. 'Whoever took those things must have had a key to open the chests,' she said. 'So who would have a key?'

'The lord Hugh. Master Serlo. Mistress Tova, and maybe Gytha?' Bertha offered. Then she laughed, and shook her head. 'But that's silly. Why should any one of them want to cause harm to the manor – or to Hamo? Unless . . .' She stopped.

'Unless?' Janna prompted, dreading to have her suspicions confirmed by the carpenter's daughter.

'Well, Gytha's mother wants her to marry the reeve. Serlo has a good position and is held in great respect. He owns his cottage and the gore acres around it and, whatever happens to my lord Hugh once Hamo inherits this property, you can be sure that Master Serlo will keep his position here. But Gytha is determined that she'll wed my lord and no other.'

Janna nodded. This she already knew. She waited for Bertha to explain herself.

'I'm wondering if Gytha knows anything about Hamo's disappearance? It's terrible even to think it, but if something happens to Hamo then my lord Hugh will inherit all Dame Alice's fortune, including this manor. That would please Gytha greatly. Hamo is the greatest barrier to her becoming the lord Hugh's wife and the lady of his manor.'

'Gytha?' Janna hadn't considered the young beauty before. She wondered if there could be any truth in Bertha's words.

'Gytha must know that if my lord Hugh inherits nothing when Hamo comes of age, he will need to marry someone with a fortune. He certainly won't wed her,' Bertha continued, unconsciously echoing Janna's own thoughts on the matter. 'Maybe Gytha knows something about Hamo's disappearance? Maybe she's even the cause of it?'

'It's possible, I suppose,' Janna said dubiously. Did Gytha have the courage or the guile to carry out such a dreadful mission? It seemed unlikely. It seemed even more unlikely that she was involved in any of the incidents that had gone before. While she would have had the time and the opportunity to carry them out, she had no motive and nothing to gain from any of them. A sudden thought lodged like an arrow in Janna's heart. Could Hugh and Gytha be in this together, and working for their common cause?

'Watch Gytha, see where she goes, what she does,' she told Bertha. 'If she knows where Hamo is, sooner or later she'll lead you to him.'

Bertha nodded, looking self-important and proud. Janna was relieved that Bertha hadn't taken her guess to its logical conclusion. If Gytha had everything to lose when Hamo inherited the land from Dame Alice, so did Hugh. Whichever way she looked at the problem, it always came back to him. He, more than anyone, had good reason to kidnap Hamo, as well as the means and opportunity to carry it out. He would not have to use force. The boy would go with him willingly. She was about to say so, but found that Hugh's name stuck in her throat. She could not say it out loud, because she still didn't want to believe it. She would hide, and watch, and wait until she found proof of his culpability,

Janna decided. Then, and only then, would she call Hugh to account.

'I'd better go,' she said, and scrambled to her feet. Bertha stood up to accompany her. Edwin gave Janna an apologetic smile. 'I'm sorry you have to face this alone,' he said. 'But I'll come out of hiding just as soon as those travellers leave the manor, I promise you.'

'And then?' Janna queried. 'Will you come on to Winchestre with me?'

Edwin and Bertha exchanged glances. She spoke up for both of them. 'It is our wish to be wed, if the lord Hugh permits it,' she said. 'I have asked my father to take Edwin on as an apprentice and he has already agreed to it. Edwin's life lies here now, with me.'

Janna nodded in understanding. 'Good luck to you then,' she said, 'and I wish you both great happiness.' She turned to Bertha. 'Please keep close watch on Gytha and, if you have any further ideas about Hamo's disappearance, either of you, please tell me.' She gave Edwin a farewell salute, then followed Bertha out through the cottage, taking time to give her younger sister an awkward wave as she passed.

Needing to find shelter, Janna headed off towards the forest for the night, all the while keeping a lookout for telltale flickers of light from the searchers, and listening anxiously for sounds of the hunt. She'd sworn never to pass another night up a tree again, and so she looked around for somewhere else she might shelter – and found it in the sheep shed where she and Edwin had hidden once before. With relief, she hurried towards it, sure that she'd be safe there for the night, for it must already have been searched by others as well as by herself.

She debated gathering leaves and straw to make a softer bed, but decided against it. Even if she cleaned out the shed in the morning, she was bound to leave signs of occupation behind, signs that could be misinterpreted. With a sigh of resignation, she cleared a small patch of the hard flinty ground free of sheep's mundungus, and lay down. She was exhausted, but her thoughts churned endlessly, keeping her fretful and awake. Hamo. He must be feeling so frightened, and so alone.

And Hugh! Her suspicions seemed impossible when she recalled his kindness, his gentle touch as he comforted her after her mother's death. His kiss . . . Her body ached and burned with memories of Hugh.

At some time during the night she heard the sound of voices and leapt up, trying to judge whether she was safe, whether she had time to run. She opened the door a crack and peered out across the water meadows. The weary villeins were returning home, their torches burned as low as their spirits judging by the snatches of conversation that came her way through the still night air. Hamo was not found then. The hunt would start again at dawn. She dozed, awoke, and dozed again until a gradual lightening to the east told her that the sun would soon rise, and the searchers with it.

She scrambled to her feet and rolled her shoulders to ease their stiffness, then rubbed her arms to generate a little warmth. She was cold and hungry. She could almost smell the fresh bread baking in the kitchen, the rich scent of pig roasting on a spit, and was tempted to sneak back to the manor and ask Mistress Tova for something to break her fast. Instead, she slipped into the forest to find something to eat. Some mushrooms, hastily collected and eaten raw, helped ease the hollow emptiness in her stomach, while a few early raspberries added a touch of sweetness at the finish. The golden aura of the sun peeping above the horizon spoke of a fine day, a fact that added to her rising spirits, her confidence that Hamo was still alive and would be found.

Hugh – or Gytha? Janna shook her head, sure that the answer lay with the one who stood to gain the most from Hamo's death. She resolved to keep herself hidden until Hugh's return. After that she would follow him. If Hamo was alive, his first call must surely be to check on the boy, and when he did so, she would be there, following in his footsteps. She took comfort from the thought that if she was wrong, Bertha would be watching Gytha, ready to pounce if necessary. In the meantime, Janna sought shelter, needing to evade Serlo's watchful eye. She found an old beech tree close to the path through the forest, and climbed high into its dense, leafy crown.

Serlo was the first to come out of the manor, leading a group of villeins. Judging by their yawns and dragging steps, they had been woken early and given little time to break their fast. Janna stayed motionless in her hiding place as they crossed the river and came on into the forest, passing close beside her hiding place. She hardly dared even to blink in case someone caught a flicker of movement. She watched them disappear down the path, and wondered if they were also searching for her. If Serlo had bothered to send some bread and ale to the barn, or even taken the victuals to her himself, he would know she was gone. Everyone would have been warned to keep a lookout for her, and for Edwin.

The sun rose higher, warming the chill from the air and lightening the sky with its rosy rays. Janna's eyes felt heavy with sleep after her wakeful night. She lay along the length of a branch, and felt her eyes close in the drowsy summer heat. A swarm of gnats found her. She flapped an irritable hand at them but they continued to bite and tease her until she found herself thoroughly wide awake. She listened for sounds of the search but heard only the discordant clanging of the bell. Then there was silence.

To keep herself awake, she cast her mind back to what Eadgyth had told her about beeches. The tree had many healing properties but, of more importance to Janna right now, was something else Eadgyth had said. 'The beech is said to protect lost travellers. The old ones especially revered it because they believed the ancient gods wrote upon its bark and so the tree received their knowledge and wisdom. Even today, if you write a wish on a beech tree, it will be granted.' After a moment's reflection, Janna pulled out her knife and laboriously began to inscribe her father's name on the smooth grey bark. J O H N. 'Please let me find him,' she whispered, as she cut into the hard wood.

The long morning wore on, and Janna was almost asleep when the thudding of a horse's hooves jerked her upright. Hugh! She peered through the leaves to make sure, and recognised the green cloak coming towards her. He was riding the reddish brown steed he'd been on before, and he was moving fast. There was no time to lose if she wanted to keep him in sight. She slid down through the lofty branches, grabbing hasty handholds along the way, until she missed her footing and fell. She crashed down into thick leaf litter below the beech, landing almost in the path of the speeding horse. Startled by her sudden appearance, the horse reared and whinnied in fright. Its hooves lashed out and pounded the air. Hugh clung tight to the reins. As he fought to stay in the saddle, he tried to gentle the horse to stillness with his voice. 'Whoa there, easy up. Easy now.' He kept on talking until at last his mount stood calm. Then he looked at Janna, and frowned with displeasure.

'What on earth do you think you're doing?' he said curtly. 'You could have killed us both!'

'I . . . I'm sorry, sire.' Janna bent her knees in a hasty curtsy, tried to correct it to a bob, remembered that Hugh knew she wasn't a boy, got her feet tangled up, and fell over. Scarlet-faced, she scrambled up again, cursing her clumsiness and the ill-luck that had precipitated her descent. She had hoped to follow behind Hugh without being seen; she hadn't expected to confront him like this.

'Why were you hiding up a tree?' From the determined set of Hugh's jaw, Janna knew he would not leave without some explanation from her. She struggled to find something convincing to tell him, but nothing came into her mind. Eventually, she decided to stick to a version of the truth.

'I'm hiding from Master Serlo,' she explained.

Hugh was still gentling and patting the horse. As the bell tolled out once more, his frown deepened. 'There is no sign of Hamo, then?'

'No, sire.' Janna shook her head, almost convinced that Hugh's concern sounded genuine. 'The search has gone on all night, but he is not found.'

Hugh's lips tightened. There was a look of real distress in his eyes. 'I must find Serlo,' he told Janna. 'But before I do, tell me why you are hiding from him.'

'Master Serlo believes that I stole some things from the storage chests in the undercroft, but I swear to you, sire, that I did not.'

'If Master Serlo accuses you of theft, I am sure it is for a good reason. No!' Hugh held up a hand to stay Janna's outraged retort. 'I hold you in good faith, Johanna, and so I am sure he is mistaken in his belief. But what about Edwin? Your *brother*?' There was a wealth of sarcasm in the word.

Janna sighed. His question was fair, but she was unsure how to answer it. 'I have spoken to Edwin and I swear he knows nothing of it either.' Janna hesitated, but decided to continue with the truth, partly because Hugh already knew it. 'He has gone into hiding, sire, because he recognised the travellers who are staying at the manor. They come from his lord's own manor near Tantone, and Edwin is afraid they will return him there if he is found. He's trying to stay hidden for a year and a day so that his lord can no longer claim him.'

'That's what I suspected.' Hugh dismounted then, but kept tight hold of the horse's reins. 'And is there any good reason why I should not hand Edwin over to Master Siward so that his lord can make his own decision about him?'

'He . . . his lord is a violent man, sire. Edwin told me he was beaten regularly. In fact I have seen the scars of it on his back. The other villeins were also beaten. Even the lord's own family were victims of his rage.'

Hugh nodded thoughtfully. 'That accords with what Master Siward hinted at, but you haven't told me everything, Johanna. Or has Edwin not told you that when he ran away, he took his lord's favourite steed with him?'

'Yes, Edwin told me what he was accused of, but no, sire, he did not take the steed. He denied knowing anything about its theft, and I believe him. But he knew no-one else would, and so he ran away.' Janna hesitated. 'For certes, there was no sign of any horse when I met him in the forest, sire.'

'Humph.' Hugh was silent for a few moments. 'And what is Edwin to you, that you defend him so vigorously, Johanna?' There was a slight edge to his voice.

Janna smiled, rather flattered by Hugh's interest. Should she tell him he had nothing to fear, that Edwin was already in love with Bertha? A quick check with the reality of her situation wiped the smile from her face. She must never forget, for one moment, the reason behind her interest in Hugh. 'Edwin was hiding in the forest, just as I was, sire.' Better not mention her stolen purse, Janna thought. 'We decided it would be safer for both of us if we travelled together, and that's why we made up the story about being part-Welsh and everything.' Shamefaced, she looked at Hugh, willing him to believe her, to believe them both.

'You seem to tell lies so readily, Johanna, that I wonder how far I can trust you now?' Hugh's eyes rested on Janna with a steady gaze that cut right through her so that she felt as if her heart and soul were being peeled open. Whatever

Hugh found on his inspection seemed to satisfy some of his doubts, however.

'Very well,' he said curtly. 'I shall speak to Serlo. I shall make sure he knows you are innocent and must be left free. But for all your faith in Edwin, I will speak to him myself. I will find out the truth.' He hoisted himself back into the saddle. 'You will bring him to me tonight, Johanna, in secret if you wish. There is no need for the travellers to see him. But you must make him come or I shall believe the worst of him and then not only the travellers but the whole shire will be looking for him. He will be caught, he will be tried in my manorial court and, if necessary, I shall have him hanged.'

Janna gulped, knowing from Hugh's tone that he meant every word of his threat. 'There's something else you should know, sire,' she said, in a small voice.

'What?'

'Master Serlo locked me up in a barn, but I . . . . I managed to escape.'

'And how did you do that?' In spite of Hugh's grave expression, Janna thought she detected the hint of a reluctant smile about his mouth.

'I cut through the thatch at the top of a wall. There's a bit of a hole there now.'

Hugh clicked his tongue in disapproval. 'I believe I've underestimated you in the past, Johanna,' he said then, 'but I won't make the same mistake twice. And I'll make sure that Serlo doesn't either.' He dug his heels into the horse's flank and it took off across the water meadows. Janna watched the horse and its rider cross the river and head for the manor house. She had no chance of keeping up with Hugh, but for all that, she must follow after him in case he led her to Hamo. The idea that he might have had a hand in his cousin's disappearance disgusted and repelled her. She so desperately wanted to trust him, yet she could not get past the thought that, with Hamo out of the way, Hugh would be Dame Alice's sole heir. He would be free to marry anyone then – including Gytha. Janna's mouth turned down in a sour grimace at the thought.

Her mood, as she followed him across the water meadows, was not improved by the memory of Hugh's last injunction. How was she going to persuade Edwin to come out of hiding and face him? He would think she had betrayed him, and in truth, Janna felt as though she had, although Hugh had given her no choice in the matter. With a heavy heart, she wondered what she could say that might make Edwin trust Hugh's word, and change his mind about staying hidden.

Trust Hugh's word! She tripped over the thought, and almost laughed at the bitter irony of it. It seemed disaster awaited them all, whichever way she looked.

She was almost at the manor house when she heard the distant sound of hoofbeats. She stopped to look behind her, and her heart turned over when she saw Godric. Surprisingly, for she had not known that he could ride, he was mounted and coming her way. As he rode closer, his face set so cold and hard against her, she knew that she was not forgiven. She looked beyond, to the party riding behind him. In front were Robert of Babestoche and, beside him, Dame Alice, his wife. The dame had a kerchief to her eyes; they were scrubbed red and raw from crying. At once Janna looked down to hide her face from them. She stepped quickly out of the party's way. Her heart went out to the mother of the missing child, knowing how frightened she must feel, and how bitter her grief would be if her only son had come to harm. Silently, desperately, she prayed that Hamo would be found alive. She also prayed that Godric would not blurt out her secret.

To her relief, and also to her shame, Godric ignored her. He rode past her, taking Dame Alice, Robert, their small entourage of servants and the laden sumpter horses on towards the manor. None of them spared a second glance at Janna, but she was shaking with fright and reaction as she stared after them. Robert of Babestoche here at the manor! She could hardly believe that the man who had wished her dead, who had incited the villagers against her and stopped at nothing to bring his wish to fruition, was now within reach. She groaned aloud as she recalled all those who could bear witness against her, if they had the mind to do so. Cecily would hold her tongue, she was sure of that, but would Godric? Or Hugh? Or Hamo, who was just a child and could know nothing of discretion?

She remembered then, and with a heavy sense of despair, that Hamo was not around to blurt out the truth. But she was still in danger and so she must hurry to those who might, albeit unwittingly, spell her doom with a careless word. She must warn them, for her sake, to be silent. She would start with Hugh, who didn't understand the danger in speaking her name aloud to his aunt. She would start with Hugh, in the hope that he would lead her to Hamo.

ELEVEN

THE GROOM WAS leading away the mounts ridden by Godric and his party, but there was no sign of them, or of Hugh, when Janna entered through the gate. She hurried up the stairs to the hall and, greatly daring, pushed the door open a crack and peeped through.

Alarm took her breath away. Hugh was in there already, along with his guests. Cecily was also in attendance, red-eyed and shamefaced. Only Gytha seemed to be enjoying herself as she plied them all with refreshments. Janna scowled at the young woman before turning to Cecily. How could she catch the tiring woman's eye, and ask her to pass on the warning to Hugh not to divulge her identity? Impatient and perturbed, she jiggled and bobbed about in an effort to attract Cecily's attention. At last Cecily looked her way. Her eyes widened in surprise. Janna beckoned to her, then stepped hastily back out of sight.

'Janna! What are you doing here?'

'I escaped. But never mind that now. You have to warn my lord Hugh not to tell Dame Alice or Robert that I've survived the fire.'

Cecily frowned. 'But what reason shall I give for such secrecy?' she asked nervously.

Janna was silenced. Cecily's secret couldn't be told, but without that truth nothing else made much sense. 'I've already told him that there are some who wish me harm,' she said at last. 'Could you just remind him of that, and ask him to keep my true identity a secret from everyone, including his own family?'

'Very well.' Cecily gave a reluctant nod. To Janna's relief, she set off at once and, without ado, bobbed a curtsy to the dame and then drew Hugh aside. At once Janna shut the door and escaped down the stairs and into the yard. Bertha ran over to her.

'You shouldn't be here, Janna,' she said breathlessly. 'Serlo's told everyone you're a thief on the run. Edwin too. People are out looking for both of you now, as well as Hamo.' In her agitation, she'd grasped hold of Janna's sleeve. She clutched onto Janna, her face tight with distress.

'Don't fret, mistress. And don't make a scene and attract attention our way.' Janna gently disengaged Bertha's fingers. 'I've spoken to my lord Hugh and he knows I am innocent, and Edwin too, but he still wants to see him tonight, in secret if necessary. If Edwin wants to stay here at the manor, you'll have to persuade him to come out of hiding. Do you understand?'

To Janna's relief, Bertha nodded. It was one hurdle out of the way. 'Have you been watching Gytha? What have you seen?'

Bertha drew a quivering breath. Janna knew her fear and distress was on Edwin's account, not her own. She waited for Bertha to compose herself.

'Gytha spent part of the morning out with a search party. She stayed with them all the time and only came back to the manor when she saw my lord Hugh return. She's upstairs with him now.' Bertha's eyes brightened with sudden amusement, her good humour almost restored as she continued, 'I was following Gytha as you told me, and I heard my lord tell her to make herself useful for once, and prepare some refreshments for his family. I must say he didn't sound very loving, or even very friendly.'

Janna stood still while she absorbed Bertha's information. 'You've done well,' she said slowly. 'Will you keep on watching?' She was fairly sure Bertha was wasting her time, but if she told her so, Janna knew the girl's suspicions might move on to a far more likely prospect. Besides, she might have misjudged Gytha, underestimated her pride and her ambition. The thought of Gytha's guilt was some consolation to Janna, even if she couldn't quite believe in it.

Bertha nodded, and walked back to keep watch on the stairs leading up to the hall. She flicked a hand in farewell, and Janna returned the gesture. She wondered what she should do while Hugh was engaged with his guests. Every instinct prompted her to join in the search, but she was sure there was no point to it, for if Hamo was going to be found, he would have been found already. Rather than rush around pointlessly, Janna decided instead to follow the leads she'd come up with, in the hope that Hamo's whereabouts might become clear to her. She could only pray that she would find him in time to save his life.

She could start by looking for Hamo's ball. As she began a careful search of the yard, she wondered if it was still there to be found. Even if Hamo had left his ball lying around, it was quite possible one of the young searchers she'd previously encountered in the barn had already made off with it. Hamo's ball was a prize worth having, being made of leather stuffed with dried beans, rather than the straw-filled pig's bladder that was the usual plaything of urchins. Without much hope, she poked and pried about bush and barn, and came at last to the reluctant conclusion that the urchins must indeed have found the ball first, for her careful search revealed no trace of it at all. Either it had been stolen, or Hamo had taken it away with him. It occurred to Janna then that there was still one place left for her to search. At the same time, perhaps she could also solve the mystery of the disappearing dog?

She hurried across to the kitchen garden, and peered behind the barrels where she'd first spotted Bones in hiding. She chided herself for being fanciful as her keen eyes scoured the area and found nothing. Disconsolate, she looked around the neat garden with its rows of herbs and vegetables, an abundance of food which brought juices seeping into her mouth when she remembered her scant breakfast.

She walked past a large bush of rue, and stopped to search for any signs of who might have been picking posies from it. Perhaps there was a footprint, or even something dropped which might help her identify the culprit. A pale glimmer deep within the foliage caught her eye, and she plunged her hand into the bush to investigate.

'Yes!' She seized Hamo's prized treasure with a shout of triumph. As she held the ball aloft, her spirits took a sudden nosedive for she understood now, without any doubt at all, that Hamo's disappearance was linked to what had gone before. It was a deliberate act by someone who wished him harm.

Hugh, she thought, with an ache of sadness that wrenched her heart. She must stick by him, tight as resin to a tree. Sooner or later, he would lead her to his cousin. She left the kitchen garden and positioned herself at the side of the barn where she could see but not be seen. There was nothing for it, now, but to watch and wait until Hugh emerged from the hall and went about his business once more.

Her feet were tired and her spirit weary from watching when Hugh finally clattered down the stairs from the hall. He was accompanied by Godric. They stood together, conferring, while Janna fumed impatiently. She desperately wanted to tell Godric what was on her mind, and enlist his help in tracking down Hamo, but she could not while Hugh was present. Of course it was quite possible, she conceded as she watched them part, that Godric would not speak to her. She could waste time with him instead of going after her prime suspect. Who, then, should she follow?

Caution won. She followed Hugh, even though she was sure Godric had seen her. He would think she was running after Hugh. It would turn him even further against her. She longed to speak to him, to try to explain, but she could not. Not when Hugh might be on his way to check up on Hamo even now. So she skulked about watching Hugh, ducking for cover behind walls and trees every time he looked around in case he spotted her.

He seemed in no hurry to join the search for Hamo, going first to the kitchen where he spent some time. When he came out, he was followed by Serlo. They spoke a few moments longer, and then Serlo strode off while Hugh went into the kitchen garden. Janna sidled after him, and watched him pull an apple from the tree. The apples were still not quite ripe and she suspected he was about to give himself a bellyache, but he made no attempt to eat it, walking instead towards the stable. Janna felt a sudden leap of hope. Could Hamo be hidden somewhere inside? She broke cover to creep after Hugh and took shelter in a stall while she waited for her eyes to become accustomed to the dim light.

'Johanna. Why are you following me about the manor?' Hugh's voice sounded weary and impatient. A hot blush flamed Janna's cheeks as she stumbled reluctantly from her hiding place.

'I . . . I . . .' She could think of no excuse that might explain her actions.

He stroked the horse's nose while he waited. The silence between them lengthened to snapping point. It was Hugh who gave in first. 'Was there something you wanted to say to me?'

Yes! But Janna was afraid to ask the questions that tumbled into her mind, for Hugh would know then that she suspected him of abducting Hamo.

'I . . . I wanted to change Arrow's dressing,' she muttered.

At once, Hugh lifted the horse's hoof so that she might inspect it, gentling the horse all the while. Watching him, Janna found it impossible to believe him responsible for deliberately injuring the animal, or for carrying out any of the other acts that had plagued the manor. He loved Arrow – just as Janna was sure he loved his cousin Hamo, as well as the manor that had been entrusted to his care. Janna knew Hugh to be kind, and she had thought that he was honourable. Gytha might not be quite so honourable, but Janna doubted she had either the resourcefulness or the will to snatch Hamo and bring about all the 'accidents' that had gone before, or even the wit to think of leaving posies of rue to mark what she was doing. But if not Hugh, or Gytha, then who?

Once again, something niggled at her memory. Was there something she'd overlooked, had someone said something that might shed new light on the people who lived and worked here?

Rue for repentance, rue for regret. But Eadgyth had said it could also be used to curse an enemy.

The significance of everything that had happened at the manor suddenly shifted and began to change, forming a different pattern altogether. And with the new pattern came an unexpected name. Perplexed, wishing she had time to sift her thoughts and make some sense of them, Janna bent to the task of removing the dressing. 'The wound is healing well, my lord,' she said, 'but you should not ride Arrow for a while yet.'

Hugh nodded. He produced the apple and held it out to Arrow. 'Don't forget I want to see Edwin tonight,' he said, over the sound of the horse's happy crunching. 'I've been speaking to Master Serlo, and I want some answers from you both. Too many accidents have been happening lately, seemingly without any explanation. There were no accidents until you and Edwin arrived at the manor.'

'We arrived at the manor before you did, sire. There were no accidents until you came home from Babestoche Manor.' Janna knew she was taking a risk, but perhaps it might provoke Hugh to deal honestly if he thought others suspected that his might be the hand behind all the incidents. And if he was innocent, as she was beginning to suspect he might be, then the more he could tell her, the closer they might come to understanding the reason for Hamo's disappearance. Feeling a little fearful, she kept her head bent while she replaced Arrow's dressing and waited for Hugh's reaction.

He went very still. 'What do you mean by that?' His tone rasped harshly.

Janna stood her ground, not allowing herself to be intimidated by him. 'I mean nothing by it, sire,' she said, in as respectful a tone as she could muster. 'You and Master Serlo seem to hold Edwin and me responsible for the troubles here. I'm only pointing out a fact in our defence.'

'Hmm.' Hugh inspected her closely. Janna flushed more deeply under his scrutiny, all too conscious of the rough smock and breeches that she wore. Automatically, her hand went to her hair, to smooth and tidy it. It was a shock to feel only stubble under her hands. Hugh lifted a sardonic eyebrow, understanding only too well her unconscious attempt to remind him that she had once been beautiful.

'Do you know anything about these accidents, Johanna, anything at all?' he asked in a more conciliatory tone.

Janna hesitated, then made up her mind. If she was going to defend herself and Edwin, and test him at the same time, she might as well do it properly, she thought. 'I know that a posy of rue has been left at the site of every mishap.'

'Rue?' She could have sworn his surprise was genuine, along with his question: 'What do you mean?'

226

'I mean that a posy of rue was left at the henhouse at the time the fox got in, and another was found beside the lamb that was slaughtered. I found a posy of rue near the byre after the animals escaped and destroyed the new wheat, and there was also a posy attached to the haystack next to the one that was fired. I found rue at the stable door on the day Arrow's shoe worked loose and the nail went into his hoof and . . . and I saw a posy of rue at the door of the undercroft, from where the woollen cloth and silver goblets were stolen.'

'And where are they now, these posies of rue?' Hugh sounded thoroughly bewildered.

'I . . . I was afraid that Edwin and I would be blamed for all that was going wrong, and so I destroyed them,' Janna confessed.

'You've told me lies in the past, Johanna. Why should I believe you now?'

And why should I believe you know nothing about what I'm telling you, Janna thought in turn. 'Because it's the truth, sire,' she said instead. 'I told lies in the past because I had to protect myself, but I have no need to tell lies about what's been happening here. Neither does Edwin. He *likes* it here, he wants to stay, he's told me so himself. Why should he try to destroy something when it is the means to his escape from his lord as well as his future livelihood?'

Hugh nodded thoughtfully. 'And Hamo?' he said carefully, going to the heart of the matter. 'Is his disappearance part of this same puzzle?'

Janna looked at him. Was he testing her, seeing how much she knew, or suspected, or did he really want to know? His face was gaunt, lined with worry and fatigue. She was almost sure his concern was genuine. 'A posy of rue was left outside the undercroft where he was playing with his ball,' she said carefully.

'You said goods have been stolen from the undercroft,' Hugh rejoined swiftly.

Janna nodded. 'And by someone who has a key to the chests, for they were all locked, sire.'

'And how do you know that?'

'I searched the undercroft when I found the posy of rue, just in case Hamo was hidden there.'

'Was he?' Hugh seized her arm. He sounded truly fearful as he begged, 'For God's sake, tell me if you know where he is, Johanna!'

'I do not know, sire. I wish I did.' Baffled, Janna shook her head while the last of her carefully constructed assumptions fell apart in the face of Hugh's anguish.

Hugh let go of her arm and began to curse under his breath. Then he turned on Janna. 'I must go out and search for the boy. You have given relief to my aunt in the past, Johanna. Will you see her again? Perhaps mix up some posset to ease her mind, for she is in great distress.'

'I can't!' Janna answered without thinking.

'Why not?' Now Hugh sounded cold and hard as he continued: 'I will pay you for your ministrations, if that is what is on your mind.'

'No! No, sire, it isn't that at all!'

'Then why will you not go to my aunt? Cecily begged me to keep your secret, she says you believe people wish you harm, but you cannot fear my aunt, surely?'

'But I do, sire. I fear everyone.' Janna stopped and took a

deep breath. She remembered what Hugh had said in the past about his aunt's marriage. Would he be sympathetic to her cause? 'I especially fear my lord Robert,' she said carefully.

Hugh frowned, but he didn't say anything. Janna knew she had come too far to back out now. She must go on, although she would not tell him everything she knew. She wouldn't betray Cecily. 'I asked you once before to keep my identity a secret,' she said. 'It was because I feared him. I believe it was he who incited the villagers to set fire to my cottage, even though they knew that I was inside. In fact, I suspect that was part of the plan, for the lord Robert wanted me either dead or gone from the manor. I want him to think he has succeeded in this. Indeed, my safety depends on it.'

'Why should Robert want your death? What do you know about him?'

It was a fair question, but one Janna was not prepared to answer, at least not without Cecily's permission. She stayed silent while Hugh waited for an answer. At last, when he saw she would say nothing more, he heaved a sigh and said softly, 'My aunt married unwisely when she chose Robert but, by calling in the priest to marry them at the church door, she now has the sanction of the church on her marriage and therefore cannot undo the union, no matter how much she might have come to regret it. That is why she summoned me for the birth of her baby, and that is why I stayed on at the manor for such a long time afterwards. It was because she suspected that Robert has turned his affection elsewhere. How am I doing so far, Johanna? Do you know what I'm talking about?'

His question caught Janna by surprise. She gave a reluctant nod.

'And I suspect you know a lot more than you're telling me?' Hugh waited for Janna's reply, but she stayed silent. Her own mother had died because Robert had tried to silence Cecily, but without proof Janna couldn't accuse Robert of anything. That hadn't stopped him trying to silence Janna with the willing aid of the villagers he'd incited. And she knew he'd try again if he realised his secret hadn't died with her.

'Perhaps you're not prepared to betray any confidences?' Hugh ventured.

Janna nodded again, relieved that he seemed to understand her position.

'Then tell me!' He grasped her once more by the arm, and thrust his face close to hers. 'Does any of this have anything to do with Hamo's disappearance now?'

'No. At least, I don't think so.' Janna looked up at Hugh, conscious of how closely they stood together. She could see the stubble of his beard, and smell the sweat on him after his hard ride through the forest. She closed her eyes, feeling suddenly faint with longing.

'Johanna.' His voice was gentle. 'I keep saying that I won't underestimate you, and then I go and do it all over again.' He gave a rueful laugh. 'But you still haven't told me why you've been following me about the manor, when you could have come straight to the stable if you really wanted to change Arrow's dressing.'

His question brought Janna back to the reality of her position. She blinked, and stepped away from him. Yet she

230

could not break the tie she'd sensed between them. How far could she trust him with the truth?

'I'm looking for Hamo, sire. I wondered if you . . .' She found she could not go on.

'If I . . . know where he is? If I can lead you to him? Do you think I have him hidden somewhere?' There was a hard edge of anger behind the question.

Janna tilted her chin, assuming a bravery she did not feel. She found she was incapable of answering his question.

Hugh gave a short, hard laugh. 'I can assure you I don't know where Hamo is, and I'm every bit as concerned for his safety as you are. If you have any thoughts about where he might have strayed, I beg you to tell me so that we can look for him there.'

'I don't think he has strayed, sire. I believe he's been taken.' Janna felt a sudden doubt as she said the words. Had her longing for Hugh led her to misread the situation? For a brief moment, she didn't know whether or not to hope that she had. Then she reminded herself that everything pointed to abduction rather than happenstance.

'Taken? But why? And by whom?' Hugh looked stunned as the full import of Janna's words struck home.

Could her suspicions be correct? A name was on the tip of Janna's tongue, but she found she could not utter it. Not yet, not without further thought. Not without proof. 'I don't know, sire,' she said instead.

'But you thought I was responsible?' Hugh nodded before Janna could answer the question. 'Yes, I can see why you might think it in my interests to have Hamo out of the way.' He took hold of Janna's shoulders and grasped her tight. 'You must believe me, I know nothing of any of this,' he said earnestly. His jaw set into a determined line. 'But by God, you can be sure I'll get to the bottom of it. No-one will be safe from my questions, no-one.' He let her go and took a step back. 'Not even Edwin,' he added. 'Go and fetch him now. I will question him along with everyone else.' And before Janna could protest, he strode out of the stable.

τwelve

Janna looked down at the ball she was still clutching in her hand. All her fine theories about Hugh's guilt had been blown away, and she was more than glad of it, for there was someone else now to take his place. She'd seen and heard several things that could suggest a possible motive for what had been happening, but before she could do anything to find Hamo, she would first have to prove that what she was thinking could be true. Edwin would have to wait. She had far more important things to do right now than go looking for him.

Taking care to keep her face hidden lest Robert or Dame Alice should see her, she went in search of Cecily. She didn't have to look far. The tiring woman was moping about the kitchen garden once more. Bones was with her, still tied to the old piece of rope. Even as Janna watched, the dog lifted a leg and sent a liberal spray over a patch of parsley. Janna pulled a face, hoping that the cook was as punctilious as her own mother had been when it came to washing herbs before using them.

'Cecily,' she called, in case the tiring woman hurried away now that her charge had done his duty. She tucked Hamo's ball behind her back as she approached. Bones barked and wagged his tail, and she bent to give him a pat, pleased that he stood four-square on his paws, seemingly without discomfort.

Cecily gave her a woebegone smile. 'I'm glad Serlo saw sense and let you go free, Janna.'

Janna grinned in return. 'Actually, I escaped. But it's all right, my lord Hugh knows about the missing goods. He knows I am not to blame, and he has spoken to Serlo about it.' Surprised, the tiring woman opened her mouth to question Janna further. 'Will you tell me again about the last time you saw Hamo?' Janna hurried on, unwilling to waste time on explanations.

Cecily's eyes filled with tears. 'I left him over there.' She flung out her hand towards the staircase which led upwards to the hall.

'And he was playing with his ball?' Janna confirmed.

Cecily nodded.

'This one?' Janna pulled it out from behind her back and showed it to the tiring woman.

Cecily gasped. 'Where did you get that?' She took it from Janna and peered at it as if it might reveal the secret of Hamo's whereabouts.

'I found it here in the kitchen garden, hidden within a bush of rue. And I found the dog here, too. I think he'd been beaten. He was frightened.'

'But . . . who? Why?'

'I'm working on it.' Janna took Cecily's hand. 'Try not to worry,' she said gently. 'I think I'm close to finding an answer. If I'm right, none of the blame for Hamo's disappearance will fall on you.'

'Do you know where he is? Is he still alive?' Cecily's face shone with new hope.

'I hope so.' It was as far as Janna was prepared to go right now. She released Cecily's hand, frowning as she noticed a patch of tiny blisters on her own hand. They were itchy and sore. Janna scratched them absent-mindedly. 'You said you were called away to speak to the cook about Hamo's meals. Who called you away?' She waited for an answer, willing Cecily to speak the name in her mind.

'Master Serlo,' Cecily answered readily. 'I asked his advice about Hamo. I wanted to know what Hamo might do about the manor farm to keep him occupied, for he is such a bright and merry boy, I knew he would not be content to stay by my side all the time. I thought Master Serlo might arrange for him to learn to ride, perhaps, or become more proficient with his swordplay, for I know he loves to pretend to fight just like his cousin Hugh. Serlo suggested I speak to the cook about providing good fresh food for Hamo, for he is growing apace and is always hungry.'

Serlo! No-one had been more assiduous in the search for Hamo than the reeve. No-one was more proud of the manor farm. In Hugh's absence he had taken charge of it as if it was his own. He had nothing to gain from setting a fox amongst the hens, or killing a lamb, setting fire to a haystack, destroying the new wheat or laming Hugh's horse – or even snatching a child. He had nothing to gain but the destruction of Hugh's reputation. Janna's next thought sent her heart plummeting down to her boots. Serlo might have started out with the intention of discrediting Hugh in the eyes of his aunt, perhaps hoping that it would further his own interests.

But snatching Hamo meant a larger purpose altogether, a purpose Janna couldn't bear to think about.

If there was anything in Serlo's past to shed light on his actions now, the cook would surely know, Janna thought. She was a know-all and a gossip, and she must be made to talk. Conscious that time was passing and that the more pressing need was to find Hamo rather than working out how to force Serlo to show his hand, Janna turned to Cecily.

'I'm going to make up a posset for Dame Alice, for I believe the lady is in sore distress,' she told Cecily. 'Will you come to the kitchen and fetch it by and by? I beg you, if you value my life please don't tell ma dame, or Robert, where it comes from.'

Cecily nodded. 'I have kept your secret, as I vowed I would,' she assured Janna.

'But please tell my lord Hugh that I have made up the posset, as he asked.'

Cecily's eyes widened as she came to understand the full implications of all Janna had told her. The lord of the manor had reached an understanding with a lowly peasant who dressed as a boy and worked as a farmhand. A smile twitched Janna's mouth as she read the girl's bafflement.

'I must go up to ma dame.' Cecily thrust the end of the rope into Janna's hand. 'Please take the dog. It upsets Dame Alice to have it near by, while my lord Robert gives it a kick every time it comes close to his boot.'

Janna gave a small huff of sour amusement. She could quite well believe it of Robert. The man was a bully, afraid of no-one save his wife. And the thought of anything that might jeopardise his comfortable life, Janna amended.

As Cecily climbed the stairs and vanished into the hall, Janna tugged on the rope to lead Bones to the herbs she wanted to pick for Dame Alice's posset. Wild lettuce and valerian would help to calm and soothe her, banish nightmares and help her to sleep, while motherwort, sweet marjoram or any of several other herbs would build her strength and lift her spirits. She glanced at the dog as she picked the roots, leaves and flowers she needed. He'd been washed, his coat was clean and shining. In fact, the dog was starting to look almost handsome. 'Where were you when Hamo was taken?' she asked, sure in her own mind that Bones had been used as bait to trap Hamo, and that the dog had then been dumped, along with Hamo's ball, once the child was safely out of sight. Or dead.

She hurriedly pushed the thought away. She could not afford to give in to despair, not while there was the slightest chance that Hamo might still be alive. 'Did you see Hamo?' she asked Bones. 'Do you know where he is now?'

The dog looked at her with bright, intelligent eyes, and whined softly. Janna gave him a pat and straightened, clutching her handful of plants. She hurried off to the kitchen, with Bones trotting willingly beside her. He'd obviously decided that the kitchen was his favourite place, and he strained on his lead to get there, setting up a frantic sniffing and barking once inside.

'Get that mongrel out of here,' Mistress Tova said savagely, as she swiped a piece of bacon away from the dog's quivering nose.

Janna set down the fragrant herbs she carried. She surreptitiously slid her hand over a piece of bacon fat before dragging Bones outside. While he was busy gulping down the titbit, she tied him to a post, leaving him in view of the door so that she could watch out for him. Then she went back inside, determined to put the cook's gossip to good use for once.

The cook glanced sideways at Janna. 'Master Serlo was in here looking for you – and your brother. You're in a lot of trouble, both of you. He says there are some goods missing from the undercroft.'

'My lord Hugh knows that we are both innocent of this crime,' Janna said quickly.

Mistress Tova gave a suspicious sniff, as if to smell out the truth. 'Doesn't do to get on the wrong side of Serlo,' she muttered darkly.

It was the opening Janna was waiting for.

'Tell me about Master Serlo, mistress,' she said. She hooked a pot of water over the fire to boil, and began to prepare and chop the herbs she'd picked. 'How is it that he lives in such a substantial home and is allowed to keep all those fields for his own?'

'This manor once belonged to Serlo's family.' Unable to resist a good gossip, the cook came over and settled her bony backside onto a stool. 'The land was confiscated by William the Bastard after the great battle at Hastings,' she confided. 'The king gave this estate as well as several others to Dame Alice's grandfather, who had fought with him and so was rewarded for his service. Serlo's family lost their land and their livelihood, and were reduced to the status of villeins on a manor they had owned for centuries before that.'

Janna was silent as she absorbed the cook's information. This was the link that completed the puzzle. It was also a familiar story. Many Saxon thegns had been dispossessed of their lands after the Norman invasion. William had even taken an inventory of everything he'd conquered, right down to the last hide and plough, cow and pig, mill and fishery, and had kept a record in what everyone now called 'the Domesday Book' for it seemed like a final reckoning of their lives. But the commissioners had many arguments to settle first, so it was said, for the thegns did not give up their land and possessions lightly, while the Norman barons were always greedy to claim more than their entitlement. It had caused great hardship, anger and misery at the time. It seemed that the memory of past greatness and great wrongs did not die easily.

'Ma dame inherited the property through her own family, but Serlo still takes great pride in the estate,' Mistress Tova continued, confirming the direction in which Janna's thoughts now lay. 'It was to reward him for his good offices that my lord Hugh granted him the right to live in a cottage that had once belonged to his family and gave him the gore acres as his own, on the understanding that the work was done in Serlo's own time and that it would not take anything away from his attention to the rest of the manor.'

She hesitated, torn between loyalty to her daughter and confiding her innermost fears. 'In truth, John,' she said then, 'I have urged Gytha to encourage Serlo's attention, for I know he is keen – more than keen – to wed her. In faith, the reeve is besotted with her, he is sick with love, but Gytha will have none of him for she means to marry my lord and no other.'

Janna nodded. She'd seen how Serlo looked at Gytha, and how disdainfully the young girl treated him in turn. Serlo must know that he had a rival for her affections, and who he was. How he must hate being subservient to Hugh, especially as all this had once belonged to his own family! 'And does the lord Hugh encourage her in this expectation?' It took all Janna's courage to remain calm as she waited for the cook to reply.

Mistress Tova sighed. 'He does not,' she admitted sadly. Then she brightened slightly. 'But my lord is lonely, and my daughter is beautiful. While he breathes, there is hope for her.' She thought for a moment. 'And if Gytha's ambition comes to nothing after all, Serlo will still have her and she must have him. She will see that he has much to offer and that she could do a lot worse than take him for a husband.'

Indeed, Serlo had much to offer, Janna thought. No wonder he worked so hard about the manor, if Gytha was his intended prize. If he could take Hugh down at the same time, that would make his prize even sweeter. She recalled her first meeting with Serlo. 'See how well my flock is doing,' Serlo had boasted to the forester while she and Edwin were in hiding. His words had led Janna to believe that they were taking refuge on Serlo's own property, yet the fields he'd shown the forester were not his own but were part of the manor he oversaw for Hugh.

Janna nodded thoughtfully. Serlo's slip of the tongue should have alerted her to his real purpose right from the start. Having already reclaimed a substantial property for himself, the reeve meant to have it all. By discrediting Hugh, he hoped to drive him off the manor farm and out of Dame

Alice's good graces, leaving himself in charge. But he must have known that, even if his plan succeeded, his power could only last until Hamo came of age.

Janna's hand stilled on the knife she was using to cut the herbs. With a cold feeling of dread, she finally acknowledged the unthinkable. Hamo's visit to the manor was unexpected, as was his ducking in the river, but Serlo had wasted no time using those events to his own advantage. Hamo's death could be made to seem the result of yet another accident. With Hamo dead, and Hugh out of the way, the path would be clear for Serlo to petition Dame Alice for the right to reclaim what had once belonged to his family. She would surely be agreeable, for by that time the manor would hold only the worst of memories for her.

Janna felt sick. Her hands began to tremble so badly she set down the knife lest she cut herself. Serlo. He had been left in charge of searching the manor grounds and forest in Hugh's absence. How easy for him to lead the search away from Hamo. How easy for him to ensure that Hamo – or Hamo's body – would never be found. Was Hamo alive, or dead? A hot tide of rage swept over Janna. She clenched her hands. If Hamo was dead, perhaps buried in the forest somewhere, they might search for ever and never find him. I can't allow that to happen, Janna vowed. Alive or dead, he *must* be found.

A sudden thought lifted Janna's spirits slightly, and gave her a thread of hope on which to cling. Dame Alice would never relinquish the manor to Serlo while there was the possibility that Hamo might one day be found. Only his dead body would be enough to convince her either to sell or give the manor farm to Serlo – and so far, there was no dead body. Did that mean Hamo was still alive? Could Serlo be waiting for the hunt to be called off before causing the 'accident' that would bring about the boy's death? If that was the truth of it, then Serlo must be keeping Hamo captive somewhere – but where?

In his own cottage? It seemed the most likely place, but it was also the most dangerous. Serlo was the villeins' reeve, the first person they would call on if they had a grudge or a grievance to air. And for the same reason he was also the first person Hugh would call on. Anyone entering Serlo's cottage in search of him would find Hamo. It was surely too big a risk. But if not the cottage, then where? The fields round about? Janna considered the possibility, but only for a moment. There was no shelter out there to hide a child, not for any length of time. If Hamo was anywhere in the fields, he would certainly have been found by now.

The forest? If Serlo had managed to take Hamo there without being seen, it would make the best hiding place of all, Janna concluded. He could choose a spot, somewhere wild and undisturbed, knowing that the grave would never be found. He would be safe then to carry on his mission to reclaim his stolen land, with or without Hamo's body.

Janna sighed. This was all thought and supposition; she had no proof to accuse Serlo of anything, nor would she unless Hamo could be found to bear witness against him.

A sudden pang of doubt shook Janna as she remembered how Serlo had hidden them from the forester. He had given them shelter for he had recognised that they, too, were of Saxon stock, and his instinct had been to protect them from the terrible justice of the forest law instituted by Norman kings. Even though they'd been expected to work hard in repayment for Serlo's kindness, she and Edwin had been grateful, so grateful. And now here she was, ready to suspect him of the worst deeds imaginable: kidnap and murder.

'Gytha was always proud. Of course she has many talents as well as being beautiful.' Mistress Tova was still talking.

'Has Gytha spent any time with the young lord, with Hamo?' Janna interrupted, her certainty in Serlo's guilt suddenly shaken. No matter how unlikely it might seem that Gytha was guilty, she couldn't afford a false accusation against someone as powerful as the reeve.

'No, she dislikes the child. Oh!' Mistress Tova put her hand to her mouth, too late to take back the words she obviously wished she'd never said. 'I didn't mean it quite like that,' she said nervously. 'Gytha's very good with children, but she resents the fact that the young lord will inherit this manor when he is of age. Even so, she's very upset by his disappearance. She spends every free moment out searching for Hamo. Poor little lad. He must have run off in a great hurry, for Mistress Cecily left him alone only while she talked to me, and she raised the alarm just as soon as she realised he had run away again.'

Janna hastily finished chopping up the herbs and threw them into the boiling water. A growing sense of urgency possessed her. The cook had given her much to think about and she was anxious to get moving.

'This is a posset for Dame Alice, to help her rest,' she said. 'Let it boil for as long as it would take to milk a goat or a sheep, then take it off the fire and let it cool. I pray you, keep the mixture for Mistress Cecily, who will be along presently to fetch it for ma dame.' Not giving the cook any time to argue, she rushed out of the door, pausing only to untie Bones. Delighted, the dog yipped and ran around in circles, almost tripping Janna as she set off across the yard.

'Behave yourself!' She nudged Bones out of the way with a not-too-gentle foot, and hurried on. She had to find Hamo – and for that, she had to find Serlo.

Her hand was smarting quite badly now. Janna looked down at the rash, remembering how she'd plunged her hand into the bush of rue to retrieve Hamo's ball. She should have taken more care, wrapped something around her hand to protect it, she thought, recalling that rue was harmless enough except when the sun shone on it and brought oil to the surface of its leaves, the oil that had caused her skin to blister.

The elusive memory flickered once more, and in a sudden Janna had it, the last proof she needed of Serlo's guilt. He, too, had once had a rash on his hand, the same rash that came from picking rue. She remembered that she'd offered to make him up an ointment for it, hoping to deflect his accusations about the straying cows – and the fox in the hencoop and the slaughter of the lamb. If only she'd thought of this before, so much harm could have been avoided!

She understood now, the posies of rue and what they meant. Rue to curse Dame Alice, and to mark his revenge against her for taking his land. She would repent that theft and suffer the consequences.

She remembered how quick Serlo had been to correct her when she'd hinted that Hamo might have been taken, how

he'd called Hamo 'silly' for wandering away and getting lost
again. Janna closed her eyes and groaned aloud at her own
stupidity as she realised something else. Serlo had seen her
with the posy of rue. No wonder he'd been so quick to act
against her. He would have had a key to the chests in the
undercroft and could easily have taken the missing goods.
Perhaps his aim was to throw Janna off his trail if he
suspected that she knew what he was doing, but it was much
more likely that he meant to use the stolen goods as an
excuse to banish her and Edwin from the manor. He had
certainly used them to discredit her. He'd made quite sure
that, if she voiced her suspicions, she would not be believed.

More convinced than ever, now, of Serlo's guilt, and with
a corresponding lightness of heart that Hugh was innocent
of every charge, Janna thought of someone else who might
help in her quest to find Hamo. Someone she could trust.
Someone skilled at tracking signs, and who knew the forest
better than anyone else, better even than the forester. Godric.
If Hamo was hidden or buried somewhere in the forest,
Godric would be able to follow the passage of whoever had
taken the child.

Hamo must be alive, Janna thought. He *must* be! Her
imagination tortured her with images of the boy's bright face,
his open, trusting nature. She wondered if he could hear the
bell tolling to bring him home. He would not understand
what was happening to him, why he was being held captive.
He would be so frightened. Janna's hands clenched in
impotent rage. She would have battered the truth out of
Serlo with her bare fists if she'd thought it would help her
cause. But punishment could come later, once Hugh found

out the full extent of his reeve's treachery. In the meantime, their best hope of finding Hamo rested with Godric.

Taking care to keep out of Serlo's way, for he was everywhere about the manor supervising the search parties, Janna walked quickly to the gate with Bones yapping at her heels. She was about to pass through when Bertha pounced on her once more, and drew her into the shelter of a barn.

'You must be careful, Janna,' she said in a low voice. 'I heard the lord Hugh tell Serlo that you're innocent of all crimes and he's not to lock you up again, but the hunt is still on for Edwin. Serlo means to have you followed in the hope you'll betray Edwin's hiding place. You won't do that, will you?'

'Of course not.' There were no doubts now in Janna's mind about Serlo's guilt, but it seemed likely that Edwin was to be made the scapegoat for all that had happened. She couldn't allow that.

'You don't have to watch Gytha any more,' she told Bertha. 'I know she's innocent, and I also know who's guilty of these crimes, although I have no way of proving it unless I can find Hamo.' She glanced quickly over her shoulder to make sure they were still unobserved. 'Go to Edwin when you can, when it's safe, and tell him he's not to show himself on any account until we find Hamo.'

'Is Hamo still alive then?' Bertha's eyes shone with hope.

'Pray God that he is, otherwise we are all doomed,' Janna said grimly. She walked to the door of the barn and peered out. Serlo was nowhere in sight. 'Have you seen Godric anywhere?' she called over her shoulder.

'I saw a stranger go through the gate a little while ago,'

Bertha answered. 'Was that Godric? He walked down to the ford. I think he plans to search in the forest.'

'Good. Thank you, Bertha.' Pulling Bones behind her, Janna left the barn and hurried off in search of the villein. At the same time, she kept a sharp lookout for Serlo. To her relief, there was no sign of him or of Hugh but, as she forded the river, she caught sight of Godric. He was about to vanish into the thick green barrier that marked the edge of the forest.

'Ho! Godric, wait for me!' she shouted, and put on a burst of speed to catch up to him.

He hesitated. Janna knew that he'd heard her cry out. It was too far for her to see his face, but she could imagine him scowling as he made up his mind whether or not to obey her command.

He stayed where he was, and she was grateful for it. 'Godric!' she panted, as soon as she was within earshot. Although he'd waited, he'd turned his back on her and seemed absorbed in studying the myriad hues of green in the foliage ahead.

'What do you want?' He turned and scowled at her.

Janna bent over, holding tight to her aching side. 'You have to help me,' she gasped.

Godric's face closed against her. He took a step away. 'I have more important things to do with my time, Janna,' he said distantly. 'I'm looking for Hamo.'

'So am I,' Janna said impatiently. She straightened. 'I think I know what's happened to him. Listen to me.' And she poured out her story, trusting him with all the truth including her suspicions about Hugh, leaving nothing out in her desperation to convince him to help her. 'I know how good you are at following signs,' she finished breathlessly. 'If Hamo's hidden somewhere in the forest, I know you'll be able to find him, Godric.'

His expression remained dubious. 'People have been searching through the forest for days, trampling tracks everywhere. How will I know whether I'm on Serlo's trail or someone else's?'

'Oh.' Janna's hopes deflated instantly. 'I hadn't thought of that.' She took some comfort from the fact that at least Godric had listened to her, and that he was taking her suggestions seriously. But his objection was sound. 'Then we'll have to follow Serlo after all,' she declared, adding honestly: 'You'll have to follow him, Godric. He's watching out for me, he thinks I'm going to lead him to Edwin – which I'm not. Bertha's gone to warn Edwin. She loves him, and she'll make sure he stays hidden until it's safe for him to come out.'

Godric nodded. It seemed to Janna that he was looking more friendly as he said, 'I doubt Serlo will make any move towards Hamo in the daylight. If he's making a show of searching for him, he'll continue while people are around to watch. I suspect we'll have to wait until it's dark, Janna.'

'So you do believe me? You'll help me?' Janna looked up at Godric with shining eyes. He caught his breath, and quickly turned away. 'I'll help you,' he said gruffly. 'But I suggest we also keep on looking for Hamo.' He hesitated. 'It would be easier for Serlo to keep him hidden if he was already dead, you know that, don't you?'

'I refuse to even think it.' Bones had started to bark and Janna cuffed him gently with her foot. 'Sshh!'

'We don't want to attract Serlo's attention.' Godric turned on Bones. 'Can't you shut him up?'

But Janna was no longer listening. 'No-one's searched Serlo's cottage, of course. It's over there.' She pointed a finger to show Godric where she meant. 'I don't think he's got Hamo hidden there, but we should probably search it if we can.'

She became aware that Godric wasn't looking, and waved a hand in front of his eyes to get his attention. Suddenly, and taking Janna completely by surprise, he pulled her into his arms and kissed her hard.

'Umph . . . ssfflk.' It was too hard to protest with Godric's lips pressed against her own, but Janna did her best.

'Serlo's coming our way,' Godric muttered, before kissing her vigorously once more.

'But he thinks I'm a boy!' Janna protested, when she could speak once more.

'No, he doesn't.' Godric kept his arms around Janna, and his mouth close to her ear as he whispered, 'He saw you in the river and I believe he's been asking questions about you ever since. I also heard him ask Cecily why she thought you were a girl.'

Too alarmed by Godric's observations to think straight, Janna melted into his embrace. They stood locked together in a long and lingering kiss. To Janna's surprise, she found she was rather enjoying herself.

'That's enough,' she muttered at last, and pulled away. At once Godric let her go, but his eyes were bright and his face was flushed as he looked at her. Janna found it hard to meet his gaze. 'We've done enough kissing to convince the reeve,' she mumbled.

Godric shook his head. 'He's still coming towards us,' he whispered. 'But he might think twice about having you followed if he believes your affection lies with me and not with Edwin.' He bent to kiss her again.

'You! John – or whatever your real name is. I want a word with you!'

Reluctantly, Janna freed herself from Godric's embrace and braced herself to face Serlo. He came striding up to them with a thunderous expression. In spite of her resolve, Janna found herself shrinking against Godric, badly needing his strength and support. Beside them, Bones continued to bark.

'If it were left to me, you'd be gone from this manor by now, and with a beating to send you on your way, you and your so-called brother!' Serlo stood over Janna, glowering at her. Godric placed an arm around her shoulders and scowled right back at the reeve.

'You may have the ear of my lord Hugh, but I know how many lies you've told,' Serlo blustered, ignoring Godric. 'Unless you tell me where your brother is hiding, I'll make sure my lord Hugh finds out the truth about you, about who and what you really are.'

Several comments came to Janna's mind, not least the fact that while Hugh already knew the truth about her, he certainly didn't know the truth about his reeve. But she held her tongue, knowing that she must not, under any circumstances, put Serlo on his guard.

'Where is your brother?' Serlo thrust his face close to hers, and Janna took an involuntary step backwards.

'She doesn't know where he is.' Godric pulled Janna into the crook of his arm and held her tight.

'This is no time for courting,' Serlo growled. 'You get back to wherever you came from, and leave the girl to me.'

'I'm staying right here to help look for the young lord.' Godric kept his arm around Janna.

Serlo glared at them both. 'Very well, then. I believe the boy may have tried to find his way home to his own manor but strayed off the track and got lost in the forest,' he snapped. 'You two can go and look for him.'

It was too good an opportunity to miss, and Janna moved off with alacrity, tugging the furiously barking Bones behind her. The reeve's next words stopped her dead. 'And get rid of the dog. If Hamo calls out, I want to be able to hear him.' Noticing Janna's surprise, the reeve continued, 'I'm coming with you. And so are they.' He raised a hand and beckoned several villeins forward. Urk and his mother were among the group.

Janna had a sudden feeling she and Godric were being enticed into a trap, but there was little they could do about it now. She dragged Bones over to Urk. 'Will you look after Hamo's dog for me please, Gabriel?' she asked, including Mistress Wulfrun in her friendly smile.

'Ooh, yes!' The boy fell to his knees and began to pat Bones with great enthusiasm. The dog wagged its tail at him, but kept on barking.

'I'm sorry, mistress. I don't know what's got into him,' Janna apologised to Urk's mother. 'Do you think Gabriel could play with him for a bit, and keep him quiet?'

'Gabriel has a way with animals, 'tis true,' his fond mother agreed. She nodded. 'Go on, then. We'll keep an eye on the dog for you.'

'Thank you.' Janna wasn't sure who would take priority where Mistress Wulfrun was concerned, Urk or the dog, but she knew she could trust the woman to do her best. Keeping close to Godric, Janna followed the villeins and Serlo into the forest.

'I really am sorry about your mother, sorry that I wasn't there to physic her,' she apologised, thinking Godric must listen to her now after what had just passed between them. The memory brought a blush to her cheek, and she quickly looked away.

'I'm sorry too,' he said soberly. 'It's true what I told you before. No matter what some of the villagers might have said to you – and I know Mistress Hilde was one of them – they regret it now, and repent the action they took against you. Especially Mistress Hilde. There is no-one to make up the cream that your mother once provided, and her skin is red raw with scratching.'

Janna felt a moment of fierce satisfaction. 'You know she killed my cat, don't you? It was a warning to me, she said, not to lie with her husband. As if I *would*!'

'She lives to regret her deed. She says now that your cat walks with her wherever she goes. She is in mortal fear that it will smother her new baby. But no-one else can see the cat. No-one believes her. Her fancies have turned her mind too far from the truth.'

'You are so right!' Janna said quickly. ''Tis Hilde's guilt that torments her now, guilt for crucifying my cat!'

Godric's face darkened in remembered anger. 'I don't know how you could have held me responsible for that, Janna, not even for a moment. You should know I would never do anything to harm you. Why, I . . .' He clamped his lips together, and marched on.

'I know that now.' Janna hurried after him. 'I'm sorry, Godric, truly. I haven't been kind, or fair, to you at all, and I deeply regret it.' She felt a weight ease off her heart. She'd treated Godric so badly; it had been a burden on her conscience. She'd thought she'd never see him again so it was a great relief to her, now, to have the chance to apologise. 'Forgive me?' She gave him a tentative smile. When he flashed a reluctant grin in return, her spirits soared. Then she remembered the task that lay before them, and her joy evaporated immediately. At once she looked towards Serlo. He was watching them. In fact, he seemed far more interested in keeping them in sight than in pretending to search for the missing boy.

Fear threaded through Janna and tightened into a knot of anxiety in her stomach. Serlo had already shown himself to be quick and resourceful, and utterly without mercy. Soon enough he would make a move against them. What was in his mind? One small thought brought Janna some consolation. While Serlo was watching them, he was unable to act against Hamo. She only hoped that, when the time came, she and Godric would be able to outwit the reeve and find Hamo in time to save the boy's life.

ChIRTEEN

THE BELL CONTINUED to toll at intervals through the weary day, the sound growing fainter as they moved further away from the manor, until finally it ceased altogether. Knowing they were wasting time, Janna grew impatient, but they couldn't start their own search under Serlo's watchful eye. The sun burned fiercely, its heat penetrating even the dim forest, parching her mouth and throat. She wished she'd thought to bring something to drink, and something to eat too.

At Serlo's signal, the villeins came together late in the afternoon to eat their dinner. Janna realised their steps had taken them close to the path again as she watched the villeins settle deep in the shade on either side of it, and unstopper leather bottles of ale to slake their thirst. She swallowed hard, trying to bring some moisture into her mouth. They must be moving back towards the manor, she realised, as she heard the faint tolling of the bell sound mournfully through the silent forest.

'You can follow this track after you've eaten your dinner,' Serlo told the villeins. He turned to Janna and Godric. 'You will continue the search with me.'

'What's he playing at?' Janna whispered as Godric came over to her.

He shrugged, and produced his own leather bottle, which he offered to Janna. She took it gratefully, and swallowed several mouthfuls of ale. It was warm from the heat of the day, and tasted somewhat of leather, but it ran down her parched throat like liquid gold.

'Thank you.' She handed the bottle back, and accepted a piece of bread and cheese from Godric. 'You're saving my life here.'

'Again.' His smile took the sting from the word. With a weary sigh, Janna sat down, her back propped against a tree. Godric collapsed beside her, and they sipped and chewed together in companionable silence for a time.

Looking around, Janna read the despair on everyone's faces. They had given up hope of finding Hamo, and were only going through the motions of searching for him now. In fact, they'd given up altogether, she realised, as Serlo directed them off down the path towards home.

'Come!' He beckoned them up to follow him. Janna knew that the trap was baited and ready for them. She knew also that she was the one Serlo wanted, not Godric. His life would not be in danger if he went with the reeve.

'Get after him,' Janna hissed, thinking to seek safety with the departing villeins. 'I'll go to his cottage and look for Hamo.'

'It's you he's interested in, not me, so he won't go anywhere unless you're there too.' Godric grasped her arm and hauled her along with him after the reeve. 'If Hamo is hidden somewhere in the forest, you can protect him while I take care of Serlo. We can search the cottage later.'

255

Janna recognised the wisdom of Godric's reasoning and stopped resisting him. In single file, they tramped after Serlo, moving from light to deep shadow, and never in a straight line. 'Did he do it? Did he do it?' a song thrush called, answering its own question: 'Come out! Come out!' There was a rustle and flutter of wings as it flew off. Serlo stood quietly for a moment to make sure they were still following him, then began to push his way through the forest once more.

'I wonder where he thinks he's going?' Godric sounded puzzled as he padded after the reeve. Janna shook her head. She wondered if either of them knew, for she herself was lost, had been lost for most of the day.

'He's already been this way once before,' Godric stopped and looked at Janna. 'He's taking us around in circles.'

'He obviously doesn't realise you know the forest better than he does!'

Godric shrugged, and set off after Serlo once more, keeping a careful lookout for any sign of Hamo. Janna marvelled how silently he walked. 'Aargh!' She gave a muffled scream as a sticky spider web suddenly wrapped around her face. Frantically, she clawed it off, sure that she could feel the tickle of spider legs threading through her hair, down her neck, against her skin inside her smock. She beat at herself with both hands, hoping to squash the insect dead. Distracted by the spider, not looking where she was going, her foot sank into a hole, giving her ankle a painful wrench. She stifled a cry, but tears came into her eyes with the pain of it. She limped towards Godric, who was waiting for her. Serlo had vanished.

'It's as I thought,' Godric said, as she came up to him. 'Serlo's been leading us around in circles, and now he thinks we're lost. He's done it on purpose.'

'What about Hamo? Where is he?'

'Nowhere Serlo's leading us, that's for sure.'

'Serlo must have him hidden in his cottage after all.'

Godric lifted his shoulders and spread his hands in a helpless gesture.

'We must find Hamo. We *must!*' Janna was frantic. 'Let's go back and look, Godric. Quickly, while Serlo is still in the forest.' A horrible thought stopped her. 'Do you know where we are? Can you find your way out of here?'

To her relief, Godric nodded. 'Let's play Serlo at his own game first and buy us some time. Follow me, Janna, close as you can, and walk quietly.'

To Janna's immense surprise Godric cut away at an angle from where they'd come, and silently began to make his way through a dense grove of trees. At once, she went after him. She could only hope he knew what he was doing.

Without warning, he jumped onto a fallen branch. The sudden crack sent her heart leaping in fear. She frowned, puzzled by his antics. 'What . . .?' He pressed his finger against her lips. They waited a few moments.

Nothing happened. Janna listened intently, but she couldn't hear anything, nor was there any sign of the reeve. Godric picked up the fallen branch and hit it against a tree. The dull thud echoed through the forest. 'Janna! Come see what I've found,' he called. 'I doubt Serlo will be able to explain this away!' Again, he cautioned her to silence.

Above their heads, birds began to twitter and sing, serenading the closing of the day. But Janna knew Godric wasn't listening for birds. She strained her ears to hear if his ruse had worked, and became aware of a furtive rustling. Animal or human? Evidently Godric knew the difference for he grabbed her hand and swept her away and around a patch of holly, then pushed through a thicket of hazel, snapping twigs and swishing branches as he passed. He was making more noise than a charging boar. Putting his finger to his lips once more, he stopped and looked behind, waiting.

This time Janna could hear the faint swish of Serlo's boots on dry leaves. Satisfied that he'd taken the bait, Godric drew Janna off in a different direction, cutting silently through a long stand of tall beeches and oaks then scooting across a patch of open grassland. He gave another raucous call. 'Janna! Where are you?'

Janna was right beside him, but she'd worked out now what he was up to, and she grinned up at him. She couldn't see the reeve, but she could hear him. He was still coming their way. Godric set off again, this time moving deep into a grove of yew, an impenetrable maze of knitted branches and leaves. 'Call my name,' he whispered, and Janna did as she was bid. The note of desperation in her voice wasn't all fake. She was frightened, as much for Hamo's sake as their own, by this deadly game of hide and seek in the forest. Serlo knew, now, that they were on to him, and that they would betray him if they could. He couldn't afford to let them leave the forest alive.

'Call again,' Godric prompted, and Janna did. She listened, heart thumping hard in her breast. There was a smothered cough, and then the faint sound of Serlo's panting breath as he came after them.

Godric nodded his head, satisfied. 'Come,' he whispered. 'Quiet as you can.' He took her hand and led the way, slipping silently through the dense growth. Once out of the copse, he kept on moving in a straight line through trees and weedy clearings, picking up speed all the way. To Janna's amazement, they suddenly emerged from the forest almost directly in line with Serlo's cottage.

'Hurry!' Godric urged, and began to race down towards the water meadows. But Janna had noticed the shed where once she and Edwin had sheltered. If it came to defending themselves against the reeve, a weapon would be handy. She hastened inside to retrieve the sword, feeling a great relief to find it still in its hiding place. Ignoring the dull ache of her wrenched ankle, she sped after Godric, following him down through the water meadows and across the river.

The door of the reeve's cottage was locked and barred against them. 'The devil take him,' Janna cursed, even as she acknowledged that this spoke of Serlo's having something to hide. 'Hamo!' she called, and beat on the door with her fist. 'Are you in there?'

Silence. Godric was peering through a shuttered window, trying to see inside the cottage. 'Hamo!' he bellowed, not caring now who might see or hear them. 'Hamo!' They both stopped and listened. Nothing moved. There was no sound in answer to their calls. Janna knew a bleak despair. If Hamo was in there, he had been silenced – perhaps permanently.

Godric pulled out his hunting knife. Large and very sharp, it was the knife he used for protection when walking through the forest. Not caring about the noise he was making or the damage to Serlo's property, he hacked into the wooden shutters, tearing and splintering them. Wordlessly, Janna handed him the sword, and he wasted no time in using it to slice through the shutter, making a large enough space for Janna to crawl through. At once she put her foot into Godric's cupped hands and launched herself through and into the cottage.

'Hamo!' she yelled, as she hit the ground. She rolled over and sprang to her feet. In spite of the heat, a fire smouldered in the hearth, and Janna waited a moment for her eyes to adjust to the dim light. There was no sign of anyone. With dragging steps, she went to the door and unbolted it. Sadly, she shook her head in answer to Godric's unspoken question. She stepped aside to let him enter.

Together they opened the remaining shutters to let in the light, then began a systematic search through the cottage. Janna's eyes narrowed. Two wooden trenchers lay on a table, as if waiting for food to be placed on them for the evening meal. Two trenchers? Janna felt a sudden surge of hope. 'Hamo?' she yelled. 'It's Janna, and Godric. There's nothing to be afraid of, we're here to help you escape.' She listened intently, felt her heart double thump as she heard a noise, but then realised it was the faint yapping of a barking dog.

'I'm sure Hamo's about somewhere,' she told Godric, 'and I'm sure he's alive!' She pointed at the second trencher. 'Look! Where do you think Serlo's got him hidden?'

Godric shrugged, looking baffled. Once more they searched through several unlocked chests and around the meagre pieces of furniture within the cottage, including the coverings and frame of a rather fine wooden bed which stood hidden behind soft drapes in a small alcove off the main room. With increasing desperation, they searched even those places far too small to hide a little boy, just in case there was some clue to Hamo's presence, anything at all.

The sound of barking grew louder. A dog was coming this way. Bones? Suddenly there was a furious scratching at the door, accompanied by a series of short, sharp yips. Desperate to stop the noise before it attracted any more attention, Janna hurried to open it.

Bones shot in. Janna could swear that the dog was surprised to see her. He wagged his tail but kept on moving, sniffing at the ground until he suddenly stopped and sat, almost as if he was keeping guard. The beaten earth of the floor was covered with rushes. By the look of them, they'd been down for some time and needed changing. Janna frowned and looked more closely. The rushes near Bones seemed unevenly distributed, as if they'd been recently disturbed. Bones was still barking, but not so ferociously now. He looked up at Janna with bright eyes. Janna thought he was trying to tell her something. 'You were here before, weren't you, Bones?' she said softly. 'Where is Hamo? Do you know?'

The dog whined, and scratched at the rushes, scattering them. Janna looked at Godric. 'There's something buried down there.' She felt sick as an image of Hamo's small body interred in the earth came into her mind. 'Careful!' She flung out a hand as Godric's knife flashed out and he knelt to dig. 'You don't know what's down there,' she breathed.

Janna knelt beside him and they began to dig into the soft earth with their bare hands. The earth shifted easily, testament to the fact that it was the gateway to something below. With a feeling of dread, Janna plunged her hands deeper into the soil. She frowned as her fingers jabbed against something hard. Cautiously, she began to throw handfuls of earth to one side, fearing what might be revealed. A small wooden panel came into view. Janna frowned at it. 'Why would anyone want to bury this?' She lifted it, and the answer was instantly revealed in the dark hole beneath.

'It's a trapdoor.' Godric crawled forward and peered down the hole. 'Hamo?' he called softly.

Janna listened intently. She thought she could hear something, but even as she strained to identify the sound, it ceased. She must have imagined it, she thought reluctantly. 'I guess this must be a storeroom?' She craned over to peer down into the darkness.

'I'll go and have a look,' Godric offered.

'No.' Janna was grateful that he'd put himself forward, but she took hold of him to push him aside. 'I'll go,' she said steadily. She looked about the room for something to light her way. Her eyes widened as she noticed a fat beeswax candle rather than the rush light she would have expected to find. A fine bed. A beeswax candle. Serlo must be saving them to impress Gytha – if only he could lure her to his cottage as he must have lured Hamo. The thought stiffened her resolution to find the missing child. 'Will you light that candle so I can see what's down here?' she asked Godric.

He shook his head. 'Let me go. You don't know what you might find.'

An image of Hamo's dead body came into Janna's mind. No! She wouldn't, she couldn't think the worst. 'If Hamo's down there, and alive, he might think you're Serlo,' she said, her voice wobbling slightly with the effort to be brave. 'He'll be much less frightened if he sees me.'

Acknowledging the truth of her words, Godric gave a reluctant nod. As he stood up to light the candle from the fire in the hearth, Bones jumped down the hole in front of Janna. He started barking once more, short furious yips that echoed the urgency they all shared. Wasting no more time, Janna grabbed the candle from Godric, picked up the sword and dropped down after the dog, ducking her head under the low ceiling.

A thin shaft of light shone down through the trapdoor. The rest of the cellar was in darkness. The air was stale and smelt of damp earth. Janna held the candle out so that its light was shed more widely. A quick glance confirmed the cellar's purpose. It was crammed with barrels and chests and newly combed fleeces, the latter piled high and ready for market. Truly this was a treasure trove, and not all gained by the honest toil of Serlo's hands either, Janna was willing to stake her life on it. How long had he been planning to take over the manor, deceiving Hugh and amassing wealth at his expense so that, when the time was right, he would be in a position to make a worthy offer to the dame for her property?

Banishing Serlo's dishonesty from her thoughts, for there would be time enough for Hugh to take revenge on his trusted reeve, Janna looked about for Bones. She could hear him barking still, but the dog seemed to have disappeared.

'Janna,' Godric's anxious voice called out. 'Are you all right?'

'Yes, but there's no sign of Hamo. Come down and help me look.'

Janna dripped a little hot wax onto one of the barrels, and secured the candle to it. With the small light to see by, she and Godric began a thorough search of the cellar. Almost the first things she found were the silver goblets and the length of woollen cloth supposedly stolen from the undercroft. 'Look!' She snatched them up with a cry of triumph, pleased that she would be able to prove her innocence beyond question now.

Everything else was sealed tight. From their weight, Janna knew that the chests and barrels were not empty. She also knew that if Hamo was concealed in one of them, he must surely be dead for there would be no air inside to sustain him. Despairing, she thumped hard on their sides, calling Hamo's name. She didn't think he'd be able to hear her above the cacophony of barking, but even that might comfort Hamo, if he was alive to hear it. Where was the boy? And where was Bones? She listened for the direction of the dog's frantic barking, then followed the sound towards a row of barrels shoved against the earthen wall at the far side of the cellar. The barks came from behind them. Janna realised that there was a narrow gap between the barrels and the wall. She hoisted herself half up onto one of them in order to peer over and down into the gap between. And drew in a painful breath, and then another. The dog was wedged there, standing guard over a small, still body.

'Hamo!' Janna's cry echoed through the low chamber as she shoved at the heavy barrel barring her way, leaning all her weight against it so that she could get to him. Godric rushed to help her and, as soon as there was enough space, Janna darted in and crouched down beside the child. He lay unmoving, but his eyes, wide and staring, gleamed in the faint light from the candle. Janna put her hand on his forehead, dreading to feel the chillness of death against her fingers. But his skin felt warm, although he did not move, or say anything in answer to her frantic question, 'Are you all right?' Then she saw why. Hamo's feet and hands were tightly bound, and so was his mouth.

A great fury shook Janna. 'He's alive!' she shouted, as she crouched down beside the child and, with shaking hands, unfastened the gag that covered his mouth.

Hamo moistened his lips with his tongue. 'Are you Janna?' he whispered, and Janna nodded, swallowing over a huge lump that had somehow got stuck in her throat. Godric shoved her aside. He whipped out his knife and slashed through Hamo's bonds.

'Hamo!' Janna reached out to take him in her arms. Instinctively the child shrank away, moving as far from Janna as he could go. He cowered against a barrel. Bones pushed past Janna and began to lick Hamo's face. Hamo pushed him away.

Janna knew rage and a grief beyond anything she'd ever experienced. Serlo had done this. He'd destroyed Hamo's open, trusting nature. He had stolen his innocence.

'It's all right, Hamo.' Janna kept her hand outstretched, but made no further effort to touch him. 'You're safe now. Master Serlo can't harm you any more.'

'We have to get out of here,' Godric said urgently.

'Just wait a few moments.' Janna inched closer to Hamo, willing him to take her hand.

'I'll go for help.' Godric rose from his knees and reached up to the opening in the roof of the cellar. 'I'll tell the lord

Hugh that Hamo is safe. I'll tell his mother too. And I'll suggest the lord brings men at arms with him when he comes.'

'No, don't go.' Janna tugged on his tunic to stop him. 'If Serlo comes back, we'll need you to defend us. But we can't leave just yet. Hamo's in shock. He's going to be too stiff to walk after being tied up for so long. Just give him a little time to recover.'

Godric nodded. He squatted down beside Janna, and gave Hamo an awkward pat on the shoulder. The boy gulped, and pressed himself harder against the barrel. Godric cast a helpless glance at Janna.

'Bones found you,' she said, with determined cheerfulness. 'Do you know, he kept on barking and barking at Serlo. He knew what the reeve had done. And he came straight here as soon as he managed to escape. He showed us where to dig to find this cellar. He's a smart dog, is Bones.'

'Bones was here before.' Hamo's voice was so quiet they strained to hear it. 'Serlo told me he had Bones. That's why I came away with him, even though Mistress Cecily told me not to go anywhere without her. But Bones was missing and I wanted to find him.' His voice hardened as he said angrily, 'Serlo kicked Bones, I saw him. He *hurt* Bones.'

'I know. I know.' Janna felt somewhat reassured by the fire that had come into Hamo's voice when he spoke of his beloved pet. His silence and apathy had frightened her. She felt even more reassured as Hamo suddenly flung his arms around Bones. Miraculously, the dog had finally stopped barking.

'Look at all this!' Godric gave a silent whistle as he gestured at the riches that surrounded them. 'I'll wager my life that the lord of the manor doesn't know about this secret storeroom!'

Janna nodded in agreement. 'Serlo will be hanged for his deeds. The lord Hugh will never forget or forgive what he has done.' Her words brought home to her the danger of their position, and she stirred uneasily. Serlo wouldn't go willingly to face his punishment. In fact, he'd stop at nothing to prevent his secret being found out.

'We should go.' Godric voiced her misgivings. 'The sooner we get Hamo safely to the manor house, the better.'

And the safer we'll be too, Janna thought. 'Do you think you can walk?' she asked Hamo.

He nodded, and climbed stiffly to his feet. 'Ow!' His face crumpled and he began to hop around as he felt the prick and sting of blood flowing freely through his cramped limbs once more.

'Up you go!' Godric swung him up and hoisted him through the hole in the floor. 'Now you.' He turned to Janna just as a muffled scream rent the air. She snatched up the candle to see better, while her heart pounded in fright.

'I have the boy and this time I'll show no mercy.' Serlo's face appeared briefly as he bent down to smile at them. 'As for my cellar – no-one knows about it so no-one's going to find you here. Its contents will keep . . . but you won't.' His chuckle was cut off by the sound of the solid oak panel thudding into place, sealing them into the earth.

'No! *No!*' Janna screamed the words in defiance, while beside her Bones began to howl. She pushed against the panel, but Serlo held it down. Godric sprang to her aid and, together, they strained to shift it. Scraping sounds above told them that Serlo was shifting something over the trap-door to hold them fast. They were trapped, sealed tight into an earthen tomb. No-one knew they were down here, no-one would come looking for them. Soon enough their air would run out. The candle would flicker and die, and so would they. And so would Hamo. Janna looked at Godric in despair. 'What are we going to do now?' Her voice was almost inaudible against the noise being made by Bones.

But Godric had already seized up the sword. Arm raised above his head, he began to saw away at the wooden panel. Janna leaned over, and slid his knife from its sheath. She began to attack the other side of the panel. Silently, desperately, they sawed through the wood, neither of them voicing their fear that their air would run out before they could cut a hole big enough to escape through.

'Help!' she shouted, just in case there was anyone around to hear her. She put her full voice into the cry. 'Help! Somebody, please help us!'

Time seemed to slow to a crawl. Terrifying images ran through Janna's mind as she realised that Serlo would have to carry out his threat now that events had forced his hand. It was a miracle the child had survived as long as he had but from now on his life could only be measured in minutes, unless he was already dead. She had promised Hamo that he was safe, that Serlo could never harm him again, and she had failed him. The knowledge was shattering; she felt almost paralysed with grief and fear. 'Hurry!' she begged, although she knew Godric was as frantic as she was to escape.

The air in the small cellar was being used up; she could smell that it was gradually becoming foul with their breath. She could hear Godric panting, or perhaps it was her own gasps for air that she could hear. She put her hand over her nose and mouth to see if it would help to filter the foulness, but instantly felt as if she was suffocating. She quickly snatched her hand away and took in several deep breaths. It was not enough to satisfy her need. She looked about for Bones. He'd collapsed on the ground nearby. Janna could see the rapid rise and fall of his tiny stomach as he fought for breath. Beside her, Godric sawed on with grim determination.

The candle flickered, and died. They were lost in the darkness. Somehow, their fate seemed even more horrible now they could no longer see each other. Janna stopped cutting for a moment, and reached out to touch Godric. She needed to connect with someone. She needed to feel she was not alone. He took her hand, and kissed it, his lips warm and moist on her skin. Neither of them said anything as he released her and began sawing at the wooden slab once more. They worked in silence for a time, until there was a crack and part of it fell away.

'We're through!' Godric shouted. Janna sensed movement beside her as he reached up to feel the opening. Why was no light shining through? Her question was answered by Godric's next words.

'There's something else, something solid blocking the way,' he said dully. 'Serlo must have pulled a heavy chest over the trapdoor to make sure we can't escape.'

Janna closed her eyes, swept by a wave of fierce anger that this was to be their fate. 'Help!' she screamed again. 'We're trapped in Serlo's cottage. Somebody, please help! For the love of God, please save us!'

FOURTEEN

'BONES! BONES, where are you?' The voice sounded muffled, far away. Janna wondered if she was imagining things. She put a hand on Godric's arm. 'Sshh.' She listened intently, sure she'd heard a voice.

'Bones? Where are you?'

'Here!' Janna shouted frantically. 'We're here under the ground of Serlo's cottage! Bones is here too!'

There was a long silence. Janna suspected she must have been hallucinating after all. Perhaps it was a lack of air that made her conjure up what wasn't really there.

'Did you hear anything, Godric?' she asked at last, reluctant to give up this tiny fragment of hope.

'Something. I don't know. Yes, maybe.' He raised his voice. 'Help!' he shouted. 'We're trapped in a cellar underneath Serlo's cottage. There's a trapdoor with a chest or something on top of it.' He stopped and they listened intently. Silence. Then Janna heard a faint creaking above her head. Her heart leapt high with elation. 'We're down here!' she shouted. 'Hurry! Please, please hurry!'

There was a sudden waft of air, tinged faintly with smoke from the fire in the hearth. Janna sucked it gratefully into her lungs. A faint beam of light from the fire slanted down through the darkness of the cellar, the light becoming brighter as their saviour dragged a wooden chest out of the way. Janna bent to pick up Bones, then looked upwards to see who was there. Peering down at them with a worried expression, but as welcome as the angel Gabriel himself, was Urk. 'Gabriel, well done!' she greeted him. 'You've got here just in time! Here, take Bones.' She thrust the dog at Urk and turned to Godric.

He cupped his hands together and Janna put her foot in the cradle. Without wasting any more time, he heaved her upwards while, from above, Urk grasped her arms and hauled her through. Then it was Godric's turn. Snatching up the sword, he pushed it through the trapdoor then pulled himself up after it. 'Thank you,' he said. 'Thank you for saving our lives.'

Urk smiled his big smile at them both, and turned aside to pick up Bones. The dog had recovered somewhat, and licked Urk's hand.

Godric took only a moment to catch his breath before seizing hold of Urk and Janna and hustling them out of the cottage and into the darkening night. 'Go and fetch the lord Hugh,' he told Urk urgently. 'Tell him he must come at once. Tell him Serlo has taken Hamo. Tell him to bring men at arms to hunt Serlo down.'

Urk looked bewildered. He clutched Bones tighter to his chest. 'Bones ran away,' he said slowly. 'I had to find him. I didn't want Serlo to see me so I had to wait till he went away from his cottage. Serlo has Hamo.'

'Yes, yes I know,' Godric said impatiently. 'What did I just tell you, Gabriel?'

'Go and fetch the lord Hugh,' the boy repeated obediently. 'Tell him Serlo has taken Hamo. Tell him to come at once. He must bring men at arms to hunt Serlo down.'

'Good boy.' Godric patted his shoulder. 'Hurry, it's almost dark. There's no time to lose.'

Still the boy hesitated. 'Go!' Godric gave him a shove.

'You can take Bones with you. Look after him,' said Janna, understanding at last what was delaying their messenger. 'And thank you for finding us, Gabriel. You're a real hero!'

Urk's face split into a smile. He set off at speed, straight as an arrow towards the manor house. Janna could only hope that he would remember their message, and that Hugh would believe it.

Although impatient to be on the move, Janna forced herself to stand quietly. She peered across the fields, scanning the landscape carefully in the lambent light of the evening sky. They had no way of knowing where Serlo had taken Hamo, for there was no sign of him now. If he hadn't risked dumping the boy in the forest before, he certainly wouldn't risk going there now, not while bands of villeins might still be roaming about the water meadows in search of Hamo. Not the forest then. Where else might he go?

'I can't see them anywhere,' Godric muttered, sounding discouraged. 'You realise, don't you, Janna, that Serlo can't afford to leave the boy alive. We may already be too late.'

'No!' Janna said fiercely. 'I'm not giving up, not yet. It's not quite dark. People will be out searching for Hamo. Serlo will take him somewhere that's already been searched, where he knows they won't be seen.'

'This copse?' Godric flung out a hand to indicate the grove that stood guard over Serlo's cottage.

Janna thought for a moment. 'We'd better check. He may have taken Hamo there just to shut him up.' Her voice caught in her throat. She swallowed hard. 'But I don't think Serlo would leave him there. It's too close to his cottage. The villeins might well come in here to collect dead wood, while the pigs will soon be foraging for acorns and beechmast. Serlo would know that a grave must be found sooner or later.'

Her eyes widened as an idea flashed into her mind. 'What about the river?' She turned to Godric, her eyes full of hope. 'It's already been searched thoroughly, but no-one will question another drowning, not when Hamo so nearly drowned that first time. Come on! But we'll search the copse first, just in case.'

Sword in hand and ready for use if necessary, she set off through the trees. Godric hurried after her, sheathing his knife and uncoiling his slingshot as he ran. 'Please, God, don't let us get there too late.' Janna repeated the prayer under her breath as they inspected the small copse. In spite of their fears, there was no sign of a small body or the reeve among the bracken and weeds that grew rank beneath the trees.

'He's not here.' Janna wiped her sweating face on the sleeve of her smock. Godric nodded in agreement and, together, they left the shelter of the grove and ran down towards the river. It spread before them like a long silver snake in the dim evening light. Finally Janna stopped for a moment, and bent over, clutching hold of her aching sides.

'He'll be hiding somewhere among the trees,' she gasped, 'but where?'

At the sound of her voice, Godric glanced behind him, then turned and hurried back to her. He bent down and quickly selected a handful of flints. Janna straightened and looked towards the river, narrowing her eyes to see more clearly, watching for any movement that might betray the reeve's whereabouts. Finally she shrugged. 'We can't waste any more time,' she said. 'Let's split up. You go downriver,' she stuck a finger towards the mill, 'and I'll go upstream. Quiet as you can. Serlo mustn't hear us.'

'No.' Godric stood his ground. 'You can't face Serlo alone. We must stay together.'

Janna stuck out her jaw, looking stubborn. 'I mean it,' Godric warned. 'I'm following you, whichever way you choose to go.'

Janna clicked her tongue. 'Look,' she said impatiently. 'The closest cover of trees is over there. Maybe that's where he's taken Hamo. He can't risk the boy being seen, not while there are people about.' Without hesitation, she began to run once more, with Godric keeping a steady pace beside her.

As they came closer, Janna slowed and tried to quieten her panting breaths. Godric crept forward; she followed close behind him. It was dark in the thicket of young alders that crowded beside the river bank but, even so, they had no trouble spying Serlo. Janna felt an unutterable relief as she saw the small boy beside him, his hand held tight in the reeve's larger hand, being dragged along against his will. Alive! Hamo was still alive. He was quite silent, and Janna's fists clenched as she imagined what Serlo must have done to keep him quiet. Truly he would pay dearly for his treatment of the boy.

Godric crept stealthily forward, slingshot at the ready. He was gaining on Serlo, who was encumbered by the struggling Hamo. Janna knew how accurate a shot Godric was, but even so her heart beat hard with fear. What if he should miss, and bring Hamo down instead? She stopped, hardly daring even to breathe, frightened that she might make some noise and alert Serlo to their presence.

'Be careful,' she prayed, knowing that Serlo wouldn't hesitate to use Hamo as a shield against any attack. She couldn't bear it if, in the end, it was Godric who brought the boy to harm.

Godric had stopped now, and was busy fitting a flint into his weapon. Janna wondered which part of Serlo he would aim at, and prayed that the flint would find its mark.

Godric took another step forward. A twig cracked and snapped. Serlo whirled and saw them. At once, he pulled Hamo in front of him. Janna saw that he held a knife at the ready. No wonder Hamo had been so silent, she thought, feeling despair as she understood that they were powerless now to save him. She reached out a hand to Godric, to stop him from doing anything stupid that might jeopardise Hamo's safety. But she was too late. His arm swung around. As Serlo whipped the knife up to the boy's throat, Godric loosed the flint. For several long moments time seemed to stand still. Then, with a grunting sigh, Serlo fell to the ground, taking Hamo with him.

Numb with shock, Janna stayed frozen, listening to the fearful silence. Finally she forced her legs to move. She ran forward, dreading what she might find: that Serlo had had time to slit the boy's throat; that even now Hamo might be dying or dead. She became aware that Godric was beside her as she fell to her knees beside the reeve. There was blood everywhere. Neither Hamo nor Serlo was moving. She reached out to Hamo with a trembling hand.

'Ohhh.' It was a long drawn-out sigh of relief as she saw that the blood spattered over Hamo's tunic had come from the reeve. The flint had hit Serlo's forehead. It was bleeding profusely, and so was a long cut in his arm where his knife had sliced through his sleeve as he'd fallen.

Ignoring Serlo, Godric snatched Hamo from the reeve's limp hands and carried him to safety, while Janna bent over Serlo to inspect his wounds and determine if he was dead or merely stunned. She wanted the reeve alive to face Hugh, to know public humiliation and disgrace before the hangman put an end to his pathetic, miserable life. As she leaned closer, his hand shot out and grabbed her. She cried out, but it was too late. Serlo had her firmly in his grasp. She lunged for his fallen knife, but he was too fast for her. He snatched it up and staggered to his feet, holding her in front of him as a shield against any further harm.

'Drop the sword.' She felt the prick of his knife against her throat. Frightened into silence, she obeyed his command.

Godric put Hamo down. He rose to his feet, knife in hand, and faced the reeve. Janna stared at him in despair. He could do nothing to save her without risking her life at the same time.

The reeve pulled Janna closer. He pressed himself against her; his arms became a tight band around her, trapping her tight. She couldn't move; there was nothing she could do to free herself. Fighting panic, she waited numbly to see what would happen next.

'Give me my life, or I'll take hers.' Serlo's voice rumbled behind her. Godric nodded acceptance. He dropped his slingshot and slowly sheathed his knife.

'No!' Janna's mind suddenly cleared. She remembered how she'd been trapped like this once before. She knew there was a way out after all. Before Serlo could move, she raised her foot and stamped down with all her strength onto his instep. He stumbled, loosening his hold as he struggled to keep his balance. Janna wrenched herself free and ran towards Godric. With a wide gesture, he swept her out of his way while, with his other hand, he pulled his knife out of its sheath. There was a glint of silver in the dim light, then Janna heard a thud.

Serlo lay on his back on the ground, with Godric's knife embedded up to its hilt in his chest.

'Your life, Serlo, instead of hers.' Godric walked to the reeve, gave the knife a twist and pulled it out. Serlo's fingers plucked feebly at the air, then fell nervelessly to his side. He gave a faint sigh and his body went limp.

Knowing that he was no longer a danger, Janna rushed over to Hamo. He was curled up in a ball. His eyes were wide with terror; his whole body was shaking. Not giving him any chance to retreat this time, she scooped him into her arms and held him close. For one long, heart-stopping moment, he stayed rigid. Then, with a strangled yelp, he burrowed into her and began to cry.

'You're safe now,' she comforted him. 'You really are safe

now. Serlo's dead. He'll never harm you again.' She glanced sideways as a faint drumming came to her ears. Horses! She caught a glimpse of torches.

'We're here!' Godric shouted. 'We're down by the river!'

The drumming sounded louder. 'Is the boy safe?' Janna recognised Hugh's voice, and felt an overwhelming relief. She bent over Hamo, fighting tears. 'Your cousin Hugh is here,' she told him. 'He'll take you back to the manor, Hamo. Your mother and father are there. They'll be so glad to see you. So glad.' A sudden thought brought fear to Janna's heart. 'Don't tell them my name,' she said urgently. 'Please just call me "John".'

'John,' Hamo echoed. There was a moment's silence, and then came the question. 'Where's Bones?'

Janna didn't know whether to laugh or cry. She hugged Hamo tighter. 'Bones is safe too,' she said. 'Urk has him, he's looking after him for you. Urk saved Bones and he also saved us. He let us out of the cellar so we could chase after you and Serlo. You're safe now, Hamo, I promise you. Everything's going to be all right. Everything.'

The nightmare was over. The knowledge filled Janna's mind and heart, and left her overflowing with joy.

FIFTEEN

THE MOMENT OF peace and thanksgiving was quickly over as Hugh leapt off his destrier and hurried over to check for himself that Hamo was alive and safe. Not wasting any more time, he pulled Hamo up onto Arrow and galloped back to the manor house with him. A joyful pealing of bells told of their safe return. Meanwhile Hugh's men at arms fashioned a litter and carried Serlo's body home, stashing it safely in a barn to await burial. He had escaped justice on earth, he'd cheated the gallows, but he would have to account for his actions in the highest court of all. Janna hoped that he would be condemned to hellfire for ever.

Hugh had summoned Janna and Godric into the solar and now they sat in comfort, with a hot bowl of pottage and a meat pie to bring new warmth and life to their tired bodies, and a jug of ale to wash it down. Hugh had expressed his thanks, as well as the gratitude of Dame Alice, and had then set to questioning them about the night's events and what had gone before. Between them, Janna and Godric had given him a full account of all that had led up to this moment. But Hugh had still more questions for them.

'What made you suspect Serlo in the first place?' He looked to Janna to answer his question.

Janna paused mid-chew. 'Lots of little things,' she said indistinctly, then hastily swallowed her mouthful. 'When we first came here, when he saved Edwin and me from the forester, he talked about "my sheep".'

'Saved you from the forester?' Hugh quirked an eyebrow.

'It's a long story,' Janna said, continuing hurriedly, 'I thought, from Master Serlo's words, that the manor belonged to him.' She gazed up at Hugh, blushing slightly and hating herself for it. 'I didn't know it belonged to you. I wouldn't have stopped here if I'd known that.'

Hugh's eyebrow rose higher.

'I also saw the way Serlo looked at Mistress Gytha, and the way she looked at you.'

'Me?' Hugh spluttered. 'But Gytha is just a child!'

'She's old enough to wed – and she has a certain amount of ambition in your direction,' Janna commented dryly.

Hugh shook his head in wonder. 'I had no idea her thoughts lay with me. Although I must confess I had . . . er . . . noticed lately that she was . . . er . . .'

He could hardly have failed to notice what Gytha had been so determined to display! Janna hid a sly smile.

'. . . but I thought, when the time came, that Gytha might make a match of it with Serlo,' Hugh stammered on.

Janna interrupted his musing. 'And Serlo was desperate to have her. But he understood her ambition only too well. He knew he had to improve his station if he was to have a chance with her, and it was to be done at your expense.'

'Hence the spate of so-called "accidents"?' Hugh ventured.

Janna nodded. 'But it went further than that. He was stockpiling goods to sell at St Edith's fair at Wiltune, or perhaps even at Winchestre. Mistress Tova told me he takes several cartloads to the fair every year, your produce as well as his own. You'll see the quantity of chests, barrels and fleeces which he has stored in his cellar. There's far more than he could have come by through honest toil.'

'I certainly knew nothing about them,' Hugh said grimly, 'but I should have questioned Serlo earlier. Although we've had fair seasons for some time now, the manor farm has not been as productive as I'd expected. I had no idea Serlo was robbing me blind.' He shook his head and growled in anger.

No wonder you were so keen to visit your aunt and make yourself agreeable, Janna thought. She wondered if the dame had asked questions of Hugh, if she'd been having second thoughts about leaving him in charge of what should be a profitable manor.

'It's a hard lesson to learn, but I will be less trusting and I'll take more of the reeve's duties on my shoulder in the future,' Hugh continued.

'The woollen cloth and silver goblets Serlo accused me of stealing are also down in the cellar,' Janna added, anxious to clear both her and Edwin's name. 'My guess is that Serlo planned to sell them as well.'

'I see now how his mind worked.' said Hugh. 'With Hamo gone and me discredited, my aunt would have been anxious to cast off this manor with all its unhappy memories.'

Janna nodded in agreement. 'Serlo couldn't have known that Hamo would visit you, but once Hamo vanished the first time he saw how a second disappearance might work in his favour. I think he snatched Hamo with the intention of drowning him, but he was unable to carry out the deed because Mistress Cecily was so quick to raise the alarm. With so many villeins out searching, he knew he'd be noticed. So instead, he decided to keep Hamo alive for a little while longer. My guess is that he planned to take him away in one of the carts with all his goods for sale, and drown him some-where along the journey, past where anyone might have searched the river for him before. Once Hamo's body was found, he could then approach ma dame with his offer.'

Hugh's lips tightened. He muttered a savage oath against his once-trusted reeve.

'I'm sorry Serlo is dead and that you cannot bring him to an accounting for his deeds,' Godric ventured. 'I would not have thrown my knife at him by choice, but I knew that if I let him get away with Janna, he would have killed her rather than let her go free to speak the truth about him. I have never killed a man before but if I had to, I would make that choice again.'

'You made the right decision. I am glad that you were there,' Hugh reassured him. 'I only wish it had never come to this. If I'd read the signs right from the start, all this might have been avoided.' He looked at Janna. 'Why did Serlo leave rue at the scenes of his crimes? What was he thinking?'

'I didn't understand, until the cook told me how Serlo's family had once owned this manor. It seems they were forced into servitude after the Conquest. The rue was both his curse and his message to your family to repent that theft.' Janna didn't add that she felt a sneaking sympathy with the reeve's grievance, although she could never condone what he had done.

Hugh nodded thoughtfully. 'You have all my gratitude for finding Hamo and opening my eyes to Serlo's true nature.'

'Don't forget Gabriel . . . Urk,' Janna said quickly. 'But for him, we would have died in that cellar. If he hadn't come in search of Bones, and then faithfully conveyed Godric's message to you . . .' She shuddered, marvelling at how narrowly they had all escaped death.

'Urk will be rewarded, as will his family. But for my part, I am indebted to you for rescuing Hamo not once but twice, and bringing him home alive.' His warm smile encompassed both Janna and Godric. 'Please be assured that you have a home here for as long as you like, and for ever if you wish it.'

Janna's mouth went dry. She couldn't find the words to answer him. But Godric spoke up.

'I thank you, my lord, and I would indeed like to stay here.' He shot a quick glance at Janna, then said hurriedly, 'But I am tied to Dame Alice's manor. I cannot leave without her permission.'

'You can leave my aunt to me,' Hugh said confidently. 'I have lost my most trusted reeve. Although the villagers will elect a new one, I'd like to have an honest man by my side, if you'll agree to it, Godric?' A mischievous smile tugged at the corners of his mouth. 'I venture to suggest that you would be far more to young Gytha's taste than Master Serlo ever was.'

Speechless, Godric and Janna exchanged glances.

Godric found his voice first. 'I have my own cot and land at Babestoche, sire,' he said. 'If I came to you – '

'You would not lose by it.' Hugh cut him off. 'Master Serlo's cottage and lands lie vacant now. They are yours, as my reward to you for saving Hamo's life.'

'That . . . that is very generous of you, my lord.' As Godric absorbed the full extent of Hugh's generosity, his face blazed alight with hope and high expectation. He turned to Janna, but before he could say anything, Hugh addressed her directly.

'And Edwin?' he queried. 'What has become of him? Has he had a hand in any of this business with Serlo?'

'No, sire! He planned to stay in hiding until your visitors left the manor and it was safe for him to come out. But if you wish to speak to him, you'll find him sheltering with Bertha, the carpenter's daughter.'

Hugh tilted his head to study Janna. 'And will he want to stay here with you, do you think?'

'Not with me, my lord. He wants to stay here with Bertha.'

'And so he shall.' Hugh's mouth curved into a wide grin. 'What about you, Johanna? How can I reward you for your deeds this day?'

Janna gazed up at him, at a loss for words. A reward? It was something she hadn't looked for, didn't want. Unless Hugh could help her find her father? Could she ask him to do that?

'I must confess, I would like you to stay on at the manor, but in a lady's attire if you please,' Hugh continued. 'I cannot get used to you in the guise of a man.' His gaze narrowed slightly as he looked more closely at Janna's smock and breeches. 'Where did you find those clothes you wear?' he asked.

Janna was thrown by the unexpected question. She blushed deep as she wrestled with her conscience. 'I . . . I stole them, sire,' she confessed.

'From the barn that burned down so suddenly on my aunt's demesne?'

Janna pondered what to say. It had been an act of defiance to set fire to the barn, to pay back Robert of Babestoche something in kind for his evil deeds. But she'd also wanted to hide the evidence she'd used to deduce his true nature, as well as the evidence of her theft. She could explain all that to Hugh, but would he understand? Worse, would he tell his aunt? If she was charged in a manorial court for her misdeed, the penalty would be heavy indeed.

She was saved from having to answer as the door from Hugh's bedchamber was suddenly flung open. Dame Alice bustled into the solar, closely followed by her husband.

At the sight of Robert, Janna quickly turned aside. She bowed her head as she hastily rose to make her obeisance.

'Please, sit down and finish your supper.' In spite of her red eyes and obvious exhaustion, Dame Alice's face shone radiant with relief. She took a handful of silver coins from her purse and set them down on the table in front of Janna and Godric. 'This is your reward for bringing my son home safely,' she said, her voice trembling with emotion. 'But no silver, or words, or anything I can do, can ever convey to you my most heartfelt gratitude.' She took Janna's and Godric's hands and held them tight. 'Thank you,' she said huskily.

'It was a pleasure to serve you, ma dame.' Godric spoke for both of them. Janna was desperately racking her brains for an excuse to flee the room. Had Hamo spoken her name? Did they already know who she was, or had Hamo remembered to keep her secret?

'I know you, of course, Godric, but I don't know your companion. John, is it?' Unexpectedly, the dame reached out and took Janna's chin, raising her face towards the soft candlelight that bathed the solar. Janna had no choice but to look at her, and also at Robert, who was standing behind his wife.

The dame sucked in her breath in a sudden hiss. 'Could it be . . . are you really Johanna?' she asked, in a tone of wonder.

'His name's John,' Hugh said harshly, suddenly awake to the danger Janna faced. 'And if you've finished your supper, John, you can go now.'

'Not so hasty, Hugh!' the dame protested. But Hugh's words came too late to save Janna. As she'd looked at the dame, so had she seen realisation dawning on Robert's face: a flash of involuntary fear, followed by an expression of fierce resolve that told Janna he would not be intimidated by her knowledge, and that he would kill her rather than risk his affair with Cecily and his role in her own mother's death being found out. She was in mortal danger once more.

'Come, John. Come with me.' Hugh grasped Janna's arm and marched her out of the solar and into the hall. Godric snatched up the silver coins and followed them.

'I'm so sorry,' Hugh apologised, once they were safely out of hearing. 'I didn't tell them you were here. I thought they would stay in my bedchamber with Hamo.'

'The lord Robert knows who I am. He recognised me,' Janna whispered. She was shaking with fright. She had never before encountered such anger, such vicious hatred. Now that Robert knew she was alive, he would have to act to silence her. She was filled with dread at the very thought of it.

Hugh looked thoughtful. Then he said, 'They'll be going home soon, and probably taking Hamo with them. There'll be no danger to you then, Johanna. In the meantime, I am sure I – and Godric – can keep you safe.'

Beside Janna, Godric stiffened. 'I can look after Janna perfectly well on my own, sire,' he muttered.

'But I don't want to be looked after by anyone!' Janna retorted angrily. 'How can I live any sort of life if I'm constantly watching over my shoulder just in case the lord Robert returns here to visit?'

'You would be safe with me if we were wed,' Godric said eagerly. 'I have a cottage and land of my own here now. I have more than enough to support a wife.'

Hugh's glance swivelled quickly from Godric to Janna. He seemed suddenly unsure of himself.

Janna took a moment to consider. She'd hurt Godric's feelings once before on this matter; she must not do so again. Marrying him would not answer her problem, but how could she explain that to him? How could she explain to both of them the idea that had been forming in her mind ever since Hugh had told her of the abbess's knowledge of her mother, the idea that now seemed absolutely perfect? It would keep her safe from Robert's wrath. It was the answer to everything.

'Even if we were wed, Godric, that would not keep me from harm,' she said steadily. 'I still know my lord Robert's secrets.' She stole a quick glance at Hugh. He did not know what Janna knew: that Robert had murdered her mother and

287

also the reason why. Nor must he find out, for it was Cecily's secret. But Godric knew everything and he was the one Janna was anxious to convince. 'While I live, I am a threat to him, and he knows it. I had thought, by pretending my death and changing my identity, to keep myself safe. My strategy has come to naught. All that's left for me now is to find a place of refuge, of safety, where my lord Robert will not be able to touch me.'

She tilted her chin and faced them both. 'I have decided to seek shelter at the abbey at Wiltune.'

'You're going to take the veil?' Hugh exclaimed, thunderstruck. Godric said nothing, but Janna saw his face crumple. He looked absolutely shattered.

'No! No, but I will stay there for a time.' Long enough to talk to the abbess. Janna raised her hand to touch the purse at her waist, felt the outline of the precious parchment, the letter from her father. She had another reason for going to the abbey. She smiled at the thought of it. If she could, if she was allowed, she would stay long enough to learn to read and write. If she could only read her father's letter, it would help her find him, help her solve the secrets of the past. Her heart felt lighter; new courage flowed through her veins as, at last, she saw the way ahead. 'I thank you for your offer, my lord, and for yours too, Godric.' Impulsively, she caught hold of his hand and held it to her cheek. 'You are very dear to me, but my mind is made up,' she said firmly.

'Then, with your leave, sire, I will escort Janna to Wiltune.' Godric still looked stunned as he turned to Hugh.

'Tonight,' Janna added. Not for anything would she spend another night here, not now that Robert knew who she was.

'Tonight,' Hugh confirmed, but he looked every bit as unhappy as Godric about Janna's sudden decision. 'But are you quite sure . . .?'

'Yes, my lord,' Janna interrupted. 'I am quite, quite sure.'

The iron gates of the abbey clanged shut behind Janna. Godric looked at her, and felt a great desolation in his heart. 'Goodbye, Janna,' he said quietly. 'God go with you.'

'Goodbye, Godric.' Janna stretched her hand through the gate, and drew him closer. She puckered up her lips and blew him a kiss, then gave a rueful smile as she heard the tut-tutting disapproval of the nun waiting behind her to take her to the abbess. She would miss Godric; she would miss them all, she realised. After living alone with her mother for so long, she'd found a place within the small community of Hugh's manor. It had given her new confidence to know that she was liked and valued there, and that she could make a life for herself even without her mother's guidance. It was hard, now, to walk away from everyone she had come to know. It was especially hard to walk away from Godric, and from Hugh.

She'd escaped from Robert, but not from her own heart, she realised. Perhaps time out from the real world might give her a chance to get her emotions in order, as well as giving her the opportunity to learn the skills she needed for the journey she must make if ever she was to find her father.

Perhaps time out might give her the chance to forget about both Godric *and* Hugh? Janna knew that she would do well to succeed in that, for while she was locked in here, Gytha would have the run of the manor and be free to choose whoever might have her. Looking closely into her own aching heart, Janna knew that in Gytha's shoes, she would find it hard to make a choice between Godric and Hugh. Better perhaps to be in her own shoes here at the abbey, with no choices left to her at all.

'Come,' said the nun. She beckoned Janna forward and Janna followed, turning her back on Godric, and on the outside world. In an effort to scrape up some courage, she set her shoulders square and tilted her chin. One thought gave her comfort. She was Johanna, daughter of John. Wherever she went, and whatever she did, she would make her father proud of her. Finding him was her goal now. For the time being, romance would just have to wait.

GLOSSARY

aelfshot: a belief that illness or a sudden pain (like rheumatism, arthritis or a 'stitch') was caused by elves who shot humans or livestock with darts

ague: fever and chills

alewife: ale was a common drink in the middle ages. Housewives brewed their own for domestic use, while alewives brewed the ale served in alehouses and taverns. A bush tied to a pole was the recognised symbol of an alehouse, at a time when most of the population could not read.

apothecary: someone who prepares and sells medicines, and perhaps spices and rare goods too

besom: a bundle of twigs attached to a handle and used as a broom

breeches: trousers held up by a cord running through the hem at the waist

boon work: at busy times in the farming year (such as haymaking and harvest) villeins were required to work extra days in the lord's fields. In return, they were given food and ale.

canonical hours: the medieval day was governed by sunrise and sunset and divided into seven canonical hours. Times of prayer were marked by bells rung in abbeys and monasteries beginning with matins followed by lauds at sunrise; then prime, terce, sext, nones and vespers at sunset; followed by compline before going to bed.

'caught red-handed': literally with blood on your hands, evidence that you had been poaching in the king's forest

cot: small cottage

cottar: a medieval villein (serf) who occupied a cottage and a small piece of land on his lord's demesne, in return for his labour

demesne: manors/land owned by a feudal lord for his own use

Domesday Book: commissioned by William I after he conquered England in 1066, the book is a meticulous reckoning (for taxation purposes) of who owned what in England, from manors, mills and land holdings down to slaves, pigs and ploughs

farthing: one quarter of a penny

feudal system: a political, social and economic system based on the relationship of lord to vassal, in which land was held on condition of homage and service. Following the Norman conquest, William I distributed land once owned by Saxon 'ealdormen' (chief men) to his own barons, who in turn distributed land and manors to subtenants in return for fees, knight service and, in the case of the villeins, work in the fields.

forest law: from William the Conqueror's time, royal forests were the preserve of kings and the 'vert' (living wood) and the 'venison' (the creatures of the forest) were protected and managed. The laws caused great hardship to the peasants, who needed timber for building and kindling, while hunger tempted many to go poaching – but they faced punishment, and sometimes even death, if caught with blood on their hands.

gore acres: the odd corners of fields too awkward to plough

gorget: a cape with a hood, worn by the lower classes

hayward: manorial official in charge of haymaking and

harvest, and the repair and upkeep of hedges and ditches

heriot: a death duty to the lord of the manor, usually the best beast, and sometimes also some household goods, such as metal utensils or uncut cloth. This constituted 'payment' for the loss of a worker.

hue and cry: with no practising police force other than a town sergeant to enforce the law, anyone discovering a crime was expected to 'raise a hue and cry' – shouting aloud to alert the community to the fact that a crime had been committed, after which all those within earshot must commence the pursuit of the criminal.

kirtle: long dress worn over a short tunic

leechcraft: a system of healing practised during the time of the Anglo-Saxons, which included the use of herbs, plants, medicines, magical incantations and spells, charms and precious stones.

medale: a drinking festivity after the lord's meadows have been mown.

mortuary: death duty paid by a villein to the parish priest – usually the second-best beast

nostrums: medicines

phantasmagoria: the fantastical illusions of dreams

ploughshare: along with the coulter, the iron cutting parts of a plough. The coulter is a blade or wheel that makes the preliminary cut through the soil; the share is the cutting blade of the plough.

posset: a hot drink with curative properties

pottage: a vegetable soup or stew

reeve: the reeve (steward) was usually appointed by the villagers, and was responsible for the management of the manor. Shire reeves (sheriffs) were appointed by the king to administer law and justice in the shires (counties).

requiescat in pace: Latin for 'rest in peace'. The letters RIP are still carved on tombstones.

rush light: a peeled rush dipped in hot animal fat, which made a primitive candle

scrip: a small bag

skep: a beehive fashioned from woven straw and covered with a cloth to keep out rain

strip fields: a system of farming was practised in medieval time, whereby two fields were ploughed and sewn for harvest in summer and winter, while a third field lay fallow

sumpter horse: a packhorse used to transport goods

tiring woman: a female attendant on a lady of high birth and importance

villein: peasant or serf tied to a manor and to an overlord, and given land in return for labour and a fee – either money or produce

water meadows: the farm land on either side of a river that floods regularly

week work: two or three days' compulsory labour in the lord's fields

wortwyf: a herb wife, a wise woman and healer

AUTHOR'S NOTE

T HE *JANNA MYSTERIES* is set in the 1140s, at a turbulent time in England's history. After Henry I's son, William, drowned in the White Ship disaster, Henry was left with only one legitimate heir, his daughter Matilda (sometimes known as Maude). Matilda had an unhappy childhood. At the age of eight, she was betrothed to a much older man, Heinrich, Emperor of Germany, and she was sent to live in that country until, aged twelve, she was considered old enough to marry him. Evidently she was beloved by the Germans, who begged her to stay on after the Emperor died, but at the age of twenty-four, and childless, Matilda was summoned back to England by her father. For political reasons, and despite Matilda's vehement protests, Henry insisted that she marry Count Geoffrey of Anjou, a boy some ten years her junior. They married in 1128, and the first of their three sons, Henry (later to become Henry II of England), was born in 1133.

Henry I announced Matilda his heir and twice demanded that his barons, including her cousin, Stephen of Blois, all swear an oath of allegiance to her. This they did, but when Henry died, Matilda went to Rouen (Normandy) for his burial while Stephen went straight to London to gather support, and then on to Winchester, where he claimed the Treasury and was crowned King of England.

Not one to be denied her rights, Matilda gathered her own supporters, including her illegitimate half-brother, Robert of Gloucester, and in 1139 she landed at Arundel Castle in

England, prepared to fight for the crown. She left her children with Geoffrey, who thereafter stayed in Anjou and in Normandy, pursuing his own interests. Civil war between Stephen and Matilda raged in England for nineteen years, creating such hardship and misery that the *Peterborough Chronicle* reported: 'Never before had there been greater wretchedness in the country . . . They said openly that Christ and His saints slept.'

I became interested in this period of English history while researching *Shalott: The Final Journey*, when Callie meets Matilda at Arundel Castle as part of her quest. As this new series began to fall into place, I realised that this time of shifting allegiances, of fierce battles and daring escapes, of great danger and cruelty, formed a perfect setting with many plot possibilities. Janna's travels will bring her into the company of nobles, peasants and pilgrims, jongleurs and nuns, spies and assassins, and even the Empress Matilda herself.

With England in the grip of civil war, secrets abound, loyalties change and passions run high, and Janna will encounter the darkest side of human nature: the jealousy, greed, ambition, deceit and fear which so often lead to betrayal and murder. As well as solving the mystery of her past, Janna's mission is to find out the truth and bring the guilty to judgment, but she will need great courage and insight to escape danger and solve the crimes she encounters along her journey.

For those interested in learning more about the civil war between Stephen and Matilda, Sharon Penman's *When Christ and His Saints Slept* is an excellent fictional account of that history. On a lighter note, I have also read, and much enjoyed, the *Brother Cadfael Chronicles* by Ellis Peters, which are set during this period. While Janna's loyalty lies in a different direction to Ellis Peters' characters, her skill with herbs was inspired by these wonderful stories of the herbalist at Shrewsbury Abbey.

I have set the *Janna Mysteries* in Wiltshire, England. Janna's quest for truth and justice will take her from the forest of Gravelinges (now known as Grovely Wood) to royal Winchestre, seat of power where the Treasury was housed. I've kept to the place names listed in the *Domesday Book* compiled by William the Conqueror in 1086, but the contemporary names of some of the sites are: Berford – Barford St Martin; Babestoche Manor – Baverstock; Bredecumbe – Burcombe; Wiltune – Wilton; Sarisberie – Sarum (later relocated and named Salisbury); and Winchestre – Winchester.

The royal forest of Gravelinges was the only forest in Wiltshire mentioned in the *Domesday Book*. While it has diminished in size since medieval time, I have experienced at first hand how very easy it is to get utterly lost once you stray off the path!

Wilton was the ancient capital of Wessex. The abbey was established in Saxon times and became one of the most prosperous in England, ranked with the houses of Shaftesbury, Barking and Winchester as a nunnery of the first importance. Following the dissolution of the monasteries during the reign of Henry VIII, ownership of the abbey's lands passed to

William Herbert, lst Earl of Pembroke. Some 450 years later, the 18th Earl of Pembroke now owns this vast estate. A magnificent stately home, Wilton House, stands in place of the abbey and is open to visitors.

While writing medieval England from Australia is a difficult and hazardous enterprise, I have been fortunate in the support and encouragement I've received along the way. So many people have helped make this series possible, and in particular I'd like to thank the following: Nick and Wendy Combes of Burcomb Manor, for taking me into their family, giving me a home away from home and teaching me about life on a farm, both now and in medieval time. The staff of the Pembroke Arms, who also looked after me while I was in England. Tony Caceres, who introduced me to the fascinating history of Govely Wood and its surrounds. Mike Boniface, warden of Grovely, who guided me through the forest by day and ensured that I also saw it (and the badgers!) at night. Pat Sweetman from the USA, who warned me about rue, and who kindly shared her knowledge of herbal medicine with with me. Gillian Polack, mentor and friend, whose knowledge of medieval life has helped shape the series and continues to give it veracity. Linsay Knight and the team at Random House for their faith and support, and Eva and Zoe for their insight and meticulous care. Finally, my husband Mike, who understands that I often need to live in another place and at another time – my gratitude and thanks to you all.

ABOUT THE AUTHOR

FELICITY PULMAN'S FIRST novel for Random House Australia, *Shalott*, won the Society of Women Writers Award in the Young Adult Reader category in 2001. *Return to Shalott* and *Shalott: The Final Journey* continued the story of five Australian teenagers zapped into the romance and intrigue of King Arthur's court at Camelot. Felicity has also published two novels from the Guinevere Jones television series and *Ghost Boy*, a time slip adventure for younger readers about the Sydney Quarantine Station. Many of Felicity's short stories have won prizes, including the inaugural Queen of Crime Award, the KSP Science Fiction/Fantasy Award and the Dymphna Cusack Memorial Award.

Felicity is currently keeping busy researching the medieval world of the *Janna Mysteries* and the civil war between Stephen and Matilda in the 1140s. When she's not scribbling notes and soaking up the atmosphere in the English country-side where the *Janna Mysteries* are set, Felicity lives near the bush and the beach in Sydney, and enjoys swimming, surfing and snorkelling, bush walking and bush regeneration, and spending time with her family.

Felicity is available for talks and workshops with schools and groups. You can contact Felicity through her website at: www.felicitypulman.com.au

Janna Mysteries
BOOK THREE

Lilies
FOR
Love

Love, revenge, secrets
and murder in medieval England

FELICITY PULMAN

JANNA MYSTERIES 3:
LILIES FOR LOVE

Love, revenge, secrets . . . and murder!

Taking refuge at Wiltune Abbey brings Janna closer to finding her unknown father, but she cannot escape those who mean her harm or those who need her help, especially when it comes to affairs of the heart.

Janna's stay at the abbey is complicated by pet-keeping nuns, old grudges and new rivalries, but things get really dangerous when she encounters Mus, who is not the 'mouse' he pretends to be.

Meeting Hugh and Godric at St Edith's fair throws Janna's emotions into new confusion, while Hugh's childhood friendship with the beautiful Emma turns deadly after Emma's brother insists that Hugh honour his promise to marry her.

Who is leaving lilies at the shrine of St Edith, and why? Janna believes the answer lies with her friend Agnes, but can she persuade Agnes to forget about her disfigurement and find courage enough to leave the abbey and follow her heart?

Janna's greatest challenge is to find someone who will teach her to read. But just as she seems close to reaching her goal, the tumultuous drama of the civil war between the Empress Matilda and her cousin King Stephen comes right to the door of the abbey.

Lilies for Love is the next exciting step in Janna's journey towards solving the mysteries of the past, while charting her passage to adulthood and an understanding of her own heart.

Available now at all good booksellers

Read on for an extract from *Janna Mysteries 3:*
Lilies for Love

ONE

THE GREAT GATE clanged shut, its metal bars vibrating with the impact. It seemed to Janna that the sound held an awful finality. She shuddered as she realised what she had done. True, she'd sought sanctuary at the abbey from those who wished her harm – most especially Robert of Babestoche, whose secret she held close to her heart – but in doing so, she had cut herself off from the world, and from all those whom she'd come to love. But Janna knew she had no choice. While she lived, her knowledge, her very presence threatened Robert's status as the husband of Dame Alice. There was no place other than the abbey for her to hide in safety.

She looked behind her through the darkness to where Godric still lingered beyond the gate. In the light of the flares that lit the gatehouse, she could read the misery on his face, a misery she was sure was reflected in her own expression. More than anything she wished she was free to follow her chosen path: her quest to find her unknown father and seek justice for the death of her mother. She really didn't want to be trapped here with a convent of women who had given their hearts and minds to the Lord Jesus Christ. Janna couldn't understand why they'd want to do that, how they could bear to shut themselves away.

She became aware that Godric was beckoning her to come back to him. Beside him, a horse neighed softly. Although Janna didn't know how to ride, Godric did, and he'd brought her to the abbey on horseback, fleeing along the path beside the river to safety at Wiltune Abbey. Janna frowned. Her mind was made up, her path chosen. She couldn't return to the outside world, not now, not until her mission was accomplished; not until it was safe.

'Janna!' Godric called softly. 'I forgot to give you these.' He held out his hand. Janna saw the glint of silver coins in the hollow of his palm.

'Take them!' he called. 'Take them all. Thanks to my lord Hugh's gift of land and my new service to him, I have no need of any further reward, but you still have your way to make in the world.'

Tempted, Janna hesitated. She could not afford to be proud. Apart from the few objects secreted in her purse, which held value only for her, she had nothing to offer the abbey in return for food and shelter. The coins would help to buy her a way in, and smooth her path when, later, she took to the road in search of her father.

Turning her back on the ill-tempered and sleepy nun who had admitted her and was now leading her to an audience with the abbess, Janna hurried back to Godric.

'Are you quite sure you want me to take it all?' she asked, as she opened the drawstring of her purse.

'Of course.' He carefully poured in the coins. Janna beamed her gratitude.

'Hrumph.' The sound of a throat being cleared warned Janna that the porteress had returned and that they were being watched.

'God be with you.' She couldn't resist touching Godric's hand one last time. 'And good luck. Take care of yourself, and thank you.' There was so much for which she needed to thank Godric, she realised. He had come to her aid on so many different occasions. 'Maybe we'll meet again one day,' she said, trying to sound hopeful but not succeeding.

'HRUMPH!' This time the throat-clearing was an ultimatum.

'Be sure that I will come to you if ever you call, wherever you may be!' Godric ignored the watching nun. He seized hold of Janna's hand, raised it to his lips and kissed it. 'I would not leave you, Janna. Not ever! Not unless you wish it.'

'I know.' Reluctantly, Janna disengaged her hand from his. 'I know.' She swallowed hard over the lump of misery that had lodged in her throat, and hastily turned away from him. If only they could wed, if she could trust in his protection, she might have begged the porteress to unlock the gate and let her free to go to him. But she knew that even Godric, who would give his life for her, could not protect her at this time, nor could he help her to fulfil her quest. This was something she must do, and do alone. In truth, she preferred it this way, for she was not ready yet to commit her life, or her heart, to anyone's keeping save her own. But she felt a great dread for the future. Following her chosen path would take all her courage.

She turned away and, with reluctant steps, returned to the porteress, who scowled at her. 'I can't think why you've come here,' the nun muttered. 'Dressed up in men's clothes, and carrying on with that young man right here at the abbey gate. Who do you think you are?' She clucked her disapproval. 'If you had not come from Dame Alice's nephew and with a message for the abbess, be sure I would never have admitted you.'

'I am grateful that you did, mistress,' Janna murmured.

'Sister!' the nun snapped. 'My name is Sister Brigid.'

'And my name is Johanna.' Silence met Janna's offer of friendship. With lips clamped tight, the nun led Janna across an open yard to a building set on one side of the entrance to the church. She walked through a small parlour and rapped on a door. Together, she and Janna waited for an invitation to enter.

'Come in.' The voice sounded weary, and rather impatient. Feeling curious, in spite of her low spirits, Janna followed Sister Brigid into the private quarters of the abbess.

The receiving room was large and lit by torches in sconces on the walls. Richly embroidered tapestries hung between them, glowing in the bright light. A fat wax candle set in a silver candlestick sat on a table littered with written sheets of parchment. Janna stared at them, for the symbols looked different from the letter written by her father. These were set in long columns and divided by lines. She could not make sense of them at all. Her gaze moved on around the room. A gold cross hung above a small altar, exquisitely chased and decorated with coloured gemstones. The stools had fat cushions to soften hard wooden seats, while the box bed Janna glimpsed through an open door contained a thick mattress and was piled with more cushions plumped down on a warm, woollen covering. She wondered if the sisters of the abbey lived in the same comfort as their abbess. Stairs to one side led to extra rooms above, quarters perhaps for the nobility, even royalty, who were rumoured to stay here from time to time. For certes, the abbess was living in great comfort and style.

Fascinated, Janna dragged her gaze back to one of the wealthiest and most powerful women in the land. Her mother had once told her that Wiltune was one of the largest abbeys in England, with vast estates, mills and other resources spread over several shires. 'The abbess is the king's tenant-in-chief. She holds the entire barony in return for the service of five knights, should the king call for them in times of war,' Eadgyth had said. Janna wished she'd thought to question how the abbess managed to provide five knights, living as she did in a house full of women.

At their entry, the abbess had risen from her work. She scowled suspiciously at Janna. 'Who is this ruffian, and what do you mean by disturbing my peace so late at night?' She spoke in Norman French, addressing the question to Sister Brigid. It was clear she didn't expect Janna to understand her. Janna bent her head, thinking it wise to pretend that the abbess was right in her assumption.

'She says she's a girl, and she bears a message from the lord Hugh, nephew to Dame Alice. I would not have admitted her else.' Sister Brigid's face pinched into a disapproving frown. 'She was accompanied by a youth and he kissed her hand!' There couldn't have been more venom in the nun's voice if she'd accused Janna of dancing on the altar of Christ. She gave the brief message signed with Hugh's seal to the abbess, who perused it silently.

'Johanna?' she said then, reverting to the Saxon language. 'Daughter of the *wortwyf*, Eadgyth?'

Janna knew a moment's panic before she managed a reluctant reply. 'Yes, Sister uh . . . um . . .?'

'Mother Abbess. We thought you were dead. The lord Hugh begged me to say a Mass for your soul.'

The abbess's expression had darkened into a thunderous frown. A sinking feeling told Janna what was coming next. She wished she'd thought to ask Hugh not to mention her name so that she could, once again, invent for herself a new identity. Now, it was too late. She braced herself.

'Out of the goodness of my heart, in Christ's holy name, and in spite of your mother's disgrace, I gave her the piece of land and the cot that was your home – and you repaid my generosity by burning it to the ground!'

'No! No, I did not.' But Janna's protest went unheeded. The abbess was practically spitting with rage.

'You might not have cared to stay there any longer, but there are many others in need of shelter and land on which to grow their food. How dare you destroy what I gave so freely!'

Freely? Janna opened her mouth to defend herself, then closed it again. It was useless to point out to this self-righteous, miserly old bat that the land had been unworked and the cottage a tumbledown wreck when Eadgyth had first moved in. The midwife had told Janna how hard her mother had worked to repair the cot, and to turn the surrounding untilled earth into the garden that had sustained them both. She and her mother had always worked hard, and had often gone hungry in order to pay the rent demanded by this greedy, grasping abbess, handing over silver coins and produce from their garden as well as several of their birds and animals. The unsaid words almost choked Janna, yet she knew the abbess would not believe that it was the villagers who'd burned down her cot and who'd almost succeeded in burning her alive at the same time. Not unless Janna told her the full story, and perhaps not even then. But there was far too much at stake for Janna to speak up, to tell the truth, and so she stayed silent.

'Not only that, but you led everyone to believe you had died in the fire! You have even disguised yourself as a youth.' The abbess's tone was full of contempt. 'Was that so that you did not have to pay for the destruction of my property, and heriot for your mother's death?'

'I . . . no, that's not true. No!'

'The girl has coins to pay, Mother,' Sister Brigid piped up unexpectedly. 'I saw her *companion* pour silver into her purse.' She flashed a spiteful glance at Janna. It was clear she thought the worst of her relationship with Godric.

The abbess stopped abruptly. She ran her tongue over her top lip as she considered the possibilities. 'The lord Hugh asks me to give you shelter, and so I will,' she conceded, 'but in turn I demand recompense for the cot and garden you have destroyed by your wanton action. And as your overlord, I also claim heriot for the death of your mother.'

'That's not f—'

Janna's outrage was stifled as Sister Brigid's hand clamped hard on her arm.

'It's the custom,' the nun reminded her.

With an effort, Janna smoothed her face into calm acceptance, but inside she raged at the injustice of it all. No wonder

Wiltune was such a wealthy abbey! The midwife's account of the abbess's treatment of her mother should have warned her how greedy and grasping she was. Janna was quite sure that Dame Alice had stayed true to her word that she herself would pay the heriot due, but it seemed the abbess did not scruple to be paid twice. Angrily, Janna untied her purse and pulled out a handful of silver. The abbess reached for it with eager hands. 'There is also the matter of your food and shelter,' she said, not taking her eyes from Janna's purse.

Seething, Janna pulled out the last of the coins. 'This is all I have, Mother Abbess,' she said. 'What is left is for my use. It is of value only to me.' She patted her purse, hearing the comforting crump of her father's letter, feeling the lumpy trinkets through the rough fabric, tokens of his affection for her mother; feeling, too, the small figurine she had found in the forest. On no account would she hand over any of her treasures. She would rather leave the abbey and face an uncertain and dangerous future than part with any one of them. She folded her fingers around the small figurine, taking comfort from the carved shape of a mother and her child. It gave her the strength to face the abbess and wait for her future to be spelled out.

'Very well,' the abbess said grudgingly. She considered a moment and then said, 'Harvest is about to begin, and extra hands are needed. You may stay so long as you are prepared to help in the fields, and do not disrupt the life of the abbey. We lead a simple life here, a life of contemplation of God and his mysteries. There is no place here for those who do not believe in Him. Do you love the Lord God and his Son, Jesus Christ?'

Faced with such an unexpected demand, Janna hesitated. She could lie and say yes. It would smooth her path and make her life a whole lot easier. Or she could be honest and say no. The one and only time she'd ever been into a church, Eadgyth had dragged her out in a rage against the priest's preaching. She'd railed against him, calling him a narrow-minded bigot, an opinion which Janna had shared, although in the end her mother's actions had helped persuade the villagers to turn against them. She could not tell the abbess 'yes', for it was not true. Nor could she say 'no', for she would be thrown out of the abbey, left to the mercy of Robert of Babestoche and all those who followed his lead. Even worse, she would lose her only chance of finding out more about her mother and, more important, learning to read and to write so that she could make sense of her father's letter. In that lay her salvation, the answer to all her hopes: the secret of her father, of her own heritage, and the chance of bringing to justice the man responsible for the murder of her mother.

'Well?' the abbess demanded impatiently.

'I am here because I don't know Him,' Janna said slowly, sticking to the truth as closely as she could. 'I am here to learn.'

'Humph.' The abbess gave her a narrow look full of suspicion. 'You may stay here as a lay sister, for the moment. I am not prepared to accept you as a postulant in our convent. For one thing, you have no dower.' Her eyes rested on the pile of silver coins on the table in front of her. She looked up then and, as her glance met Janna's, she had the grace to look slightly ashamed. 'I will not accept you into our community until you have proved yourself fit to serve the Lord,' she amended. 'You may live and work with our lay sisters. They tend the garden, do the cooking, keep the abbey clean and help out in the fields when necessary, leaving my sisters free to say their prayers, to worship the Lord, engage in contemplation, or keep busy with more important tasks on the Lord's behalf. Be sure that I will keep close watch on you to make sure you are worthy of my trust.'

'Thank you, Mother Abbess.' The words stuck in Janna's throat. She bowed her head so that the abbess could not see her anger and dismay. I don't have to stay here forever, just until my mission is complete, she reminded herself silently, taking some comfort from the fact that being locked within the walls of the abbey was not a life sentence. Or was it?

Janna Mysteries

BOOK FOUR

Willows FOR Weeping

Murder at Stonehenge, and a
letter that could change the fate
of a medieval kingdom at war …

FELICITY PULMAN

Available at all good booksellers in March 2008

ShALOTT
RETURN TO ShALOTT
ShALOTT: ThE FINAL JOURNEY

By Felicity Pulman

Zapped back in time to the medieval court of King Arthur, Callie and her friends invoke the legend of the Lady of Shalott ... with terrifying consequences.

'Infectiously readable and admirably comprehensive'
Viewpoint magazine

'This spellbinding story weaves together the past and present to create a tale that is at once dark and dangerous, and tantalizingly dreamlike. *Shalott* is unputdownable.'
Maggie Hamilton

'This is an unsettling, unusual, intriguing and moving novel, rich in character, action and mystery, full of the atmosphere of Arthurian legend' Sophie Masson

Available now at all good retailers